THE EXORCI'S TOUCH

AN ASHSTRIKE SANCTORUM NOVEL

KIMBERLY M. RINGER

KIMBERLY M. RINGER

THE EXORCI'S TOUCH

An Ashstrike Sanctorium Novel

KIMBERLY M. RINGER

Contact Information: www.kimberlymringer.com
Header Photo: DepositPhotos
ISBN Paperback: 978-1-957447-07-0
ISBN E-Book: 978-1-957447-08-7
First Edition: August 2022

Author Comments

This book carries a lot of my own personal grief. In February 2022, my mother passed away, and I dealt with it, the only way I knew how. I wrote the feelings. So while this is a work of fiction, and the story is its own, there are glimpses of my own pain in Jesse and Maddie.

I would not have gotten through what I have in 2022 so far, if it were not for my husband, little human, Hype Girls, Kate, and the Romance Riot. I cannot tell you how much I appreciate everything you have done for me.

Elisabeth and Tara: There are no words for the love and support you have given me. Whether it was to help in all things that are the author life, or just talking me off the ledges, and letting me rant.

My Little Human: I love you to the stars and back. You are the best thing to ever grace my life.

Content Warning

Unaliving

Sexual Assault

Slavery

Dubious Consent

Family Death

Language

Violence

Depression

Explicit Adult
Content

Stabby, Physical
and Gun
Violence

Ashstrike Sanctorum

The Overseeing Primals

Minstrel
Always an Astral & Seer
One Other to be determined

Astral Primal   Exorci Primal

Astrals and Exorci's

Species Primals

Species Heads

Kismot	Therugi
Werewolf	Immortals
Bacri	Seers
Aamanti	Phrenic
Changling	Ovexa
Iamu	Angels
Puroklets	Witches
Kir	Vampires
Calassei	Fae

Ashstrike Sanctorum Creature Registry

Astral:	Encforcer / Emissary with Daggers
Angels:	Winged creatures
Changling:	Humanoid shapeshifter
Exorci:	Executioners
Fae:	Elusive, secretive, not much is known
Immortals:	Humans turned immortal by the dark Moesia witches
Ovexa:	Super talented tracker and used as investigators
Phrenic:	Physic / Mind control
Seers:	See the future

THERUGI:	DEMON CLASSIFICATION CATCH ALL
VAMPIRES:	DRINK BLOOD FOR SUBSTANCE
WITCHES:	USUALLY TALENTED IN HEALING POWERS, SOME VARIATIONS

ELEMENTALS

CALASSEI:	CONTROLS AIR
IAMU:	CONTROLS FIRE
KIR:	CONTROLS EARTH
PUROKLET:	CONTROLS WATER

SHIFTERS

AAMANTI:	DRAGON
BACRI:	EAGLE / OTHER BIRDS
KISMOT:	MOUNTAIN LION
WEREWOLF:	WOLF

CONTENTS

CHAPTER 1

MADDIE

"Come on, Maddie!" Beth pulled me by the arm toward the entrance to the bar, but I stumbled.

"Fuck, Beth. Let me keep my feet under me." I muttered.

"I don't know how you can be so clumsy." She smiled, but her eyes flashed in amusement, showing the Kismot animalistic side of her.

"Not all of us have the reflexes of a cat, Beth."

When we got inside, there weren't that many people, and I let out a relieved breath. I was exhausted and wanted to bail on tonight, but it was our weekly ritual to meet at Stevie's Bar at the end of a long week.

Stevie's was nothing more than a single large room with an L-shaped dark wood bar, matching barstools, a small dance floor on the far wall, and a few tall bar tables closer to the door. The walls, in the light, were a dark blue, to match the leather on the stools, but otherwise there were just basic recessed lighting in the ceiling.

We slid into our usual table in the corner, and I leaned against the wall. "Two drinks, and I'm out. Remember our deal."

"Yeah, yeah, yeah. You always say that. Maybe you will get the balls to talk to mister tall, dark, and handsome tonight."

"I don't even know who you are talking about." I said, but my gaze instantly moved over to the bar, where mister tall, dark and handsome was sitting. He had been here every Friday night for the last month, and while I had definitely noticed his long dark hair, sunglasses, just too long scruff of a beard, leather jacket and gloves, I was also certain he hadn't even given me a sideways look.

"Really?" Beth snorted. "Which is why you are totally not eye fucking him right now, right?"

"Okay. Fine. I've noticed him, but I'm too plain for someone like that. Leather jacket, leather gloves, and the motorcycle sitting outside, that I'm sure belongs to him... besides, I'm not really the bad boy type."

"Maybe they should be?" Beth caught the eye of the bartender and raised her hand, circling it for a round of drinks. He nodded and started getting them ready. "The clean-cut boys certainly haven't done anything for you."

"Beth..."

"Go get our drinks. Tell Joel to put it on a tab for us." Her green eyes sparkled as she pulled her long red hair back, making the freckles on her face stand out more.

"I told you two drinks." She just raised her eyebrow at me, and I sighed. She was right. We would be here until she deemed us ready to go. I shook my head and chuckled.

Maybe a little dancing and letting loose tonight wouldn't be a bad thing. I weaved my way through the barstools and tables, and when I got to the bar, Joel asked, "Your tab or Beth's?"

"Make the bitch pay tonight." I smiled with a wink, taking my drink from him. When I turned to meet back up with Beth, mister tall, dark, and handsome's eyes lifted and met mine. My heart stopped, and I wasn't even sure I was breathing. His gold eyes were piercing and captivated me so wholly, I forced myself to take a quick breath and bit my bottom lip.

His bottom lip dropped, and he looked down. He let out a small sigh and, with two fingers, motioned for me to come over to him. I nodded and looked over to where Beth was. Holding a finger up to her as my heart beat faster, I took a quick drink of the rum and coke in my hand, and another, before I turned the corner and sidled up to the stool next to him.

I put my drink on the counter and wrapped my hands around it.

"What's your name?" His baritone, gravelly voice said.

"Madilyn. Maddie for short." I took another quick sip of my drink, before looking up at him. "Yours?"

"Jesse." His eyes seemed to study me, and there was something hesitant in that gaze.

"What?"

"There's..." He shot back the rest of his drink, and when he looked back at me, he said, "You registered with the Agency?"

I blinked. "I'm sorry. What?"

He gave me a knowing look and said, "I can feel it. Not full blooded, but there is a line there."

I let out a huff. Just my luck. Just as I said, he wouldn't be interested in me. He wants Sean. "Of course you are. Is that why you've been here for the last month? I've noticed you watching. Is that why you are talking to me? Because of Sean? I have nothing to do with my brother, okay? My best friend just broke up with him because he needs to get his shit straight. I have nothing to do with him or whatever bullshit he's gotten himself into."

"What are you talking about?"

"You're an Astral, right? Sean's so fucked up that they sent an Astral after him, and you want me to tell you where he is?" I stood up from the stool so fast it tipped, but it righted itself. "I just told you I don't know where he is, okay?"

I turned, and he put his hand on my forearm. I felt a charge go through me, and when I looked down at his hand, he removed it quickly, cussed and turned to grab a napkin, dipping it in his drink, and wiping my forearm down quickly.

He looked down at his hand and muttered, "Shit."

"What?" I asked, and his head shot up to look at me.

"Oh, thank the gods." He muttered and went to examine a small hole in the finger of the glove.

I looked at him carefully, and then realization and fear went through me. "Oh, fuck."

His eyes met mine, and he let out a long sigh. There was sorrow in his eyes as he sat back down on the chair.

Oh, fucking hell. Sean was in so much trouble, the Agency sent an executioner after him?

"The Agency has seriously sent an Exorci after Sean?" I blinked at him, and when he looked at me, his eyes narrowed at me.

"Again, I don't know who that is."

"You are Exorci though?" I asked, just loud enough to be heard over the music that started playing. A small nod as I looked at my arm, and realized why he freaked out over the hole in his glove. "But you aren't here for Sean?"

"No, Maddie." Gods, the way he said my name. It heated something deep within me I hadn't felt in a long time. It had been too long since that side of me had been awakened. Sure, I'd found one-night stands, but no one that legit made me wet just saying my name.

"Then why?"

"Why am I talking to you?" He huffed a small laugh and asked the bartender for another drink. "Is it too much to believe I was weak for your beauty?"

"Smooth." I crossed my arms and rolled my eyes. He gave me a droll look, and when he opened his mouth, I said, "I know this is going to be rude, and feel free to tell me to fuck off, but..." I hesitated just long enough, he smiled and met my gaze.

"How can Exorci have sexual relations or any kind of a relationship with anyone without killing them?" His voice was quiet, but heated as he looked down the length of me before meeting my eyes.

I nodded. "I mean, theoretically, that simple touch should have killed me."

"Most Exorci can have relationships with humans. It's the others that are... problematic. Your line must be diluted just enough that my fingertip brushing your forearm wasn't enough to do anything." His head tipped to the side, "You didn't answer me though. Are you registered with the Agency?"

"Last of my line, unless I marry someone registered of course." Then I whispered and looked back at my drink, "Bacri, non-shifting. My great grandfather was a Bacri, an eagle shifter, but neither I nor my mom have any ability to shift. At this point, my brother and I are the last line listed in the Agency's records."

He shook his head and said, "I'm sorry. I can't."

I let out a breath, and said, "Look. I'm not looking for a commitment. I'm not even sure why I came to sit down over here next to you. My life hasn't had the best of luck when it comes to males."

"It's too dangerous." Jesse said, slamming back the rest of his drink. He looked at me, and there was something that looked like longing in his eyes as he said, "You are beautiful, Maddie, and I appreciate the talk, but I won't take the chance."

Then he got up, and when he turned to leave, I reached out and grabbed his forearm. He looked down at my hand, and finding some sort of stupidity, I said, "So, lunch. Tomorrow. Alexanders on Stevens Creek near Valley Fair. Noon."

He looked at my hand a moment longer and met my stare. I released his arm, but didn't look away. There was a pull toward him, but I ignored it. This was stupid. I was quite literally putting my life in danger, but for a month, I'd had something pulling me toward him, and for more than just his rugged good looks.

He nodded, and said, "I'll see you tomorrow."

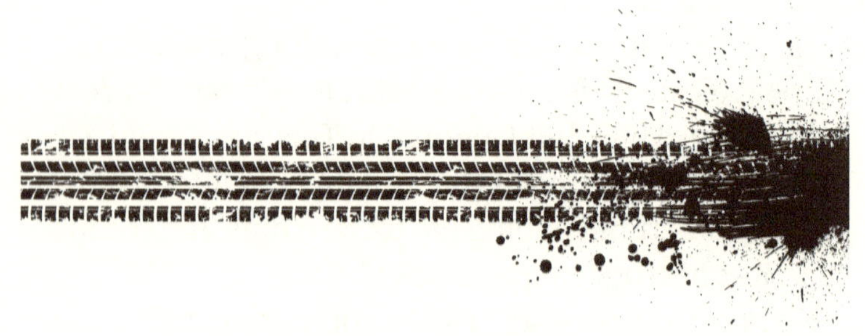

CHAPTER 2

JESSE

I stared at Alexanders on the other end of the parking lot and my heart raced. There was something about that little touch yesterday when our skin made contact. It should have killed her, but instead it sent a spark of life through my hand and right into my chest.

I saw her walk up to the front of the restaurant and look around from where I was parked behind a large truck. Her long brown hair fluttered in the wind, and caught on her plump lips. I sighed, closing my eyes for a moment, and seeing her face last night. Her golden eyes had taken my breath away. Her golden skin had been set off by the dark red she wore, that I hadn't been able to ignore her anymore. When I opened my eyes, she took a large deep breath, before steeling herself and going in. Shaking my head, I secured my helmet on the clip of the bike, and headed for the door.

Every step I took, I warred with myself. There was the rational part of me that said this was stupid and reckless. Only there was this other part of me that couldn't stop myself from taking one foot in front of the other. There was every reason not to.

I couldn't touch her. There is no way for us to have a real relationship. I couldn't give her any kind of physical relationship.

My hand hovered over the door handle, but a phantom something shoved me toward this girl. Yes, I had been watching her since the first time she and her friend practically skipped into that bar a month ago, long brown hair flowing down her back, a wide smile amplifying those apple cheeks, and bright hazel eyes sparkling with excitement. Wrapping my hand around the handle, I pulled the door open, quickly glanced around and saw her sitting at a table along a row of windows, staring out toward Stevens Creek.

"For one, sir?" I looked at the host and then back to Maddie.

"My companion has already arrived." My voice was low, and she couldn't have heard it, but Maddie's head swung around, those gold eyes meeting mine as I headed in her direction.

"May I sit?"

"I wouldn't have asked you here if I didn't want you to." A small smile crossed her lips, along with the most adorable blush on her cheeks.

I slid into the booth and leaned on the table, studying her for a long moment. "Why did you, Maddie? I mean, let's get right to it. You are beautiful, and if I were not who I am, I would beg for a proper date with you."

Her eyes snapped to mine, and she said with a scoff, "beg for."

"You are one of those girls who either doesn't believe in their own beauty, or is constantly fishing for the complements, aren't you?" I leaned back and crossed my arms. "Don't play games with me. If I'm going to take a chance with your life, the least you can do is play me straight. I won't put up with it, because every time I touch you, I will put your life in danger, little bird."

"I don't live life dangerously." She whispered after a sharp inhale of breath.

"Then what am I doing sitting here? Because that is *exactly* what you are doing. With these gloves on or not," I threw my leather clad hands up for her to see. "If my skin touches yours, you will die, Madilyn."

"I didn't yesterday."

"You were lucky." I took a deep breath as the waitress walked by with a large tray filled with different dishes. "My... abilities... are a bit more potent than others like me."

Her head cocked to the side, her eyes brightening, and I smiled. Bacri, no matter how diluted, always had that same head cock, and I chuckled. There was bright intelligence in those eyes, and that could be a good or bad thing.

"When you say that, you mean to say that even, say, our waitress would fall to your touch?"

"It happened once. Only once, but I won't let it happen again."

She sat back, letting her hands fall into her lap, her shoulders drooping, before saying, "Let me ask you this."

I waited, and when her eyes looked outside, I found myself focusing on the curve of her jaw, the length of her throat, and my mouth watered at the want to touch her. I was so ingrained in my own thoughts, she snapped her fingers in front of me, but smiled, "Jesse."

"Sorry. What was that little bird?" I swear I saw her cheeks redden just slightly more.

"How about you let *me* decide what risks I'm willing to take. Let's have lunch. Talk. *Then* I'll tell you whether I want to take the risk."

The waitress showed up then asking, "Sorry for the wait. My name is Sarah. What can I get for you two?"

I was still looking at her. I had given her the straight truth as to how she could die with the simplest of touches, yet she was still asking for me to have lunch. She lifted her eyebrow as to say, '*You gonna give me at least that?*'

I shook my head and huffed a small laugh. "Blue cheese burger, with fries and a coke, please."

Madilyn's smile grew as she said, "California Chicken Club, fries, and a root beer."

When I handed the menu over to the waitress, she looked me up and down, then back to Maddie. Her entire body was tense as her eyes slid back to me and asked in a low voice. "Is everything okay, ma'am?"

"First date jitters. I'm fine." She smiled up at the waitress, who looked back over her shoulder and plastered a professional-looking smile on her face.

After she walked away, I shook my head. "First date?"

"Okay, pre-first date."

"Pre-date?" I raised an eyebrow at her, and she chuckled softly. It warmed me right down to my cock. I couldn't help the smile on my lips now.

"Oh, the almighty Exorci Jesse Westbrook does smile."

"How do you know my last name?"

She gave me a droll look and said, "I'm not an idiot. I'm Agency listed. Everyone knows the names of the Exorcis in the area. So you tell me you are an Exorci and your first name is Jesse, and you don't expect me to put it together?"

"Alright." I shrugged, then looked at her, "So what do you want to know?"

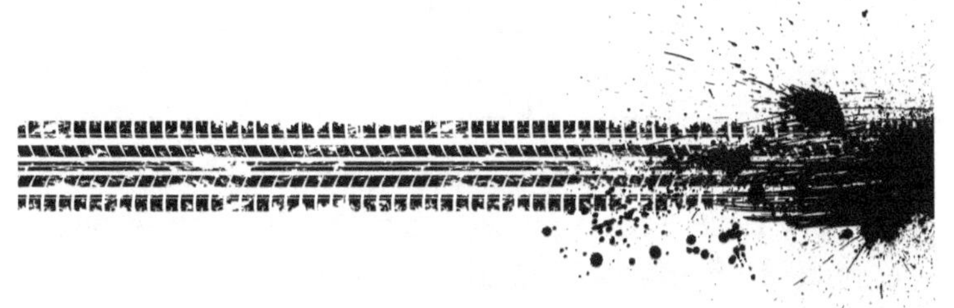

CHAPTER 3

JESSE

-TWO YEARS LATER-

I watched as Maddie writhed underneath me. I pumped my fingers in and out of her, rubbing her clit with my thumb as she rode my hand. She was so close to shattering, and with a smirk, I pulled my hand away. She whimpered as her eyes met mine. "Jesse, if you don't fill me with that delicious cock of yours, I'm going to finish this myself."

"Don't you worry, little bird." I said, sliding on the specially made oversuit. To anyone else it looked like a compression long sleeve shirt, and full legged swim pants, with a small hole for my cock. There were also the special condoms I had to have made. All for this brunette beauty laid out before me.

I slipped one of the condoms on, tucking the edges under the shorts. Maddie looked me up and down as I took a step towards her and slowly rubbed against her.

"Jesse. Please." Her head was tipped back, hips grinding against me, as her back arched. She laid there begging and pulling at her nipples. The sight of it ruined me every time. I plunged into her, and she cried out in pleasure, tightening around my cock.

It took a deep breath and a ton of control to not lose it right there. Maddie unmade me. I ran my gloved hand down her thigh and lifted her leg, pushing deeper inside of her. Her hips rolled against me, and I couldn't help the growl that came from deep in my chest.

I pulled out of her and when her eyes met mine, I slammed back in, rolling my hips against her clit. The O her mouth made was pure perfection.

Slowly, I picked up speed, until I was unable to stop the flood that was coming.

"Fuck yes, Jesse. Harder." Smirking, I obliged, and pounded into her.

Feeling her tighten around me, I groaned, as I pulled out just as she was on that edge, pumped her with just the head of my cock before pinching her clit and slamming back into her. Her walls clamped down and spasmed as my balls tightened, and I slammed into her over and over again, fucking her through her orgasm.

"Jesse!" she screamed as she rode through another orgasm that hit with the force that her whole body stilled, and I released deep within her.

I smiled at her passed-out form. She was the most beautiful thing I had ever held, but my heart sank knowing I couldn't keep her. Gods, I loved her with every ounce of my being, but how could she be with someone who couldn't truly fuck her the way she deserves? Every time I was playing Russian Roulette with her life, even with all the precautions I took.

I buttoned up my pants and finished cleaning my equipment before packing up. There had been Exorci who had been able to have sex with humans with no issue. Their toxins weren't potent enough to penetrate through their skin. I made that mistake only once. While the act was completed, by the next morning, she had died. Any supernatural I touched would be dead in moments. Humans typically could live through contact from an Exorci, but there were a few of us that were more potent than others.

I wouldn't take a chance with Maddie. When we had first met, I almost had a heart attack when my glove had a hole in it and I had touched her forearm. One second of my skin in contact with her and she could drop in moments.

My phone rang as I slid my leather gloves back on. Looking at the caller ID, I groaned, but reached over, and said, "Yeah."

"Come by the office. We have a problem. You're being sent out." Minstrel Carlos said. "The Primals have an assignment for you."

"Won't be able to get to Fresno until later this afternoon."

"I'm at the Astral office in San Jose. I have the file here." He huffed a laugh and muttered under his breath. "This will teach me to set up an Astral with her bonded up north. I really need to find a replacement. I don't know how she managed her Astral work and being a project designer."

"No offense Minstrel, but that really sounds like a you problem."

"That it is. Now, I'll see you in an hour, or are you not done with the Bacri yet?" He said it teasingly, but also with a note of warning.

"Leave Madilyn Taylor out of this, please." I tried to say it with a bite, but it was just a whispered promise to the world.

"I'll see you in an hour, Westbrook." He hung up, and I just stared at Maddie laying on the bed.

"What am I doing?" I whispered as I ran my hand through my long brown hair and pulled it away from my face. I reached into my riding jacket and pulled a leather cord out and tied it back. I loaded my things and carefully pulled the blanket up around her shoulders. She turned her head up toward me and with her eyes half open, I inhaled her vanilla cinnamon scent and kissed her shoulder through the blanket before saying, "Sorry, little bird. I gotta run."

"Let me know when you are back in town." She mumbled.

"Of course. You'll..." I trailed off, because my heart did that sinking thing again.

"Be careful Jesse. I love you." She said, turning toward the door as I slid my pack over my shoulder.

"Love you too, Maddie."

CHAPTER 4

JESSE

I walked out of her apartment and sighed as I leaned my forehead on the door. My gut was telling me that was going to be the last pleasant time with her for a long while. I groaned as the feeling sat and swam in my stomach. "Fuck."

My gut had always treated me well, and had often told me when things were going to go sideways. I sighed again, pushed off the door, and jogged downstairs. As I walked out the door, a lady with two kids and arms full of groceries headed toward the building. She tipped her head at me as I held the door for her, before she said, "Thank you, sir."

"You're welcome." I winked at the little girl. When I looked back at her mom, she was looking me up and down, and there was a hungry look in her eyes. I just nodded at her again. "Have a good day."

When I got to my bike, I unlocked the helmet lock, slipped my helmet on as I threw my leg over the seat, and pushed the start button. The engine roared to life, setting off the two alarms to the cars parked on either side. I chuckled, because I had parked away from everyone, to prevent this very thing from happening. Not my fault they parked on either side, with the entire parking lot practically vacant at this time of the day.

I loved my bike, though, and had paid more for it than many paid for a car. But 2500cc's didn't come cheap, and the six-cylinder engine was a force to be reckoned with. I rolled out of the spot and looked up to where Maddie's empty apartment window was. My heart flipped and sank again. I tried to bury that feeling as I pulled out onto the street heading for 880. When I got off at The Alameda and headed toward the University, my phone rang and I clicked the button on my helmet to answer. "I'm sitting at the light. Calm down."

A light chuckle came through, and I revved the engine to make a point. "Just wanted to make sure you didn't forget where the Astral office was."

"Not likely, since Astral Primal Alpha Jade Romero gave me numerous assignments from behind those desks."

Another chuckle and he said, "I'll see you in a few minutes, Westbrook."

"Asshole." I muttered. The window to the F150 next to me rolled down and a middle-aged man asked what kind of bike I was on. "Triumph Rocket 3."

He whistled and his eyes roamed the length of it, and I smirked. It was a hella sexy bike, and I had decided it was worth the money after the first trip to Carson City for a job. It handled the curves of Highway 50 beautifully, and my ass didn't hurt when I arrived.

Parking at the other end of the parking lot, I hung my helmet on the custom clip, and went inside the Spanish style building. The access panel clicked open when I pressed the entry card against it, and the door slid open. A small simi formal reception area sat up front with a mess of glass and dark wood cubicles. I didn't know how anyone could do anything in this sort of environment, but I also knew my circumstances were much different from the rest of the world. I nodded to the Therugi who sat at the desk, and she smiled brightly, "I'll let him know you are on the way back."

"Thanks, Janet."

I opened the heavy dark wood door with the old Norse protection rune encompassed with a circle, and two daggers crossed behind it etched on the door to find Minstrel Carlos Medina was standing there looking at me with a serious look on his face.

"Shit. Where am I headed?"

"Colorado. Grand Junction to be specific. There is a witch that has gone rogue." Carlos said, handing me a code to access the file on the Agency's app.

"Why do I have to go to Colorado? It will take me a couple of days at best to get out there." I asked, opening the app, punching in the access code, and then looking back at him while it loaded on my phone. "Isn't Melissa available? She's usually hanging out in the four states."

"Melissa is on another assignment in Utah at the moment, and it's taking a bit of undercover work to get her close enough to her target." He released a long breath and said, "It wouldn't take you days to get there if you would just fly, ya'know."

"There is something about being locked up in a pressurized box that makes me twitchy. With my abilities, you don't want someone trying to restrain me or pat me down." I said with a wry smile.

His eyes brightened, and he smirked. "That would take a bit of paperwork. Though we could get you TSA clearance. I have pull with the government and may be able to get you cleared to just get on a plane."

I looked down at my phone and started swiping through the file, seeing the long line of infractions on the witch's record. She had been busy, that's for sure. The majority of it would not be on the local authority's radar, but definitely on the Agency's. This time, though, the police had started asking questions. "Isaac can't pull the locals off it?"

"Clarisse Héroux" Minstrel Carlos said.

"Is that supposed to mean anything to me?" I said, still scanning the pictures and information.

"She hexed, then poisoned her. Look at the *Deceased* tab." When I did and then her name, I sighed. Dried blood ran from her nose and mouth, but her eyes were missing. No other trace of blood at all. My eyes, however, focused on the slightly pointed ears. I raised my eyebrows and looked up at him. "She's the daughter of the Brokville Mayor. Bastard child. He won't claim her."

"The mother Fae? Or the father?" I asked. "Where are they in all of this? You don't wanna piss off the fae, so where do we stand?"

The fae had only come out of hiding about a thousand years ago. They had stated that they had watched the Ashstrike Sanctorum for a long time before coming forth. The problem was they had some truly unique abilities, and some of their older tales told of jumping through portals to other lands. Even of a war over five thousand years ago that wiped out most of another world. They were elusive as the Angels themselves.

"The father. The Brokville Mayor is Fae. Mother is human. Clarisse was half-blood. Since there is high visibility on this, the Fae Primal is calling for action, swiftly. Hence why they aren't waiting for Melissa to finish her assignment in Utah."

"Supernaturals are forbidden from being in office. How did the Agency even allow this to begin with?"

"Small town, mostly supernaturals. A supernatural has usually held office there, but is forbidden from running for anything beyond Mayor."

"Again, why am I being hauled all the way out there?" I closed the app, and set my phone on his desk.

"Because you are the best."

I gave him a droll look. "That's an awesome legacy. The best hired assassin for a private agency."

"I'm sorry Jesse. I know it's a hard, lonely life." He paused when he saw me turn my head to the side. "Madilyn Taylor."

"Don't, please. I know it's a risk. I need to distance myself, but I can't. There is something about her." I whispered.

"Jesse, I know the special apparatus helps, but you are putting her life in danger."

"It's torture. I can't get enough of her. I can't fully give myself, because if I do, then I lose her. It isn't something I forget." My fists were balled up, and I concentrated on releasing them.

"Be careful."

"You've made your point. You can let Isaac know I'm on the way, but I'll be a couple of days." I waited for his confirmation, which took a long moment as he studied me, and when he did, I turned and left the room.

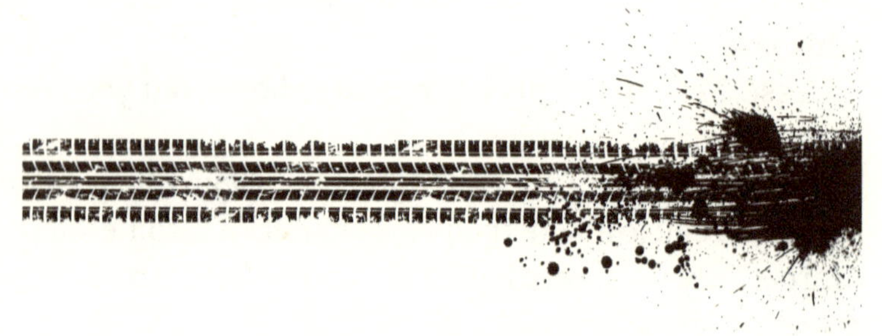

CHAPTER 5

MADDIE

"So where is your man headed this time?" Beth asked as I sipped on my milkshake. I had woken up this morning saying goodbye to Jesse again.

"Don't know. Didn't say." I looked at my phone and craved just a message that he was okay.

"I'm assuming you fucked like rabbits last night." She said, stuffing a bite of her salad into her mouth.

I rolled my eyes and blushed, knowing Beth said it just to get to me. In comparison to her, I was a prim princess. Jesse was my third serious boyfriend, and he had taught me most of what I know about sex. I'd lost my virginity at sixteen, but at that age, what do you know other than opening your legs, and letting the boy do what he wants? It's all about him at that age, anyway. Or at least that is what I thought.

It wasn't until my last ex that I learned I was worthy of receiving at least some pleasure. That all came to an end after I caught him cheating on me, a few times, and the realization that there was just too much gaslighting, I found the courage to walk away. It had been with Beth's help, but I did it.

There had been a few Mr. Right Now's and one-night stands before the day that Jesse walked into my life. When I saw him at the bar that first night, I had felt that tug in the world, and I've been like a moth to a flame ever since. He was all I wanted.

My phone vibrated on the table, and on the screen was a message from my brother, Sean, telling me he had to go to Colorado for an assignment.

"Jesse?" Beth asked, bringing me out of my thoughts.

"No. Just Sean saying he's going to Colorado for work." I muttered in disappointment.

"Still can't get information on what exactly his new job is? I mean, I'm glad to see he's kicked his gambling habit and has stayed off the heroin, but it would be nice to know what he is doing for twork now."

"I know, but he really seems healthier." I shrugged and said, "Said he'll be there for a few days."

Beth absently swirled her drink and then sighed.

"You want him back?" I asked without really asking. I knew how much she loved him.

"Depends on if he can stay clean. I'm also not going to assume all that gambling debt. I have to protect myself."

I nodded. Even I had pulled back from Sean for that very reason.

"Anyways, Jesse." Beth said, switching subjects. She was deflecting because it hurt to talk about Sean. I knew the feeling, and didn't blame her. "You really don't know where Minstrel Carlos is sending him this time?"

"I don't. Doesn't really matter. I'd really rather not know, because if I do, then I'll start wondering if I know who it is he's dealing with."

She chuckled and shook her head. "I know you've told me how he protects you, but I'm surprised you would even continue to—"

"I love him, Bethany Jayne Wilson." I cut her off.

"And I love Sean, but I had to walk." She leaned back, and said a bit defensively, "I didn't walk because I don't love your brother. I would have married him if it weren't for the drugs and gambling."

"To be fair, those are totally legit character flaws that are not easily overlooked."

"And the fact Jesse can kill you, me or any other supernatural with just the brush of a finger isn't a legit character flaw?"

Beth was a Kismot I had met randomly at San Jose State. All supernaturals could feel the extra pull of another supernatural. The stealthiest of us, though, were Astrals. They were the ones who were basically an emissary with daggers and could hide their "otherness" from us. They could move fast as lightning, and you wouldn't know what happened, until it was over.

"We are very careful." I muttered, then took a long draw of my milkshake.

"I still worry for you, Maddie."

"Besides, his touch killing me isn't a character flaw. It's no different from me being from a line of Bacris or you a Kismot. His ability just isn't shapeshifting. It's a toxin excreted from his skin that happens that kills supernaturals instantly."

"And humans."

My eyes popped up to hers, and while there was sorrow there, her eyes had a hardness to them that hit me in the gut. "Once. That was just once, and it was why he didn't want to even start anything with me."

"Yet, if he asked you to marry him, you would in a heartbeat."

"Yes, I would." I didn't hesitate. "I love him wholly. That includes him being an Exorci."

"He still killed a human." She shrugged, taking another fork full of her salad.

"And you say that like no kismot has ever killed a human before. I know they have. I also know that your own sister did it on purpose."

"She was protecting her mate."

"And when Jesse did, it was an accident. So many Exorci had been able to sleep with humans, he thought he would be able to as well. He was sixteen. Didn't know it was even going to be a problem until the next morning when they found her." I let out a long breath. "That wasn't his fault."

She stared at me for a long time before she finally nodded her head. "They test the level of exorcorotoxin in an Exorci's skin now because of it, so that is some progress."

"It is. I just wish it wasn't at Jesse's expense." Putting a fry in my shake, I smiled and when I ate it, Beth wrinkled her nose. "What?"

"I have known you for eight years, and I still can't get used to you doing that."

"You don't know what you are missing, my friend." I took another and dipped it dramatically into the shake, bringing up lots of the chocolate frozen goodness before popping it into my mouth.

She just tipped her head back and laughed.

CHAPTER 6

JESSE

It was dark, barely any light coming from the light of the moon, which would mean it would be hours before anyone would find the body, and I would be long gone by then. Slowly, I walked up to the house and noticed that the front door was ajar. I closed my eyes and centered myself and could feel death slowly filling the space ahead of me.

Shit. If someone had gotten to the witch before me, Isaac and Carlos were going to be very pissed off. I opened the door with a light push and saw the witch on the floor, throat slit from ear to ear. Much further and they would have decapitated her. Amateur, quick job.

There was a rustling of movement in the kitchen, and I tilted my head and listened. The ping of energy from them was really faint. Whoever it was, was a supernatural, but last of their line or not registered supernatural. I froze as I wondered if it was possible this was the work of an Astral, but why send me if an Astral was here to dispatch the witch? I looked back at the witch. The tangy, tart smell of her death was filling the house already. Typically, the smell of death wasn't a problem, but it was something about a witch's death that always caused my stomach to swirl in that sour kind of way.

I slowly removed my leather gloves and tucked them into my pants pocket. Making my way across the living room, I saw just the outline of someone at the sink.

"Amateur." I said, causing him to jump and turn. He wore a ski mask, and there was just enough light in the room that I saw his eyes widen.

"Exorci."

I let a feral smile cross my face as he took in my six-six muscular frame. He was shorter than I, maybe six one, and scrawny.

He lunged for me and I dodged the movement, and tried grabbing his wrist to put an end to everything quickly, but he was fully covered.

"A precaution, because we never know when we will run into one of you fuckers." He said in a voice that was familiar, but not.

He swung the knife and caught the top of my hand as I danced out of the way. Whoever this was being careful, but when he kicked out, I grabbed his ankle, and held it in the air. He pulled on it, and the motion moved his pant leg up.

I smirked. "Maybe you should have tucked your pants into your boots." He pulled on my grip, but I had a firm hold on him. "Before I kill you, who sent you after the witch?"

He pulled yet again, and when I didn't release his foot, I sighed, and slid my other hand up his leg, and he fell to the floor.

It was strange, though. His eyes turned toward me, sadness filling them before he said, "Tell her I'm sorry. Tell my sister I'm sorry."

I blinked. He shouldn't be able to talk to me. He should be beyond a doubt dead. "What?"

"Exorci. Tell... my sister... I'm sorry." Then he took one last shuddering breath and was gone. I toed him with my boot and kneeled down next to him. I watched his chest for a moment, and when it no longer moved, I removed his mask.

Then the face under the mask caused every cell in my body to freeze solid. The smattering of freckles across his nose. The apple shaped cheeks, the... gods, even the golden eyes were the same, even in the vacant stare. All the features I loved so much, on a male face.

Oh gods, it really is him. I tried to calm my breathing. Fuck. Fuck. Fuck. Fuck.

I blinked and stared at his face.

Fuck!

When air filled my lungs again, I reached into my pocket and pulled out my phone. I dialed the number and when Minstrel Carlos answered the phone, there was a clear, "Speak."

"We have a problem."

"Explain."

"The witch is dead, but not by my hand. Someone beat me to it."

"Do you know who?"

"Sean Taylor." I let out a long breath before continuing, "Which is the problem. He fought me and I'm the one still standing."

"Sean... Taylor." I could practically hear the wheels turning.

"Maddie's brother." I forced the words out.

"I can see how that is a problem for you."

"Minstrel, while personally it really fucks things, what in the absolute fuck was Sean Taylor doing in Colorado?"

"Murdering your target, apparently."

"Obviously, but why? How are Sean and the witch connected?"

"Look into it, Westbrook. I'll let Isaac know you will be hanging around a bit longer than we originally thought.

I woke up to my phone going off. For five days, I tried to find the connection. For five days, I dove into every aspect of Sean's life for any connection to anything here in Colorado, and I couldn't find a damn thing. Except for the witch. The witch had some contact with a Jaysen Flinch with an area code of 650. That was the closest connection to anything back home. A phone number with a Bay Area area code.

I didn't even look at the phone, but just put it to my ear and said, "Talk."

"Jesse."

I stopped breathing. "Maddie." I let her name out in a whisper. I knew why she was calling, but I couldn't say anything. She was crying and probably had been for hours. "Hey, little bird. It's going to be okay. Tell me what's wrong."

I hated having to play the part, but she couldn't know. She couldn't know that I was the one who killed him, that I was looking into him and what his connection to the witch was.

"It's Sean. He's dead. Got in some trouble in Colorado, and they found his body at a witch's house outside Grand Junction. The local officials say his body appears to be clean, though. So at least it doesn't appear to be drugs. They don't know what killed him. I told them to run an autopsy, but then Minstrel Carlos said he would handle it. He's been dead for a week, and I'm just now finding out about it. Minstrel Carlos said it was because they didn't even identify Sean until yesterday."

I stayed quiet and just let her talk. She rambled on for a few more moments before saying, her voice soft and careful, "Can you come home?"

My gut tightened because I knew I needed to be there for her. Needed to hold her and tell her everything would be okay. I also really needed to stay here and find out what the connections were, and why Sean was even involved. But I'd also been through the witch's house from top to bottom at this point. I wasn't so sure there was much more to do here.

"When is the funeral?"

"I... I don't know yet. Hopefully, this weekend. Minstrel Carlos is setting everything up. Agency and all." Her voice trailed off, then she hiccupped through some more tears. "I really want you here. I know you are working. Can you ask Minstrel Carlos for a short leave? Please?"

My fingers ran through the hair at the top of my head, and I gripped it tight. "Okay. Give me three days. I need to finish up before I can head out. Then I'll ride hard and fast to get back to you, okay?"

"Thank you, Jesse." The relief in her voice almost undid me. She paused for a moment before saying, "Beth's here with me."

"She okay?" Sean and Beth had a long fucked up relationship. One of the smartest things Beth had done was to leave Sean.

"She's pretty torn up. You know her though, she's trying to be strong for me. I'll be better when I'm in your arms, though. So, hurry, please?"

"I need three days at a minimum. I can't get there any sooner." I stretched the truth, but it was a long two-day ride at best.

"Where are you?"

I chuckled, "You know I can't tell you that, little bird."

"Three days, huh?" I could hear her wheels turning. "At least I know you are still on the west coast. Possibly even still in California if you have to spend a day or two cleaning up."

"Maddie."

"I know. I know. Can you blame me for wanting to know where my heart is?" I could picture the smiling smirk on her face, and couldn't help the smile that crossed mine. Only there was that sinking feeling again in my chest.

"Three days, Maddie. I love you."

"Prove it when you're home." Was her only response before she hung up.

Groaning, I got up and leaned on my knees, staring at the wall with all the notes, photos and red string interconnecting everyone, except for Sean. Sean was the enigma. He didn't fit. I'd dug into the witch, and linked her to fourteen other murders on the west coast, the highest profile case being the Brokville Mayor's daughter. I was sure that the only reason the police hadn't gone on a literal witch hunt was because of the Agency's involvement.

What also bothered me was that I couldn't find the piece that fit the victims together. They were of all races, shapes, sizes, and religions. There was nothing that showed any kind of pattern. Only three of the victims seemed to even have any connection to this Jaysen Flinch in the Bay Area. One was an accountant in San Jose, another a sales clerk for a grocery store in Mexico, and the other was a ranch hand in Portland.

There was very little in the way of cross over for any of the victims.

I went to the bathroom, washed my face, and grabbed a protein bar before leaning on the doorjamb, staring at the web on the wall again. "Shit Sean, what did you get yourself into? Why did you have to be there? Why did it have to be me?"

I grabbed my phone and pressed a few buttons, immediately connecting me to Minstrel Carlos. "Jaysen Flinch. What, and who is he?"

Silence for a moment, but I heard some clicks of the keyboard before he said, "He's on the list, but human classification. Not sure exactly why a human is on our registry, but I'll look into it."

"That answered the *what* of that question, but *how* about answering the who?" I bit back. Him being human just meant that I was on my own finding him.

"He had a record until five years ago, when it was sealed by Court Order." Carlos hummed a bit, before a few more clicks had him saying, "He has friends. High up friends."

More clicks.

"Carlos." I drew out his name. I was losing patience and didn't have time for these games.

"Hold on to your handlebars, Westbrook." Few more clicks of a mouse, and he said, "There are several felony drug possessions with intent to sell that didn't stick, and he's been questioned in a few suspicious deaths, but again, nothing."

"Well, there is the Sean connection." I started taking down my notes and string and putting them all into folders.

"Care to elaborate?"

"There are three murders that the witch committed that connected the deceased and the witch to Flinch." I closed up the folders and stuffed them into the saddlebag before starting in on my personal belongings. "The witch had multiple calls from a 650 number—"

"650?"

"Yup. So now we know why he was here. He must have been working for Flinch. Probably something to do with his gambling debt." I said in realization.

"Exorci, what are you talking about?"

"Sean Taylor had a bad history of heroin and gambling addictions. Sean may have been getting his fix from Flinch too, but it was my understanding he hasn't touched the stuff in a while. Hence why I said he probably is into him for money." When Carlos didn't respond, I asked, "Can you pull Flinch's financials? Any companies? Anything and everything on him?"

"It will take a couple days, but yeah."

"Good timing. I'm assuming you are still in San Jose?" There was a grunt of confirmation. "Okay. When is Sean's funeral?"

"I have it organized for Sunday. I'm assuming I'll see you there?"

"Leaving now. After I spend a night with my girl, I will get back to this. I let out a long breath.

"I'll have the information you want at the funeral."

"Thanks." I turned off the phone and stuffed it in my jacket pocket, before tossing everything into the saddlebags. It took less than five minutes to pack up and walk out the doors. A text to Isaac that I was leaving town so he could re-secure and sanitize the safe house, and I was starting the bike.

I had just buckled my helmet when the phone rang again. I declined the call and chuckled when Isaac immediately texted how I was being rude.

> **Just started the bike. Will be hard to hear you.**

> **Minstrel Isaac:**
> **Fine. I need a report.**

> **You'll have one in a few days.**

> **Minstrel Isaac:**
> **Not good enough, Exorci. I have people to report to as well.**

> **Then call Minstrel Carlos. He can update you.**

> **Minstrel Isaac:**
> **You are supposed to report to me on this one, Exorci.**

He wasn't really wrong, but considering the circumstances of this case and everything else that had intertwined my personal life, Isaac could back the fuck off.

> **There are ties back home.**

Minstrel Carlos can bring you up to speed.

I put my phone back in my pocket and pulled back out onto the road to head home. I wasn't sure how I was going to face Maddie, but if she wanted me there, that's what I was going to do.

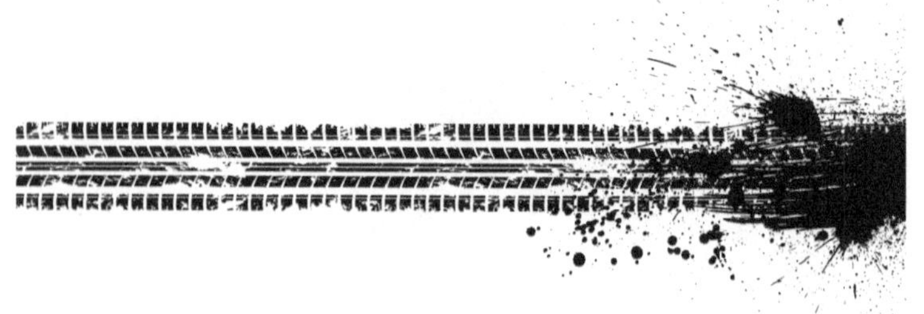

CHAPTER 7

MADDIE

"I'll get it." Beth said, when there was a knock on the door. I sighed and got up to make another cup of coffee. Probably another relative sending flowers. My apartment was filled with the fucking things. They didn't make me feel better, and I didn't want them. It wouldn't bring Sean back. I grumbled as I poured another cup of coffee. I clunked the pot back onto its spot and got the creamer out of the fridge. The funeral was tomorrow, and once it was done, I was sending all these flowers to a convalescent home where someone could enjoy them. The toxicology report that came back said no heroine or other drugs were in Sean's system, and that was a relief to both Beth and I.

After putting a splash of creamer in, I reached for the sugar to add to my coffee when a deep voice said, "How many cups have you had today, little bird?"

I turned and flung myself into his arms. "Jesse." I cried into his chest. I wrapped my hands around his waist as he pulled me closer. He kissed me quick on the top of my head where my bun sat, and I sighed.

"When did you get in?" I pulled back and looked up at him. He looked tired.

"Drove straight here. I haven't been by my condo yet." He said, taking my cup of coffee from the counter and drinking it. He made a face and looked at me disapprovingly.

"I'm distraught. Don't judge me about my coffee."

"How many cups today?" His eyebrow lifted, and I pinched my lips together.

"Beth!" He shouted over his shoulder.

"Yeah, Jesse?" She was leaning against the doorjamb.

"How much coffee has she had in the last two days?"

"Well, considering she hasn't slept more than a couple hours since she found out about Sean, too many." Beth said, and when Jesse studied her, I realized she hadn't really slept much more than I have.

"Traitor." I said, squeezing Jesse tight, before taking my cup from him and draining it. I went back over to the pot, made us each a new cup, and then handed him the pinkest fairy mug I had. He gave me a small smile, but turned back to Beth.

"How are you doing, Beth?" She just shrugged at him and took a sip of her tea. "You gotta give me more than that. Have either of you even showered since the call?"

"Jesse." I chastised.

"You are supposed to be taking care of each other." He stepped back, drank from the mug, and pinched his nose. "Little Bird, I worry about you on a normal day when I'm away."

"Then don't go away again. Stay." The words were out before I could think them through.

"You know that isn't realistic." He muttered without looking at me.

Silence filled the room, and it was Beth who finally spoke up, "Since Jesse is right, in that we should probably shower, I'll jump in first. You two need to talk."

I stared Jesse down as he stood in my kitchen drinking from the pink fairy mug. When I heard the faucet to the shower turn on, Jesse finally looked at me. There was heartbreak in those eyes of his, and I didn't know what to do with it.

"Maddie, you know I would love nothing more than to stay here with you. I want to be here for you. I want to..." He set the mug down, and I saw his hands fist and release.

"You want to hold and make love to me like a normal man." I finished for him. It wasn't that we hadn't had that discussion.

Shame lined his face. "I..."

Putting my hand over his gloved hand, I squeezed it. He gripped my fingers, held it tight, and just looked at me. "I don't blame you, Jesse."

"I know." He pulled me close to him again, and was careful where his hands touched, since I only had a short-sleeved t-shirt on. "I know."

I pulled back and sat up on the counter, and wrapped my legs around his hips, pulling him closer to me. He held me like that the entire time that Beth was in the shower. When she came back into the kitchen, she smiled and said, "Go Maddie. You're up."

Jesse gave me a sad smile, kissed my shoulder, and helped me down from the counter. "I'll be here when you get out."

Nodding before I left the room, I turned toward him. "Thank you for being here."

He gave me a sad smile, and just said, "Go. Get cleaned up."

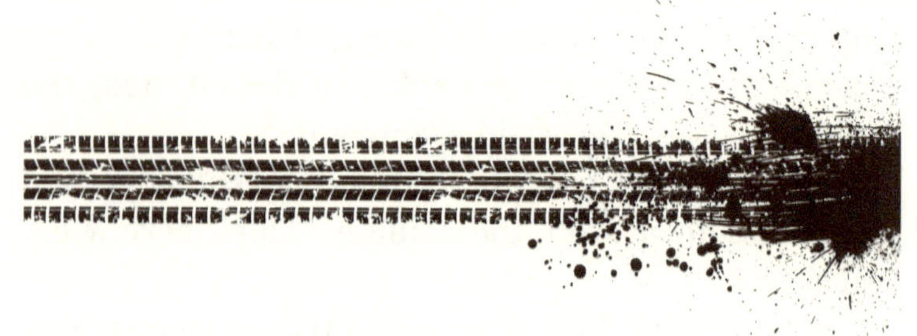

CHAPTER 8

JESSE

I took a deep breath as she headed toward the bathroom and looked at Beth.

"You know something." Beth said, crossing her arms.

"You also know I can't say anything that is Agency related." I said carefully.

Her eyes narrowed at me, and then she cocked her head to the side. "His death is Agency related?"

"Of sorts." I ran my hand through my hair, leaned against the counter, and rested my head on the upper cabinets. Her face contorted as she tried to put the pieces together. "There are connections, but I don't think he was completely out of his troubles. I'm working on it. That's really all I can say, Beth. I'm sorry."

"You said you were three days out. You got here in two and a half."

"Had to finish up where I was and then once on the road, only stopped when I had to." I shrugged, but met her stare.

"Where were you, *Exorci*?"

"I can't tell you that, *Kismot*." Beth flinched, but knew what I was doing. If she wanted to use titles, I would use fucking titles. I would hide behind those fucking titles for as long as I could to protect Maddie.

"Are..." I raised an eyebrow at her, knowing what she was going to ask, but she shook her head. "When you say he wasn't completely out of his troubles... what do you mean?"

I looked toward where Maddie was still in the shower, and said, "Beth, I know you are hurting and want answers just as much as Maddie does, but I can't tell you anything. More than that, I don't want to tell you anything that will hurt either of you."

"Fuck. What did Sean get himself into?" She growled more to herself than demanding an answer from me. She knew I wouldn't budge on this.

My phone rang, and when I saw who it was, but before answering it, I turned to Beth. "Go get dressed. We will go out to get something to eat, because something tells me neither of you have had a proper meal in three days."

Beth nodded, and when I lifted my phone to my ear, I said, "Yeah."

Carlos sounded exhausted as he said, "We have more info on Flinch."

"What do you have?"

"I'll gather it together and give you a drive with all the information on it." He paused and said, "You back in town?"

"Just got in. I'm at Maddie's. Beth Wilson is with her."

"The ex-girlfriend?"

"That's her." I took a deep breath and let it out slowly. "Beth realizes I know more than I'm saying. I'm not breaking the laws. Just keep in mind that these aren't stupid women. They know I know more than what I am saying."

"Another reason is this is a mess for you to be involved with."

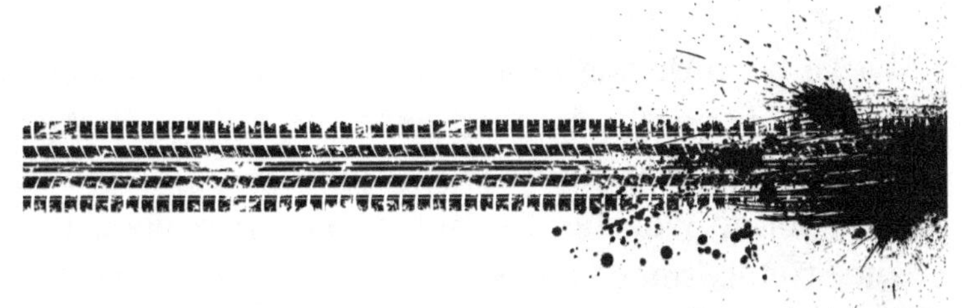

CHAPTER 9

JESSE

I drove Beth and Maddie to the gravesite a couple days later. Minstrel Carlos had arranged for Sean to be cremated, but Beth still wanted a little service for him, so Carlos made sure it happened. When we arrived, I scanned everyone there, and noted that a lot of the local Agency players were here.

The memorial service went smoothly, and tears were shed from a lot of people I didn't know. I wondered how many of them actually knew Sean in reality. We stood and waited for the room to clear.

"Hey there, Jesse." Said a voice I would know anywhere.

I turned to see Astral Primal Alpha Jade Romero. Next to her was a tall, blond muscular man, that I assumed was her bonded. "Astral Primal Alpha." I nodded my head, and she just scoffed.

"We've been through too much shit not to consider each other friends, so stop with the bullshit titles, Jesse." She smiled, and then said, "Jesse, this is my fiance, Kolton Webster. I know we haven't really had a chance to talk since I moved. I'm sorry about that."

Pulling my glove up, I shook his outstretched hand. "Nice to finally meet you, sir."

"Nice to meet you. Didn't think there would ever be a man who would make this workaholic settle down. You'll have your hands full." I said to Kolton.

Jade laughed. "He's just as much of a workaholic as I am." There was a blush to her cheeks, and it was nice to see her so happy.

"*Mija!*" Carlos came over and gave her a quick kiss on the cheek and then nodded to Kolton before saying, "There are a couple of other Astrals here who would like to see you."

"All in the day." She sighed dramatically. She turned to Maddie and said, "I'm sorry for your loss, Maddie. I had worked with Sean a few times, and while he had his demons..."

"Thank you, Astral Primal Alpha." Maddie said with a nod of her head.

Jade turned to Carlos and said, "Seriously, I need a shorter title."

There was a long string of other people both Agency and not, who came to give Maddie their condolences, but there was a man standing at the back of the hall that hadn't taken his eyes off Maddie, and it was making me edgy. There was something familiar about him, but I couldn't place it.

When he pushed off the wall, the light from the window fully hit his face, and I stiffened.

"What is it?"

"Beth." I said carefully. "Stay with Maddie. If anything happens, get her to my condo. Understood?"

"Yes, Exorci." I hated the title, but it was clear she knew I had just gone on the clock.

I took long strides toward him, and when his dark eyes met mine, he nodded out the door. Nodding for him to follow me around the corner, I slipped a glove off. There was no way I was going to take a chance on Maddie or anyone else getting hurt.

"Mr. Flinch, care to tell me why you are here?" I tried to hide the fact I was gritting my teeth.

"Sean Taylor was a... business associate of mine." He said carefully.

"Meaning you were giving him the heroine? Funding his gambling debts?"

"Sean did odd jobs in an effort to pay off debts. Luckily, there were contingency plans in place if there were ever a mishap." He said, straightening his jacket cuffs.

"Sean's dead. His debt is paid in his death." I felt my blood pressure rising, but tapped it down. My little bird would not be paying this man off. She would *not* be responsible for what Sean did.

"Oh, but I didn't kill him, did I? No. *Someone* else caused his heart to stop beating." He sighed dramatically. "Now I'm out a bit of cash. A substantial amount of cash."

"That sounds like a personal problem."

"I'll get repaid, Mr. Westbrook." I narrowed my eyes at him as he patted my shoulder and turned to walk away.

I grabbed his hand with my gloved hand, and said, "Don't put a hand on me and what's mine. Am I clear?"

"Go inside and be with your girl, while you can." He slid a card into my hand and strolled off.

"What the fuck?" I muttered, looking at the business card he gave me. *Ivy Grace Entertainment.* Along with an address of the club adorned the front of it. I knew of the club, but when I looked up to where Flinch was, he was striding toward a line of black sedans.

Carlos was watching him walk away as well, but came up and handed me a small flash drive. "Here is everything we have on him."

"He threatened Maddie. Can we put some protection on her? Any Astrals need some work? I'll pay them out of my own funds."

"Unfortunately, I don't have any extra hands, Jesse." He looked off in the direction Jaysen Flinch was and as we watched him get into a blacked-out sedan, he said, "How did he threaten her?"

"It was veiled, and nothing that would hold up in court." I ground my teeth as I said it and slid the glove back on just as shots rang through the air.

I took off running before the reality of what happened fully hit me. Astrals were surrounding someone on the ground. Two jumped out of the way as I burst through the line they had made.

When I got back to the front of the room, Maddie was crouched over someone on the ground. The shiver of death filling the room washed over me and then there was nothing but fear.

No.

Not Maddie.

No.

I bent down and pulled her to me. Her hands were covered in red, but not her blood, I realized. Beth was laying there, red spreading across her stomach and chest. Her gasps were short and wet.

I turned to where Minstrel Carlos was behind me, already on the phone. When his eyes met mine, a quick blink told him the ambulance wouldn't get here in time. I looked around the room, and saw two other Exorcis coming toward me. The look on their faces told me they felt it too.

"Jesse." Brandon said with a shake of the head and Nickolas also shook his head at Carlos when their gazes met, giving him the same information.

"Maddie, Little bird." I pulled her away from Beth.

"Jesse, help her."

"Minstrel Carlos has already called 911. They will be here soon." She grabbed onto Beth's hand, and Beth's eyes met mine. She looked at me, large brown eyes pleading, and in short quick gurgling breaths said, "Please."

"The ambulance is on the way, Beth. Hold on." Maddie begged.

Beth shook her head, and looked at me. "Please."

This time it was me who shook their head. I couldn't do it. I couldn't kill Beth, too. Brandon and Nickolas stood behind me now, and her eyes met theirs.

"I'll do it." Brandon's voice was both a grate to my ears, but also the sound of soothing salvation.

"No. The ambulance is coming and they will fix you, Beth." Maddie pulled away from me, but pulled Beth closer to her.

Beth's breathing was coming in wet gurgling breaths. Death weighed heavily in the air. I didn't know how to help Maddie. "Little bird." I said hesitantly.

"No. They can help!" She turned back to Beth, tears streaming down her face. "They will take you to the hospital. They will get you all fixed up. You'll come home with me. I can't lose you, too, Beth."

"Ms. Taylor." Brandon looked at Nickolas and me before he said, "I'm assuming Jesse has told you how our abilities work."

She looked at me wide eyed, to the two men behind me, and then back at me. "You... you can feel it?"

I nodded, but Beth's rattle caught our attention. Brandon crouched down next to her, and he removed his glove and held it over her chest. "If you want it to end now, darling, you have to touch me. I will not force this decision on you. You are free to wait to see if the ambulance comes, but..."

Beth looked at Maddie then, and when their eyes met, Maddie let out a sob, but nodded. She lifted her hand and put it in the sign language formation for 'I love you.'

Maddie mirrored it, touching their fingers together, but didn't release Beth's stare. There was a serene smile that crossed Beth's face, and it was as if the knowledge of final peace calmed her, her body relaxed. Beth reached up and threaded her fingers through Brandon's, and a second later, she was gone.

CHAPTER 10

MADDIE

Beth's eyes went blank after she threaded her fingers through the Exorci's. It was instantaneous, and I wailed as tears fell down my cheeks. First my brother dies, now my best friend dies at his funeral?

Jesse's hands landed on my shoulders, and I heard him say, "Thank you. Brandon, for giving Beth the option."

"No one should suffer. Death was here; it was just waiting."

"I know, but thank you for giving her the choice." I felt Jesse give me a long kiss on the back of my head, and then he whispered softly in my ear. "Come on. Let me take you home."

"Beth." I whispered. I couldn't let her go. I couldn't just let her lay here on the cold ground. I looked up to where Brandon was kneeling, and there was pain in his eyes as well. He hadn't let go of her hand yet. I looked at it, and he gave it a gentle squeeze before he said, "It was her choice. She decided to release herself."

I knew that, but I felt hollow inside. I dunno what I would do if I didn't have Jesse. I leaned back into him, and Brandon's eyes fell on Jesse. He bunched his eyebrows in question, and I felt him shake his head.

"I know the dangers of being with Jesse. Please don't." I croaked. There was an edge to my voice I didn't even recognize. I looked down at Beth, just as the doors burst open, announcing that the ambulance and paramedics had finally arrived.

Jesse pulled me back, and I curled up into him. Minstrel Carlos was dictating instructions left and right, but I didn't hear anything. I crunched Jesse's shirt in my hands and sobbed into his chest.

Paramedics shouted orders for chest compressions as the gurney lifted, and they wheeled the remains of my best friend away.

"I'm taking her home. You know where to find me." Jesse said.

For three days, Jesse had stayed and taken care of me while I sat on the couch, staring into nothing, or wandered around the house straightening nothing. Jesse made sure I ate, even though the first day, I just threw everything up.

This morning when I woke up, wrapped in a blanket, and Jesse's arm wrapped tight around me, I felt a little more like me. I smiled as I rubbed my thumb back and forth over his long-sleeved shirt he always wore.

Realizing my bladder was about to burst, I slipped out of bed and went to the bathroom. When I was done, I looked at the drawer, and slipped on a pair of specially made latex shorts that we used.

I leaned against the doorjamb for a moment, watching him, and even in sleep, he was the most handsome man I had ever seen. The way this man flipped me inside out... There would never be another man who would own my heart the way that Jesse Westbrook did.

"Hey, little bird." He said, pulling me against him as I crawled back into bed.

"Hey." I kissed his chest, and when I looked up at him, my stomach tightened in that way only he could make me do.

Running my hand down his side, pulling him closer, his eyebrows lifted. "You must be feeling better if you are getting those kinds of impulses."

"Jesse, I always crave you and never get enough of you. I'm just feeling broken inside right now." I couldn't explain it. There was this gaping hole inside my chest where Beth and Sean had been that I couldn't touch, and his presence was like an anchor, holding me still in a world spinning out of control.

That pulsing between my legs was a distress signal that could only be answered by Jesse Westbrook. He rolled over on top of me, and reached up to where the disposable gloves sat as he bent down and kissed my collarbone through my shirt. Kissing lower and lower, his teeth nibbled on my breasts and when my back arched up into him, he bit down on the nipple.

"Good gods." I moaned.

His hand went to between my legs, and stopped as he cupped me. "My little bird, prepared."

His hand ran over the smooth material of the special shorts that I was wearing. I wrapped my legs around his hips and flipped him over onto his back, so I was straddling him. His eyes heated as he said, "Someone wants to go on a ride." He licked his lips and curled his fingers in the waistband, pulling them away from me before letting it release with a snap.

I moaned at the sting it gave me, and groaned my hips along the length of him through his sleeping pants. He hardened against me the more I moved, and as the smooth material moved against me, I felt myself get wetter with each roll of the hips. Jesse met me with every thrust and pitch against him, and when his breathing quickened, I lifted myself to my knees.

He froze, and I smirked. "Eat me, Jesse."

There was no hesitation as he moved further down the bed, and wrapped his arms around my hips, and pulled me down onto his mouth. The feel of his tongue through the thin material had me moaning and lightly grinding against him. When Jesse latched onto my clit, I sat down on him and rode his face hard. I looked down at him, and his eyes were on me. Love and lust filling every corner of them. When he winked, our signal he needed air. I cocked an eyebrow, smirked, and ground against him a few more times, before lifting and allowing him air to breathe.

"Little Bird is feeling," he let his tongue drag across the center of me before finishing, "feisty this morning."

"I swear Jesse, if you don't make me cum all over your face, feisty is going to be the least of your worries."

His answer was to run his tongue around the tight opening, and an unbidden, "Fuck." Groaned out of me.

Jesse chuckled, and I looked down at where his head was just peaking back out from between my legs. "Make. Me. Cum. Jesse," was his only warning as I sat back on his face and rode him. He didn't hesitate. Only licked and sucked.

He pushed up on my hips, and said, "Face the other direction, little bird."

I flipped around and saw his cock sticking straight up in his pants. "Speaking of feisty." He pulled me back down on his face and attacked my clit. Nips, sucks, and the lapping that had my hips moving of their own accord. I bent over and ran my lips across his cock through his pants. I felt the vibration of his moan enter me, and then his finger was pressing against my ass as he clamped down on my clit. My hips moved in short thrusts against him, as my hand moved across his cock.

I had just had the thought of thinking that a good way to die would be by Jesse spilling himself deep down my throat, when an orgasm rocketed through me so strongly I froze. Everything went silent. There was nothing but Jesse's finger inside me and flicking my clit with his tongue.

When it subsided, I collapsed and rolled off to the side of him. I was working on catching my breath when he got up and out of bed. "Where do you think you are going?"

He turned and looked down. I smiled at the wet spot on the front of his pants. "Looks like I need to clean us both up."

I heard his phone go off a couple times when he was in there, but when he returned, he had a washcloth and was sliding on a new pair of gloves.

Putting the washcloth down for a moment, he slid the shorts off before picking it back up and wiping me down. He tossed the washcloth in the hamper and the shorts into trash before pulling my shirt down and kissing my stomach.

His phone went off again, and he sighed, resting his head just below my heart. "I am not answering that."

As if his phone knew that he was ignoring it, the phone rang, and he groaned. "If that wasn't Carlos' ringtone, I would ignore it, little bird."

I reached over, grabbed it, and handed it to him.

"Talk fast. I'm in the middle of adoring a beautiful little bird right now, Carlos." His eyes had moved very slowly up my body as he said the words, and when they met mine, they heated.

Until he blinked and it all vanished. "It's only been three days though... Yes, sir. I'll meet you at Mavericks in ten."

He hung up, laid his head back down on my stomach, and whined like a baby. "I don't wanna."

I ran my hands through the tips of his hair and smiled. "I know. Do you have to leave, or just meet with Minstrel Carlos?"

"I don't know. I'll let you know." He groaned as he got out of bed and got dressed. When he slipped on his jacket, my stomach tightened.

"Gods, I love you in that jacket."

"You love me regardless. Now, be good, my little bird."

"Aren't I always?" I huffed a laugh, but gave him a devious look that had him shaking his head with a small smile. "I love you, Jesse."

"Love you too, Maddie." He kissed the top of my head and headed out the door.

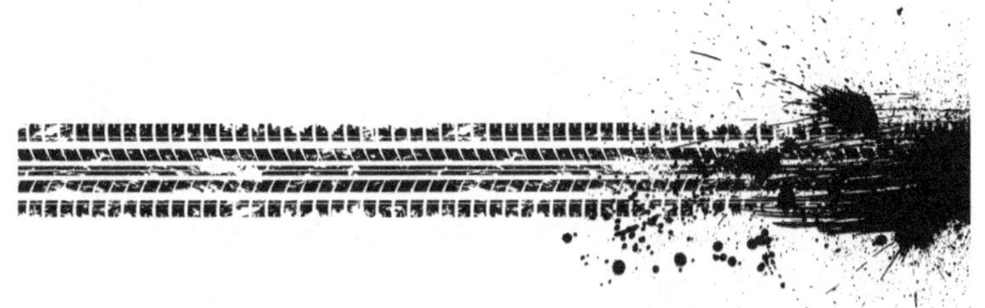

CHAPTER 11

JESSE

Thirty minutes later, I was meeting with Carlos at a restaurant with a tablet opened to a private, secured file.

"This was all you could get on Flinch?" I shuffled through a few of the files, but it wasn't much more than what was on the thumb drive he had given me at the funeral.

"I'm sorry, Westbrook. For the last few years, on paper, he's a clean citizen who pays his taxes. The worst thing he's done is get a speeding ticket going over the

Grapevine coming from LA, and he paid it on time, with no penalties."

I leaned back in the leather booth as the waitress dropped off the deep-fried onion between us. Reaching over and plucking off a couple pieces, I dipped it in the ranch before popping it into my mouth. I ran through everything I knew about the man.

"Do you know what the connection really is to him and your girl's brother?" Carlos asked, leaning forward on his elbows and pulling a piece off for himself.

"Like I told you before. I know Sean had a bad gambling problem, and from what I've been able to sort out, Flinch has ties to Sean's dealer. It's not enough, and I have found nothing that says he was into him for any money, but Sean was always good at hiding that until they came to collect." I pinched the bridge of my nose.

"How is she doing?"

"She's just lost her brother and her best friend. Considering she's still on this side of the ground, I'll take that as a win." Carlos nodded at me, picking another piece of the fried onion, and biting into it. "But other than a few phone calls from the other creatures and Flinch, I can't find any connections."

Carlos' phone buzzed, and he looked down. When I saw Primal Rebekkah's name on it, I raised an eyebrow. Carlos just shook his head and smiled.

"*Si*, Primal."

His gaze rose to meet mine, and he said, "Exorci Westbrook is actually sitting in front of me right now... Discussing the Sean Taylor matter... Yes, but..." Carlos let out a long sigh before his eyebrows inched together,

"Connected to the witch? ... And Oregon... I'm sorry did you say Primal—"

I tilted my head in question, and he held up a finger. "Yes Primal, I'll have Westbrook head out immediately." There was a quick jerk in his head and surprise crossed his face in a flash, before he said, "Alright, I'll have Pavoritti go with him."

What the hell? Brandon and I both? I tapped my fingers on the table and waited for him to finish. Whatever is happening must be big if the Agency was sending two Exorcis.

"Thank you, Primal." He hung up the phone as the waitress brought over our lunch and set them down.

"Can I get you two anything else?" She asked, noting my eyes hadn't moved from Carlos.

"Another ice tea, please." I turned to look at her and tried to give her a pleasant smile, but it was awkward. My mind was trying to figure out what in the hell could be going on. The waitress nodded her head and turned to Carlos, who nodded.

"Where am I going, and why is Brandon going with me?"

"Oregon. There are some demons who were working with the witch you went after in Colorado. Apparently, the Fae Primal recently appeared there."

"He never leaves Ireland, though. Any fae in the world have to go to him."

Carlos let out a chuckle as he put a piece of steak in his mouth. When he was done chewing, he said, "He has embraced technology. Though still grumbles about it not being as advanced as Álfheimr before its fall."

"Yet they claim to have just come out of hiding a thousand years ago. They really need to get their stories straight. Have they been here all along, or did they jump through a dimensional portal?" I took a large bite of my cheeseburger, savoring the chunk of avocado on it. I studied Carlos for a minute, trying to figure out what the hell was really going on, and half waiting for him to fill me in.

Carlos took a long drink before he said, "Primal Rebekkah also said that Flinch, who she noticed you had an interest in, has also registered a flight plan out of SFO to Portland on a jet owned by—"

"Primal Theodrym Gindryl. His Royal Faeness." I said with a sigh. "But what could Flinch and the Fae Primal have to discuss?"

"That is what I need you and Pavoritti to find out."

"But why both of us?" Then my eyes go wide at the only thought I can think of. "Carlos, if you mean to tell me that our assignment is the Fae Primal…"

"No. Your assignment is actually someone who is traveling with the Fae Primal. Primal Theodrym has ordered his release from this world, and that is actually Pavoritti's assignment. You both are going because I want you to work together to get some answers.

I chewed on another bite of my burger as I thought through what he said. I swallowed and hesitated for a moment. "Information collecting is the Ovexa's job, not an Exorci's. So, again, why are we both going?"

The left side of his lips lifted in a smirk. "I'm throwing you a bone, Jesse. Letting you investigate a link between your girl, her brother, and all the other chaos that is going on around here."

A flash of shame filled me as I stared at my fries before popping one into my mouth. "Thank you."

"I want you guys to leave in the morning. Pavoritti just got done, and is spending some time with his parents. His sister's birthday is today. Day after tomorrow, you are supposed to cross paths with them at a restaurant outside of Salem."

I nodded, knowing he would send me the specifics via more secure channels.

One more night with Little Bird, then I was off again. I nodded to Carlos and said, "Watch over her while I'm gone, please. My gut is giving me that feeling. Well, it was before Sean and Beth, but..." I let out a long breath through my nose. "It's sticking around, which means something else is going to happen."

"And it's rarely been wrong. It's one reason you are so good at being what you are."

"I'm good at doing what I do, because of the stuff in my skin." I hissed through my teeth.

"Besides that. There have been plenty of Exorci who just don't have the instincts or ability to stay alive this long."

I did know that. I'd watch many not make it through some of the easiest assignments. It was either their own stupidity that killed them, or they didn't have the mental makeup to be a born killer. There was no way around it. That's what I was. I was born to kill. I had resigned myself to that long ago. The pay was good, and the job had never bothered me. I loved my life, didn't have to deal much with humans, and I was ridding the world of the worst of the creature world. It was fine until Little Bird.

"What's going through that head of yours?"

I shrugged and moved some of my fries around on the plate before looking up at him. "I had no issues with the way my life was as an Exorci, Carlos. I'd like to think that we've become friends over the years, and I get to help make the world better, in my own twisted way."

"But..." Carlos pushed when I didn't say more.

"But, I hate leaving Maddie. Hate leaving her even more when I can feel that something is going to go sideways in a major way. Moreso than it already has." I met Carlos' gaze and said, "At the funeral. There was something about the way Flinch told me to spend some time with her while I could. There was a hidden meaning there, and I don't know what it was."

"Go north. See what you can find out." He put the last piece of steak in his mouth, and I eyed him carefully.

"What aren't you telling me, Carlos?"

He laughed at that. "I'm Minstrel of an agency for supernatural and paranormal creatures. There is a lot that I'm not telling you, and even more that I can't tell you."

"That isn't what I mean, and you damn well know it."

His smile faded as I saw him scan the room quickly. "There is something larger going on. There are too many coincidences. The chances that the Fae Primal, Flinch, and Sean Taylor keep coming up means there is a connection. We just need to know why and how."

I nod once in confirmation, but then add, "The fact the Fae Primal has left the Isles is eye-catching enough. Why would he chance doing that and meeting with someone shady?"

The waitress laid the bill down, and Carlos slapped the Agency black card down. Her eyes went a little wide, as she took the agency black credit card and walked off.

"Go. Spend another night with your girl and I'll get you the info you need for the road."

"Thank you."

CHAPTER 12

MADDIE

Jesse left early this morning, only saying he was headed north and didn't know when he would be back. I made him promise to call me tonight, between the non-stop kisses and sniffling on his chest. He had chuckled and said he would. I knew there wasn't much he could tell me, but he kissed my head before walking out, and I had forced myself to get up and go to work. They told me I didn't need to come in yet, and to take a few more days, but I couldn't just sit in my apartment.

Only my brain wouldn't focus. It was 3:30pm, and I was having the worst case of the mid-afternoon drop I'd had in a long time. I stared at the monitor, sure that there was some reason for going into this program, but I couldn't remember for the life of me what that was.

When my desk phone rang, it scared the living hell out of me, and I shook my head before seeing that it was just the front desk. I reached over and picked up the receiver. "Hi, Becca."

"Maddie, there is a man here to see you. A Mr. Flinch?"

Why did that name sound familiar? I could almost hear Jesse's voice saying it, but why?

I must have taken a moment too long, because Becca said, "Maddie?"

"Yeah. Put him in the conference room. I'll meet him there."

"You got it." She said as I hung up the phone, shaking my head and trying to sort out why I knew the name. I still hadn't figured it out by the time I'd walked down the long, carpeted hall to the reception area, where Becca smiled and said, "He's inside conference room two."

I opened the glass doors and stepped inside. "Sorry for the delay, Mr. Flinch. What can I do for you?" When he turned, I froze, blinked, and realized I had seen him before. "You were at the funeral."

"I was. I was a... business associate of your brothers." He was a little over six foot and dressed in a dark blue pinstripe suit. His brown hair was cut and styled perfectly so not a single hair was out of place, and I wasn't sure there was a single hair on his face where there should be a shadow by now. Did he shave just before he came in? His piercing blue eyes reminded me of a snake ready to pounce. The very thought made my head pound slightly, and I realized I would need to get some serious sleep tonight.

"My brother didn't have a business. So that means I want nothing to do with whatever you actually associated with him on."

He let out a small chuckle. "That is where you are wrong, Madilyn Nikole Taylor."

"First, get my name out of your fucking mouth." I lifted my hand and pointed at him. "Second, I had little to no contact with that loser of a brother of mine. He was my brother by blood, and I loved him for that alone, but I hated everything he was and stood for. I want nothing to do with anything that was in his life, and that includes you."

"Except that business extends directly to you."

"I don't fucking want it. So, you may leave." I stepped back and held my hand toward the door.

He reached into the inside pocket of his blazer, and pulled out a tri-folded set of papers, unfolded them, and then in a voice that practically promised death, said, "Sit down, Ms. Taylor. You and I have business to discuss."

My heart raced, and when he flopped the paperwork on the table, I made out the words *Irrevocable Contract*. My eyes scanned the first paragraph, and it was between Davidson Investments, Jaysen Flinch, individually and DBA Davidson Investments and Sean Daniel Taylor.

I looked back at the man who stood there like he owned the building. "It looks like that is paperwork for you and Sean. That agreement wasn't made with me. Sean has no assets, and I'm under no obligation to pay any of it with my personal funds."

A sly smile crossed his face as his chin lowered, and he looked at me like he was a cat playing with a mouse. I had the sickening feeling I was the mouse and was priming to be running for my life. Right now, was one of those times I wish I was able to shift and fly away for a long time. Live like my ancestors, and just escape the real world for now.

I reached deep within me, trying to find any shred of confidence I might have left and finally said, "I would appreciate it if you would leave, and never contact me again."

"See, little Madilyn, this is where you are wrong. You are a party to this contract."

"I'm not." I ground through my teeth.

"You are. This contract isn't bound by United States or California law." Triumph shone in his eyes as he noticed I knew what he was going to say. "It's bound under Ashstrike Sanctorum law."

"Bullshit." My heart sank. We were last line registered, but because we were registered, it was required we follow obscure laws outside of those of humans.

"I would not be here if it were not, because you are right, under human law, you would be under no obligation to pay his debts, but you are not human. While you and Sean may have been last generation registered, non-shifting Bacri, you were still registered, and therefore are bound by our laws. So, I say again, Ms. Taylor. Sit the fuck down so we can discuss business."

There was an audible single pound in my head as I slowly took a shaky step toward the chair, and when I reached it, I fell into it. All my hopes of actually being rid of my brother and his problems were disappearing into dust.

I spread my hands over the contract and started skimming through the terms, most of which were pretty standard to any business contract you would find. Indemnification, insurance requirements, the usual. It was very standard until I got to the assignment and binding effects clause.

The covenants, conditions, and regulations of this agreement shall be binding upon all heirs, executors, administrators, successors, biological creatures inheritants, and assigns of parties hereto. This includes any amounts due to Davidson Investments or Jaysen Flinch, or their heirs, executors, administrators, successors, biological creature inheritants, and assigns.

While that seemed to cover why I was being held accountable for the contract, it was the following paragraph that made my heart stop.

If one Sean Daniel Taylor becomes no longer living, Sean Daniel Taylor passes all obligations for payment onto one Madilyn Nikole Taylor. If Madilyn Nikole Taylor is unable to pay off all amounts due by said call date listed above, then said Madilyn Nikole Taylor shall work for Davidson Investments and / or Jaysen Flinch in whatever capacity, said party requires. Madilyn Nikole Taylor, hereinafter "Token", shall be the property of Davidson Investments and / or Jaysen Flinch, who has complete control over all actions of Token, who will comply with all instructions, until such debts are paid. Non-compliance shall be handled in accordance with section XXIV. Forfeiture below.

My eyes popped up to the man leaning back in the chair across from me. I hadn't even seen or heard him sit down. He was smiling, knowing he had me hook, line, and sinker. His claws were in the mouse, and at first glance, I didn't have a way out.

"I'll petition the Agency for a release." Even I heard the shake in my voice.

"Go ahead. It's ironclad." He was enjoying this.

I looked back at the paperwork, and angry, hot tears stung my eyes. I was barely able to choke out, "How much?"

"You will be working for me for a long time, sweetheart. But if you really want to know the amount, the full accounting is attached to the contract, current as of the date of his death. You also won't tell anyone of our 'special' relationship."

"What if I refuse?"

"Section twenty-four, forfeiture, doll." He nodded his head in a gesture for me to look at it. When I did, I realized I really was either owned or a dead woman. Short version... I didn't do what he said, I didn't pay, I was dead. He owned me. My fucking brother sold me and signed me over to this man.

My owner stood, straightened his jacket. Looked me up and down, tilted his head to the side. "You can start at Ivy Grace."

"The strip club?"

His eyes heated slightly as he looked me up and down again, and moved so he could look at my ass. Mr. Flinch formed his mouth in a small O as he let out an appreciative breath. "You would look fabulous up there, doll. Be there at ten tonight."

Without saying another word, he smiled and walked out the door.

I just watched as he whispered something to Becca, who giggled and blushed incessantly and walked out the door like he hadn't just ruined my life even more than it already was.

It took me way too long to gather my wits, but I crumpled the paper in my grip before I walked back out.

"He was nice."

I gave her a droll star and shook my head. "I'm going home." I didn't give her a chance to say anything and strode out.

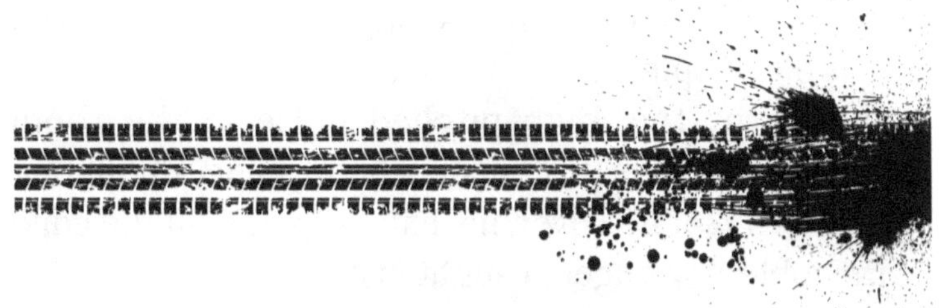

CHAPTER 13

MADDIE

When I got home, I drank half of the bottle of gin that was in the cupboard. Beth must have brought it over at some point. I yelled, screamed and tore up all the family pictures that had any photo of me and Sean happy together as kids.

He fucking sold me. Didn't even have the courtesy to fucking tell me I would be owned by an unknown man and corporation. Now, I was expected to arrive at Ivy Grace at ten o'clock tonight to do who the fuck knows what? Maybe I'll just be a server. The tips would help pay the bills, at least.

When I was done tearing through every album I had, I flopped onto the couch and chugged another long draw from the bottle. I'd been laying here for a long while, the room blissfully blurry, and as long as I didn't move too fast, it didn't spin.

There was this high-pitched noise in the room though, and when I rolled over to my side, my phone was lit up. I reached over, my hand slipping off the edge of the table. My fingers caught just enough of the edge of my phone that it fell onto the floor.

"Fuuckkk."

The noise stopped, and I sighed into the cushions. Only a moment later, the noise was back, and I looked down to where my phone rang, and saw "Jesse ♥ Westbrook".

I grabbed the phone and sat up quickly, too quickly. In the process of trying not to throw up as the room spun, and my stomach doing its gymnastics routine, I had answered the call.

"Little Bird, are you okay?"

"Humm?"

"I've called ten times."

"I'm sorry... Jesse. I..."

"Madilyn, are you drunk?" The worry in his voice made me blink and sobered me a little bit.

"No." I sighed. "Maybe a little."

"Maddie, why are you drunk? What happened?"

"Nothing." I laid down, took the small cream couch pillow, and pressed it against my eyes to keep the light out, and willed the world to right itself.

"Don't lie to me." He heaved a heavy sigh, and I winced. "You don't drink unless something happened."

I chewed on my bottom lip and pondered what to tell him. "I'll be fine Jesse."

"You will, because I'll help make sure of it. Now, tell me what happened, my little bird." The sound of my pet name on his lips brought a small smile to my face.

"One of Sean's old business partners came to visit me at work." I couldn't tell him everything. I needed to find out exactly what being owned by Jaysen Flinch even meant. If it was just working at his club until he tired of me, then I could handle that. Jesse could handle that. Until then, I would not tell Jesse anything else.

"What did he want?"

"For me to pay Sean's debt, of course, under Agency law." I huffed a laugh, and I realized just how thirsty I was. Water. I needed water. I sat up slowly, keeping my eyes closed. Before I opened my eyes, I waited for everything to right itself in my head. Fuck. I really had drunk more than my share. Crap. I needed to get sober before going to Ivy Grace tonight.

I blinked, and widened my eyes a bit a few times to try to get things to focus, but nothing was right. "Fuck. Remind me not to drink half a bottle of gin, babe."

His throaty chuckle came through, and it made me smile. "Don't drink half a bottle of gin, Maddie."

"Asshole."

There was a huff of a laugh. "You've called me worse. Usually when you're on the edge of orgasm, and I deny it."

"Yeah. Def called you worse then." A small smile crossed my lips.

"I love those whimpers, though. Getting back to why you drank half a bottle of gin... How much does Sean owe?"

My gaze flicked to the papers on the counter, but it took a minute for my brain to track the movement. The room went a little wobbly, but it righted itself. "I don't know."

I still hadn't looked at the accounting at the end of the contract. I'm sure it was hundreds of thousands of dollars. I should burn it.

"You... don't... know?" The words were slow, and then he grunted. "Don't you think that is something we need to know?"

"I'm meeting him tonight for more information. I've got it, Jesse. I'll work it out. Get a second job. I'll do what I have to." My voice was clipped, and I knew it was partially the gin, partially frustration, and partially anger.

"We will do what we need to do." He corrected. Fear coursed through me, burning some of the haze off.

"No." There was no way I was giving this man access to an Exorci. That would be mass murder, the likes that would end us both up on an extermination list. I wasn't going to do that to Jesse.

The silence that came from him was telling. I could almost see the raised eyebrow. "I'll work it out with him tonight, and figure it out."

"We will talk more about this when I get home, okay?"

"When is that going to be? Any idea?"

"Planning to have your boyfriend come over while I'm gone?" There was a smirk to his tone that had me chuckling.

"Well, maybe I'll have him work off whatever this debt is."

"Little Bird..."

"Jesse, you know whatever is left of my heart only belongs to you." I smiled, because whatever this contract was getting me into, I would do whatever I could to protect him in the process. "I love you."

"I love you too, Little Bird. Now go drink some water. Lots of water. Take a shower and eat a sandwich."

"Yeah, yeah."

"Don't sass me. I bet the room is spinning right now."

I huffed a laugh and tried not to shake my head because yes, the room was indeed spinning.

"I'll call you tomorrow and we can talk about a game plan for this Sean thing, okay?"

"Tomorrow." I sighed, just to get the conversation to stop. I didn't know what Flinch was going to require.

"Good night, Maddie."

"Good night, Jesse. And be safe."

He didn't answer, but there was a long pause before my phone disconnected. I knew he couldn't make that promise. Every time he left, he could easily not come home.

Water.

First, I needed to get up and make my way over to follow Jesse's instructions.

Water and food.

Then I could deal with Flinch and Sean's never-ending task of fucking me over.

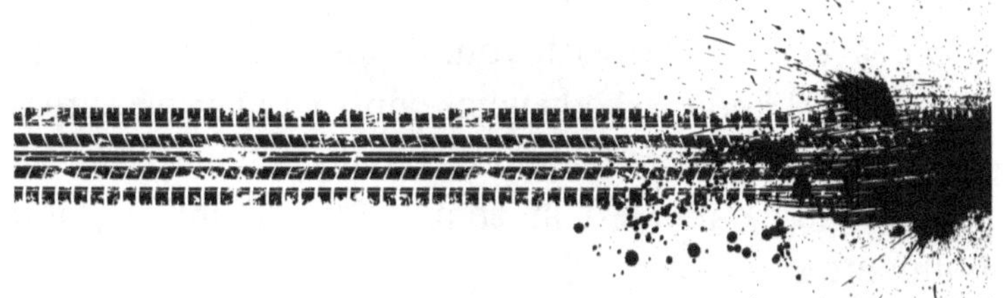

CHAPTER 14

MADDIE

Dressed in plain blue jeans, black fitted t-shirt, sneakers, and my hands in my black leather jacket, I walked, head held high, up to the doors of Ivy Grace. I bypassed the long line of people waiting to get in, and when I reached the bouncer, he indicated the long line.

"I'm here to see Jaysen."

"Name?" He turned toward a touch screen that was installed next to the door.

"Madilyn Taylor."

He pressed a few buttons, then froze and turned to me. "Sean's sister?"

I sighed heavily. "Unfortunately, otherwise, I wouldn't be here."

He looked me up and down, and then with sad eyes, just said, "I'm sorry. For everything. His death, and what Jaysen will do with you." I raised an eyebrow in question. "I know exactly what contracts Jaysen enters into. Therugi. Hellcat Demon, actually."

I actually chuckled at that. "You do make good bouncers."

The door opened then, and a tall lanky man, whose red hair was long, thin, and straight, looked at me with reflective eyes that didn't really show any iris, said, "This way, Ms. Taylor." I nodded to the bouncer and followed the man in.

I could hear the too thumpy music, but we turned before the bend toward the main room. I was led down a hall with black painted walls and dark hardwood flooring. There was just barely enough lighting from tiny starlight sized lights in the ceiling to illuminate the walkway. We reached a pair of frosted glass doors at the end of the hall around a corner, where the creature opened one, waited for me to walk in, and closed it, where I heard an audible click of the lock.

Flinch's eyes moved across the page, and then a small smirk decorated his lips. There was a push against my head, and a small pop in my ears. Gods, I really shouldn't drink like that again.

"Good evening, Ms. Taylor."

I just stared at him. When he dipped his head again, I shook my head and moved to sit down in the chair. I was tired, and just wanted to get some sleep. "So, what is the plan, Mr. Flinch?"

"You work off Sean's debt." When I didn't react, he tilted his head to the side. "You didn't look at the number, did you, Ms. Taylor?"

I meant to. Shit. "Stop playing around, and just tell me what I'm going to be expected to do, and for how long."

He tipped his head back and full-on belly laughed. "You seriously did not look at the number."

Shrugging, I gave him a blank look and said, "I'm assuming it's a few hundred thousand. I know he liked to gamble."

"Oh, Ms. Taylor. You will likely never pay off his debts." At my confused look, he leaned forward and said, "You will start off serving drinks. You will be paid minimum wage, and all your tips will go to the debt. If you get enough of an audience, I'll let you move on to being a dancer, where again, you'll get a minimum wage, and all tips will go into the debt payoff. From there, if you prove yourself, then you might be able to do some odd jobs here and there." He looked me up and down, a glint in his eye that pressed on me in the most uncomfortable of ways.

"While here, I'd like to go by 'Nikki', please." My voice sounded small, even to my own ears.

"Fine. Go get dressed. You can talk to Danella. She can get you settled. You will work here six nights a week. Mondays off. I want you here ready to work at 9pm. You'll work until you are done."

For reasons I didn't know, I didn't fight him, and stepped out of the room to find this Danella person.

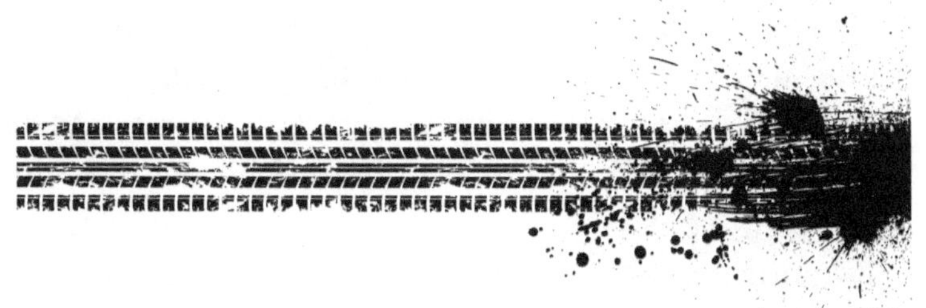

CHAPTER 15

JESSE

Sitting at the swanky restaurant overlooking a river, with Brandon, we looked like two business men looking over contracts and having a business meeting, like half of the other patrons of this overpriced place. We had received a change of location when we were just outside of Redding, California.

Brandon drove his M5 up to Portland, and I had to admit, it was comfortable for a car. I preferred the bike, but he didn't complain when I put the window down to get the air on my face.

"Can I get you gentleman anything?" The server asked. He was human, and didn't realize that most of the people in the restaurant tonight were, in fact, not human. Fae had been slowly coming in and filling the tables throughout the restaurant.

"Ice tea please." I asked as my eye caught the tall blond male walking in the door. His gaze scanned the room, and when he reached Brandon and me, there was a twitch in his shoulder before he gave us an imperceptible nod.

Brandon clocked it as well, nodded and said, "For me as well."

The Fae Primal walked by us, and by the time he walked by, there was an envelope on the table. It quickly disappeared into the false piles of papers I was studying. I watched him sit in the back corner booth facing us with two other fae.

"Carlos wasn't lying. Shit." Brandon muttered. "Flinch just walked in."

It took every ounce of restraint to stay seated in that booth and not wrap my hands around his neck, squeezing. When he walked by a couple tables away, I shivered at the spark that went through the air. My gaze popped up to meet with Brandon's. He mouthed a 'what the fuck?' and I blinked.

Why was he emanating a power? He was human. There was a groan from the fae that sat at the tables between us. The sound seemed to follow in his wake as he made his way to where Primal Theodrym Gindryl was sitting. My eyes flicked in that direction, and when the Primal narrowed his eyes at Flinch, they then flicked to me, then back. It was all in my peripheral vision because I couldn't take my eyes off Flinch sitting there, his arm draped over the top of the bench, with a small smirk on his face.

Brandon reached for the envelope and opened it. "Dorin Moreano. Apparently Primal Theodrym found him sleeping with his daughter, and a month later, found out she was with child."

His jaw tightened and his voice was tight as he told me the rest. "Moreano stabbed her when she was about three months along, killing the child growing within her." He slid the photo over to me, and I glanced at it.

"He's the one sitting on the edge." I scoffed. "How much easier could this be?"

"Why doesn't he just take care of it, though?"

"If they were not mated, then it would be a scandal in his house. I doubt anyone knew she was pregnant. Something like that would have been announced." I ran my hand through my hair. "I'm more concerned why Flinch is meeting with the *oh so secretive* Fae Primal. What is their connection?"

"Want to go have a chat?"

"Wait for them to order dinner. You can do a drive by." I looked back to Brandon. "Do you have any remote comms?"

"Always carry them." He pulled a couple from his jacket.

"Any chance you could get one in Flinch's pocket and one next to the Primal?"

"Is it time to be a klutz?" He smiled at me, like he was excited about the idea.

I huffed a laugh and shook my head. "However, you wanna do it, brother. It's your assignment."

Smiling, he handed me one of the earpieces, and I discreetly stuck it in my ear. He stood, straightened his dress shirt, tossed his gloves on the bench seat behind him before he walked in that direction, as if heading for the bathrooms. I tilted my head down as if I was studying the menu and pulled it in front of me, but I could just see where Brandon "tripped" over the leg of a nearby chair. I barely saw the comm land in Flinch's jacket pocket, and as he tried to get up, he stumbled, where Dorin Moreano tried to help him up, but just fell when he grabbed his hand.

There were a couple of just too loud exclamations, my head popping up with half the restaurant. A couple of fae had jumped up from a nearby table and had thin, delicate daggers in their hands. "Careful, boys." I muttered, more to myself than to the fae ears around me.

"*I'm so sorry, sirs. Tripped over de leg der.*" Brandon was laying on a serious fake accent, and clear as day, I heard Flinch. "*Be careful, swine. You don't know who you deal with.*"

"*Again, I'm so sorry.*" He stood, brushed off his pants, and rushed to the bathroom. I watched as the Primal, pulled Moreano up, and gestured for a couple of his companions to take him away. He was good. I would give him that. No indication that he knew he was dead.

"*What is wrong with your guard?*" Flinch sneered.

I saw the Primal's eyes narrow on him. "*First, stop trying to use your abilities on me, Flinch. Second, he has a blood flow condition that will randomly make him pass out. It will pass."*

His abilities. So, we didn't imagine that wave of power. What and who is Jaysen Flinch? It took a lot of strength to stay in my seat. Brandon's voice over the comms brought me back to reality. "Jesse."

I click the small button on the earpiece and grunt.

"Flinch is more than he seems. I could feel it."

"Hummhum."

"Be right out." Then the sound clicked, and Flinch was bitching about how one of his largest debts just died on him, and he was going to enjoy picking up that payment.

My eyes flicked to him, and I was half out of my seat when Brandon was there with his hand on my shoulder. "Sit down. We don't know he was talking about your girl."

"Don't let one idiot ruin the line." The Primals voice was light and thick in an accent that only came from the most rural of areas in the Isles. *"He can be replaced. The debt you are collecting. Think they can help out?"*

"Maybe. Need to give them time to see first. Give me a month. I have some tricks up my sleeve." Flinch had a smile on his face that made a growl come out of me. If he was talking about Maddie, I would kill him. He wouldn't lay a finger on her.

"Are there any shipment issues?"

"Nah. Everything is set to arrive on time." Flinch took a deep breath before continuing, *"But there are a couple of roadblocks that I'm gonna need to take care of."*

"I don't need to know that. Just make sure the Agency stays out of all of it."

Flinch's chuckle was menacing. *"They don't even have me on a radar. We are good there. Don't worry about that."*

My eyes met Brandon's. "I thought you said he was clean. That there was nothing but a speeding ticket."

"That's what Carlos said. He was human, with a clean record over the last few years. It matches what I have been able to find, too. There were a couple of charges brought against him over the last few years, but he's got friends, or he is legit clean, because they were all tossed out. Just disappeared into oblivion."

"We are done then." The Primals dismissal was absolute. I could feel the wave of power in those words from here.

Brandon's eyes met mine again, and I said, "Why would he risk coming for that discussion? None of this makes any sense. He could have taken care of the household issue at home."

A shadow fell over our table, and there was no doubt who was standing there. My eyes moved slowly, almost too slowly, as I turned to face him. He smiled at us and dropped the mic in front of Brandon. "Dropped something, sir."

"Thank you for returning it to me, Primal."

"I'm sure you have questions. Tomorrow morning, Crown Horizon. Penthouse. Be there at eight. I'm heading home immediately after. I've been gone too long as it is."

I blinked at him. "Yes, sir."

Then he was gone.

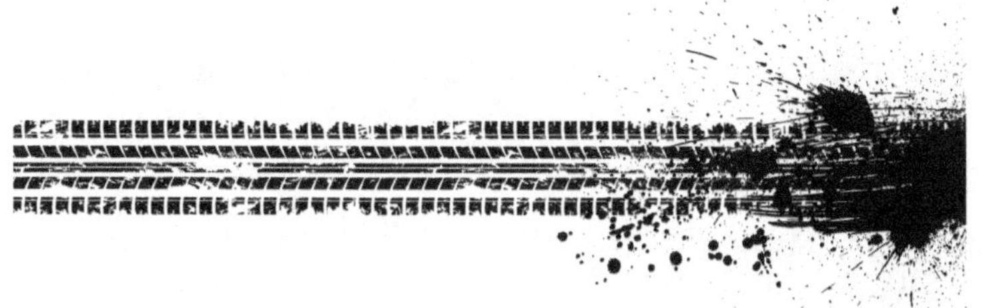

CHAPTER 16

JESSE

Last night we had gone back to the hotel room, and discussed it all. I had even called Carlos, but the asshole put me straight to voicemail. There may have been a long string of vulgar statements made.

Flinch was a creature and somehow had kept it from us, from the Agency. That sinking, spoiled feeling sat in my stomach again. I had no proof, but I knew this was all connected. Flinch, Maddie, Sean, the Primal, the witch, … all of it.

We were heading downstairs on our way to meet with the Primal, when my phone rang. When I saw the name, I answered it with a, "You better have some fucking answers."

"I've been working on it all fucking night, Exorci." Carlos' voice was drained, and it took some of the wind out of my sails. It forced me to take a long, deep breath.

"Please tell me what you've found. This is too close for comfort."

"I know, but Jesse. I can't find anything. That's just it." I stopped and looked at Brandon. When he gave me a questioning look, I said, "Carlos said there's nothing."

Brandon's voice was incredulous. "That's impossible. There is no way that amount of spark isn't registered."

Carlos' tone was hesitant, but said, "You are sure you weren't just picking up on the Primal's? Rumor is his is pretty present and could rival all the currently sitting Primal Primes."

"No, the Primal's differed from Flinch's. The Primal's was clean, clear power. Raw power. That of mythology." I still couldn't get over the feel of it.

We reached the car, and Brandon leaned toward the phone and said, "Seriously, Carlos, it's his. Not the Primals. This isn't Jesse making shit up."

I threw my bag in the trunk and went to the passenger seat, and slid in. Leaning my head back, I sighed, "What does this mean? How can he be a creature with that much signal... but not be a listed creature?"

"I..." Carlos trailed off, and it was at that moment, I leaned my head back in realization.

"Carlos. Don't you dare tell me that the thing that the Primals fear they will do, is exactly what is happening?" I groaned.

"What are you talking about?" Brandon said, starting the car and pulling out of the spot. I held up a finger.

"Let me look into it." Was all that Carlos said before he hung up the phone.

Brandon slammed on the gas as he turned onto the main road toward the meeting spot. "Start talking, Jesse."

"So, Carlos says he isn't registered, which there is no way that could be legit."

"Creatures of that power do not go unnoticed and not be on the Agency's list."

"Unless—"

"No, unless." Brandon was taking the corners a bit faster than was probably needed, and when he pulled into the valet, he slammed on his brakes, making the valet's jump back.

"Yup. Carlos is going to look into it."

"Well, fuck. That's gonna cause ripples." Brandon threw his door open and threw the keys at the scared kid. "We won't be long. Keep it close."

Neither of us spoke as we went to the penthouse at the top of the hotel. When we got there, there were four fae warriors standing guard in the entryway to the main door. The one closest to the door said, "While you don't need weapons to harm our Primal, should you not leave him in the pristine condition he currently is in, you will not get on that elevator."

Instead of opening the door to allow us entry, we were told to take five steps back. The Primal stepped out of the room, handing his suitcase to the man behind him.

"I will keep this short. I will not tell you my connection to Flinch, but you should be cautious of him."

"What is he?"

The Primal just smiled. "He's done his job well. That's beneficial."

Brandon knew not to push it, and I wanted to, but Brandon said, "What shipment is he organizing for you? Why do you need anything in the US? You control all of Europe."

He shrugged, and with a sly smile said, "I'm expanding my opportunities. Right now, it's in silks, if you must know."

"Silks..." I drawled out, and he shrugged. Again, with that arrogant shrug.

"Now, I need to get home. I have family and business matters to attend to."

"Why did you even leave? Just to have us take care of a problem for you? Why didn't you handle it in-house?" I asked, a little disbelieving this appeared to be the only reason he had left his sanctuary.

He looked me up and down before saying, "I wanted to see just how good the Pacific West Coast Exorci team was." There was an appreciative nod of his head. "Both of you are worthy of your titles."

I blinked, looked at Brandon, who was just as confused as I was. When I looked back at where the Primal was, he was standing in the elevator with his warriors. "It was good to meet you both. I wish you good health and love."

Just as the doors closed, he winked at me, and I felt a very strong shiver go down my spine, then jolt into my stomach, instantly making it sour again.

"What in the fuck was all that?" Brandon ran his hand through his short brown hair and groaned in frustration.

"I don't know." I was still staring at the closed doors when I groaned, "But why does it make that pit in my stomach feel worse?"

Brandon's head, still tipped back, rolled toward me. "Seriously, man. I feel like we are in a viper nest, and while we are armed with all the toxins, they are still going to eat us alive."

My phone rang in my pocket. "Yeah."

"You leave Portland yet?" Carlos' voice was tight as it came through the phone.

"Just finished with the Fae Primal."

"On the way back, stop and see Jade at the compound."

"What why?" I looked at Brandon, and he was looking at me with a question in his eye.

"Rose Porter saw something."

My eyes narrowed, but I stopped breathing. It was never good when you got a call that Rose Porter, Seer of the Ages, saw something. "What? Does it give us any answers to Flinch or why the Fae Primal actually left his castle?"

"We could only be so lucky." It sounded like he had flopped into his chair before he sighed dramatically. "She wouldn't tell me anything. Made a big deal about only telling you, and that she wouldn't do it any other way other than in person."

"What if I wasn't available?"

A huff of a laugh came through the line. "That is exactly what I told her, but she just said that she knew you and Brandon were in Portland and that you could take the scenic route home."

"Of course she did."

"Alright." I ran my hand through my hair. Getting home to Maddie was just going to have to wait. I turned back toward Brandon and told Carlos, "Tell Ms. Porter that we will be there in about six hours."

Pulling up to the compound, Jade met us at the door.

"Jesse Westbrook."

"Jade Romero."

We stood there staring at each other, and finally she came over and punched my shoulder. "You need to come up here to visit me. Do you understand? I don't want to admit I've missed your face."

"Hey, life has been a bit crazy since you found your bonded. We've talked on the phone. You've seen my mug via video chat."

She wrinkled her nose. "I'd actually prefer to see your mug in person. Don't tell anyone else that, though."

I laughed, and she gave me a huge hug, but when we pulled apart, she whispered, "Ms. Rose is waiting for you over at the Ranch office."

"Don't suppose she told you why I had to appear in person, did she?"

Jade gave me an even look, then looked past me and yelled, "Chantel, you gotta use your legs!"

"Yes, Astral Primal Alpha!" the girl, who I assumed was Chantel, yelled back.

"And no, Jesse. She didn't. You know how Rose is."

I sighed and shrugged. We walked inside the giant auditorium that had mats set up for various different sparing lessons for the trainees. I gave her an assessing look then asked, "Where is Kolton? I want to talk to him."

"Probably playing in horseshit."

I sputtered, and raised an eyebrow as Brandon said, "I'm sorry what?"

"The Porter Ranch is a horse rehabilitation facility."

"Why do you want to talk to my Bonded?"

I let a small smile lift the corner of my lip. "Make sure he's treating you right."

Her dramatic eye roll even made Brandon chuckle. "Like Carlos would let him treat me any way other than a Princess."

"Hey, Brandon and I have to deal with Carlos now. You were much easier to deal with. Carlos is just stressed all the freaking time. You at least know how to take a joke."

"Try living with the man." Jade's attention went over my shoulder again, and I turned to survey the room. Jade had stepped up beside me. "Chantel's parents were killed six months ago. She's dove headfirst into her Astral training. Nine. She's nine, Jesse."

"How did they die?"

"The official report is a burglary gone wrong in Sac." Without moving my head, I looked at her, and she did the same, meeting my gaze. "The real story?" I nodded. "An Ovexa was tracking some vampires making their way through downtown. Chantel's family had gone to dinner, and the vampires got bold. Grabbed her mother, killing her instantly. Her dad was slowly fed from. The Ovexa got there just in time to pull Chantel away and get her to one of the safe houses."

"What happened to the vampires?" Brandon asked, his eyes trained solely on Chantel. I'm sure he was seeing his little sister. Their parents had died at the hands of a rogue Changeling when he was only fourteen. He fought to stay with his sister and basically raised her on his own.

"They are in the deepest depths of Alcatraz."

"Good." I muttered.

"Why weren't they extinguished? Why not call us in?"

A small smile came across Jade's lips. "Chantel. She said she didn't want to have them die easily."

"Let me guess, they are both close to the burning?"

"Yup." Jade's lips said with a pop. "Said she wanted them to know what it was like to die slowly, like they had done to her dad."

"How close to death are the vamps?" Brandon said after a long minute.

"Hum?" Jade asked, obviously lost in her own thoughts.

"You said they are close to the burning." Jade nodded. "So, almost 200 years old?"

"198 and 194."

"Good. I hope they have a few years of pain before they finally die. Fucking bastards." The tone of Brandon's voice was pure Exorci, and I sighed watching the girl.

We stood in silence for a long minute, and when Chantel flung her leg around the neck of her sparring partner, she used her nimbleness and momentum to bring them down, pinning them to the mat. "Down!" the monitor said.

Jade took a step closer to me, one much closer than any other creature ever would, and I had to physically hold myself back from taking a step back.

"Jesse," Her voice was low, but just loud enough that Brandon and I could hear her. "I know you are looking into a man named Jaysen Flinch."

I felt my muscles tense, and that sour feeling in my stomach returned.

"Chantel's vampires... they were on his payroll. I don't know what they've done for him, or what exactly the connection was, but one of his shell companies came up on their bank records." Jade turned to look up at me, and I turned my head to face her. "I asked some of my contacts at Alcatraz to see what they could find out, and they both refused to talk. The vamps have gone two months without feedings. They've received protein shots, but they aren't getting fresh blood."

I took a deep breath before nodding. "Why does everything come back to Flinch?"

"What do you know of the Fae Primal?" Brandon asked Jade.

She shrugged. "Not much more than you do. You've at least seen and spoken to him."

Brandon's eyes narrowed.

"Rose." I said in understanding.

"Rose." She smiled back at us. "She knows everything. Since I've dealt with the wolves, she has had no blockages to her vision anymore."

"How are things with the wolves?"

Jade let out a heavy sigh. "Complicated, but Aaron's a huge help."

We all turned to watch Chantel again, and after a minute, Jade's shoulder bumped my arm. "Go, see Rose."

"Okay."

"Hey, Jesse?" I raised an eyebrow at her. "Everything will be fine. I'm here for you if you need anything. You know that, right?"

"Yeah. Thanks." I said as Brandon and I headed out of the building to his M5.

When we slid in, Brandon heaved a heavy sigh and said, "Why did that sound like Jade knows more than what she's telling us?"

"If it had anything to do with Flinch, I think she would have told us. Which makes the fact that it sounds like she knows more, even that much more problematic. Means it's personal."

"Your girl?" Brandon said, starting the car with a roar, and turning toward the connecting road they had put in.

"Or your sister."

Brandon shuddered at the thought and shook his head. "But Ms. Porter said she needed to see you. Not me."

My stomach swirled again, and I tapped my fingers on the armrest. "Yeah."

Five minutes later, we pulled up the gravel driveway to the main office building and when I stepped out of the car, Kolton turned around and smiled brightly. "Jesse!"

"Hey, Kolton. I see Jade was wrong."

He rolled his eyes. "Oh, is that so?"

"She said you were rolling around in horseshit."

He rubbed the back of his neck and huffed a laugh. "Yeah, I just changed. So, she wasn't wrong." His eyes flicked between us. "Ms. Rose is inside waiting for you. She wants to see you alone, Jesse."

Brandon's "fuck" was almost worse than Kolton telling me to go in alone. Then he looked at me and asked, "Want me to call to check on her?"

"No. I need to see what she says first." I looked at Brandon, whose eyes held nothing but concern. "I'll help with anything you need, man."

Nodding, I stepped inside to see Rose Porter, the infallible seer in all of the Americas.

No sooner was I across the threshold, was I wrapped up in her arms. I'd only physically met her three times, and all since Kolton and Jade had become Bonded. Ms. Rose was a myth, a legend, among the Agency. Most of all, she was someone I considered a friend. Since Jade had moved up here, I'd talked to Ms. Rose a lot more, and she was warm, friendly, kind, and stern as hell. No one crossed Ms. Rose Porter. May the Gods forever torture the soul that kills Ms. Rose Porter.

I froze as she shifted, doing a mental check of each connection of our bodies, and where I had any exposed skin. I really didn't want to be the cause of killing the woman. Then I noticed how she had slid on her long sleeve sweater, even though it was a solid 75 degrees outside, and wrapped her hands up in the ends of her sweater. I couldn't help but smile softly at the fact, she was being careful too.

"Jesse. It's so good to see you again." She finally said, pulling back. I let her make all the movements.

"You too, Ms. Rose."

"How are you doing?"

I raised an eyebrow at her. "I don't know, Ms. Rose. How am I? I'm scared of what you saw, especially that you thought was so important, I had to be told in person."

"I could have told you over secure channels, but then I wouldn't have been able to see your handsome face."

"There are lots of pretty faces around here. You don't need my ugly mug." She gave me an even look. "Ms. Rose, does this have to do with my Little Bird?"

Her entire face morphed from the cheerful woman we all knew and loved into something sad and hesitant. "Jesse."

I took a step back, and fear coursed through me. "I won't kill her. Whatever she does, I won't do it. I'll stop whoever dares to try."

She actually laughed. "You are right about that. You won't kill her."

There was something about the way she said it, though. Her voice was almost humorous, but there was an edge of warning to it, too. "Tell me."

"She's falling, Jesse. She's in a bad situation, that I don't... I can't see it all, but things are going to get much, much worse before they get any better for the two of you."

"This is what I get, Ms. Rose?" I could feel the anger rise in me, and I didn't know how to stop it. "Riddles. This is what you brought me here for? Riddles?"

"No. You have to stop Jaysen Flinch. He is only the first step in something larger." She pinched the bridge of her nose. "There is someone else, someone powerful, hanging in the distance, but I can't see him. Only Flinch is hanging around you and Madilyn Taylor, though."

"We have been trying to find out what Flinch is doing. I don't understand any of this, Ms. Rose."

"Jesse..." The gray in her hair shimmered, and she stared at the wall. I waited for it to stop, and when she blinked and turned toward me, there were tears in her eyes. "Madilyn Taylor may not be able to be saved."

"I've already told you. I will stop anyone who tries to kill her." I ground my teeth, but my stomach went sour and hollow again.

"The Bacri Primal will be involved. I don't know how or why. I see him talking to her, commanding her, but I don't know the specifics." She rubbed her face. "I'm telling you what I know, Jesse. I'm telling you so that you might be able to protect her through this, okay?"

"It's still all riddles. I don't understand any of it."

She let out a long breath. "I know, but I'm hoping you can find the pieces to be able to understand it, and then save her. For both of your sakes."

"For both of our sakes?" I scoffed.

A small smile as she nodded. "There are glimpses of you two being happy together. Truly happy."

I stared at her for entirely too long, my mind completely blank. "How can there be both her demise, and us being happy together? One can't support the other."

Not to mention, I can't touch her. I can't have Maddie the way I want, the way I craved.

Ms. Rose just smiled and shrugged. "I don't get to know those connections, Jesse. I know they exist, but I only see what I see."

I nodded.

"Head home. I'll let Carlos know you were a good Exorci and stopped by to see an old lady." There was a teasing tone to her voice that made me smile through it all. If it were anyone else, I would have wrapped my bare hands around their neck, but Ms. Rose always got a free pass.

Instead, I wrapped my interlocked hands behind my neck and looked up at the ceiling. "I guess I'll go try to find answers to your riddles. See what I can do about stopping Flinch before he *completely* destroys my life."

"I'm sorry I don't have all happy news, Jesse, but there is light at the end of the tunnel. There is happiness for you."

"If she dies, Ms. Rose. I'm out. There is no happiness left for me. She is my forever."

"She is." Ms. Rose said, pulling me in for a hug. I didn't hesitate, and wrapped my arms around her shoulders.

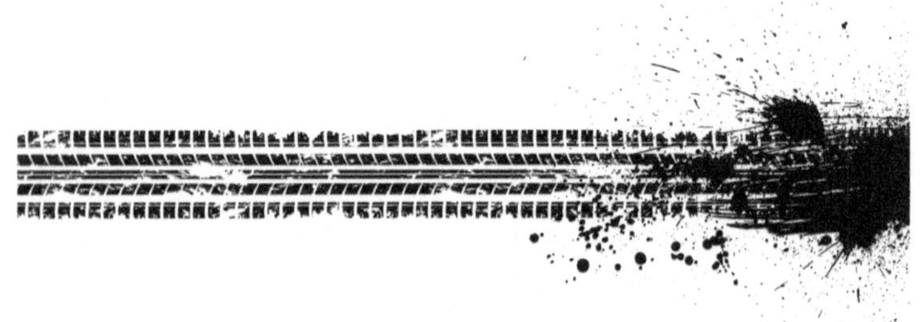

CHAPTER 17

JESSE

Brandon dropped me off at my apartment, and as I tossed my keys into the little blue bowl next to the door, I called Maddie.

"What?" She bit into the phone.

"Well, hello to you too, Madilyn." I rolled my eyes. I was too short-tempered to deal with shit tonight, but needed to hear her voice.

"I'm heading to work." She sighed, and I knitted my eyebrows together.

"What?"

"Sean's creditors are holding me accountable, so I picked up another job to help pay them off." I heard her car start, and the phone connect to the internal sound system in her car. A moment later, I heard her drive over the grate on her way out of the apartment complex, and out onto the Almaden Expressway. The silence was way too long for my liking, and just when I was about to call her on it, she sighed. "When do you get home?"

"Just walked into my apartment. Was hoping to shower and then come spend some time with my girl. See what we can do about the Sean money situation."

"I got it covered, Jesse."

I growled into the phone, "Little Bird."

I heard the deep breath she took and the click of her blinker before she said, "Seriously. I got it."

"Maddie. Look, I realize I was gone longer than I was planning, but there is no reason not to let me help you."

"I know it was only a week this time. I also understand how your job works. I'm not mad. Just overwhelmed, okay?"

I let out a grunt as I stripped my clothes off and sat on the edge of my bed. My phone dinged in my hand, and it was Carlos telling me he needed me to head to Barstow in the morning. "Fuck."

"Where are you going now?"

I huffed in frustration. Why couldn't I have one day with her? Maddie's voice came through, clipped and pissed. "Nevermind, you can't tell me. You can't tell me anything."

"Maddie." I chastised.

"Don't Maddie, me. You've hardly been here since Sean died. I need my boyfriend to be here for me right now, and instead he is working and going all over the Pacific Coast, killing people."

"Little Bird..."

"Oh, shut up, Jesse. Like I said, I know how your job works, and it's taking precedence over me right now, and I'm pissed and hurt." I opened my mouth to tell her I was here tonight, and she was the one busy, but before I had the chance, she said, "I know you told me when we first started this together that this was the way it was, and I've mostly been alright with that. I've even been alright with you not fully able to fuck me, but I'm emotionally raw right now, and... I just got to work. Call me when you get back and have time for your girlfriend, Jesse Westbrook."

The line went dead, and I stared at my phone. There was absolutely nothing going through my head then in a flood, the realization hit. My little bird was hurting, and she wasn't wrong. I hadn't been killing people, but I had been up to Portland, watched Brandon neutralize a problem, talked to the ever-elusive Fae Primal, saw Jade, Mrs. Rose, and then came home. All the while my Little Bird needed me to be there for her.

I grabbed my phone and sent the message to Carlos.

Have Brandon take it? Or someone else?

I stared at the screen as I saw it go from *Delivered*, to *Seen*, to three little dots dance across the screen.

No. This is your assignment. I'm sending Brandon to Irvine. Nikolas is in Anchorage.

I need some time with her, Carlos.

I don't have it to give you.
I'm sorry Jesse. I don't know what's going on, but the West coast is blowing up. We've been too lax or something, but orders are coming down from the Primal Prime's left and right.

I grit my teeth.

I'll try to find some time soon for you.

Fine. Send me the details.

Those dots popped up on my screen again, and I sighed.

Access Code: 255386
I'm sorry, Jesse.

It's one of many reasons why Exorci's don't get involved.

I punched in the authorization code, and the file came up on the Agencies app. I read through the specifics of the job, and groaned. Seems a Kir got handsy with a Purkolet without her permission. "Stupid ball sack."

There was a strict law within the Agency. There was no running from it, no question whether you would be extinguished from this life if you were found guilty of sexual assault. It was only a matter of time.

In this case, there was undeniable evidence. Her father had come home while he was mid-act. She had fought and there was a ton of physical evidence as well.

Tomorrow I would get up early and happily drag his carcass in front of the Purkolet family, where they could watch the light fade from his pathetic eyes.

I put my phone on the charger and sighed. I had exterminated so many sexual predators, they almost didn't faze me anymore. It was just another job, and I didn't like how that sat with me. Putting some of the worst scum out of existence. These should be the jobs that I run and fight for.

There was a time when I would already be on my bike en route. My gaze shifted to the black dresser that sat on the opposite wall, to a photo of a beautiful brown-haired woman with apple cheeks and bright eyes. Maddie was leaning against a tree, cutting an apple with a knife. I had caught her with a slice of apple on the knife, halfway to her lips, with the most adorable smile.

Guilt slammed into me.

She wasn't wrong. I had been here for only a few days after Sean died. Then I left for a week. She wouldn't be fine after just a few days. No one could expect her to be.

Gods. I could only hope that she would never find out it was my hand that had pulled the life from him.

Running my hands through my hair, I growled, "Why me? Why *did* it have to be me?"

I knew Sean was going to end up dead before he became an old man. Only I figured it would be his drug addiction, or because he owed money to the wrong bookie, or he got a loan from the wrong person. Not because he ran against me and I accidentally killed him.

When I met with the Gods after my last living breath... We were going to have a long talk.

CHAPTER 18

MADDIE

-Two Months Later-

"Nikki." Flinch said with a fake warmness that had a shiver going up my spine. I suppressed it because it was never a good thing to be called into Flinch's office. Everyone who worked here loathed the little black envelopes. If there was one at your station, you knew it meant one thing and one thing only. Jaysen Flinch was summoning you, and you answered or suffered the consequences.

No one ever *really* talks about what exactly they are, but you hear things. Cut hours. Higher debts. Sex. Special assignments where you were required to have sex with his patrons. More sex. Then there were the more secret assignments that men and women would go out on, but we never heard exactly what anyone was doing.

"You've done well these last few weeks." For two months, I'd been trying to keep my head down in hopes he would just forget about me. Figured I couldn't be so lucky.

"Thank you, Mr. Flinch."

"I think it's time for you to move up. Of course, it will come with extra write offs. I'm moving you to special projects that only my best dancers are allowed."

The way he said it made my skin crawl. "You mean to whore me out?"

"Only if they pay for it, or it's part of business." There was a noncommittal shrug to his shoulders. "There are other jobs to be done. I believe your special abilities will come in handy for us."

"No." My voice was firm. I wasn't going to be whored out. The only person who was ever going to touch me, or not touch me as it would be, would be Jesse. Sure, we've had our issues, but he'd tried to be here more lately, regardless of the disagreements we had had over me paying back Sean's bills and how much more I'd been drinking. I closed my eyes, my head was pounding, and maybe Jesse was right about the gin. I just might swear it off for life. Gin and I had become friends, but if gin was going to give me a headache like this, then maybe Jesse was right. That I could do with a little less of it.

"You read the forfeiture clause. You know what happens if you don't perform your duties to me." He rose slowly to his feet, hands flat on the glass table before me, and met my gaze. That pounding grew louder in my head. "Sean owes me a substantial amount of money, and I will get my return on it, Ms. Taylor."

"How much?" I hadn't been able to bring myself to look at the amount. When I had gotten home after that first night working at Ivy Grace, I had been so pissed that I burned the contract, and its subsequent accounting, in my sink. I sighed though as the pounding in my head became louder.

When Flinch smiled again, it felt like the lights had dimmed, and I had this quick flicking image of spiders running over his teeth. He jerked his head, and then said, "Three million, seven hundred and eighty thousand dollars."

The air left my lungs in one large swoosh. My whole body froze. "Sean owes you almost three point eight million dollars? And you are trying to get that out of my pathetic hide?" There was a part of me that was terrified to every cell, but I laughed at the hilarity of it. "How did you allow that measly little sack of shit to rack up that much debt to you? Seems like bad business after the first few hundred thousand."

His eyes flashed, and he said, "Stand up."

Without thinking, I did. I jerked my head to the side and rolled my head, trying to clear the instant pressure in my head that came with the motion. Something more than just a gin hangover was messing with my head.

"Take your jacket off."

Again, without thinking, I did, and as I placed it on the chair, I felt my body lengthen as I stuck my ass out and wiggled it.

What in the actual fuck was going on? Was he feeding something into the air?

"Turn around." He looked me up and down and licked his lips.

"Come here." I walked around the desk and stood before him. His hand lifted and ran over my arm, up my neck, and then he was running his thumb across my bottom lip. Heat flooded through me, but something wasn't right.

"On your knees."

I knelt and looked up at him, realizing I was batting my eyelashes at him. He undid his belt with a smirk, and pulled his cock out, bouncing the tip of it over the plump portion of my bottom lip. As my tongue snaked out and licked the tip and through the slit of it, fear tore through me. Nails embedded themselves into my brain as he thrust down my throat. The salty taste of him perennating every corner of my mouth.

It was as if I was in the back of my mind in a dark corner watching myself. Watching myself moan and deep throat him. There was nothing about this that I wanted, and when I tried to push through my outer self to stop, the nails punctured deeper. That inner version of me gripped my head as I realized what I was in fact dealing with and just how fucked I was.

Flinch was a Phrenic.

I heard myself moan at the taste of him, but rebelled against it. I didn't really want this, but while my mind thought that, my whole body responded to him, and reacted wholly different. My breasts tightened, my nipples hardened, and I swear I felt myself get wetter as I swallowed him over and over again. His hands rested on my head as he thrusted down and grunted like an animal. There was nothing I could do. He had total and complete control of me.

I tried to shake it off, but I couldn't find where that connection, that link, was to sever it. If I even could.

"Swallow bitch." Then he shoved himself down my throat and emptied his balls.

When he was done, he smirked down at me, slowly releasing the claws in my head. "Good job, Nikki. Now go. You have a set to do. I wanna see that ass on stage."

I couldn't control the smile that crossed my face, or the swing in my hips as I walked out of that room.

I strode into the dressing room, trying to keep myself from vomiting. When one of the other girls, Crystal, asked why I was late, I kept my head down and my voice low. "Was meeting with Flinch."

She smiled and winked. "Good job, girl."

There was a knock on the door, and Nathan, one of the bouncers, popped his head into the room. "Nikki, you are up in five minutes."

"Thanks!" I shouted over my shoulder and prepared for the night, even though I really just wanted to take a hot shower and melt off every ounce that was Jaysen Flinch from my existence.

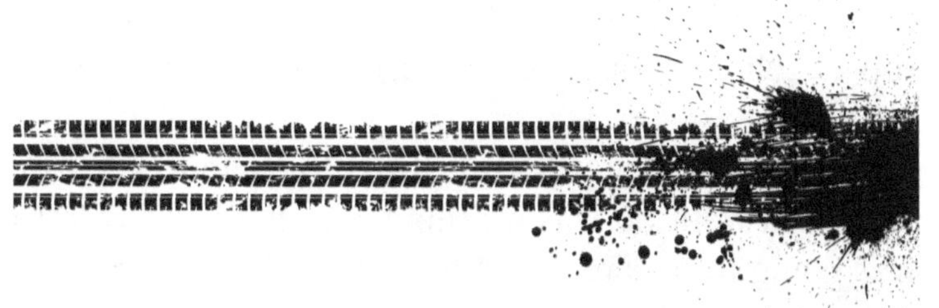

CHAPTER 19

MADDIE

I rushed into Westwind and had just gotten to my desk when there was a shadow over my shoulder. I jumped, spun around to find my boss standing behind me.

"Maddie." His eyes made quick work of my appearance. I looked down and cringed. My shirt, which I had grabbed from the pile on the kitchen table, was wrinkled, and I hadn't noticed the stains on my jeans. When Fred's eyes met mine again, he said, "Are you okay? I mean, I don't expect you to be peachy keen since it's only been a month and a half since your brother died, but… are you okay?"

"Fine, Fred."

"Really? Because you look like hell. You look like you didn't sleep at all last night, are making mistakes left and right on your work, when you are usually one of our top-notch admins, and you barely made it in on time today."

He wasn't wrong. I got maybe thirty minutes before my alarm went off this morning saying if I hadn't left I was going to be late, and I had noticed more errors in the reports and other things I had been handling.

I glanced at my computer screen. Not to mention, I was seriously behind on emails.

"It's been rough Fred, but I'm fine."

"You're not."

I took a deep breath. "Look, there is a lot I'm having to deal with Sean's estate, and it's not something that is going to go away. I can't get out of it."

"I get that Madilyn. As a friend, I hope you understand I am worried about you, but as your boss… as your boss, there are concerns about your ability to handle your workload and handle your job duties." He let out a long sigh. "Go home. Get some sleep, do some laundry, and come back tomorrow."

"Fred, I need to work. Going home won't lighten the workload."

"But you having to do it over again, because you can't even see straight right now, isn't doing you any favors either. Go home. Get some rest and we will see you tomorrow morning." He held my gaze as I stared him down. "I'm taking the Johnson and Robinson project from you. Jackie and Hayden will take over."

"Fred!"

He held a hand up. "They have tight deadlines, and you aren't able to meet them. I'm serious when I say your workload and job duties are failing Madilyn. Consider this an official warning." He slipped a piece of paper in front of me, which was indeed a formal warning. "I'm sorry Madilyn. I'm hoping things get better soon in your personal life."

It felt like a punch to the gut. I'd always taken such pride in my work, but what could they expect? I just lost Sean and Beth. Luckily, all the usual shit was pretty easy. The boy had no assets, there was nothing to collect from. It was this damn contract with Flinch.

When I looked up from the paper, Fred was gone, so I collected my things and snuck out to head home. By the time I got in the car, tears were streaming down my face. I sat in the driver's seat, just staring at my phone for a long minute. My fingers moved across the screen by memory as I sent a text to Jesse.

Please tell me you are home.

I waited way too long to see the Delivered, change to Seen, to the three bubbles come across.

What's wrong, little bird?

Meet me at my apartment.

I started the car and tore down the street home. I needed Jesse. I needed to feel something. I needed to feel needed, and not an obligation or a means to a debt collection.

Fifteen minutes later, I pulled into the mostly empty parking lot, my car clunking over the grate, and I saw Jesse look up, pulling his helmet off. When his eyes met mine, they narrowed in confusion. I threw the door open and ran to him. Jesse caught me in his arms, wrapping tight around me.

"What's wrong, little bird?" His arm wrapped tightly around my waist and his other hand went to cradle my head.

I buried my head into his chest, letting the smell of leather envelope me. I couldn't stop the sob that wracked through my body. He wordlessly reached down and swung me up into his arms.

This. This is what I needed from him for the last two months. He'd been trying so hard to be here, and keep the Agency happy, but he seemed to go out on more and more jobs since Sean died.

As he carried me up to the apartment, I let the tears flow. Reassuring sounds came from him, and when we got to my door, he set me down, pulled his keys from his pocket and opened it. I turned to go in, but once again, he swooped me up and took me into the bedroom.

"Get undressed and into bed." He ran his hand over my hair, and I leaned into it. "You look like hell, Little Bird. When was the last time you slept?"

The distress in his voice twisted my gut, but I was so exhausted, I couldn't fight him. "Got about 30 minutes before I went into work this morning."

He let out a sigh through his nose and shook his head. "Madilyn Nikole Taylor."

I met his gaze. "This second job kept me up all night. I got home, ate half a bagel, and got about 30 minutes in the chair before I had to leave."

There was a quick nod before he asked, "And why are you home now, and not at Westwind?"

I looked down at myself and cringed. I looked like I rolled out of a dumpster. "Fred came in, gave me a written warning, because I've been exhausted, and having a hard time keeping up on my work."

"And you still won't tell me the name of the club you are serving for?"

"No." I turned my head from him and stepped away, stripping my clothes. Distractions. I have to distract him. He can't know who I'm working for. He had been looking into Sean's death, but had said he hadn't really found anything concrete to link together. If he linked Flinch and Sean's death, he would know I was working Sean's debt off to Flinch. Would likely know just how royally fucked I was.

Jesse hitched a breath when I slipped the shirt off and tossed it in the corner into the plastic hamper. Distract him. Keep him distracted, Maddie. Unbuttoning my jeans, I bent over as I dragged them off my hips and down my legs. The growl behind me brought a smile to my face, and when I was completely naked, I looked over my shoulder, grinning at him.

"You are such a fucking tease, woman." He tipped his head back and groaned, "I don't have my equipment with me either, so climb into bed, and I'll make you some food. Then you are going to sleep."

"Yes, Jesse." I rolled my eyes, and before I could take another step toward my bed, he was there, arms around me, carrying me.

"I said to bed, little bird." He laid me down, kissed my temple, where my skin tingled, and a jolt of awareness slipped over me. That was really close to the hairline. I ran my fingers across the spot, carefully, and felt them tingle as well.

A pan sizzled from the kitchen a couple minutes later, and the smell of bacon filled the house. I looked at my fingers, and then in the direction of the kitchen. I ran my hand along the spot again, and I swear his lips must have touched skin.

No. I must be imagining it. I would be dead if they did. Right?

I was still staring at my fingers when Jesse came in and cocked an eyebrow at me. "Under the blankets."

I nodded and scooted back on the bed, bringing my feet up to slide up under the blankets. "You didn't need to cook me anything. A bagel and cream cheese would have been fine."

He looked offended at the statement, dipped the fork in the eggs, and lifted it to me. "Eat."

"Jesse. Seriously, you didn't need to cook up a full breakfast for me."

An irritated growl rattled in his chest as he lifted the fork again. I took the bite he offered, and it was delicious. I reached for the bacon, and he smirked before swatting my hand with his nitrile gloved ones.

"You won't cook for yourself. The only time you get a hot meal is when I take you to dinner or I cook for you. So shut up and let me feed you." The loving, dominating tone of him had me pressing my legs together, and the corner of his mouth lifted as he clocked the movement. "Woman. I swear."

"There might be some dental dam in the bottom drawer." I whispered as he lifted another fork of eggs, and it froze just out of my easy reach. I lifted my eyes to his, leaned forward slowly, taking the bite. His eyes heated and flicked to my bedside table.

"Food. You need food. And rest." He ground out, in a marvel of strength that I didn't know he could muster. He had never been concerned about ensuring his satisfaction. Jesse was always concerned about my enjoyment. I had read a book once that called that sort of behavior *a pleasure dom*. Jesse fit the description, but I didn't know enough about the whole BDSM set up to call him that. Beth had teased me once about Jesse being my dom, but I just rolled my eyes at her.

Jesse held up a piece of bacon, and I took it from him. His eyes flicked to the drawer again, and then he handed me the rest of the bacon and instructed, "Eat. I'm gonna go clean up. If you finish the bacon by the time I get back, lay down and try to get some sleep."

The corner of my lip twitched up, and I folded my arms under my breasts, shifting them upwards, and this time, Jesse didn't suppress the groan from him. "Little Bird. Sleep. Please."

I slipped a piece of bacon into my mouth and savored the crunch of it. Jesse shook his head mumbling how I was going to be the death of him or something as he headed back to the kitchen. My phone dinged, and when I saw who it was, I wrinkled my nose and sighed.

Make sure you are on time tonight. Special projects.

I'll be there.

I stared at it for a long minute, crunching on the bacon and listening to Jesse wash the pans in the kitchen. Special projects. Just what would that be? He had hinted at me having to sleep with people as part of the job, and I would rather die. Anything. Anything other than that.

I was so wrapped up in my own thoughts, that I didn't hear Jesse come in. "What's got you thinking so hard on your phone?"

"Nothing." I sighed when he raised an eyebrow at me. "I was hoping to get tonight off, but no dice."

CHAPTER 20

JESSE

There was so much she isn't telling me, and it was driving me crazy. "Put your phone down and try to sleep."

"Come lay down with me?" Her voice was so worn, there was no way I could deny her. "Please, Jesse."

Pushing off the doorjamb, I pulled the blankets up to her chin once she slid down into them. "You sure, little bird?"

She gave a slow, sleepy nod, before I walked around to the other side of the bed and grabbed one of the throw blankets. I wrapping my arm in it, I curled around her. She pulled it tight against her chest and muttered. "I love you, Jesse."

"Love you too, little bird." I kissed the back of her head, and within moments, she had fallen asleep.

As I laid there listening to the soft snores of my girl, that sour, empty feeling settled into my gut. Ms. Rose had said that things were going to get worse for us before they got better. She had also said that Maddie may not be able to be saved.

I would protect her. I had to. I... I couldn't lose her. Pulling her close, I inhaled her vanilla cinnamon scent, and just wished I could be by her side all the time. While that wouldn't work for my job at all, it also certainly wouldn't work for Maddie, since she wouldn't even tell me the name of the club she was serving at night. Why wouldn't she tell me? Sure, I could research it, but she had asked for privacy, for me to trust her. It was one of the hardest things I've had to do. I trusted her, but to not know, to not be able to make sure she was safe... gods it was so hard, but I respected her decision, even if I didn't like it. I almost caved one night and followed, but my bike isn't the most inconspicuous of vehicles out there.

I sighed as I felt her breathing next to me. She's safe. She's in my arms, and I wasn't going to force her to tell me. Not when I was holding onto the one secret that could ruin us both.

A buzzing against a hard surface woke me, and I realized it wasn't my phone but Maddie's. She was curled up in my chest, her soft snores luring me back into security. I was just about to fall back asleep when it went off again. I reached over her, and grabbed it, to turn it on 'Do Not Disturb', but when another text came in, I froze at the name that came up on the screen.

'*Ivy Grace*'

Maddie woke up then, and mumbled, "What's wrong?"

I felt my blood pressure rising, but took a deep breath. Maybe she didn't know the club was owned and operated by Jaysen Flinch. My eyes slid to her, and I prayed Sean hadn't executed a contract with him. His contracts always contained an ownership clause over another person in the family.

"Your phone was going off." I held it up, and it buzzed again. Her eyes went wide for a split second before she forced herself to relax. "Mind telling me why Ivy Grace is texting you? One of the most popular creature strip clubs in the bay area?"

She took a deep breath, as she wiped the sleep from her face, and then got up out of bed. Maddie swayed her hips as she headed to the bathroom, and I got up, setting my arms to either side of her, caging her to the wall.

She wants to play, I'll play.

"Little Bird." I whispered along her chin, and I saw the way her skin prickled, and her nipples quickly hardened. Shit, her body was so responsive, this was going to be torture on both of us.

"Humm?"

"Why is Ivy Grace texting you?" I held my breath as I put my hand in her hair and gripped it tight. The moan she gave me instantly made my cock hard. "Maddie…"

Her eyes popped open, and her gaze met mine. "It's the second job I picked up to pay Sean's debts."

"How much does he owe? They can't collect against you." I whispered against her ear, and I pushed my leg between her legs, and raised it, so she was barely on her tiptoes. Her hips moved slightly against my thigh, a light moan coming from her, and I couldn't help the smirk that crossed my lips.

"Maddie. Ivy Grace." I commanded, but moved my leg against her, inciting a whimper of pleasure from her.

"I'm usually a server. Sometimes I fill in on stage, Jesse." I pulled her hair back a little further, and she froze when my face was just an inch from hers. Gods, I wanted to kiss her. Run my tongue along her throat, take this hand that was on the wall and thrust it between her legs, and really make her scream for me.

"Who do you report to?"

"Danella Johnson." Her breathing was getting more ragged as she ground against my thigh, her wetness seeping through my pants. Oh, to taste her. Fuck. "You said you would give me privacy for this."

"Your phone woke me up, little bird." I released her, but pinned her with a stare. "Don't move."

I backed away toward the dresser, but her heated gaze didn't leave mine. I bent down into the drawer and grabbed a set of disposable gloves.

"Jesse." She begged as she sagged against the wall.

"I got you, little bird." I slipped my hands into the gloves, tucking my sleeves into the ends, and ignoring my phone going off in my back pocket. When I reached her, I wrapped my hand against her throat, and the sexiest whimper came from her.

I let my other hand run down her side, and when I brought it around to the front, her legs unconsciously widened to allow me full access. My thigh instantly resumed its previous position, and she was absolutely soaked now. I let my fingers slide down between her folds, and she tipped her head back, rolling her head slightly to the side. She couldn't move it much with my hand there, but gods, her submission was pure gold. One day. One day, we would be there.

My thumb circled her clit, as I thrusted two fingers into her. Her legs all but gave out, and she shifted so she was seated on my thigh more than anything.

"Tell me the truth, little bird." I whispered against her cheek, being so careful of the distance between us. She wrapped her arms around my neck, gripping onto the back of my shirt. The fabric pulled away from my neck, leaving her arms dangerously close to the flesh there. I pulled away from her, giving her a warning look. "Maddie."

Her voice was pleading, but said, "I'm being careful. I promise. I don't want to jeopardize anything with you."

My phone vibrated in my back pocket again, and I ignored it as I took a half step toward her again, and said, "You swear to me you are an occasional dancer, and only run drinks at Ivy Grace."

She met my gaze, and as I slid my hand back between her thighs, I pinched her clit. Her eyes rolled into the back of her head as she breathed, "I swear on everything that we are, Jesse Westbrook. I swear on my love for you, that all I have done at Ivy Grace is be a server and occasionally dance. I will even tell you I have done no private rooms. No patrons have touched me."

There was a flash in her eyes that made me realize she wasn't telling me everything, but she had given me this much, so I smiled and said, "Good girl. Now cum for me."

It was the only instruction she needed before I was rewarded with her tightening around my fingers as I plunged them in and out of her.

Once she was completely spent, I carried her back to the bed and covered her back up. I headed to the bathroom to dispose of my gloves and put some new ones on, but by the time I got back to the bed, she had drifted back off to sleep.

My phone started going off again in my pocket, and I answered it without looking. "I swear, if the world isn't on fire, I'm going to encircle my hands around your neck."

"Exorci." The voice on the other end of the line was not that of Carlos or Brandon.

"Primal Emma." My eyes flicked to Maddie, kissed her on the top of the head, grabbed my shoes before backing out of the room and closing the door. "What can I do for you?"

What in the hell was the Exorci Primal doing contacting me directly? She always went through Minstrel Carlos.

"I need to send you on a special project."

"Ma'am?"

"Minstrel Carlos Medina will be advised you are unavailable for the foreseeable future. He will also deliver the documents within the hour, leaving them on your kitchen counter."

"Ma'am?" The question hung in the air for a long minute, before I asked, "May I ask why this isn't going through normal channels?"

"You will understand when you see the file."

"Yes, Primal Emma."

"I need you on the road tonight, if you've slept."

I looked in the direction of Maddie's bedroom and sighed. "I would like to have one more night..." I trailed off, when I realized she would be at work, anyway. "But I can get on the road tonight. May I know the direction I'm going?"

"North, across the country line."

"Noted." I ran my hand through my hair. "I'll be home in a couple hours, pack and get on the road after I review the file. Am I reporting directly to you, Primal?"

"Myself or the Primes. No one else is to know of this. You are bound by Agency law. This mission never occurred."

"What mission?" I let a small chuckle come through.

"Ride safe, Exorci." Was Primal Emma's huffed response.

I tossed my phone onto Maddie's coffee table, and leaned back on the couch, resting my head. What in the fuck was going on with this world, that I was constantly on the move? I have never been this busy. Four to five missions a year, tops. I mean, all the work was doing wonderful things for my bank account, but I didn't really have anything I wanted to spend it on. I didn't need a big house, so my little condo was fine. I had the bike of my dreams, and it wasn't like I could go on elaborate vacations.

I must have dozed off, because I woke up to Maddie, kissing the top of my head, and stroking my shoulder. "Jesse."

I rolled my head in her direction, and blinked my eyes open, mumbling, "Hi, little bird."

She had showered and rolled her hair up in a towel. Maddie had a pair of short blue jean shorts and a black tank on, and as I let my eyes drift down her long legs, I shifted on the couch, because fuck, I wanted to just bend her over the back of this couch and have her begging for me to allow her release.

"Jesse. You can't look at me like that, when I am ten minutes from leaving to go to work."

That cleared my head. "Ivy Grace."

She nodded. "It's slowly paying off Sean's debts."

"Please be careful, Little Bird." I stood up and wrapped my arms around her.

She squeezed me tight, pressed a kiss to my chest, before she looked up at me. "I love you."

"Love you, too." I kissed a long kiss to the top of her head and sighed. "I'm gonna be gone for a bit."

She stiffened in my arms, and I squeezed her close. I looked down into her bright hazel eyes, and there was worry and sadness there. "How long is a bit?"

"I don't know. All I know is I'm going north."

Her eyes narrowed slightly, and she asked, "Didn't they send you the info through the app?" I shook my head. "Why not?"

I pinched my lips into a thin line and held her gaze. Realization hit her. "This never happened. Shit, Jesse. Who are you going after?"

Her head twisted and rested back on my chest, and I sighed. "I don't know. I don't know anything right now."

She relaxed a little in my arms, and said, "Call as often as you can please?"

"Of course."

She released me, pulled the towel from her hair, and padded off to the bathroom. "Can you throw a bagel together for me real quick?"

"On it." I watched her disappear back into the bedroom and groaned. Canada. I was going to be at least a couple of weeks from her. Maybe longer, depending on what was waiting for me at home.

I rubbed the rest of the sleep from my face and went to make Maddie her a quick dinner. Something more than a blasted bagel and cream cheese.

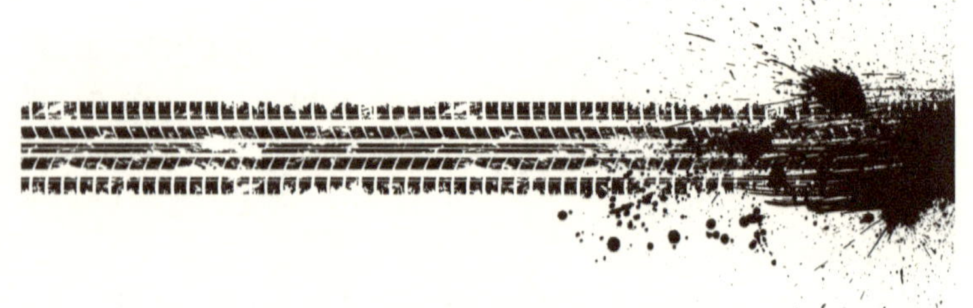

CHAPTER 21

JESSE

When I got home, there was indeed a manilla envelope sitting on the kitchen counter. In big black letters, written across the front of it, said, "JW". I tore it open and pulled out the blood red folder. A stamp stating it was confidential sat diagonally across the front, and I shook my head, looking at it.

"I need a drink." My bar was fairly stocked, and I pulled a bottle of Tullamore Dew whiskey down. Without looking, I opened the cabinet door on my right, and reached in for a couple ice cubes before plunking them down into the glass.

I looked at the file again, as I twisted off the cap, and filled the glass halfway. The file felt like a brand sitting on the counter.

Any extermination for a creature or head would go through the usual channels of the special app that was created for the Agency, and therefore would go through the Minstrel for the region. If an Exorci was handed a file, with no digital record, you had seriously fucked up. It always meant it was off the record and the assignment didn't exist. This could be for any number of reasons, but it always contained the signature of all three Primal Primes.

A red file, though? A red file meant this was more than an extermination. It was an execution high up. Whoever's name was on the inside of that file was at least a Species Primal, Astral, or Exorci. I only knew of three exterminations of this kind to have occurred since the formation of Ashstrike Sanctorum over two thousand years ago.

I took a sip of the whiskey and let the smooth rich liquid slowly make its way down my throat. "What in the fuck is going on in this world?"

The Fae Primal comes out of hiding, has us exterminate one of his men, which could have been done by his own people, the constant extermination of creatures lately, and now the extermination of... I ran my fingers over the folder, and pulled the front back and let it drop open. When I saw the picture of the person there, I let out a groaned, "Fuck!"

I tipped the rest of the amber liquid back and sighed.

Name: Ashton Clarke

Creature: Exorci

Age: 38

Place of Birth: Winnipeg, Manitoba, Canada

Discovery: Accidentally killed a werewolf girlfriend in twelfth year schooling.

Family: No known links to any family. Orphan and went through the system, aged out with no adoption.

Education: AS in Psychology, BS in Psychology Specialist from University of Toronto. Paid through academic and track scholarships.

Creature Assignment: Mid-North America

A fellow Exorci.

I was being sent to kill a fellow Exorci. I knew of only one other Exorci who had ever been exterminated. One in the entirety of the Agency's existence, once. He had a mental break and went on a rampage through multiple creatures communities, and the Primals at the time quickly put an end to it.

I scanned the file and reviewed the infractions. Multiple unsanctioned deaths, digital fraud, and embezzlement from half of the companies on the stock market by the looks of it. Governments from all over the world were looking for him. It looked like Interpol had made pretty good progress in locating him, narrowing down his location to Alberta, Canada, but didn't have anything else.

The Agency, however, thought he had taken refuge within the Mitsue Bear Clan, north of Edmonton. I called bullshit. There was no way she would harbor someone like this. Her soldiers would tear him apart.

I let out a heavy sigh and tipped back my glass, only to realize it was empty. Going back to the bar and refilling my glass, I kicked it back and refilled it again.

Three. Maybe four days on the bike. Doable, but shit. A fellow Exorci. No wonder they were keeping this off the books. The Astrals and Exorcis were supposed to be untouchable. If there was discourse or problems within our ranks, chaos would insure among the creatures. Two thousand years ago we were entrusted to keep order.

I took another sip of my whiskey and ran my hand through my hair, gripping my neck as I thought through it. How had he gone under the radar so much? How had the Agency not been able to pick up on this before the human authorities did?

I rifled through the paperwork some more and noted some odd gaps in the file.

My phone pinged, and the screen popped up with 'Little Bird'.

Ride safe. Come home to me.
I love you Jesse Westbrook.

As I looked at the message, my gut tightened. I took a deep breath, letting it out in a long release through my nose.

I love you, Little Bird.
I'll always come back to you.

My eyes flicked to the file again, and I dialed Primal Emma.

"Exorci."

"Primal." I waited a long moment before I said, "I have questions."

"I suppose you do. It's only the third in history."

"Third?" My eyebrows shot up. "I knew of Shen Kim in the 1500s, but didn't know there was another."

"Annabella Nikolakova." Her voice was quiet. "You know your history on the Russian Imperial Romanov family?"

"Who didn't know of Princess Anastasia?" I huffed. "Movies have been made a hundred times over about her... Primal, are you saying..."

"That Nikolakova and the Princess Anastasia were connected?" A huffed laugh came over the phone. "Princess Anastasia and Nikolakova were involved. When Princess Anastasia wanted to end the relationship, Nikolakova went rogue."

"History says that the family was shot... a well-done cover up. Right. There would be no trace. Such a powerful shifter family, gone, except for Anastasia." I shook my head.

"She lived. With the help of the Agency, of course, was relocated to Poland, where she lived out the rest of her life. Finding a new family. The bear shifter line continues, a be it, in secret. Rumors swirl around the connection, but no one will ever find one." There was silence for a long moment, and I knew Primal Emma knew why I was calling. "You read the file?"

"I have."

"There are also rumors he might be the cause for a lot of problems up in Edmonton. It is not really the point now. The Primal Primes have called for action. We have to clean house, Westbrook."

"I get that. I just never thought I would ever have to take the life of a fellow Exorci."

If we had been on a video chat, I knew she would have been nodding in agreement. The Exorcis and Astrals were the creature police. We handled everything. We had to take care of our own, though.

"Primal, there are holes in the records. As if disappeared completely, or someone wiped his actions for a while."

She huffed a chuckle. "You noticed that too, huh?"

"I realize that my record will say I was nowhere near Canada during this assignment. Say I was in Los Angeles or something, but... *who* is protecting Clarke?"

"I don't know. It's someone high in the ranks for sure, and they know how to hide themselves. They have access to hackers and security that have led all the Agency's best to dead ends." She let out a heavy sigh. "Did you notice one of the dead spots?"

I reached over to the file and started scanning it again. There, not more than a few months ago. He disappeared from everyone's radar, only to pop up in Grand Junction, Colorado, at the same time I had killed Sean. "Please tell me this is a coincidence?"

"You know I don't believe in them."

I tipped back what was left in my glass and slammed it down on the counter. "What the fuck is going on?"

There was a long silence before I growled, "I know I'm asking for personal reasons, but what is going on?"

"Rumors. A whole lot of rumors."

"Okay, give me the rumors, then?"

"The Ovexa and Exorci are working together to try and figure it out exactly, but someone is working through all the major corporations of the world, and trying to turn any creatures employed by those corps against the Agency."

"To what purpose?"

"That is the question. Ovexa Finn said that he spoke to a Kir working for Royal Petroleum, who said he was broached by a half fae. Apparently, all they did was try to say how the Agency had been in control for too long, and that there should just be one creature overseeing things."

"So, we can have another situation like we did when the Agency was created? That didn't work then, and in today's world, it would be even worse. Sure, there are all kinds of issues with the Agency, but if only one creature oversees things, we are going to end up in a worse state than we are now. If that creature deems another as lesser, that undoes centuries and centuries of work to equal things out just to the point we have." I took a long, deep breath. "I'm sorry. I shouldn't have gone off like that."

"You are not wrong." I smiled because that could have been taken in a few ways.

"Primal, why was the Exorci in Colorado at the exact time I was sent there for the witch? Why was Sean there? Why did Sean kill the witch? What is their connection? Other than Jaysen Flinch."

Primal Emma let out a very loud, deep sigh. "Ovexa Finn is looking into it. You keep looking as well. We will find the connection."

"Can I ask a personal favor?"

"Ask, Exorci."

"Can you verify whether a contract was made between Sean Taylor, Bacri and Jaysen Flinch?" I rarely asked for favors from Primal Emma, but I had to know. Now that Maddie was working at Ivy Grace, I had to know.

"I'll look. Now, get on the road, Jesse. It's a long trip."

"Yes, Primal." When she disconnected the call, I put my phone down, staring at the red file on my counter. I really wanted another drink, but if I had to be on the road soon, I needed to be sober, so I spent the time looking back at the file and reviewing the information again. I would need to burn it by the time I got to the border.

I knew that once I went through the checkpoint, any record of me going through it, or any hotel along the way, would immediately disappear, but I couldn't risk it. The documents didn't exist.

This trip didn't exist.

This extermination didn't exist.

I straightened and headed to my bedroom to pack for the trip that I wasn't going on.

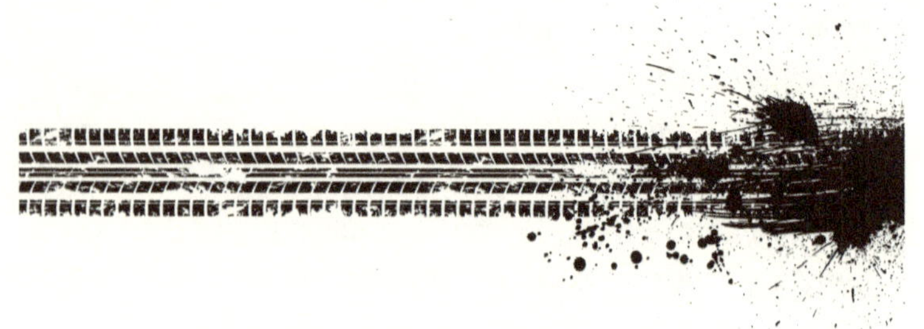

CHAPTER 22

MADDIE

It only took three days for Flinch to leave me another black envelope on my dressing table. Cheryl, one of the other dancers, gave me an apologetic look as she finished getting ready, and squeezed my shoulder before heading on stage.

Of course, this was how today was going to go. I had already received a second warning at work this morning. One more and I could lose the job, but Ivy Grace was keeping me up all night, and my sleep schedule was crap. Getting maybe three hours a day, I was living off caffeine, more specifically energy drinks. I looked at the lime green can on the counter and cracked it open, chugging half of it, before I picked up the envelope.

I tried to shove down the flashbacks of what the presence of that black envelope caused. The last two times... I winced, took a deep breath, smelling something musky in the air and centered on that. I took it and tore it open, pulling the small black card out.

His scratchy handwriting said, 'Dress in all black. Long pants, long sleeves. Hair up in a bun. Black socks. Black running shoes. All are in the bag under the bench. 10:15 go to the last door on the left, then down the hall. Wait there.'

I blinked in confusion at the note. I was to be covered up? There was a sack under the bench with a white tag bearing my name. I crouched down and untied it. The soft black fabric of the bag pooled around the contents, and when I pulled them out, I found a long sleeve black turtleneck, thick black leggings, black socks, and black sneakers. Setting them on the bench counter in front of me, I quickly stripped and changed clothes.

There was a knock on the door, and a tall black-haired man came out and said, "Nikki."

I twisted and looked at him, and my voice caught in my throat. He was ruggedly sexy. I let my gaze run up and down him, and swallowed hard, squeaking out, "Yeah?"

"Put your hair up into this hat on the way down." Then he opened the door wider, waiting for me to step out. When I did his voice was low, and borderline seductive, as he said, "I'll be your team leader, of sorts, at least that is what Flinch would call it."

"Team leader?"

He nodded. "Flinch assigned you to help with some of our special projects. I know this is your first time, so I'm just going to have you on watch duty. When we get to the van, I'll give you an earpiece to wear. It has a mic in it, so you can tell me what you see."

I nodded, but my head started replaying all sorts of scenarios. "What I see?"

"Bacri right?"

"Yes, sir." I muttered, and I thought I saw him take a slightly slower step. "Non-shifting though."

"You have the eyesight benefits, though." It was a question, but said as a statement, so I just nodded. "Which is why you will be the lookout."

We reached the door, and sex on a stick opened it for me, where a black van, complete with blacked-out windows and open side door, waiting for me, apparently. I stepped in, abandoning all self-preservation at the building threshold. I was under orders, and it was this or death. I could die either way, but...

I sat in the second row seat, without another word, as he slid into the seat next to me, shutting the door, and then the van was taking off down the street.

My team leader sat close to me, watching me a long moment, and when I took in a deep breath, there was something calming and soothing in his scent. It didn't take long, but I was leaning my head against the window, fighting to keep my eyes open.

"Nikki." Someone was touching my shoulder, and I jumped. My head whirled around to face the offender. I could just make out a man's profile in the dim lights of the van.

Shit. I fell asleep? I groaned and rubbed my neck. My eyes flicked around the van, and it was just the two of us. His hand was still on my shoulder, his thumb moving back and forth. "You okay, Sweets?"

I bristled at the name. "Sweets?"

"Well, you weren't responding to your name, and you look good enough to eat." The smirk and blush that accompanied the up and down look he gave me had me warm and cold. While Jesse did everything he could, I missed the real skin to skin contact. I blinked. What the actual fuck Madilyn? Get your shit together. You don't really want any other man touching you.

"I'm not going to hurt you, Nikki." He said, interrupting my thoughts. "It is time, though. I'll need you up on the roof. Here is the earpiece. Push the button here." He pushed the exposed end of the earpiece and there was a faint red light that circled the area. "If you see anyone coming up, see the cops, security, or anyone else, that would be a problem, just say something."

I nodded and studied him. "What do I call you?" He raised an eyebrow. "I'm going to go out on a limb here, and assume that you work for Flinch, and that you don't use your real name, just like you probably assume that Nikki is not what I normally go by."

A bright smile crossed his face, and he reached over and put the earpiece into my ear. The feel of his skin was like a wildfire to my senses. When he had it secured, he let a couple fingers trail across my cheek, and it took a lot of effort not to lean into it. "You can call me Maverick, Sweets."

"Maverick." I whispered the name.

"Fuck, Sweets. Be careful how you say my name. I may actually have to try to seduce you, because the way you just said my name..." He let out a long breath, his mouth in a delicious O.

I bit my lip at the sight of it, and cursed myself again. When he regained control of himself, his head ticked to the side. "Tired?"

"Yeah, trying to still keep my day job while I work all night at the club. Still got adult bills to pay."

His eyes narrowed, then bent down to rifle through a bag. "Do you trust me?"

I huffed a laughed. "Do I have a choice?"

He pulled a small bottle out and pulled out a dropper from it. "It's a concentrated dose of a substance that works like caffeine."

"I won't take drugs, Maverick. It's a hard pass." I turned in my seat to face him more fully. Where Jesse was all rugged rough and tumble kind of sexy, Maverick was more clean cut kind of rugged. He had just the smallest of a beard that he obviously intentionally kept short and shaped. Hell, even his eyebrows were perfectly shaped, and the way his eyes heated as he looked at me had me blinking to push away the thought of pushing his plump lips to mine.

"It's not like that. Not at all. Think of it like a NoDoz."

"So not any worse than the energy drinks I've been downing like water?"

He laughed at that, and it was such a joyous sound that I wondered what he was doing here? "The energy drinks are likely doing far more to your system than this will."

"Alright."

"Open your mouth for me, Sweets." When I raised an eyebrow, he lifted the corner of his lip and there was a flash of white teeth and he dropped his voice and said, "Please?"

The way he said that simple word had my mouth watering. There was this part of me that wanted to drop to my knees and put something else in my mouth.

Shaking my head to clear the improper thoughts, I pushed that urge down and opened my mouth, sticking my tongue out. When he leaned forward, his eyes flicked to my tongue, to my eyes, and then back to my tongue, as he dropped four drops on it. The taste was bitter, but his eyes met mine again, and I curled my tongue back into my mouth. I swore I heard a growl come from him as I did it. I had to admit; it was slightly satisfying to see him react like that.

"Maverick! Time's ticking." Someone from outside of the van said.

He reached over, took my hand, and helped me out of the van. He held it a moment too long, before squeezing it and letting it go. I took a deep breath before I asked, "So, where do you want me?"

Maverick let out a small cough that made me blush. The man standing a few feet away chuckled. "Man, Mav. I haven't seen you this flustered in a long time."

"Shut the fuck up, Chip."

"Yes, sir." Chip turned and started going through a bag, but I noticed the genuine smile on his face. A blond and another dark-haired man just chuckled as they went through their respective bags.

"Where do you want me stationed, Maverick?" I tried to keep my tone smooth, but it was a little harsh as well. I was used to being hit on. Ivy Grace was a strip club and bar. It was bound to happen, but Mavericks seemed more... real. Most were grabby or through slurred compliments. Mavericks were natural, sweet, carrying and genuine. They flowed off his lips, and I didn't know how I felt about it.

He turned to face me, and the little light coming from the streetlight illuminated his face. He was beautiful. Different from Jesse. More clean cut, but the dark shadow of a scruff was definitely doing things for his looks. He had dark eyes, ones that warmed when they met my gaze. He held it for a moment too long before he sighed and said, "The building to my right. There is an open stairwell that will take you to the second floor. The door should be unlocked. Go down the hall, and there will be a fire door. Behind it will be the stairs to the roof. You should be able to lie down along the roofline and see us going into the building here to our left."

My eyes flicked up to the roof line and then back down to the building that was at least 100 yards to my left. "That's why you need my eyesight." I gaged the distance again and then looked in the opposite directions. "Large parking area. Lots of open space. Will not only give me the space to see someone coming, but it leaves us vulnerable to being seen by the parking cameras."

"Beautiful and smart."

"Flirt."

"Only if it's working." I gave him an even look before he jerked his head toward the building I needed to be at. "Go. Let us know when you are set up, and we will move. It's a tight deadline. When we're done, go out the door to the other side. I will be there to pick you up."

I turned to leave, and bit the inside of my cheek to keep from saying, '*promises, promises.*' Seriously, what is wrong with me? My heart belongs to Jesse. Why am I flirting back with this man? I should just tell him my boyfriend is an Exorci and put an end to it right now.

Before I knew it, I was laying down facing the Goldleaf Trust Corp. building. I pressed the button on my earpiece and said, "In position, Maverick."

"Good girl."

I coughed to cover up my own moan, and when I looked in his direction, I could see him rubbing his face. The smile that crossed mine was one that hadn't appeared in a long time.

As I watched them climb up the side of the brick building, I realized that the crew I was with were all shifters. Only shifters would be able to scale with that sort of ease. Movement off to the right caught my attention, and I realized it was just a bird in a tree. Narrowing my eyes, it appeared to be a red-shouldered hawk. Not something uncommon to the California Coast, but it seemed to watch me.

The building, I was supposed to be watching the building. When I looked back, there was no one. I couldn't see anyone on the walls, on the roofline, in the parking lot in front of me, anywhere. They must be inside now, doing whatever it was they were doing in there. Curiosity plagued me, but the more I looked around, the more I decided, I probably didn't need to know. This was Flinch and if he was a Phrenic, then it was likely not something entirely by the letter of the law.

I shifted back toward where the hawk was, and it was nowhere in sight. My gaze moved across the lot, and I was a little surprised by how much I could see up and down the main road. I wasn't exactly sure where I was, since I had fallen asleep, and therefore hadn't paid attention to where we had gone. This time of night, I could be anywhere in the South Bay.

Flashing lights caught my eye off to the left, and I clicked the button again. "Maverick. We got flashing lights coming from the...west."

A grunt and then I heard a few gun shots ring out, and I froze. A loud groan of pain and another voice came through. "How bad is it, Mav?"

"We got humans incoming. Let's move." Maverick said, but his instructions were through pants.

"They are pulling in on the east side. Move it boys." I said through gritted teeth. A loud caw pierced the air, and my head tipped up to the sky. The bald eagle circled high above me, let out another cry, and then flew west. "Please don't let that be a scout?" I muttered.

"What was that, Sweets?" Maverick's voice was strained, and he grunted, as I saw them crawl out of a hatch on the roof and make their way down the side of the building. Only they were missing one, and the one I thought was Maverick was only using one hand to jump down. In fact, once he got to the fire escape, where the others continued down the wall, he ran down, and then jumped from the second story landing.

"Not your concern. The only concern you should have is getting your asses into that van and picking me up. Move faster." I growled as I stood and ran to the stairs, taking as many at a time as I could.

I just heard one of the other guys say, "Damn. I like her. Tells you exactly how to fuck off, beautifully, I might add."

I couldn't help but chuckle as I hit the bottom landing and shoved the back door open. To my relief, the van was there, door open. I jumped in, and the driver, the man who I think was Chip, slammed on the gas before the door was shut and I had a chance to sit down.

Next to me, Maverick was holding his arm. "You're shot."

He gave me the 'No *shit sherlock*' face, and then a voice behind me said, "Nikki, switch spots with me, so I can look at it."

I blinked and nodded. I climbed over the seat and let the blond man take my seat next to him. "You are all shifters."

"What gave us away?" The blond working on Maverick said.

"The way you all scaled the building. Even a well-practiced human wouldn't be able to scale it like shifters can. Also, you are down one. What happened?"

"Hack. He was a fox shifter." He said, and Chip hit the gas as we hit the highway. "I'm Bell. Kismot. Chip, he's a bear."

I twisted back in my seat and made eye contact with Maverick. "Wolf." Then there was a sly smile that heated me in all the right places.

"Of course you are."

"What is that supposed to mean? You've known me for no more than a couple hours." Then he snarled at Bell.

"Got it." Bell said, his fingers covered in blood, but he held up a bullet, fully intact. "Lucky asshole. When we get back, you should shift and rest for a while. You'll heal faster."

Maverick gave him a small nod, and then leaned his head back. "Please tell me someone grabbed Hack's bag before we left?"

"Yeah, we got it, boss."

"Did he shift before..." I swear I saw his throat bob slightly. "Before he died?"

"Yeah. I'm sure Flinch will cover it, but if nothing else, they will just think he's a critter who got in where he shouldn't have and got caught in the crossfire." Chip's voice was soft, and I thought he was holding back a bit of emotion, too.

We were silent for a long time, and when we pulled onto Stevens Creek, I finally asked, "Is it the same team every time?"

"Flinch, he pairs us with who he thinks we will work best with. Close enough to protect each other, but not so close that we will band together against him." Bell said, but his eyes went to Maverick and to Chip before he looked back at me. "But jokes on him. Our hatred for all being under contract to him has bound us. I would die for these two. For you too, Nikki. You didn't even sign the contract you are held to. Neither did Maverick. I signed when I was young and dumb. Chip... well, that is his story to tell."

"Short version, Nikki. I signed because it was the only way to get my sister the chemo and radiation treatment she needed. She's alive because I sold myself. My nieces and nephews have their momma because of that. I won't apologize for it."

"Shit." It was long and drawn out as I looked at each of them.

When my gaze met Mavericks, he just shook his head. He reached over the seat and cradled my cheek, rubbing his thumb across my cheekbone. It was warm, and I felt the blush, but not that same tingling feeling I got when Jesse touched me. "We all have a story, Sweets."

"And you all know mine."

"No. We don't." Bell said carefully as we pulled into the parking lot and circled around to the back side of Ivy Grace. "We know that your brother, Sean Taylor, who, whether you loved him or not, is a right fucking asshole for binding you to Jaysen Flinch. That is it."

"Not much to tell other than that. I have my personal life drama, but when it comes to why I'm here, well, that's the long and short of it. Sean's a fucking dickwad and signed me over to fuck me over, even in death."

Bell's eyes widened slightly as he looked to Chip and then to Maverick, who smiled softly, huffing a laugh. "So, there it is."

"Nikki, can you help Maverick out?" Chip asked. "Bell and I will take what we retrieved to Jaysen."

I nodded and watched as they stepped out.

CHAPTER 23

MADDIE

"Nikki?" Maverick's voice was soft as he said, "I have to tell you something."

"What's that?"

"I know that this will make me a right asshole, but I know you have a boyfriend. I know who and *what* he is." I blinked. Jesse and I have kept it largely under wraps. Well, until Sean died, and he and the other two Exorcis helped with Beth. "I know you would have told me. I know I shouldn't be flirting with you. I also know I can't help it."

Swallowing, I met his gaze. "Maverick, Jesse and I are complicated."

He chuckled. "I suppose it would be considering he is an Exorci. Don't worry, I'm not going to ask for details."

"Good, because you won't get them." I stepped out of the van and went to help him out, but he just hopped out, and with a grunt, closed the door with his good arm.

"Regardless, we are a team, and I don't want there to be any issues. I want you to trust me, so I'm not trying to keep secrets."

"Which means you know that my real name isn't Nikki." I opened the door into the hallway, and he slid in, opening a door right next to it, holding it open for me.

Once it was shut, he turned and backed me up against the door. "That's right Madilyn." He bent his head down, ran his nose along my neck. "I also can tell that you are aroused, and if you were not spoken for, I would be buried deep within you right now."

Then he took three steps back, heaving large breaths. He gripped his neck tight, and when his breathing evened out, he said, "I had to approve of you being on the team, so I followed you. Jaysen only gave me an address and asked me to report back on the girl who lived there. I didn't know anything. I swear.

"When Exorci Jesse Westbrook pulled up and carried you into your apartment that day, I admit I was intrigued. How was a Bacri involved with an Exorci? That *particular* Exorci, at that. Then I noticed how he never really touched your skin. It was always your clothing, kissing your hair, your covered shoulder." His face turned beat red as he said, "My imagination went wild when I heard you screaming his name in pleasure one night."

"Maverick..." I said his name almost as a warning, but there was something about this man.

"Please call me Ian when it's just the two of us." His voice was pained, and I didn't know why, but I nodded.

"Since you know my story, are you willing to tell me yours? Bell said you're in by assignment."

"My Dad." He walked over and sat on the couch, that I hadn't even noticed. Hell, I hadn't noticed anything about the room until now. It was pretty scarce, but since I walked into it, all my attention was on Maverick... Ian.

The couch and a cream and black rug were really the only furnishings. I walked over to the door, ensuring my back was to him, as I sighed and locked the door. "Please tell me."

I went and sat on the opposite side of the couch, brought my knees to my chest, and rested my chin on them. Ian's eyes stayed on mine as he thought through it.

"I've been obsessed with you since Flinch had me follow you. I've watched you every day since that assignment." He took a ragged breath, rubbed his face, shaking his head and looking away to the wall. We both knew how that sounded. "Why do I want you so bad? What is it about you that puts me at ease and makes me want to spill everything to you?" His voice was soft and held a tone of awe that pinched something within me.

"I can't answer that for you." I was attracted to him, but I knew my heart belonged to Jesse. Regardless of everything, I knew that my heart was his. I just hoped he didn't break it beyond repair.

He winced as he turned to face me. "My dad and mom had fertility issues after I was born. They wanted more pups, but couldn't seem to carry them to term. Flinch had access to some fae technology that would allow my parents to have more pups. Only it was at a cost my parents couldn't financially afford."

"So, your dad signed the contract. What happened to him?"

"He died in a car wreck about ten years ago."

"Ten years ago." I breathed.

He nodded and said, "I've been working for Flinch for eight years. I'll never be able to work off the money. I've just tried to accept my fate. I looked at the contract, though, and saw that he won't be able to go after my brothers and sister, if something happens to me."

"Brothers and sister? So, the treatments worked?"

A large smile crossed his face. "They did. Twin brothers and a sister. Mom's labor was rough, but she said she would do it again to get the three of them."

Someone pounded on the door, and he smiled. "Get the door. I'm gonna shift and curl up in the corner. I'll be good by morning."

Standing, I turned for the door, but before I could move another foot, he had me wrapped up in his good arm. "Thank you, Madilyn."

The way his name rolled off his tongue... oh gods, his tongue... no. Stop Madilyn. Step away.

I forced myself to take a step back, and he quickly set a kiss on my temple. There was no tingling feeling, like when Jesse did, just warmth.

I nodded and turned to go to the door.

When I opened it, Jaysen was standing there, saying, "Since you are done early, you can run drinks until four."

"I'm really tired. Can I go home for the evening, please? I haven't had a day off in three weeks."

My head throbbed, and I rolled my head around, closing my eyes to push him from my brain, but it was no use. "Go run drinks."

"Yes, sir."

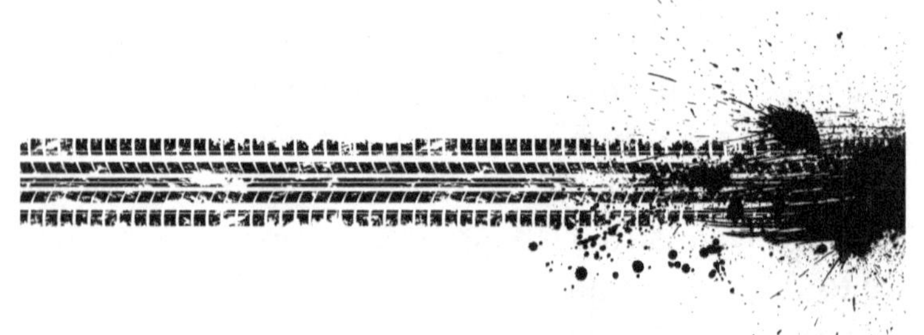

CHAPTER 24

JESSE

Sitting at the small table that had been my room for the last two weeks, I fisted my hands through my hair and growled, "Where in the fuck are you?"

My fists let go and pounded on the table just as my phone rang. When I saw the caller id, my anger banked.

"Hi, Little Bird."

"Hey, Jesse." Her voice was weary, and I looked at the clock.

"What are you doing up?"

"Just off work at Ivy Grace." I heard things clunking in the background. "Walked in the door and decided I needed to hear your voice before I got a couple hours' sleep."

"Maddie, you gotta take care of yourself when I'm working."

She was silent for a moment too long, before saying with a bit more bite than I expected, "I'm doing the best I can right now."

"You are mad."

"Damn fucking straight." She took a deep breath. "You've been gone for three weeks, Jesse. We were doing better. I was doing better with you around more. Day trips were fine, but this... this is hard."

"We've talked about this, little bird. This is my job and who I am. In a very literal sense. There are no other job opportunities for me."

"I know that. Doesn't mean I have to like it. Doesn't mean this is right." I heard her get a glass of water from the tap and take a sip before saying, "I'm tired. I need you. I need to be held, to be cherished."

"I'm sorry I can't be there right now." I muttered, feeling like a right asshole. This whole thing does suck. In any normal relationship, I would have been there for her non-stop through all of this. Been able to love her and hold her, and... "Maddie?"

"Yes, Jesse."

What was it I was going to say? "Nevermind. There is nothing for me to say. Nothing that I can say to make any of this better, to make you feel better, and nothing I can do to change any of it."

"I know." She let out a heavy sigh. "I'm going to bed. I love you, Jesse."

"Love you, too, Little Bird." I whispered through the phone.

When she hung up, I just stared at it. For twenty minutes, I stared at the phone. I wanted to go home. Edmonton was not being very beneficial in my hunt for Clarke, and I wanted to go home and hold my little bird.

Looking at the time, I decided to take another look at it in the morning... or at least in a few hours. For all the frustration I had about Maddie not going to bed yet, I laughed at the fact it was almost 5:00 am and I hadn't slept yet, either.

My phone was ringing, but mutely behind my sleep induced haziness. I rolled over and reached for it, answering without even looking at the number.

"Yeah."

"Exorci."

My eyes shot open, and I sat up. "Primal. What can I do for you?"

"I need an update."

"I got nuttin." I groaned. "I've been all over Edmonton, and found nothing."

"Nothing."

"Nothing. There hasn't been a whisper here. Are you sure he's been here? I've spoken to a few of the reps, but they haven't heard anything. I spoke to Ovexa Chales earlier this week, and he had his ear to the ground for me, and he hasn't come up with anything either. Said he would keep looking. You also mentioned the Mitsue Bear Clan. I'm trying to get in contact with them, but... until I do, or at least have something more to go on, I want to wait on showing up there."

I heard Primal Emma heave a heavy sigh and then she said, "No productive movement then?"

"None." I waited for her to respond, and when she didn't, I asked, "Do you want me to stay and keep looking, or should I just do the snooping from home?"

"Come home, Exorci. Spend some time with your girl, and you can go back once we have something."

"Primal?" Again, there was no answer, so I took that as an opportunity to continue. "How much can I divulge to Ovexa Chales? I mean, this whole trip doesn't exist. This assignment doesn't exist? How many people are we bringing in on this?"

"Ovexa Chales was key in getting us the info we had. He's already fully on board." I heard a chair squeak in the background and she let out a long breath. "He's become a ghost."

I huffed a chuckle. "The good ones know how to do that when they start to feel the heat."

"If I remember correctly, you did just that in La Paz after things got a bit... unbloody."

"Hey, I confirmed my exterminations, and *then* walked off into the ocean."

She full on laughed at that. "Only to randomly show back up here at home eight months later. You still haven't told me how you did that."

"And I won't, because I might have to use the tactic again." I rubbed the rest of the sleep from my face, got up, and went to the little kitchenette. "Back to the orders at hand. Do I stay or do I come home?"

"I already told you to come home, Jesse. There are things you need to deal with here."

"With the Agency?" My hand froze on top of the pod coffee maker.

"I need you to follow upon some things here with Jaysen Flinch." She was hiding something, and I didn't like it.

"Just say what you want to say. We've worked together for too long. You owe me that much respect. What is going on?" I stared as the liquid dripped into the cup and I took a deep inhale of the nutty coffee, waiting to wake me up.

"You asked me to see if there was a contract for Sean Taylor, and I have found nothing in regards to a contract, but... Ms. Taylor is working at Ivy Grace."

Gritting my teeth and my stomach suddenly dropping to my feet, I said, "Yes. To the point, Primal." I practically growled it at her, trying to tap down on the rage that I was feeling crawl up my spine.

"A Bacri scout thought he saw Ms. Taylor on a rooftop acting as a scout for a break in that resulted in a fox's death."

I didn't realize I even had the plastic silverware in my hand until it crunched and pierced my palm. "Fuck." I shook my hand out and went to clean it out.

"Jesse?"

"I'm fine." I let out a huffed breath before asking, "Do we have any verification? Do we know why? Has the Bacri Primal been made aware?"

Her voice was strong and meant to convey comfort, but there was a hint of worry there, too. "How do you think I was made aware? He let me know out of respect for our eighty years of friendship. He is going to pay her a visit. See what he can find out, but... if she spills blood..."

"I know. All Agency protection goes out the window." I swear if Sean signed her over to that shit, I would make the gods raise him just so I could kill him over and over again. "We don't know about a contract, though?"

"No. Like I said, Primal Berk is going to pay her a visit. See what he can find out."

"What is it about, Flinch? Why is there nothing on this man in the Agency records? Everything says he is a human, but he's completely entwined in all things Agency." Shaking out my hand, I grabbed one of the creamer packets and poured it into my coffee, now that it was finished. "There has to be some sort of connection."

Primal Emma was dead silent on the other end of the phone, and when almost a full minute went by, I asked, "That is what worries you, isn't it? That he's involved, but no one knows how or why a human is so involved and skirting the Agency politics and laws?"

"You said it. Not me."

"Great." I grumbled and took a sip of the magic bean juice. I was going to need a lot of it before getting on the road. "Since there is nothing left for me here, then I'm going to pack up and head home. See what I can find out from Maddie."

There was a small noise of acknowledgement before she said, "Report in once you've got something. I'll be in touch. Safe travels, Exorci."

When the line went dead, I threw my phone onto the bed.

Fuck. If Maddie was indeed under contract, she was royally fucked, and there was only so much I could do. Flinch would kill her before letting her out of it.

First thing, first. Get home. Second, see Maddie.

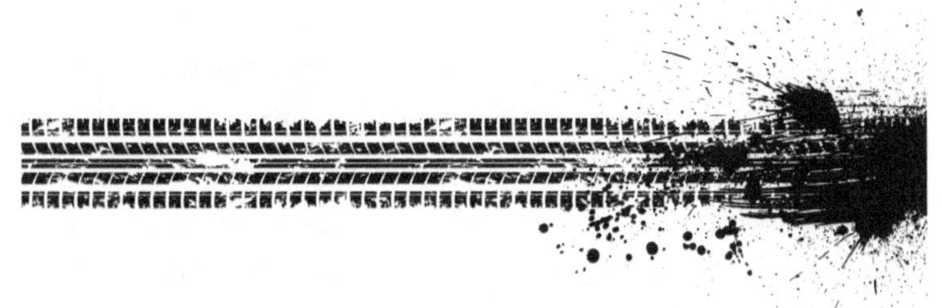

CHAPTER 25

MADDIE

"Thank you, Jackson. Yes, I'll have those reports to you by the end of the week."

"Great. We meet next week to finalize the plans and I want to make sure that the funding all works." Jackson said as he shook my hand and walked out the main door.

"Maddie?" Sarah, one of our Admin Assistants, asked from behind me. I turned, and she looked nervous. "There's someone here for you in conference room three."

"Okay. Who is it?"

"I don't know. He's lean, but... are you okay? He looks like someone I wouldn't want to meet in a dark alley." Her eyes flicked in the direction of the conference room, and I forced a smile on my face.

"I'll be fine. If you hear screaming though..." and what, have her call the police? If it was anyone Agency, it wouldn't matter. The police wouldn't be able to do anything. If it is anyone from Flinch, then, well, I was equally screwed.

She nodded and squeezed my arm as I walked down the hall and opened the door. It was one of the two conference rooms that weren't glassed in, and once I opened the door, I instantly wished that Sarah had put him in one of the glass rooms. The Bacri Primal was standing in my office. This was never good.

I dropped to my knees, head down, and laid my arms out to my side. "Primal."

"You can stand." I slowly rose to my feet, but kept my head down.

"What can I do for you, Primal Berk?"

"Lift your gaze to me and answer honestly."

Shit. This was an inquisition. Could I avoid looking at him, and twist the truth? No. That would only make things worse.

"Are you currently working at Ivy Grace?" He asked, the second my eyes met his. He pulled on my heritage and commanded full obedience and truth.

"Yes, Primal." I could, however, keep the answers short.

"Are you under contract with the owner, Jaysen Flinch?"

I gulped. "Not by my hand."

The Primal's shoulders released slightly. "Are you working at the club only, or has he sent you out on other jobs?" I swallowed hard. I'd been on four look out assignments. Why couldn't he just ask me yes or no questions? "Bacri Madilyn Nikole Taylor. I require answers."

"I've done additional assignments."

"Including being a look out for the break in which resulted in the death of a fox shifter at Goldleaf Trust Corp.?" I swallowed hard.

Due to the contract, I was somehow magically bound not to speak of my assignments for Flinch, but I was also bound to tell the truth to the Primal. My Primal. My mouth opened, closed, and my throat tightened as a small squeak came out.

Primal Berk noticed my struggle, and came to stand in front of me, causing me to back up to the wall. He met me step for step, and when I couldn't move anymore, his head lowered so we were nose to nose.

His eyes shifted to his eagle form as he repeated his question. "Were you the lookout for a break in that resulted in the death of a fox shifter at Goldleaf Trust Corp.?"

I felt the pull in both directions to answer and to not answer. My voice squeaked again, and I tried to answer with just a shake of my head, but couldn't move my head.

"You cannot physically answer, can you?"

"No sir, I cannot." He backed away and released his hold on me. I sagged in relief.

"You realize that is an answer in itself, right?" He gave me a small lift of the lips as he said that, and I just nodded.

"So, you did not sign a contract with Jaysen Flinch, but are bound by it, under antiquated bullshit law." He tipped his head to the side in a way that showed so much of his eagle form that I was momentarily jealous of him. I had always wanted to shift, and right now, there was a part of me that wanted to do so, and just fly away. "Why didn't you come to the Bacri office to petition its release?"

My eyes met his as hope flared in my chest. "Is there? Is there something you can do to nullify it, I mean?"

"I'll get a copy of it. How much was your brother into him for?" Of course, he knew Sean had a problem. It would have been reported to him for years.

"3.8 million." My voice was small, and I played with my fingers. "I suspect I'll never work it off."

Thankfully, the Primal just nodded. He looked out the small window before he said, "Try to stay a scout. I can keep you somewhat protected from the Primals if you are still a scout, but the second you draw blood, I'll have no choice but to revoke Bacri protection." His eyes met mine and held them as he said, "Is that clear, Madilyn Taylor?"

"Yes, Primal."

"I'll be in contact." He strode for the door, and I was left feeling empty and cold. I hated Primal magic. I gathered my files that had fallen to the floor when I had dropped in greeting to the Primal, and took a deep breath to settle myself before walking out and to my office.

He would look into seeing if I could get out of the contract. I just had to stay as a lookout.

My phone dinged, and there was a fluttering feeling that filled my stomach when I saw it was Maverick.

You free for lunch?

Really backed up here at work.

Maverick had only kinda backed off the flirting. The longer Jesse was gone, the bolder he got. I sighed, looking at my phone.

Too bad, because I brought it anyways.

There was a knock on the window next to me, just as I was passing Sarah's desk, and we both jumped at the sound. When I saw him standing there holding up a bag, I shook my head and smiled.

"That hunk was waiting for you?" Sarah said.

"Apparently." I muttered. I held up a finger and then texted him.

I'll be right out.
Just need to put some files down.
I'll meet you at the picnic tables to your left.

Maverick looked in that direction and nodded, heading over there.

"Did you and Jesse break up?"

"Nope. He's traveling for work. Maverick is just a friend." I said, smiling at Sarah. "I'm taking a quick lunch, and then I'll be back. Can you scan the information in this file over to me and get the plans from Fred? I need to finish up some reports for Jackson."

"Sure thing." She smiled, and then added, "Jesse and Maverick. No wonder you aren't sleeping. I wouldn't either if I had those two in my bed."

"I don't have either of them in my bed right now. I told you, I've had to pick up a second job to pay off some of my dipshit brother's bills."

She just looked at me like I was full of bullshit. Fine, let her believe what she wants.

"Oh, Maddie. Was everything okay with that guy who just left?"

"Yeah, in fact I'm hoping he can help me with the Sean situation." I looked out the window and saw Maverick unpacking some food, and I couldn't help the smile on my face. I could see myself between the sheets with him, but he wasn't Jesse. And Maverick wasn't mine. "I'm gonna go eat."

As I walked out the door, I warred with myself. Why was I so attracted to him? I sighed. It was the attention. I was getting attention from a very good-looking man, which made me miss Jesse even more. Gods, I missed Jesse. He called every night and we would talk, but he had been gone for a month now, and I... dammit, I missed him.

"Hey, Sweets." Everyone in our group had taken to calling me 'Sweets' as a nickname.

"Hey, Maverick." I said, swinging my leg around the bench and sitting down. "And why did you bring me lunch today?"

"Because I know that you probably didn't pack anything and would plan on working through lunch." He kept his head down, but he wasn't wrong. "I know you are having a rough go. You didn't sleep at all this morning, did you?"

I shook my head. "And neither did you, by the looks of it."

"I got three hours in. Woke up, thinking about you." His voice trailed off, and there was an adorable blush to his cheeks. Before I could say anything though, he met my gaze and said, "I'm trying, Sweets. You know I got it bad for you, but I'm trying to be as respectful as possible, okay?"

"I know, Maverick." I grabbed a fry and popped it into my mouth. "I might be a bitch for allowing it, but I can't be mad about free food. You know I cherish you as a close friend. I'm sorely lacking in those right now."

His dazzling smile was all I needed. It was the comradery that held me together anymore. Having someone I could talk to, who related to what I've had to go through. They understood the hard decisions. They understood what it was like to be in a no-win scenario. They understood what it meant to have us all be a unit.

"One thing I've noticed about you is that you don't take care of yourself. You wouldn't eat if it weren't for Jesse or someone else feeding you. Someone had to pick up the slack while he's out on assignment. So why not your friends?"

"I eat." I admonished, and to emphasize the point, I picked up my burger and took a giant bite, and raised my eyebrow.

"Good girl. Now don't forget to chew." I covered my mouth to keep from spewing the burger back at him, and I tried to stifle a laugh. "In your mouth, please, Sweets. I'm not into the regurgitation thing."

I chewed, drank a bit of the Dr. Pepper he got me, and when the last bit was down, I took a fry and threw it at him, muttering, 'asshole.'

"All joking aside, you are gonna need your strength tonight." His voice was low, and he didn't make eye contact with me. He just slowly took a fry and took a bite.

"That will be four nights in a row, and I didn't get the Monday off he promised me at the beginning." I took another bite, chewing slowly. "Not that I expected him to have any of my best interests at the forefront of his mind."

I looked back toward the office and could see Sarah watching me carefully. When Frank walked by, my heart sank at the defeated look on his face. "I'm gonna lose this job if this keeps up. I need it. I'm barely surviving."

"Jaysen ain't given you anything from your jobs?" Maverick asked before taking a long drink.

I shook my head. "Everything goes towards Sean's debts and I'll never be able to pay them off."

"How much?" He asked before he popped the last of his burger into his mouth.

"3.8."

Maverick choked and sputtered. "Million?" When I nodded in confirmation, he said, "Fuck. I'm in for 600K, and know that I'll never pay it off because he's adding thirty percent interest. My father didn't even blink at that fact, apparently."

"I know I've said this before, but I am sorry."

He gave me a small smile, and then it fell. "Well, someone is about to make your day, regardless of the news I just gave you."

I blinked at him and cocked my head to the side. "Why?"

Maverick lifted a finger and pointed over my shoulder. I turned, and I couldn't believe it. How had I not heard him drive up?

"Jesse?" I knew a shit-eating grin was all over my face, and I looked back at Maverick, who smiled back. There was something in his eyes, and I couldn't help but feel a small pang of guilt for putting it there. Swinging my leg around the bench, I got up and said, "Be right back."

My feet had hardly touched the ground before I took off at a run toward Jesse. When I reached him, I launched myself at him. His arms wrapped around me as he swung me around.

"Hey, Little Bird."

"Hey, yourself." He put me down, giving me a long kiss at the hairline on my temple, and once again I felt that tingling. I turned, keeping an arm around his waist, "Come on, I want you to meet someone."

When I looked back at where Maverick was, he was stuffing our trash into the to-go bag. He met us halfway, and I smiled up at him and said, "Jesse, this is Maverick. He's a very close friend, so I expect you to be nice."

Jesse raised an eyebrow at me before turning toward Maverick and extending a gloved hand out to shake his hand. "Nice to meet you, Maverick."

Maverick didn't take it, but looked at him with that dazzling smile. "No offense, man. Wolf." He pointed to himself. Jesse chuckled, and Maverick picked up the pleasantries. "It's nice to officially meet you. Sweets has told me quite a bit about you."

I felt Jesse stiffen his arm, and Maverick must have caught the movement because his lip twitched before saying, "I'll see you tonight, okay?"

I let out a heavy sigh before saying, "Yeah, I'll see ya there." He turned to leave, but I hollered back, "Hey, Maverick?"

Turning to look back at me, I said, "Thanks for bringing me lunch and making sure I ate."

"Anything for a friend." Then he strode off, and I watched as he threw the trash in the bin, headed off into the parking lot with his hands in his pockets and shoulders hunched a little in defeat. I tried to convince myself in that moment that he knew where we stood, but I needed to do better about drawing a line.

"You met at Ivy Grace?" Jesse interrupted my thoughts, and I nodded.

"He's been a good friend, Jesse. A damn good friend." I looked over my shoulder back at the office and felt Jesse sigh against me.

"So, your lunch has already been taken. Sorry I didn't get here earlier. I haven't even gone by the condo yet." He turned me to face him, disappointment in his eyes.

"If I had known, I would have told Maverick to shove off, but I didn't know you were coming back today." I leaned in and he held me tight against his chest. The smell of fresh air, sweat and leather filled my senses, and I couldn't help but relax into it.

"I'm not mad, Little Bird. I knew I was taking a chance. It's already one. I knew you very well could have already gone to lunch, or had just gotten back." His head lifted and I could tell he was looking at the picnic table. "I just didn't expect you to have company for lunch."

"Is it that I had company for lunch, or that I had male company for lunch?"

"He called you 'Sweets', Little Bird." He leaned back to look at me, and I rolled my eyes at him.

"It's a stupid nickname. Maverick isn't even his real name. Obviously, everyone at Ivy Grace has an alias." I leaned back in his arms and narrowed my eyes at him. "You've been gone for weeks, Jesse. I made friends at work. A couple spilled over into my private life, so you are gonna have to get used to a few males calling me Sweets."

He studied me for a long time before he sighed. "You work tonight?"

"Yeah. No idea what time I'll be home, either. When I get done here, I need to go home and nap for a few hours. Didn't get much last night." I bit my lip, because I couldn't tell him what I was doing. He would lose his shit. Go down and take care of Flinch on his own.

Ordered by the Agency or not. So I did what I did best, deflected. "Otherwise, I would tell you to meet me there, and then prove to me just how much you missed me, because *fuck*, I've missed you."

I smiled as I felt him harden against me. "Keep talking, Little Bird, and you won't be going back into that office."

"Yeah, yeah, yeah. Promises, promises." I teased, but he pushed his hips toward me, and I knew it was a promise he would keep, if I so much as gave him the go ahead. "I'm already on thin ice here. I'm working so much, I'm not sleeping, so I'm..." My voice hitched, and I took a deep breath.

"Shhh..." He pulled my head against his chest. "We will work it out. I promise you that."

I took a step back and looked up at him. He really didn't know how deep in shit I was, and I didn't want him to worry. I didn't want him to have to carry my burdens. I just nodded and said, "I need to get back inside. I'll call you when I get off work here tomorrow, and you can work on making things up to me for being gone so long."

"Deal." He kissed the hairline on my forehead this time, and again I felt that tingling feeling. "I love you, Little Bird."

I pulled his jacket back and my lips tingled as I pressed them to his chest through his t-shirt. I sighed, taking in the leather and the smell of him again.

"I love *you*, Jesse Westbrook. Don't you ever forget it."

CHAPTER 26

JESSE

This had been the longest twenty-eight hours I have had to endure in a long time. Being gone from Maddie for this last assignment was hard, but the distance was enough to chill me out a little bit. I reached her door, shifted my backpack and the bag in my hand, and slipped the key into the lock. She wasn't supposed to be home for another half hour, and I wanted to get dinner started for her.

Yesterday, Maverick had met her for lunch, and I barely contained my jealousy. I could tell how much he wanted her. The way he looked at her as they sat at the table, the way he deflated when he finally saw me walking toward them, and the hunched, defeated way he walked away... I mean, I couldn't blame him, but fuck if his eyes didn't say everything that didn't need to be said. She tried to reassure me that there was nothing between them, but I'm not stupid. I knew my little bird loved me, and it wasn't that I was threatened by the wolf... I just... stupid jealousy. He could be here for her when I couldn't.

Taking a deep breath and opening the door, he stopped when he got into the living room and sighed. "You gotta take better care of yourself, little bird."

I toed the laundry along the way into a pile and made my way to the kitchen, where there was a stack of dishes in the sink. Dropping the bag of groceries on the counter, and my backpack on the chair at the table, I slipped a pair of gloves on and got the water on the stove and unloaded the bag.

I checked the water, and it was still warming up, so I got to work on picking up the rest of the house. It wasn't a pig-sty, it was just unkept. There was a string of laundry from the front door to the bedroom and another to the couch. I could almost see her stripping on the way, and then face planting onto either the bed or couch to get some rest. How involved was she at the club? Of all the clubs... she had to get a job at the one that I found linked to her brother.

After rinsing the dishes in the sink, putting them in the dishwasher, and getting a load of laundry started, the water was finally ready. Putting the tortellini pasta into the pot to cook, I started in on the red sauce.

I let my mind wander as I stirred the red liquid, adding seasonings here and there, until it was just right. I reached over and checked the water and then there was a soft, "I really missed your cooking."

"You could do more than just bagels and cream cheese. I've taught you a few things in the kitchen, little bird." I turned, put the spoon down, and faced Maddie. "Didn't hear you come in."

She shrugged. "I've learned to walk quietly lately. Keeps some of the creeps off you at Ivy Grace, but I don't wanna talk about that. All I know is that if that isn't tortellini and Jesse's garlic cheesy bread, then I am walking out of here and getting fast food."

I blinked at her and feigned hurt. "You would rather have fast food than anything else I would cook if it wasn't your favorite meal?"

"Well, my favorite meal is your cock, but since you're cooking, I guess that isn't really an option right now." Her lip twitched up as she took two sultry steps toward me and wrapped her arms around my waist. "I really have missed having you here when I get home."

"It's because I cook for you."

"Oh, shut the fuck up. We've already determined I miss your cooking, but I just miss having you here." She kissed my chest, and leaned her forehead against it, taking a deep breath. I kissed the top of her head and sighed contently. We stood like that for a moment before the sauce sputtered.

Maddie chuckled. "Let me change, and I'll make the bread."

"Only a robe, little bird. I don't plan on you being clothed long after dinner."

"Yes, Jesse." She rolled her eyes dramatically, but the smile and light in her eyes was worth it.

When she returned, I froze. "When did you get that?"

There was a gentle smirk on her face as my gaze trailed from her knees and up her body. The robe was likely supposed to be white, but was so shear, that it left nothing to my imagination, and my cock swelled to full attention. "A few weeks ago. Bell was with me. My car had broken down, and I needed to get some new pole shoes, and he offered to take me while Maverick fixed it."

I felt my eyes tighten just slightly, but then I ran my tongue over my lips and groaned. "If I hadn't gotten your favorite, I would abandon dinner, but..." I bit my knuckle and groaned. I took my fill, and she even turned around and bent over to allow me a full view of her full ass, and when she spread her legs so I could see down the center of her, I nearly lost it in my pants right there.

I rubbed my face and tipped my head back. "Fuuuccckkk, Little Bird."

She stood up, giggling. "Just reminding you what is at home for you."

I slipped my gloves off, and reached for a replacement pair and growled, "Don't you think for one second that I don't know what is here and at my disposal."

She hummed as she reached for the knife to cut the bread in half. "Your disposal? Huh?"

Sighing, I turned and checked the pasta again, and it was perfect, so I removed it from the heat and drained it. "Little Bird, are you telling me you don't want my personalized attention this evening?"

"Jesse," she whirled around and pointed the long-serrated knife at me, and I held back a smile at the stern look she gave me. "If you don't have me cumming multiple times tonight before I have to be *there*, then we are going to have a major problem. Do I make myself clear?"

"And since when do you think you have the ability to make demands, my little bird?" The heat in her eyes flashed as I dropped my voice into that octave that always had her melting. Slowly, I took a few steps toward her, and turned the heat off on the sauce. The gulp she took was adorable, and I stood before her, taking the knife from her hand, and bent close to her ear. "You are going to go sit at the table, while I finish the bread, and make you a plate. Then, when you are done eating, you are going to sit there while I enjoy *my* dinner." Her hummed whimper was adorable, and then I chuckled, "And I won't be eating the pasta or bread. So, go get the shorts on. Now."

Her grip on the counter tightened, and I saw her knees buckle slightly. When she turned, I smacked her ass, and watched her practically skip into the bedroom to do what she was told. I took a deep breath, because I really needed to get myself in control.

By the time she came back into the kitchen, I had placed a towel on the tabletop and was pulling the bread out of the oven. She reached for a plate out of the cupboard, and I cleared my throat. When she gave me a questioning look, I raised my eyebrow at her. "I believe you were given your instructions, little bird."

She paused, and I could see the question in her eyes, on whether or not to push the matter. Maddie gave a quick nod and went to sit at the table.

"Jesse?"

I looked over my shoulder as I cut the bread and said, "On the table, Maddie."

Her face flushed, but she complied, sitting on the edge, hands in her lap, feet resting on the chair before her. I made a plate, and when I reached her, she started to spread her legs, but I shook my head. She pressed her knees together and threaded her hands together.

"How was your day?" I asked, as I lifted a forkful of food to her. She shrugged as she took a bite.

When she swallowed, she sighed. "I'm on real thin ice there." I gave her another bite, the heat in her eyes hadn't stopped, but she knew the game. We were having a moment of normality, before the world caved in.

"I told you, we will work it out. I've got money. You won't have to worry about anything for a while. I wish you would let me help you with Sean's debt. Tell me how much and who to get the money to." I lifted the fork to her mouth, and her eyes refused to meet mine as she leaned forward to take the pasta in her mouth.

"Can I have some bread, please?"

"Maddie." My voice was soft and I didn't—

"No." Her gaze met mine, and there was determination. "No. I'm not talking about his debts. Not during our first night together in way too fucking long,

Jesse Westbrook." She waited until I nodded and then her gaze looked down and slowly back up. "Now, may I please have some bread and a glass of water?"

I let the side of my mouth lift. "Good girl, asking for water instead of something else."

"I know how to get what I want."

"Yes, my little bird does." I gave her a piece of the garlic cheesy bread and went to fill another glass with some water. When I returned, though, she reached for the water, and I flicked my gaze down between her legs before handing it to her. She gulped down the glass of water and smiled at me as she opened wider.

"Fuck." I drawled, but was on my knees a moment later, pulling her hips to the edge of the table. Her hips rose as I moved closer toward her.

Slowly, I ran a gloved finger over the center of her, and I saw how wet she was through the material. Then I ran my tongue down the center, but avoided her clit.

"Jesse."

"I haven't forgotten your demand for multiple orgasms, little bird. And you are already so close. Aren't you?"

Running my tongue up the middle of her again, she hummed her, 'Yes', just as I flicked her clit.

Gods, I wanted to taste her. Taking my fingers and pressing against the material, my finger pushed inside of her just as I wrapped my lips around her clit and sucked. It was mere moments before I felt her tightening around me. Curling my fingers, I flicked her clit again and again, extending out the pleasure.

"Didn't even have to make me work for that one."

Her breathing slowed as she came down, and I languidly lapped from one end of her to the other. She ground against me, and I heard her slap against the wall. I hummed a laugh against her as I lifted her hips, and circled the tight opening of her ass.

"Jesse." Maddie's breathing came in short quick breaths as I stuck my thumb against it, moving back to her entrance, and pressing my tongue inside of her. Alternating, entering her pussy and ass, her breathing became more and more labored. I could tell she was trying to hold still, but her hips moved involuntarily. "Gods, I've missed this."

"What do you want, Little Bird?"

"You... in me... now." The last word came out more as a growl, but I just chuckled at her.

"Give me at least one more." Then I clamped down on her clit, and thrust into both her ass and her pussy as she rode my face, my fingers pumping in and out of her.

My poor little bird was so deprived of special attention, she didn't make me wait long before she screamed in ecstasy. When she came down, I flicked my tongue over the bundle of over sensitive nerves, and as I felt her thighs quake next to my cheek. I stood, pulling my fingers from her.

I stood up, pulling her by the hand with me. Letting her settle against my chest, she attempted to catch her breath.

Her fingers dug into my shirt, and she took a big breath before looking up at me and said with as much energy as she could muster, "Get your equipment on, Jesse. You are not done with me yet."

"Oh, I know that, Little Bird. The question is, do you need me to carry you to the bedroom, or are you capable of walking?"

In answer, she pushed me back and jumped off the table, taking the towel with her and hurrying to the bedroom. I was quicker, though, and reached out, gripped her by the back of the neck, and pulled her back to me. She moaned at the feel of my grip.

"I love you, Little Bird. On the bed, on your knees."

"Yes, Jesse."

CHAPTER 27

MADDIE

Gods, it was nice to have Jesse home. I knew I missed him, but no one made me feel the way Jesse did. Just having him in her apartment was enough. Of course, the sex tonight was divine, and the eight orgasms that he had dished out like Halloween candy sure helped.

Jesse had made the time to stop by the store and get everything to make my favorite meal, all before I had to leave to go to work. There were questions in his eyes, sure, but he didn't ask them. Jesse didn't want to bring the world down on our short time together tonight.

Sure, I was going to get there just in time, but the boys could get over it. I pulled into the parking lot, and when I got to the back door, swiped my card, the door blew open.

"*There* you are." Maverick growled. His nose flared, and he closed his eyes for a moment to gather himself.

"Don't. You've known where we stand from the beginning, Maverick." I said, stepping past him. "I'm assuming there is a black envelope and *another* night out on the town?"

He grabbed my arm and made me face him. "I'm sorry, Sweets. I didn't expect it to hit me like that. Knew you would be with him. Thought I had expected that. Just…"

"Didn't want it to happen." My voice was low, but I looked down at his hand still gripped in mine. I squeezed it. "I haven't been fair to you. I shouldn't have allowed you to continue flirting at all. Hell, I shouldn't have reciprocated."

He pulled me closer and put his hand on my cheek. "You have done nothing wrong. I'm a wolf. I'm domineering, possessive, and…" He studied my face and opened his mouth.

"If I were not with Jesse, I would likely be yours right now." The words hurt coming out, only because they were true. I was attracted to him. He was fucking beautiful, but my heart wasn't his. "It's not fair to you, and I'm sorry."

"Don't be sorry, Sweets." He bent down and put his forehead to mine. "I will wait for the day that he fucks up enough that you walk away. You are worth waiting for."

"You'd be a rebound. An emotion fuck. How is that fair? You need to find a good woman, a good *wolf*, who will treasure you for who you are, and not treat you as a second choice. I'm sorry, that is what it is, Ian." I whispered the words, because we were having a very private discussion, in a very public hallway, in the back of a club that owned our lives. My heart clenched at the truth in my words.

"Look at me, Sweets." He waited, and when my gaze met his, he said, "I said this once, but I'm gonna say it again. I will wait for you. Jesse will mess up, and I'll be here waiting. I don't care how mother fucking pathetic that sounds. I'm going to wait for you, Madilyn, until my dying breath."

Then he kissed my nose and took a step back. I had to make myself take a deep breath and fight the urge to lean into him. "Go, get dressed. We needed to leave ten minutes ago."

Nodding, I turned and hurried down the hall. When I reached the dressing room, there was indeed a black envelope sitting at my station, with a black bag next to it. The envelope tore quickly, and I read the same instruction I had had for almost a week. *Report to Maverick after changing.*

I quickly changed and hurried back down the hall. I should have tried harder to remove Jesse's scent from me. I mean, it isn't like it... hell, I didn't know how it worked. When I got to the van, Chip was in the driver's seat, Bell was in the passenger's seat, and Maverick was sitting in the back, door open, waiting for me. I stared at him a moment, and he tipped his head for me to hurry up. I jumped in and slid into the seat on the other side of Maverick, trying not to overthink anything he had said earlier.

Maverick slammed the door shut as Chip pulled away from the club and sat down next to me. Wrapping an arm around the back of me, he bent down to whisper in my ear. "I'm sorry for my behavior earlier, but what I said stands."

"I don't know why you are whispering. Bell and Chip can hear every word." I turned my head toward him and smiled. I reached up and held his cheek for a moment, like he had to me earlier, and it was surreal to have him lean into my touch. His nose nuzzled my wrist before his hand covered mine, and he put a kiss to the palm of my hand.

"We heard everything you declared to her earlier as well." Bell said, and I met his gaze in the mirror. He knew what that declaration was. I did, too, and I really didn't want to think on it.

"What are we doing tonight?" I muttered, trying to change the subject, and pulled my hand back into my lap, where I played with my fingers.

Maverick shifted next to me and said, "You are gonna do what you do best, Sweets. Keep an eye out for trouble."

I took a deep breath. "And what are you guys doing?"

Maverick took my chin in his fingers and got close. "Keep you safe and out of harm's way. We will get what we need, and you will just stay out of the way and stay safe."

I ground my teeth. "You don't control me, Maverick."

"I do while we are out here. I won't let you get hurt, Sweets." His eyes met mine and didn't move.

"Nor will we." Chip said from the front. "Face it, Sweets. We are here to be the muscle and if anyone is gonna get hurt or captured, it's gonna be one of the three of us. Not you."

Maverick's eyes softened slightly. "Madilyn..." My name on his lips was heartbreaking. "You are a scout. A lookout. The day you have to take a life will be the day I have failed you." He released my chin, and I nodded.

I didn't know if I could take another being's life. Could I? I knew they had so much blood on their hands they were dripping from it. Could I carry that weight around?

Maverick's eyes widened just a bit, and I nodded. "I'll be a good little eagle scout." He reached up and flicked the end of my nose. "Again... what are we really doing?"

"Cracking a database with no external access for information on an ice demon up in Canada. She's one of the most powerful elemental demons. She's refused to work with the elementals, but doesn't get involved with her Therugi side either."

"Daphanie Davies. Flinch wants to work with her on something, but we have no way to contact her." Bell said, semi-distracted. At some point, he had pulled a little laptop out and was clicking away.

"You are going into an Agency building?" My eyes went wide, and my heart raced. What were they thinking? "They will send Jesse, Brandon, or Nickolas after you for this."

"Tonight should be easy. Just gotta get Bell to the terminal, cover him while he gets what we need, and then get out." Maverick's voice held something back, though, and I knew it wouldn't be that simple. If it were, I wouldn't be here, and it wouldn't be the whole team deployed. Bell had been sent out on data collection solo before, and this would have qualified for that.

"What aren't you telling me?" I looked out the window, and decided, if they didn't want to tell me, I would accept it, but we had been doing this for a while now, and they should trust me with more information.

"A lot, Sweets. Just keep us covered, okay?"

"As you command." His hand was on mine and squeezed. He knew I wasn't happy with the answer.

The thirty minutes of silence in the car was interesting. Out of the corner of my eye, I could see how Bell and Chip would catch Mavericks in the mirrors, and every time, whether he realized it or not, he would squeeze my hand tight. I didn't have it in me to pull away from him, even though I should have.

Gods, I was a right toxic bitch. I should try to cut all ties, all contact, everything with Maverick. It wasn't fair to anyone. Most of all Jesse. Maverick, at least, knew what he was doing. Jesse... I took a shuddering deep breath, and I saw Maverick cock his head to the side, but I shook it off. He rubbed his thumb across my hand, and when we pulled off 280, I did pull my hand from his.

"The Cupertino Agency campus..." I looked through the window.

"You will be across the street at the corner store." He handed me the earpiece, and I pushed it into my ear. I clicked the button on as he did the same, and I snapped. He nodded, and I turned it off.

"There are cameras everywhere. Security too. Not to mention the Astral and Exorci in training here." My eyes shifted to each to each of them.

"That would have been nice to know beforehand, Flinch." Maverick gritted out of his teeth. After a couple minutes of contemplation, he said, "Bell, you know of any other options for access to the building?"

"Nope. There is a rotation every fifteen minutes, so we have a small window to roll through."

"Noted." Maverick's head turned to me. "We good to go, boys?"

"Good to go." They confirmed from the front seat.

"Let's drop Sweets, then we circle around and get the job done."

He opened the door, and I sighed, but before I stepped out, I looked at each of them. "If any of you get hurt or die, you best hope there is a good hiding place in hell, because I'm coming for you."

"Yes, Sweets." Chip and Bell said from the front, but Maverick had a humorous glint in his eye and just smirked.

Stepping out, I rounded the corner to the corner store, and went up the fire escape. When I got to the roof, I saw the van go in, but I had visual on the guys for the moment. Reaching up and pushing the button, "Entry point?"

"North end, back corner."

"I don't have visual from here. It's a blind spot."

"The van will be blocking the door, anyway." Bell's voice came through.

"If it's all blind, why in the fuck am I playing scout?" My question was met with silence as I saw the van drive down the small alley behind the building along the main road.

"Going in."

I sighed, and muttered a soft, "Copy."

It was agonizing on that rooftop waiting for anything and everything. Then I saw it.

"Bell, tell me you have what you need?"

"Need ten."

"You don't have it. Squad coming in from the south on the roof."

Gunshots rang through the air, and I didn't wait.

"Since when did Astrals use guns?" Chip growled. Just before I hurled myself down the fire escape, I looked over at the building.

"The roof squad is still accessing via the roof." I jumped and landed on the ground in a crouch. I pounced up and took off across the busy street. I heard honking behind me, but I couldn't be bothered. If something happened to my boys,… to Maverick, I would never forgive myself.

I reached the van, just as they busted through the back door. I threw the doors open, and just as they were jumping in, I was pulled backwards, with a knife at my throat.

Leaning back, I brought my foot down on whoever was holding me, but they compensated for it. So instead I jabbed my elbow into the side of their stomach as they were holding the knife, and it dropped. I whirled around, bringing my leg up, nailing them in the nose when they bent over. As they ducked out of the way, a man with a red E badge slowly removed his leather gloves, and I laughed. I actually laughed. I had seen Jesse do that on so many occasions, that I just tipped my head back and laughed.

It was a distraction tactic, because I realized I was further from the van than I thought I was. Maverick's head popped out of the side of the van, and I heard him in my ear. "Keep him right there, Sweets."

"Exorci Trainee, huh?"

"You are a pretty one." His voice was gravelly, but not in the way that had me in a puddle with Jesse.

"Aren't you supposed to have extermination orders before you touch me?" I half smiled at him, and the fire in his eyes was dark. "But what if I'm human?"

"Then my touch won't be a problem, will it? And if you are human, you already know too much, and I can get my Astral associate to come over and help."

It was then that the van bolted backwards, clipping the Exorci, causing him to whirl around toward me. I felt his hand on my forearm, but I kicked out, nailing him in the balls, before Maverick's arms were around my waist and hauling me into the back of the van.

"Got her. Go! Go! Go!" The van bolted forward.

My arm tingled and my foot hurt. I had not worn my ball buster shoes, and sneakers were not the right shoes for this.

"Bell, get me the first aid kit." Maverick's tone was all commanding wolf. My eyes widened, and as he rubbed my cheek, something felt wet. "Say something, Madilyn." His voice was full of panic, and fear, true fear, laid in his eyes.

"Let me up, Maverick." He had me pinned between the seats when we fell into the van, and I really wanted off the floor. It was making my stomach a little woozy.

"Careful, Madilyn. You're bleeding." Maverick said in a low hushed tone, but there was relief there as well.

"I'm fine." I crawled up into the seat, and he popped open the first aid kit, and went to work on the gashes that lined my forearm.

"How are you even alive right now?"

"Umm. Self-defense classes, thanks to Jesse, actually." I took the earpiece out and put it in the cup holder. "With all the trouble that Sean had been in, he thought it might be a good idea, in case one of them wanted to use me to get to Sean."

"No, Sweets. How are you not dead by the Exorci's touch?"

"He didn't touch me, or I would be dead." I rolled my eyes. "Maverick, remember I know how to move around an Exorci. The Astral must have gotten me."

He grunted, dismissing my comment. I grabbed his chin. When our eyes met, I spoke through clenched teeth. "For years I have learned and perfected the art of moving around an Exorci so that I stay on this side of the earth. Are we clear?"

"Yes, ma'am." There was a bit of a proud smirk on his face before he brought his attention back to my arm. "Will you please let me get this cleaned and wrapped up? You're getting blood all over the seats."

Shaking my head, I stuck my arm out, and said, "Thank you."

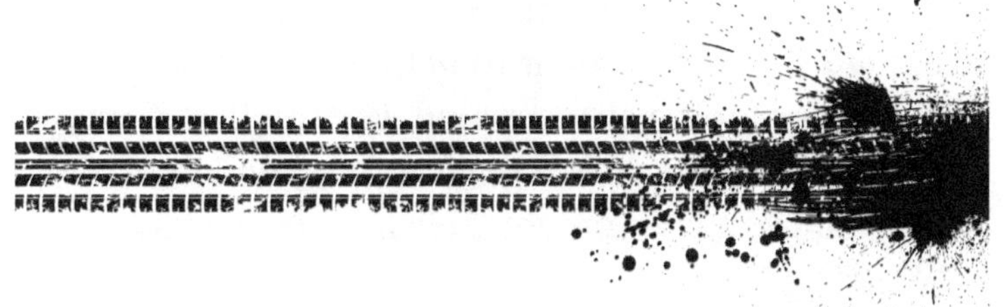

CHAPTER 28

MADDIE

I hung my keys on the hook by the door just as Jesse came out of the kitchen. Confusion, and then something that looked a lot like panic and worry, flashed across his face. "I didn't expect you home for a couple more hours."

"Yeah. Got done early." I tugged on my sleeve.

He looked down at it and sighed. "What happened?"

Shrugging, I turned to head toward the shower. "There was an incident, and I got scratched."

He grabbed my elbow and slid the long sleeve shirt back. "That is a hell of a scratch."

Jesse's eyes scanned me from head to toe. He noticed I was in all black, and not the short shorts and crop top I had left in. I could see his mind working. "Maddie."

"Jesse." I quipped. "I'm not playing games tonight. I'm tired, I'm sore, and I want to get a couple hours' sleep before I have to be at Westwind. For the first time in a *very* long time, I have a chance at four solid hours."

"Where were you tonight?" He asked carefully.

"Working."

"I know that. *What* were you doing tonight, Maddie?" His voice cracked, and I couldn't not tell him. He likely knew, or had suspected, that there was a contract. Had probably even tried to find out through his connections with the Agency.

I looked at my feet. "Doing special projects. I didn't lie to you, Jesse. I started by running drinks and cover occasional dances. Then I was dancing, and running drinks. Now I dance and do special projects, but I'm not going to talk about it tonight."

"Damn it, Little Bird." When I turned to face him, his hands were in his hair and he was staring at the ceiling. "Why didn't you tell me that Sean signed a fucking contract with Jaysen Flinch?"

I froze. It was as if literal ice had started flowing through my veins. My heart stopped, started, and then... "How?"

"I'm not stupid. I know how the Agency works. I know what those loopholes are. Fuck, I've been trying to find out if your asshole of a brother signed a contract with Flinch."

I just blinked at him. I knew he had been looking into things, but...

"Maddie, you said you were running drinks and danced occasionally. Okay, I get that. You were working there to pay debts, but not to literally *pay debts*." Jesse came to stand in front of me and his voice was thick, and there were tears in his eyes. It broke my heart as he fell to his knees and wrapped his arms around my legs. "How much? How much did that fucking piece of shit brother of yours sell you for?"

I swallowed. This is why I didn't want to tell him. It wasn't something he could fix. It wasn't something that he could fuck me into a better mood for.

"How much did Sean Taylor sell my little bird for?" He repeated. The tears that fell and ran down his cheeks broke me.

"3.8 million." I hardened myself, because I wouldn't let this be the destruction of our lives. "I'll never be able to pay it off."

Jesse went stone still. "I'll empty everything I have to help pay it off. I'll sell the bike. I'll buy a smaller condo. We'll combine households to conserve funds. I'll do whatever I need to help, little bird. I'll talk to Primal Berk."

"I've already spoken to Primal Berk. He's looking into the contract, but I doubt that there is anything that we can do." I sighed. The weight of everything that happened tonight and the exhaustion of my life over the last few months. I just wanted to sleep. "Maverick has been looking for a way out, too."

He stood quickly and then grit out, "I don't care about fucking Maverick."

"Well, you should, because he saved my life tonight. Bell and Chip too, so you better *start* caring, Jesse Westbrook." My voice was clipped, and then I leaned against the wall. "I'm exhausted. I'm going to shower and then go to bed. Are you staying or going home?"

"I'll stay." He said, his voice catching on something in his throat. I had never seen Jesse like this. "If you will let me."

"Of course. Come, hold me as I sleep." Then I turned and headed off to bed.

"Little Bird." Jesse was shaking me awake.

"Hummm." I groaned as I pulled the blankets back over my head and heard Jesse chuckle.

"It's 8:15, Maddie. You are late for work." His voice broke through the haze.

"Shit. Shit. Shit!" I cursed, throwing the covers back. "Why didn't my alarm go off?"

"I'll make you some toast while you get cleaned up." Jesse muttered. There was something about the way he said it that gave me a pit in my stomach.

After brushing my teeth, brushing my hair back into a ponytail, and putting a pair of jeans and black v-neck t-shirt on, I walked out into the living room, just as

Jesse walked around the corner, toast in hand. "What's wrong?" I asked.

"Didn't sleep. Was thinking of what I could do to help pay off Sean's jail sentence. Didn't realize it was so late until it was too late." I took the avocado toast from him and sighed.

"There isn't anything we can do, Jesse. Flinch has his claws in me, and I can't get out of it."

"I'll make some calls today, see what I can do." His eyes met mine. "I love you, little bird. Now go to work. I'll see what I can find out."

"Love you too, Jesse." I gave him a quick kiss on the shoulder and he laid his hand on my head, turning to kiss right next to the messy bun I had thrown my hair into.

I practically ran down the stairs and to the car. By the time I was at the office, the parking lot was nearly full, and I had to park at the opposite end of our office.

When I rushed in, almost an hour late, Frank was standing at the entrance, and said, "My office. Now, Maddie."

Shit. I took a deep breath, bracing for either a major ass chewing, or my walking papers. "Yes, sir."

Sarah and Becca's apologetic looks had my stomach swimming. My heart raced, because it was those looks that told me this was the straw that broke the camel's back. I was getting fired.

Frank followed me, and when we reached his office, he closed the door and didn't even offer me a seat. "Maddie, I really hope you get your things sorted out, but we can't do this anymore. You are late entirely too often, you aren't sleeping, so you are making mistakes, and are really behind schedule. I've reassigned all your projects."

I nodded. "Westwind deserves better than what I have given you since Sean died. I am sorry about that. I'll pack up my desk."

His head snapped up. "I expected a fight."

Shrugging, I looked out toward where the rest of the office was. "My life is falling apart, Fred, and while I'm not sure what I'm going to do to keep a roof over my head, I also understand where you are coming from. I'm not surprised by this."

He handed me my termination packet, with all the extra EDD documents, before saying, "I won't fight unemployment. I know you are working a job overnight that is killing your sleep schedule... can it help out?"

"No." My head shook back and forth, and I felt a tear slide down my cheek. "I'm having to work directly for the guy who Sean owed money to."

"Mad—"

I held my hand up. "So, I don't get a dime of it. I can't really say anything else. It's complicated. Really fucking complicated. Thank you for the amazing opportunity to work here. Good Luck, Fred."

His eyes softened to borderline puppy dog status, before he said, "Good luck, Maddie. If you need anything, let me know."

My eyes stayed down as I walked past Becca. Sarah, luckily, was not at her cubby, as I went and grabbed the few personal items I had at my desk and snuck out the side door. I told myself I could hold it together as I meandered across the parking lot and to my car.

I held it together as I drove home, parked, walked up the stairs, and slipped it into the lock. I was even able to hold it together until I walked in and saw Jesse with his ear to his phone.

"Primal Berk, I'll have to call you back. She just walked back into the apartment... Yeah. Sure. Tonight. I'll meet you after I drop off Maddie at Ivy Grace... I'm aware. Look, I gotta go... Yes, Primal."

"Primal Berk?" I hiccupped and tried to swallow the tears, but Jesse was standing before me, and pulled me up into his arms. He carried me to the couch, and sat down where my legs were laid over his lap, and I buried my head into his shoulder and cried.

"I got fired. I hate Sean. I hate Ivy Grace. I hate Jaysen Flinch."

Jesse let me cry and pound on his chest in frustration for seconds, minutes or hours. I didn't know, but when I was done pounding on him, he pulled me tight against him. "It's okay, little bird." I felt him take a large deep breath. "We will find a way."

I knew he didn't know what to do to fix it, but I turned my face into his shoulder and just let the tears come as Jesse held me.

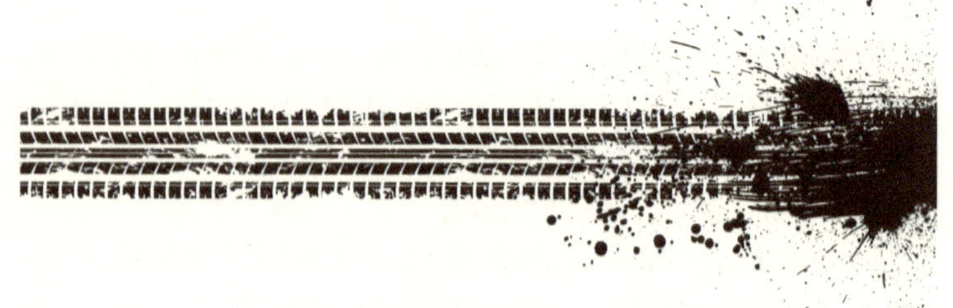

CHAPTER 29

JESSE

Maddie had been laid off for two weeks before I got the message from Primal Emma that the Alpha of the Mitsue Bear Clan contacted her and had some information for me.

When we spoke last night, she had been a little detached and cold. I didn't know what was going on, but I needed to keep working so we could pay off that sleaze of a debt collector. I had begged Maddie before I left to be careful, and not to do anything that would jeopardize her life. She agreed to try, but said she wouldn't have much choice in the matter.

I'd been away from Maddie for only four days, was worried sick, and I wanted to turn this bike around and ride hard and fast back to her arms. I was really beginning to hate this. Maddie was the single star in my life, and watching that brightness dim when I had to leave, and continue to dim every time I had to leave, was killing me. She wouldn't tell me what was happening at Ivy Grace, but I could see it killing off a piece of her soul every night.

Of course, I had tried to find out what was happening, but as far as the Agency was concerned, Flinch was mostly clean. They knew of the strip club, but he had human status in the registry. There were questions as to why a human was even registered with the Agency, but the consensus there was that it was because the club was a creature club.

I pulled up to the gate, and a dark, very muscular man who reminded me a lot of that wrestler who became a very popular movie star said, "Road is closed."

I flipped the visor of my helmet up and chuckled. "Well, good thing I'm not here to see the scenery."

"Strange place to be if you aren't here for the scenery." He raised a single eyebrow and the comparison to the wrestler / actor was complete. I couldn't help but chuckle.

Pulling my helmet off, I met his eye and said, "I'm here to see the Alpha. Could you please show me to the office or tell me where I might find Alpha?" He crossed his arms, and he would have been intimidating if it hadn't been for the fact a simple brush of my finger would stop his heart. "Primal Emma asked me to come and talk to them about Clarke."

His whole body stiffened before he nodded his head and said, "Very well, Exorci. Hold on for one moment."

He stepped inside the little shack that was stationed near the gate. It reminded me of an old outhouse more than anything, and a minute later came out and said, "Alpha knows you are incoming. Straight up the road two kilometers and you will see a gravel drive on the left. Alpha and the Soldier Primes will wait for you at the greet house."

"Thank you." He pressed some buttons at the doorway of the shack and the wheels squeaked painfully against my ears as it rolled back, allowing me through. The guard winced a little as I put my helmet back. Starting the bike up with a roar, he shook his head before stepping back inside. With a smirk, I headed up the road.

Just beyond the bend, away from the sight at the gate, the road was pristine.

Turning down the drive that looked to have been redone since last winter, I saw a guest house set back in the trees. There were two small cubs running around and playing out in front, and a tall brunette woman leaning against the door.

At the end of the drive, I pulled up to where a moderate-sized house sat, with a man leaning against the post of the porch. "Alpha is waiting for you in the greet house. You can leave the bike here." He stepped off the porch and stepped forward as I secured my helmet on the handlebars, knowing no one here would be stupid enough to mess with my bike. "This way."

We turned the corner and walked down a well-worn path about a quarter of a mile. When the large structure came into view, my eyes widened just slightly. Reminiscent of an old log building with huge windows along the roofline, it had two bears reared up with intricately engraved double doors that were at least twelve feet high.

The doors opened, and when I stepped inside there were eight large brown, black, and tan bears lining the hall, with one noticeable hole in the line, second from the Alpha. I chuckled, because while it wasn't unexpected, it was still a sight to behold. I was an Exorci, so it didn't surprise me the Alpha had their entire Soldier Prime line there and at the ready.

My boots clomped on the hardwood of the floor as I made my way to a simple one step dais where a beautiful, tall, black-haired athletic woman stood. She crossed her arms, and I chuckled.

"Well, look at you Alasie." I kneeled to one knee with my hand over my heart and paused for a moment before standing.

"Exorci Jesse Westbrook. You are far from home." She raised a delicate eyebrow before saying, "What brings you to my woods?"

"I couldn't come and check on one of the most adorable cubs I had seen in Canada?" There were a couple of low rumbles from the bears, and she waved them off.

"I haven't seen you in over a year, and you just stroll in. I would think you would have called me if this was a social visit." Her smile dropped as she became the Alpha. "Which one of my cubs have been misbehaving?"

"If you ask those in Edmonton, your entire clan, but I suspect it is actually a certain Ashton Clarke." My eyes swung to the growls that emanated to the right of me. While I knew my touch would kill them, I had purposefully left my gloves on to maintain the appearance I would not be hurting their Alpha. I gave her a droll look, because she knew I wasn't here for any other reason. Sighing, I closed my eyes a second before opening them and giving her a look because frankly, I wanted her soldiers to shut up. "Will you please advise your Soldier Primes I have no intention of hurting you, Alasie? If I were here on an execution order with your name on it, then it would be done already."

She nodded, and there were brief flashes as they all reverted to their human forms. Not that they looked anymore relaxed or anything. Each of them were in solid, dark green leathers with claw-like weapons at their hips. Her eyes focused on the empty slot in her ranks, and there was a deep breath that hitched before she let it out slowly.

"I take it you are familiar with him, and from your reaction, lost a soldier to him as well." I said carefully.

"We did." She took the step down from the dais and stood before me. She crossed her arms, holding her forearms tight. "Clarke has been causing us a bit of a headache up here. The lumber companies have been allowing their workers to carry rifles because they believe that bears have been killing their staff. We figured out it was the Exorci Ashton Clarke, and organized an eradication of our own. He wanted a bear attack? I would unleash a bear attack."

One of the Soldier Primes shifted uncomfortably, and I saw a long scar down the side of his face. Alasie turned toward him and a sad smile crossed her lips. She lifted her head and met my gaze. With pride she said, "My Primes fought valiantly against him. He was not left unscathed, but we lost one of our own. Soldier Prim Siku fell to his touch. He was buried with honor and given back to the Gods."

"What of the local authorities? I'm assuming you have contacts there?"

"I do, and he has done what he can to keep the eyes off the clan, but there are stories, and most of the population here know we exist, even without evidence to prove it. We were lucky to keep Siku's death out of their eyes."

"What happened after the attack? Any idea where Clarke went?" I ran my hand through my hair and grimaced when some of the longer ends caught on the snap. Sliding my glove off, the one nearest me shifted and there was a low grumble that came from his direction. I turned toward him, my back to Alasie, and said, "My hair got caught in my glove. Fuck. You need to go for a run or something, man. Alasie is the last person in this building I want to hurt. You are quickly becoming higher on the list, though."

A warm hand rested on my shoulder, and I looked over it to see Alasie smiling. "Exorci Westbrook isn't here to hurt me. You may all stand down."

"Ma'am." One of the guards said.

Her voice pulsed through the room with a power that I just smiled at. It was no wonder she was tapped for Alpha over her brothers. "You are all dismissed."

She stood there with her hand on my shoulder as the line of her most trusted guard strode out of the hall. When the door shut, she let out a deep breath. "I'm sorry Jesse. They are pretty on edge."

"I'm an Exorci. One touch, and their leadership goes down. I don't blame them, but I didn't even take off my gloves in here, Alasie. Not until the damn snap caught in my hair." I glowered down and played with the offending glove.

"I noted that. Like I said, you didn't do anything wrong. They are just on edge. And for good reason." She turned and sat down on the step to the dais, resting her forearms on her knees. I made my way over and sat down next to her.

"How many did Clarke kill?"

"Forty-five humans, six fox shifters, and seven of my clan." Her voice was heavy, and only one that a leader who truly felt for their people could imbue. "The Fox King worked with us. He lost his daughter in the fight with Clarke."

"Fuck. No wonder this is a file."

She stiffened next to me. "This is an extermination? Not just a recall?" Her voice was so low that I knew that even with their exceptional hearing and the guards outside, they wouldn't have heard a word. I just met her gaze and nodded. "Fuck indeed."

"Well, in that case, let me help you along. I heard after the altercation with us, he scurried off toward Prince George. You wanna stay tonight? I have a guest house that isn't being used. Soft comfy bed, hot water, flushing toilets. All the comforts of home."

"Not all the comforts." I grumbled, thinking about Maddie. Then I smiled and turned to her. "Where is Jonathan anyway? I didn't see him on the way in."

"My guards probably have him barricaded in the house." Her cheeks flushed, and I bumped her shoulder with my own. She had mated with him about five years ago. He had been a close friend of mine, but I hadn't heard anything from in a year.

As if he had been called, the door burst open, and he screamed, "Jesse Westbrook, you lay one finger on my woman, and I'll kick your ass. Exorci or not."

I placed my hands behind my hips and leaned back. "Like I would dare. She would likely rip me to shreds, you fuckhead."

I watched as a six foot–two blond-haired blue-eyed man strode in and stood before me. He narrowed his gaze at me and I just smiled up at him.

"Where is Maddie?"

"At home. She's got a lot of shit to deal with." My heart sank at the thought, and my stomach swam in that sour feeling again.

"That is Jesse speak for you are here on official business." I pressed my lips into a thin line and nodded. "Please tell me they sent you after Clarke."

I looked over at Alasie, who was beaming at her mate. "They did."

"Thank the Gods for that." He reached down, and I took his hand to get up. "Always with the leather man."

"Cloth gets eaten up too quick." I shrugged. "The leather works for the bike too, so I just go with it."

Jonathan bent down and kissed Alasie before helping her up. His hand smoothed over the lower portion of her stomach and whispered, "Did you tell him yet?"

"I haven't had time." She rolled her eyes.

"Seriously?!" I said, looking between the two of them. The smile on my face was one of pure joy.

They nodded. "We only just found out, so she can still hide it, but it won't be long."

I tipped my head back and laughed. "You are in for it, Jonathan. A mother of cubs... and an Alpha mother at that. You are royally screwed." Turning, said Alpha mother stuck her tongue out at me. I laughed and tipped my head toward the doors. "That explains why your guards were so over the top temperamental."

"Yeah. Damn supernatural sense of smell. They figured it out two days after we did."

"I'm very happy for you."

"Come on. Let's get you settled." Johnathan said, wrapping his arm around my shoulders. "Then we are going to drink beer and talk like we used to back in the States. Tomorrow you can do whatever it is you need to do."

"Yes, Chief."

Jonathon's head tipped back and he let out a belly laugh.

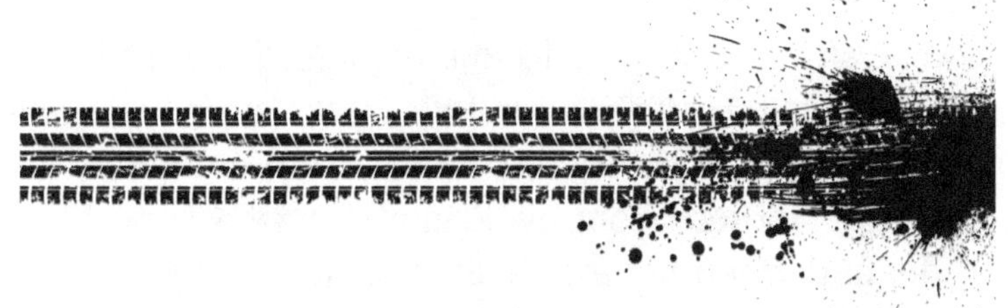

CHAPTER 30

MADDIE

I sat there, looking at that damn black envelope, when Cheryl laid her hand on my shoulder. "Another night out?"

"It would appear so. Is it wrong, I would rather have old corporate men looking at me wiggle my ass and tits than go out tonight?" I leaned back in my seat and sighed, tipping my head back.

Cheryl chuckled, but dropped low so hopefully only the closest supernaturals would have heard what she was saying. "No. I mean, at least he hasn't had you out 'servicing' his clientele yet. I've been lucky to only have to go twice, but there are girls who have been here much longer than we have, who go out four to five nights a week. He's basically running a prostitution ring." I rolled my head in her direction, too tired to do much of anything.

Ever since Jesse left four days ago, I hadn't been sleeping well. He stayed for two weeks after I lost my job at Westwind. He tried to delay it, but ultimately he was under orders from his Primal. There was nothing to do, and when he got a call to head out, he did. He apologized profusely, but he had been able to put off taking off for two weeks.

"Nikki?"

I blinked quickly and shook my head. "Yeah?"

"Are you going to open it or just head down to that hunk of yours named Maverick?"

I rolled my eyes. "He isn't mine."

"Really?" she huffed, her eyes going wide, hand plopping onto her hips, and rolled her eyes. "That isn't what he says. The whole place knows you are his."

"He wants more, but I'm with someone else." I reached for the envelope.

"I've never seen this man." Then she froze, and looked at me, "Or woman."

I smiled. "Man, but if he came here... it would be a major problem. Trust me when I say he will stay far, far away from Ivy Grace, if he has anything to say about it."

"Noted. Does Maverick know about him?" She asked carefully as she headed to the door for her set.

"He does. Even met him. Don't worry Cheryl," I added at the look she gave me. "Maverick knows exactly where I stand, regardless of the claim he has stated upon me."

"Hopefully against a wall while that beast of his fucks you straight." I smiled at her as she gave me a huge, toothy smile. "I know you. Both of your men want to throw you against the wall, and don't even give me that look. The rest of the building knows, too."

I mean, she wasn't wrong, but I had tried to step further away from Maverick. I still had to work with him, but a line had been drawn and I was holding it. He was trying to hold it as well, but the little gestures were slipping out, and I accepted them. I would notice, get the warm fuzzies, and not tell him to stop. God, I really was a toxic little shit and didn't deserve Jesse. How and why he stayed through all this was beyond me. Hell, I didn't deserve Maverick either.

Cheryl's eyebrow had raised as she waited for my retort. "Go tip someone's world, you sexy beast. I'll see you soon."

My nail slid under the fold of the envelope, and I lifted the card. "My office. Wear black."

Sighing, I dressed for another night out, and headed to Flinch's office. As I walked by the open door in the hall to the main room, the music came through. I crossed my arms over my chest and leaned against the door frame. On stage was Cheryl, who indeed was tipping some man's world. Though by the look on the woman's face sitting next to him, if she wanted, I had no doubt she could have both of them in bed tonight.

A hand landed on my hip, and the thumb moved back and forth before a deep voice said, "Hey, Sweets."

I turned and looked up at Maverick. As I took him in, my eyes narrowed in confusion. "You aren't dressed?"

He looked down at his tight blue t-shirt and dark blue jeans. "I'm clothed."

"That isn't what I mean." I bumped him with an elbow and looked back out to where Cheryl was.

"Had a message Flinch wanted to see me. Figured I'd change on the way out."

"I was told to dress and then go to his office, too."

He pulled on my hip, gesturing for us to head that way. His hand slid to the small of my back. "Well, let's not leave him waiting then."

"Why both of us? Did Bell and Chip get messages too?"

"Yeah, but just to dress and be ready in thirty minutes." He shrugged, but when he spoke, his voice was distressed. "Must be something about what your duties are."

His hand hadn't moved, except to have his thumb loop into the middle loop of my jeans in the back. He knocked on the door, and when it opened, I instantly felt that pounding in my head. I looked to Maverick, who must have felt it as well, because his eyes narrowed and crunched slightly. My body moved across the room to stand behind the two chairs that sat in front of his glass desk.

A pleased smile crossed Flinch's face, and once again, I had the thought that spiders should cross over his teeth. I tried to suppress the shudder that went through me, and I felt Maverick press his hand flat against my back in comfort. The only amount he could afford to give me, considering the situation.

Oh, gods. Maverick. The last time I felt like this, Flinch made me give him a blow job. Would he make me do something again and make Maverick watch? Would he make me do something with Maverick?

"What can we do for you, Flinch? His voice was even, and I wondered how he could do that. I didn't turn to look at him.

"Tonight, I need Nikki to go in with you."

"No." Maverick's voice was that of a dominating wolf, and I clasped my hands behind my back. His hand slowly moved to grip mine, and I squeezed it.

"You are not in a position to object. Nikki needs to be there tonight. Make sure she is armed, too." He looked me up and down, and I leaned back just slightly against Maverick's hand when the corner of Flinch's lip lifted. "I know that your boyfriend, and I don't mean Maverick, but your other one—" He gave Maverick a look that made my skin crawl.

"I'm not her boyfriend." Maverick growled.

He rolled his eyes and just said, "As I was saying, I'm sure your *other* boyfriend has had you trained in self-defense?"

"Yes. Jesse has." I drew out the word carefully. I tried to slow my heart rate. Opening my mouth to ask why, Flinch lifted a finger to shut me up as his phone rang before my voice could come, and took the phone call. His head tipped down slightly, and a pure evil smile crossed his face as he looked up and forced me to meet his gaze. "Thank you. I'll make sure to let her know we have confirmation... and evidence to support it."

The breath I took stop halfway at the way he said that. Maverick's hand squeezed, and I forced myself to take a few quick breaths. I tried to move my eyes, but my head throbbed and I felt a clawing at the back of my head. I squeezed Maverick's hand again, and when Flinch put his phone down, his eyes flicked to Maverick, who squeezed tighter on mine.

"You two are fools. Even larger fools if you think I don't know how much you want to fuck each other's brains out." Flinch scoffed, and I felt the pressure and clawing release. I took a deep breath. "Back to business. I have some information for Nikki."

I looked to Maverick quick then and back to Flinch. Jesse had always said there were times in your life that you knew life was going to change in a way so dramatic that you could feel it in the air and into the pit of your stomach. This was one of those times.

My stomach dropped, and my breathing became short and quick. I opened my mouth to say something, anything, to make it stop, but Maverick said again, "What can we do for you, Flinch?"

"Tonight, you are getting some information on the Ventana Wilderness Kismot Pride and the Los Padres Kismot Pride. Specifically, regarding the Los Padres trader situation a few years ago. There is a cub of theirs that is an outcast. I need to know the specifics."

"How? Have the Kismots even divulged that information? The Kismots are pretty close to the paw on what happens in the pride. Much more than we are in the pack."

"Everything is in a file cabinet. I've given the info to Bell. He's the collection man, so I need you three to get him in and out." He then turned toward me and said, "That phone call."

I waited and made myself breathe. Maverick threaded his fingers through mine at the small of my back and held my hand tight.

"Do you know who killed Sean Taylor?"

Trying to hide the fact that my stomach had dropped to the floor, I simply said, "No. His body was handed by the Agency. I wanted to have an autopsy done, but the Agency had already had him cremated."

"Don't you think that was strange?" He was enjoying this.

"No. We are Agency. When we die, we are disposed of however the Agency sees fit. Sometimes the family gets a say, sometimes not." I tried to keep my voice calm, but it hitched in all the wrong places.

Maverick growled low and deep beside me. "Flinch. Just say what you want to say."

"That phone call told me they have secured the evidence to prove that Exorci Jesse Westbrook is the one that killed your brother, Sean Taylor."

The world stopped.

I wasn't breathing.

I couldn't feel anything but the darkness surrounding me.

I wasn't seeing.

I wasn't...

"Madilyn... Sweets."

Maverick.

My head moved back and forth, or tried to, but two strong hands held my head.

"Madilyn." It was Maverick's voice again, and then I heard the evil chuckle from Flinch. I blinked slowly as I watched Maverick's face turn to rage.

He turned around and growled in pure wolf anger. "You think this is funny? You are destroying her, and you think it's fucking funny, you piece of shit."

"And you will be there to catch her. Maybe now you can fuck her out of your system."

"Sweets loves Jesse. We've discussed this. I know exactly where I stand with her." I blinked again, not understanding what was happening before me. "Flinch, I love her, but what you are doing is not right. I don't want her like this. Though, it isn't like you would give two shits about any of us. We are contracts. A means to an end. Not that any of us know what that end is."

There was a clawing against my brain that had Maverick and I gripping both sides of our head. I looked to Flinch, and using that Phrenic power of his, he projected his voice directly into our minds, 'And you won't. There are people I must answer to as well. There are people that I have to get this information for. I am merely one step in a staircase.'

Then the claws were out, and I stood. When had I fallen to the ground? Maverick was there, though. Holding me tight against him. "Now go. Get the information that I require."

I stood there staring at Flinch with only one thought going through my head. Jesse? Jesse killed Sean? That couldn't be. Jes—

Maverick had my head in his hands again and made me look at him. "Sweets, look at me."

Meeting his gaze, the concern in them made my vision go blurry. I opened my mouth and the only thing I could think to say was, "Jesse?"

"I don't know, Sweets." He pulled me close and said over his shoulder, "You said you have evidence of this?"

"Yes. I'll have it in a couple days. They are hand delivering it from Colorado." I heard Flinch's voice, but the words didn't sink in.

Maverick quipped, "Then why not wait to let her see it when it comes in? She's destroyed her and now she is going to be distracted until then. You've just made it harder for us tonight. Thank you, asshole."

I felt Maverick's head twist and turn like he was trying to get Flinch out of his head, but then Flinch's voice was low and demanding. "Go. Get the info I need."

"Yes, sir." Then Maverick was pulling me from the room. Once we were over the threshold, he swung his arms under my legs and carried me out toward the van.

He was muttering things, but I couldn't focus on the words.

Jesse wouldn't have killed Sean.

Jesse would have told me. There is no way he would have kept this from me.

Even if Jesse got that assignment from the Agency, he wouldn't have carried it out. He knew that even though things were not great between Sean and me, he wouldn't have killed my brother.

There was a misunderstanding.

There has to be an explanation.

No. Jesse didn't kill Sean.

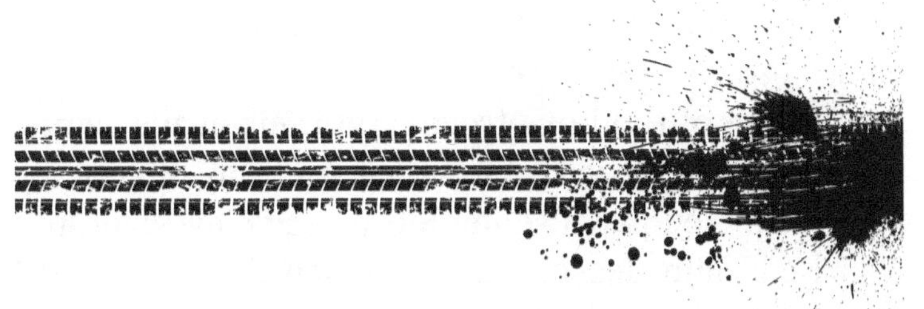

CHAPTER 31

MADDIE

"When Flinch said that you had some self-defense training, what all have you been through?" Maverick was trying to distract me. He was worried. I felt it in the small touches and the way he held me on the ride out here. Shoving the entire conversation into a box, I pushed it aside. I would deal with it after the mission tonight. After I was back home and able to rightly fall apart. After I was back home and could even begin to contemplate the allegations that were made tonight.

"Hand to hand." When he nodded, I added, "and I have a 9mm that I've been putting some range time in for over the past few years as well. That actually started before Jesse, because, well, Sean had some drug dealers who thought they could get money from me when he didn't pay up. Glad I had too, because I had to handle things myself a few times."

All three of the boys froze, and their heads swung toward me in such an animalistic way I actually chuckled. "You may use me for my eagle eyesight, but a girl can aim. Jesse..." my stomach dropped, and I stopped talking.

"Sweets, you know we are all here for you, right?" Chip said carefully.

I nodded. "I'm sorry. My world is just falling apart, and if he... if he killed Sean... I don't know what to believe anymore. Jesse has been my rock. My constant." I looked up at them, "Then I met you guys, and I know you'd be there for me..."

"It's just different." Bell said, racking his gun and sliding into his side holster.

Trying to distract myself, I turned to Maverick. "Why the guns this time?"

"Other supernaturals. The bullets are made with whatever that toxin is that Exorcis have..." His voice trailed off. My breathing hitched, and my eyes got blurry again.

It took a minute, but when I regained control, I straightened and shoved all my emotions back into that box. "So, the bullets are made for the supernatural, but if they are human, it's a bullet, so it acts the same." I slid the magazine in and racked it before sliding it into the holster on my right side. I quick loaded two additional magazines, and then put them on the magazine holder on my left hip.

I hadn't realized they were staring until I pulled my hair back and secured my ball cap, threading my hair through the back. I looked at each of them. They had all stopped mid movement, and were just watching me.

"What?"

"Just how long have you been working with guns?" Bell asked.

"Eight years. Why?"

"There is next to no lighting, and you loaded those magazines and put them into the holster that was all muscle memory. Shit, I wanna go to a range with you sometime. See just how good of a shot you are." Chip was beaming at me, and it lifted some of the Jesse fog from my brain.

"Well, hopefully you won't have to see it firsthand tonight." I muttered and turned to Bell. The look that Maverick was giving me was laid with too much emotion, and I couldn't deal right now. "Are we ready? It's my understanding that you will get paper files tonight? How does this normally work inside?"

Bell and Chip looked to Maverick. "Mav calls the shots and tells us how and when to move." Chip said carefully. "Did something happen between you two?"

"No, but she is avoiding my gaze."

"For good reason, Maverick." I whispered. I couldn't deal with him right now. I couldn't look at him with all the hurt from Jesse going through me. I didn't trust... myself.

"Okay." His voice was hesitant, but he cleared his throat before continuing. "We go in on the north side, and I want Sweets and Bell between us, Chip. Is that clear?"

"Noted." Chip said, and while he was looking at me, there was a small nod that came from Bell as well. The order was clear. Make sure the two of us are protected.

"Let's move." Maverick headed toward the north door when I saw movement near it.

"Negative. Movement up there. Can we get in through the south door?"

"We can, but it's a long hallway and leaves us exposed longer." He said, but I looked at the door and shook my head. It was a no go. They were setting up at that entrance, and if we went through them, it was only going to be a larger crowd of chaos inside. With a heavy sigh, he looked back in that direction. "South side it is."

Sliding in through the south entrance, Bell was able to hack the electronic code so quickly, even he muttered, "Well, that was easy."

"Stay alert. Nothing is going the way it should tonight." Maverick's hand was on my back as he guided me through, and I swear I felt his thumb move in comfort as we stepped into a long hall. "Between me and Chip."

I nodded, and when he looked down the hall, I saw his jaw tighten.

Ten minutes later, Bell was walking out of the room with the file in his backpack and we were making our way back down the hall. This did seem easy. Too easy.

We were almost to the door when the unmistakable sound of a bullet being chambered echoed in the silence. I twisted, drawing my gun, aimed behind Maverick, who was half turned and fired.

Chaos erupted as Bell and Chip turned, but before they could say anything, Maverick had hauled me up by the waist, my arms still outstretched over his shoulder, and rushed for the door. I aimed and took seven more shots. Bodies falling at every pull of the trigger. Maverick put me down just as we got to the door, and I nodded as he turned to let me step through.

I blinked, and just before I walked through the door, two more quick shots rang out. Maverick lunged before falling against me. I turned as Bell grabbed Maverick and found one lone person standing in the hall, gun raised. They fell moments after my fingers squeezed off the last two rounds. I dropped the magazine, only to be pulled away, and a knife held to my throat.

Sagging against the assailant, they leaned forward, and I bit down on their wrist. Just as the blade dropped from their hand, I caught it, twisting and plunging the knife into their gut. I used the momentum of my movement to pull the knife across their stomach. Pulling the knife out, I felt hot liquid spread across my hands as I kicked out, sending them to the floor.

"You bitch." The garbled sound came from the pile of person on the floor.

Anger, despair, and fear for my boys filled me. I tilted my head to the side, and I felt a wicked smile cross my lips as the feeling of pride at being able to handle this all myself wash over me. Wet gasps came from the man before me and I smiled at him with death in my eyes. "You attacked my boys with the intent to kill them. You deserve to die."

His mouth opened, and I flipped the knife in my hand and chucked it at him. It embedded at the base of his throat. When I turned, Chip and Bell had one of Maverick's arms over each of their shoulders, with wide eyes.

Maverick.

"Is he?" I couldn't even think the word.

Bell's head shook. "No, but let's get to the van and get back so we can see what we are dealing with."

That broke through the haze, and I switched out my magazine and lifted my gun. The blood on my hands caused it to be sticky and slick all at the same time. "Go. I'll cover you."

There was a grunt from Maverick, but his head still fell forward, and his feet dragged behind him.

I looked around the door before we stepped out and saw a glint of metal near the front of the building. Narrowing my focus, there were three figures lined up against the wall.

"Hold up." I mouthed, and just as I turned to take my shot, one shot rang out, and the sting hit my leg, making me lose my balance. I repositioned, pulled the trigger, and all three were laying in a heap a moment later. Looking around quickly, doing one final visual sweep, before opening the van door. The boys maneuvered Maverick in, and I jumped in the front seat, handing Bell the first aid kit before Chip was even behind the wheel.

Reaching behind me, I found Maverick's hand reaching for mine and squeezed it. There was a soft squeeze back, and I looked over at him. His breathing was labored and his chest was covered in blood. Fear racked through me, the likes I hadn't felt in a long while. I can't lose him.

Chip slid into the driver's seat, and I noticed his arm covered in blood. He was working one handed, and when he started the van and slammed on the gas, I asked, "You're hurt?"

"Went clean through. Once Maverick is settled, I'll shift and curl up in a corner. I'll be fine like he was last time. Give me a couple of days and you won't even know there was a problem."

He took a turn fast enough that Bell complained, "Chip, I need to not have him sliding all over the seat to see what I'm dealing with."

He had a headlamp on his head so he could see better, and Maverick's breathing hitched and gurgled. Blinking, all I saw was Beth laying there on the floor of the chapel where Sean's funeral was. She made the same wet breathing sounds, and I closed my eyes tight, trying to clear the vision.

"Shit. I don't see an exit wound for this one. Lung may have collapsed too." Bell said, and then made Maverick look at him as he pressed his hand over the wound on his chest. "I know it hurts like fiery pits of hell, but you need to slow your breathing. Roll over on your side. We will get the doc on you as soon as we get back. Just hang in there, Mav."

Bell handed me a phone from his pocket and said, "Go to favorites and call Ivy Grace." I scrolled through his phone and found the number and pressed the button. My fingers left trails of blood in their wake. I wasn't sure if it was the man I'd killed or Maverick's. Probably Maverick's.

"Speak quickly." My heart froze at the sound of Flinch's voice through the line.

"There was trouble. Bell is working on him, but Mav is hurt."

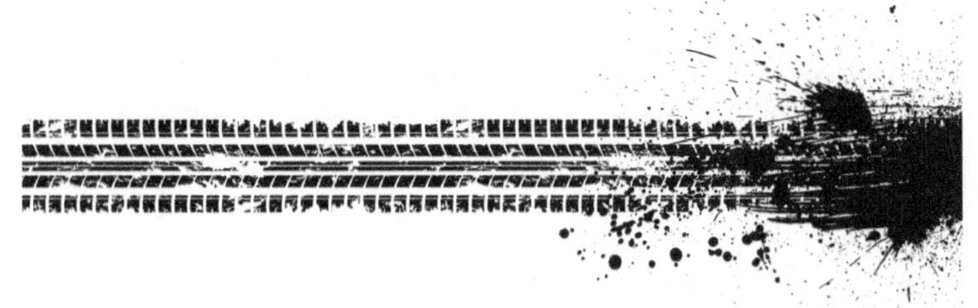

CHAPTER 32

MADDIE

Bell and Chip hauled Maverick into the back room, plopping him on a cot, and all I heard was that the doctor was on the way. I clung to his hand and stared at him as he laid on the injured side. Bell thought the bullet might have hit his lung, but wasn't sure. His breathing evened out as I ran my thumb across the back of his hand.

With the worst of the immediate threats either removed or in the process of behind handled, my mind went blank. So much had happened tonight, and I just stared at Maverick.

Claws were back in my brain, and I barely registered the tick my head gave as Flinch walked in. "What happened?"

Chip gave the report, and when the room went silent, I pulled my gaze from Maverick toward Flinch.

"You spilled blood tonight?" I nodded my head. Lots of blood. At least fourteen were dead by my hand alone tonight.

"You know what that means?"

I blinked and the memory of Primal Berk's discussion with me at Westwind went through my mind. "It means I no longer have Bacri protections. I am a Bacri without a home. It means I am Agency listed without Agency protections." I turned to look at Maverick, my voice dropping. "It means I'm a dead woman."

"Flinch, you need to have Kall wipe the footage. Now." Bell begged.

"He's already on it." Flinch's voice sounded like it was under water. "Good job tonight, Nikki. Who knew you were that good at eradicating threats? Your value has just increased."

I bit the inside of my cheek to keep from telling him I was just protecting those I loved. Yes, I *could* do it. Didn't mean I wanted to. Fourteen tonight, and I didn't hesitate one damn bit. In fact, when I gutted that fucker, I felt the thrill of it. Adrenaline coursed through me. I wasn't sure what scared me more right now, that thrill or the fact I almost lost my boys.

With that, Flinch strode from the room. The doctor and someone with an IV walked through next, and they spent the next hour with Maverick. One bullet went through his side, and that was quickly cleaned and stitched. The one that had me worried was the one to his chest. The bullet hadn't hit the lung, but had just missed it. The problem was that there was no exit wound. There was a lot of movement and medical terms flying around the room, but I couldn't focus on anything but Maverick at that point. When they finished patching him up as much as they could, Maverick squeezed my hand a little tighter.

"The fluids and antibiotics will help. You won't be able to shift until the bullet is out of you, so you need to come see me this afternoon so we can scan the area and see where it is to remove it." The doctor looked at us. "Anyone else hurt?"

"Sweets got shot in the leg, not that you could tell by the way she moved." The doctor came over and took some scissors to my jeans. My eyes slowly moved to him, and down to where my leg was. He pressed down and asked if it hurt, and I shook my head. I couldn't feel anything but the fear of losing Maverick, Chip, and Bell tonight.

The doc cleaned my leg up, used some liquid bandage, told me to rinse it and keep it clean. It should heal quickly if I could shift, and I just nodded, not bothering to correct him.

His assistant gave almost the exact same orders to Chip for his arm. I vaguely heard him and his assistant leave, but it was as if there was a single string between us. I saw all three of them turn to look at me out of the corner of my eye. It was Bell that ran his hands through his hair and said, "In case Mav or Chip don't say it... Thanks for saving our lives tonight."

I turned to face them.

"You really had our back, Sweets." Chip rubbed his face, and fidgeted with the stubble on his chin before I saw the fear and gratitude in his eyes.

"If Jesse..." I swallowed thickly before I took a deep breath and continued, "If Jesse killed Sean, I'm not sure what I'm going to do. I'm not sure I can be with him anymore, and he's gone eighty percent of the time... Shit. This is making it sound like you guys are second to him, and you aren't."

I looked over at Maverick, who gave me a small smile. He understood and reached out for my hand again. When had I let go of it? I took it and squeezed. "You guys are all I have left. I have your backs as much as you have mine. I'll do whatever I can to save my family."

Bell and Chip looked at each other and then bright smiles crossed their faces before the word came out in unison. "Family."

Chip leaned over and kissed the top of my head before saying, "In that case, sis, I'm gonna let you fuss over the pup here, and head home for some sleep."

Bell reached over and squeezed my shoulder before nodding and walking out with Chip.

"Family, huh?" Maverick's voice was weak and came out more of a strained whisper than anything else.

Frustration and irritation flared as I turned to look at him, and his eyes widened just the slightest before I started in on him. "How dare you, Ian. How fucking dare you?"

His eyebrows shot to his hairline this time, his mouth opened, but I continued. "How fucking dare you almost die on me! How dare you think that your life is worth less than mine, Chip, or Bell's? How dare you jump in front of me and take a bullet like that?"

Tears were streaming down my face, and he reached up and wiped them away. "Madilyn. I would die a thousand deaths to see you still breathing. Don't you realize that? Bell and Chip would have done the same. I was just the one who—"

"Ian... I can't lose you, too. If I lose you, there is no point in being on this side of the ground anymore." I whispered, and he pulled me against him as I sobbed. His chest shuddered as he held me, but I squeezed him tight. "Don't leave me, Ian."

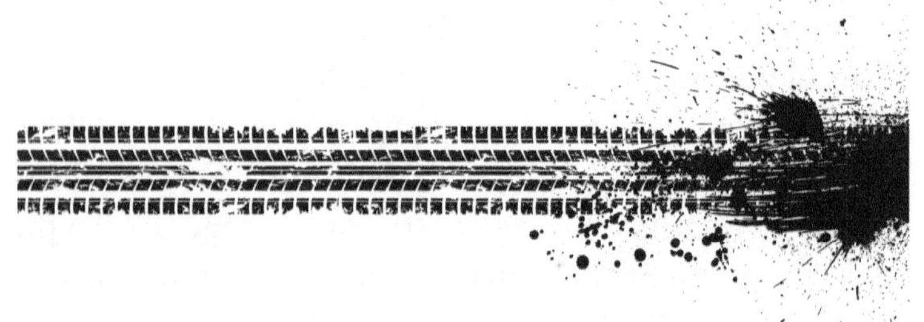

CHAPTER 33

JESSE

I woke up and stretched. There was a soft knock, and Jonathan and Alasie opened the door.

"Hey. We thought you might want some breakfast." Alasie said, putting a plate of eggs, bacon, sausage, and an assortment of berries on the small table in the room.

"And this came for you today." Jonathon said and winced as he held out a red envelope.

"I can't say I'm surprised." I sighed as I looked at the writing. It was Primal Emma's. "I've stayed and enjoyed a few days with all of you, and while it's been fun, I do need to get going. I don't want the lead on Clarke to go stale."

"You know, anytime you want to get away, Jesse. This cabin will always be available for you." Jonathon said.

"Thanks, man." I let out a heavy sigh. "But I really just want to get home and back to Maddie. I set up to have her rent auto paid from my account and groceries to be delivered while I'm gone. So at least I know she will have some food in the house. That woman wouldn't ever eat anything but bagels and protein bars if it weren't for me cooking for her."

"When are you going to marry that woman?" Alasie said with a playful smile.

"Things need to settle down first. Sean really fucked shit up for her. We are trying to sort it out, but marriage isn't really in the cards right now."

They stood there staring at me for a long time with that you have to be kidding me look.

I looked up, met Jonathon's eyes, and I felt the lines of tears there. "I can't touch her. I can't hold her. I can't truly make love to her. How can I marry her if I can't give her everything she rightfully deserves?"

"That is only an answer that she can give you, man." He looked at the plate, then back at me. "Eat. Go take care of Clarke. Go home to Maddie and fix whatever it is that is broken, but you aren't telling us everything, and that's okay, man. I get it. An Exorci has to have his secrets. Go home. Fix it with Maddie. Then bring her back here for a while and get away from all things Agency."

He took Alasie's hand, lacing his fingers through hers, before she winked and closed the door behind them.

I let out a long breath and got up to eat.

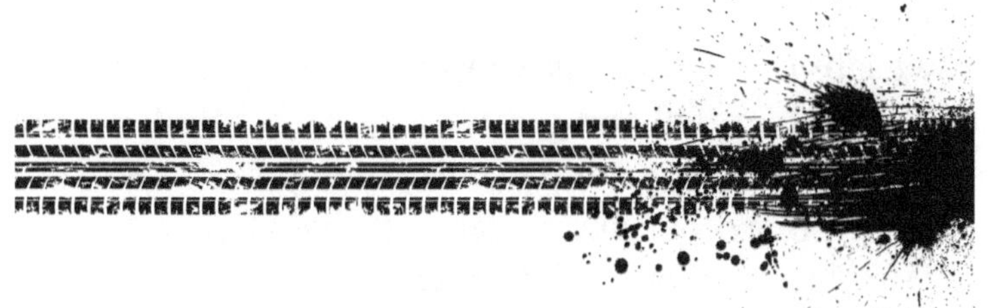

CHAPTER 34

MADDIE

I came into work with a little bounce in my step after actually getting some sleep. I had the day off from my other job I had taken to be able to keep my apartment and food on the table, and for once felt like I could actually handle tonight. That all went down the toilet when I opened the black envelope and Flinch's writing said, '*Come to my office.*'

My heart hammering in my chest, I put my purse away and headed to Flinch's office. I stopped at the doorway to the main room and watched Cheryl dance. I only hoped to be as fluid and graceful as she was. She was straight hypnotic.

Bell tapped me on the shoulder, and I looked up at him. "Hey, sis."

"Hey." I let out a content sigh. I had to admit, it was nice to know that there wouldn't be out on the town jobs this week while Chip and Maverick recovered. Flinch had let Bell and I know that we would have the week off from special projects, but to be here every night for our other duties. "How are you doing?"

"Alright. Worried about Maverick. He didn't answer my texts before I came in, but hopefully that just means that he is sleeping."

"I talked to him a few hours ago. He was finally able to shift this morning, so was going to try to get some z's in form. Give him an hour and he'll be up." Bell sighed and leaned his head on the wall.

"What does our overlord have you doing, right now?"

"Bouncer duties. Seems so boring in comparison, but I'll take it. Not getting shot at, not having to worry if you'll get hurt..." There was something there, and I took his hand and squeezed it. "When you called us family, the other night... It cemented how ya fell into my life. Seeing Mav like that scared the shit out of me. We've all left jobs bloodied and injured, but... That was the worst yet." He paused and wrapped an arm around me, pulling me in for a tight hug. "Thank you again for having our backs, Sweets." Then he kissed me on the temple and headed for the front doors.

My vision was blurry as I watched him walk away. I loved my boys. They really were all I had left. I had no idea where Jesse and I stood, and I had a very strong feeling that was what Flinch wanted to see me about. Sighing, I headed down the hall to Flinch's office.

'Took you long enough to finish with Bell. Come in.'

I twisted my neck and shook my head at the intrusion. I took a deep breath and walked in, closing the door behind me. "Yes, Mr. Flinch. What can I do for you?"

"The other night I told you I would have proof of my claim over who killed your brother."

My stomach dropped, but I refused to say anything. I still didn't want to believe it, and I knew if I showed any emotion, he would latch onto it, and this would go much worse for me.

"I received this." He reached out, and I took the small thumb drive from him. I felt clawing at my head, and my eyes popped up to meet his. "What do you say, Nikki?"

The words fell from my mouth before I could stop them. "Thank you, Mr. Flinch. What can I do to thank you for your generous gift?"

My stomach roiled because that was not what I wanted to say. What I wanted to say was for him to take the thumb drive and shove it so far up his ass he would need surgery to remove it.

"Remove your breasts from the top." He said, his eyes fixated on my chest.

My hands moved of their own accord, and pulled the straps of the lacey bralette shirt down and pushed down the black lace, my breasts spilling out over the top. Flinch took three strides toward me, and said, "On your knees."

Dropping to my knees, my tits bounced, and he moaned as his eyes heated.

My fingers gripped the thumb drive in my hand and I tried to get the pain to derail his control, but I felt his claws dig deeper.

His hands undid the belt, button, and zipper of his pants, but before he could give me instruction or do anymore, there was a knock on the door.

His glare toward the unwelcome intrusion gave me enough of a mental release that I was able to breathe.

"Call from his highness." Was all that was said at the door, before Flinch nodded and re-buttoned his pants.

"Go home Nikki. Watch it. Take the next two nights off. By then, your team should be able to return."

I stood, put my top back on, stuffed the drive in my pocket, and all but ran out of there. That was close. Too close, and there was nothing I could have done to stop it.

Bell's eyes met mine as I rounded the corner, and he was instantly there. "What's wrong?" I shook my head. He looked around and pulled me into the closet. "Sweets. What is wrong? I've only seen you that pale a handful of times." I shook my head again, tears leaking out of my eyes.

He pulled me close and just held me for a long minute as I cried. "It's okay, Sweets. We gotcha. Chip and Mav would know better what to do right now, but we gotcha."

A hiccupped chuckle came out of me, and I pulled back and wiped the tears from my face. "Seriously, Sweets. Tell me what happened."

"Flinch gave me a thumb drive that supposedly has evidence of Jesse killing Sean." I took a shuddering breath and looked up at him, unable to say the words.

"... and Flinch got in your head and made you 'satisfy' him."

"It didn't get that far, but he would have, yes."

"I really wish there was a way to stop him." His eyes seemed to burn through the walls in Flinch's direction. "He's a strong Phrenic, though. There have been people who have come in to investigate and then leave, never realizing they were even here, let alone have talked to him.

"I'm going home. Flinch told me to go and watch the video and see what is on the drive and come back in a couple days. Says we all will be returning then."

Bell pulled his phone out and sighed. "Chip is at his cousin's out of town. I can try to sneak out if you don't want to be alone."

"It's okay." I hugged him again. "Thank you for the instant breakdown help. I'll go home and curl up in bed."

"You going to watch what's on the thumb drive?"

Looking off to the side where bottles of bleach sat on the floor, I wanted to force it all down Flinches throat, but knew I would be the one who would drink it, and not him if I tried. I looked back up at Bell, and he had a smirk on his face, knowing what was going through my head, but then raised an eyebrow, waiting for my answer.

"I will, but I need to gain the courage first."

"I..." He paused and moved so his face was in my view. "I don't think you should be alone when you do. Call me, Chip, or Mav, when you are ready, okay?"

I nodded. "Thanks, Bell."

He opened the door and went back to his station at the door. Sighing, I went back to the dressing room and grabbed my things.

I sat in the car for almost an hour. My hands and feet had gone cold, and I had that damn thumb drive in my fingers, flipping it over and over in my hands.

"Fuck it." I started the car, threw it in reverse, and headed to Maverick's.

I banged on Maverick's door, the little 'three' hanging above the peephole, jiggling at the force of it. When one of the neighbors stuck their head out, I told them it was an emergency and to go back to bed. They were grumbling as they went back in when Maverick opened the door. "Madilyn?"

"Please don't push me away." My voice was small, even to my own ears.

His eyes popped open, and he shook his head. He had been asleep. That's why it took so long for him to answer and slow to react. "Never." He pulled the door open a bit more to let her in.

"I'm sorry. I should have made sure you were up. Bell said you had shifted to get some sleep and to speed the healing, and that you were going to be out for a little bit, but I didn't want... no, I needed—"

"Sweets. It's fine. Are you okay?"

"Yes. No."

"Okay, so no physical injuries that need immediate attention?"

"No." I answered, realizing that he was just trying to figure out how quick to wake up.

"Okay. Let me make some coffee and finish waking up. Then you can tell me why you are so freaked out to the point that you showed up at my door a little after... what time is it?" He looked over at the clock and shook his head. He must have been sleeping hard. "It's after midnight. Thought you would still be at the club." He headed for the little kitchenette off to the left and started making a cup of coffee in his little pod maker.

I tilted my head to the side and watched him. "You're moving better."

"Shifter healing." He looked over his shoulder and looked at me. I was staring at the counter and running my fingers through the grooves. "I'm sorry, Madilyn."

"Why are you sorry?" I asked, my mind not understanding what he could possibly be sorry about.

"I just realized." I narrowed my eyes, but he rushed over to me and put his hands on my hips, pulling me against him. "It's been three days since Flinch told you about Jesse. I'm assuming he showed you evidence, and that's why you are here?"

I took a shaky breath. "Yes, and No."

His gaze crossed each inch of my face. "You are gonna need to give me more than that, Sweets."

I reached into my pocket and pulled out a thumb drive. "He handed me this, told me to go home to watch it, and then come back in a couple of days, because then the team would be returning."

I looked down as I flipped it over and over again between my fingers.

"Why do I feel like you are leaving something out, Sweets?"

"Because I am." I leaned forward, bringing my forehead to Maverick's chest. His left hand tightened on my hip, as his right took my chin between his thumb and finger, forcing me to look up at him. "Flinch made me submit, and would have had me do a whole lot more if he hadn't been interrupted."

Understanding and something else flittered across his face. He leaned down and kissed my forehead before stepping back and making his coffee. "Want some?"

"Yes, please."

We stood there; me leaning on his counter, playing with the damned drive, and him staring at me. When my cup was ready, he handed it to me and took my hand to lead me into the living room.

It was simple. Rental low pile brown carpet, a couple of small windows, a couch with a pillow and blanket on it, and a big screen TV is all that filled the space. A small cabinet sat below the TV which housed a gaming console with a sound bar. No coffee table, no side tables. Nothing.

"Leaves room for my wolf's form to just curl up on the floor." He said, noting how I took in the room. I nodded as he pulled me onto the couch and wrapped the blanket around my shoulders. He must have been using it, because the extra warmth of it pulled away any of the chill from sitting in my car.

"So, you didn't answer me earlier." He took a sip of his coffee and waited.

"Flinch didn't make me watch it with him, and after I left his office, Bell let me cry it out in a closet for a bit. He said I need to watch it with one of you, and to call when I was ready." I took a long sip of the coffee in my cup and stared at the floor.

"So you haven't watched it yet?"

I shook my head. "I sat in my car for an hour before just coming over here. I know I should, but does it matter? If Jesse did kill Sean, then it will show that. Even if Jesse didn't, then Flinch probably had it made to make it look like he did anyways. I know that thumb drive has Jesse killing Sean on it. I just don't know whether to believe it or not."

"What does your gut tell you?"

"Since I called Jesse to tell him Sean died, he's been dodgy and cagey about what he knows and what he doesn't know about it. He's an Exorci though." I took another sip before sighing. "He knows a lot of things that he shouldn't."

I lifted my gaze to meet Maverick's, and there was pain, understanding, and something more in that look he gave me. Not pity exactly, but there was also something that looked like hope.

"Do we watch it now, or after I get something to eat in your stomach?"

"I ate before going in." He studied me a long moment and then got up, and grabbed his laptop from another room.

"Alright. Let's get this over with. Let's see just how this looks."

Maverick's hand reached out for the drive. When I hesitated, I asked, "I have questions for you before this is turned over."

Worry framed around his eyes as he sat down on the couch, laptop in his lap. "Okay."

"First, have you seen this footage before?" He shook his head. "Second, can Bells determine if it's fake or tampered with?"

"I'm sure he could. Do you want him to look at it before or after?"

"Before."

Maverick pulled his phone out and texted Bell. After a few texts back and forth, he opened the laptop and sent the file off. He closed the laptop and then looked at me expectantly.

"Do you expect this to make us a couple?"

"Sweets." He moved the laptop to the other side of him, and knelt between my legs, and put my head in his hands. "I have already told you I want you. You know that. I know exactly where we stand. And when you are ready, if you are ready, if you break it off with him, if … whatever happens relationship-wise, happens, then I will be sitting in the wind waiting for you. I…" He stopped himself, but I had vague memories of what he had told Flinch that night and I knew what he was going to say, because it was clearly written all over his face. So I just nodded at him.

He leaned forward and held me like that, taking slow, deep breaths. "I know how pathetic it makes me. I know it makes me a right asshole to be... in love with another man's woman. My parents would be disappointed in me for it, but Madilyn..." his voice was a caressed whisper. "If you were a wolf..." He squeezed his eyes shut and kissed the tip of my nose before slowly, painfully, pulling away.

"Finish that sentence." I breathed.

"Not until you are mine." He said, taking a deep breath to calm himself. "Now, how are things going at The Edging?"

I blinked and shook my head. "You practically tell me exactly how you feel about me, basically, tell me you want me as your..." I took a deep breath, because I couldn't say them. "And just like that, you are going to change topics to my new day job to avoid this conversation?"

His heated eyes met mine. "I'm avoiding it, because I'm holding on to what slim slice of dignity I have left before I say *those* words." Another deep breath and he continued, "So yes, how are things going at The Edging?"

"Fine. It's another creature club, and I'm literally only going to be dancing, so it has that going for it. The pay ain't bad. Though someone paid my rent this month. Landlord told me not to stress over it because it was paid." I narrowed my eyes at him, and half wondered if it was him. He was the only one that knew how hard up I was. Bell and Chip thought I was getting a slice of what we got out of our jobs at Ivy Grace. They were, so they thought that I would be as well.

"Wish I had thought about it, but no. Not it. Maybe Jesse?"

I shook my head. "I'm not so sure that he would have thought that far ahead in that department. That man rarely keeps food on hand at his place. Which reminds me, any chance you left me groceries yesterday?"

Again, a shake of the head. "Hummm."

Someone knocked on the door, and I looked at my phone. "It's almost two in the morning. Who could that be?"

Maverick's phone went off and he got up. "It's Bell."

When he opened the door, he rushed in and sat with his laptop open. "I've run it four times. It's clean. Sweets. You sure you want to see this?"

A knot formed in my stomach, and I thought the coffee I had was going to revisit me. I started taking slow, deep breaths. "It's clean?"

He nodded. "Is there a need to look at it, then?" Tears welled in my eyes, and it was everything I could do not to let them fall.

"Sweets, you have to breathe, nice and slow. You are hyper-ventilating." He wrapped his arms around my waist as he sat down next to me. "Play it."

Bell turned his laptop to face me, and hit the spacebar, putting the video of the man I loved with every inch of my heart, killing my brother front and center.

I watched as Sean went into the house, sliced the witch's throat open, went into the kitchen, and when he faced toward the main room, put the ski mask on. Jesse made his way through the witch's house and heard Sean in the kitchen. I watched how my brother fought him, and Jesse defended himself, and gave him a warning, before sliding his hand up his pant leg and watching him fall to his death. Only Sean didn't die right away. He didn't just drop like others who had been touched by an Exorci, his mouth moved, but there was no sound.

I watched as Jesse knelt beside my brother, watching the life leave Sean's eyes. The video cut there.

"It's all genuine. The angle of the camera was able to just catch the witch's death while still showing the entire kitchen." He sighed as I stared at the frozen screen of Jesse, looking at Sean's dead face.

I heard Bell and Maverick talking, but didn't make it all out. There was something about how Jesse probably searched the place after, and likely scoured the entire house for a clue about why Sean was there, but I heard Bell say, "Mav... the type of video this is. It's only available on the black market. It's fae tech. It doesn't surprise me that Jesse wasn't able to find the video."

"Jesse really did kill Sean. He did it, and he hid it from me. He didn't tell me. He... How could he... If he really loved me..."

Bell and Maverick looked at each other, and both were on their knees before me. "Sweets."

I looked between them, feeling my heart shatter into a million pieces. "Jesse killed Sean."

My world slowed, sped up, and then spun. The last thing I remember were arms wrapped around me before it all went black.

Bell and Maverick held me as I cried for hours after blacking out. Bell left around four in the morning and said he would update Chip. Maverick just carried me to bed, changed me from my bralette into one of his t-shirts, and tucked me in. He slid in behind me, wrapping an arm around my waist, and that was where I still was when the sound of Jesse's ringtone woke me up a few hours later.

I reached over and held it, looking at the screen. I had to talk to him. I had to find out if he would even admit it to me.

Did it matter? Could I even be with the man that had killed my family? I'd been asking myself that since Flinch first told me Jesse was the one who did it.

Just as I was going to answer it, the call went to voicemail. I waited a moment, because I knew he would call back. When he did, Maverick asked, "Are you going to take his call?"

"Yes. I have to confront this." Maverick nodded and made a sound as if he was zipping his lips shut.

I accepted the call with a "Did you do it?"

"Good morning to you, too, Little Bird. Now, you are going to have to be a little more specific? Did I do what?"

"Did you kill Sean in Colorado?" There was silence as I felt my stomach flip, and I was very grateful I hadn't eaten anything yet.

"Little Bird."

"Jesse Westbrook. Did you kill my brother?"

He let out a heavy sigh, and it sounded like the words were stuck in his throat. "I had an assignment to exterminate a witch in Grand Junction, Colorado. When

I arrived, someone else was already there, and had already killed her. I found that person in the kitchen. There was a struggle, and yes, I killed the person in the kitchen."

"Did you kill Sean?" My voice was a broken whisper, and I felt Maverick move behind me and put both legs on either side of me and wrap an arm around my stomach.

"I didn't know it was Sean until I removed the ski mask and saw his face. I freaked out and called Minstrel Carlos immediately. I didn't know it was him until after he was dead."

"Flinch gave me a thumb drive that showed me that you came in, and killed him."

"Yes, Little Bird—"

"Don't you fucking *'little bird'* me, Jesse. You killed Sean. You killed my brother. As a result, we attended a funeral that Beth died at. Because of you, I lost the only two pieces of family that I had left."

"Lit—"

"Stop, Jesse. Don't. I can't." I felt my whole body go ridged and Maverick pulled me closer, the warmth of his embrace releasing some of the tension in my body, but the tears still flowed. "I can't be with you anymore, Jesse. I could barely deal with your work schedule. You've been gone more than you've been here since you ... since you killed my brother. All of that, I could continue to work with because I do love you, Jesse Westbrook. Gods, I love you so fucking much, but I can't be with the man that killed the only two pieces of family I had left. Goodbye and good luck. I wish you the best."

Without giving him a chance to say another word, I hung up and turned into Maverick's chest. I let out a wail and pulled him closer. I felt him wince, but he only held me tighter. That supernatural hearing allowed him to hear every word. He pulled me closer and said, "It's okay, Sweets. We got you... I got you."

I fully collapsed into his arms and let it all out.

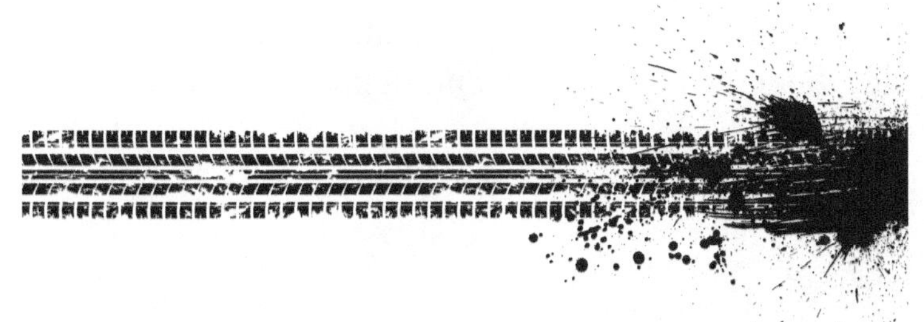

CHAPTER 35

JESSE

Tears spilled over and ran down my cheeks. My heart raced, and I stared at my phone.

Little Bird knew, and she cut me out.

Flinch told her.

I should have been the one to tell her.

I should have had that conversation in person, so she could see the truth in my eyes. The truth was that I didn't know it was Sean until after he was dead. Sean knew it was me. Sean knew *exactly* who he was up against. He had even asked for me to tell his sister that he was sorry.

Now... What was I supposed to do now? Maddie is my everything. She is my forever. There will never be someone else.

I blinked and everything inside of me went numb. Grabbing my keys, jacket, and helmet, I walked out the door.

I needed a drink, or maybe a few dozen.

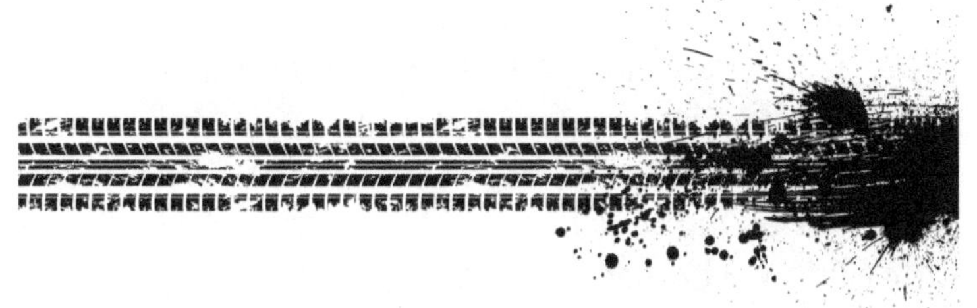

CHAPTER 36

MADDIE

I blinked against the bright light. Why is it so bright? Every muscle in my body hurt, and I stretched.

"Why are you waking up already, Sweets?"

"Fuck if I know?" Maverick rolled over and caged me in. He winced slightly at the movement, but that shifter healing was making quick work of the chest wound. "Go back to sleep. We got at least three hours before we have to get up."

I'd stayed the last three nights at Maverick's. We had even gone over to my apartment and so I could grab a few things. All three of my boys didn't want me to be left alone. Bell and Maverick had seen how I shattered that night. How I fell deeper into the pits of hell.

While we were at my apartment, someone knocked on the door, and when I went to answer it, there was another mystery grocery delivery. It was filled with eggs, bacon, sausage, pancake mix, lunch meat, sliced bread, cheese, a pound of hamburger, chocolate milk singles, and, of course, bagels and cream cheese. The boys had brought it back to Maverick's, and while I didn't know who had bought it, I wasn't going to let it go to waste.

I chuckled as I heard Maverick's soft snores. That man could sleep anywhere and in any position.

My phone rang just then, and I groaned, reaching over for it, but answering quietly. "Hello?"

"Maddie?"

"Who is this?"

"Jonathon Harris. Longtime friend of Jesse's. I haven't been able to reach him for a couple of days. Is he with you?"

"No." I said through my teeth, but took a deep breath. "Jesse and I broke up a few days ago. Please call his cellphone."

Silence for a long minute, and just when I was going to hang up, the man said, "Very well. I'll keep trying."

"Thank you."

"He loves you, Maddie." The man's words came out quick.

"Then he shouldn't have killed my brother." I quipped and hung up the phone.

I rolled back over and pressed against Maverick, waking him back up. My hand brushed over his abs, as they dipped a little lower, and I felt him hard and ready.

"Hey there, Princess. Be careful. He has a mind of his own first thing in the morning." He had taken to calling me Princess when we were alone. Said I needed to be treated like one.

I hummed against him, and let my fingers play in the hair under his belly button. My breasts tightened and my nipples became very sensitive under his shirt as I pressed against him.

Maverick rolled over onto his back and looked at me, eyes wide. "Madilyn..."

"Ian." I answered. I shouldn't feel this way about Maverick, but there had been no secrets about how he felt about me, or that I was feeling something for him. It wasn't fair, and I had laid it out.

"You just..." The heat in his eyes was scorching, and I wanted nothing more than to feel those flames.

"I know." I took a deep breath. "It isn't fair. I'll stop."

I pulled myself away from him and rolled over onto my side. I pressed my legs together and tried to will myself to calm. It wasn't fair. I had told him before it would be a rebound. A way to just feel something, even if I had been feeling something for him.

"Rolling over, Princess, doesn't help. I can smell how turned on you are right now."

"Sorry. I'll go shower. A cold shower." I threw the blanket back to get out of bed, and he caught me by the waist, pulled me back onto the bed, rolled me under him, and settled overtop of me and between my legs.

"I'm not saying no, Princess." He bent down and ran his lips along the side of my neck, and I tipped my head back. "The gods know I want to be buried deep inside of you. I just want to make sure you aren't doing it for all the wrong reasons."

He laid a small kiss at my collarbone and then leaned back so he could meet my eye.

"I told you before I feel an attraction toward you, Ian. I also told you that anything that happened between us would be a rebound, an emotional release fuck. That isn't fair to you." I reached up and let my fingers run through the three-day-old stubble on his cheeks. "I'd be lying though if having the ability and freedom to touch you like this, without any guilt—"

He leaned down, and his lips crashed onto mine. The heat of that kiss was searing. I had been kissed before, but suddenly everywhere Maverick was touching me was like a bolt of electricity. He pulled back, his breathing heavy.

"Madilyn, you know how I feel. I know you are a mess of emotions, and so if you want to fuck, then we can certainly do that. I have wanted to hear those little sounds you make as I make you cum." My legs squeezed against him of their own accord, and he smiled. "I can smell it, Princess. I want to taste it. Taste *you*."

I didn't know what to say. He pressed against my core and I moaned. "Can I have you, Princess?"

My eyes flew open and met his gaze. "Ian..."

"I know. You've already said it, multiple times. I don't care if I'm the rebound. I just want to call you mine, even if it's just for a little while, because this... this isn't going away for me. Call me selfish, I don't care. I told you I would be here when he fucked up. I told you I would wait." He lifted off of me, so I could think for half a moment. "Can I have you as mine?"

"Will you kick me out of this bed and apartment if I say no?" I didn't know why I was hesitating. Yes, I did. I was still heartbroken over Jesse, but I couldn't deny the attraction and the want to have Ian. Ian, not the façade that was Maverick.

"Hell no." He still hovered over me, not letting me make a decision based on his touch. "You will always be welcome in my bed, as mine or platonically."

"As yours?" The words settled over me, and I felt my inner thighs squeeze together again.

"Fuck, Princess. I'm trying here."

I met his gaze, and there was hesitation, and a place where I saw how he guarded his heart, and everything within him, waiting for me to tell him no. Reaching up and running my fingers through that stubble, I pulled him down to me, and said, "I'm yours."

"Thank, fuck!" In a flash, the t-shirt I was wearing was gone, and his lips were traveling down my neck, across my collarbone, and then back to my shoulder, to the meaty part of it.

When his teeth grazed it, I arched up into him, and there was a wolf-like growl that came from him that had me wrapping my legs around his hips. I could feel the restraint in him as he ran his tongue along that spot before pulling away and kissing it. He rested his forehead on that spot and took a second to breathe.

"You okay?"

"Princess, I am more than okay. I'm fighting my wolf right now, and every propriety that is my heritage."

"I'm sorry." I didn't know exactly what that meant, but stuck a pin in it to talk about later. Right now, right now, I wanted him out of those pajama pants and buried deep inside me. I ran my hands down his chest, and as I ran my hands down his sides. His eyes closed, revealing in the feeling, and his whole-body shivered. When I reached his pants, I slid them down, using my toes to get them the rest of the way off. He lifted to assist, but when I wrapped my hand around the hard length of him, his hips thrust against my hand.

His hips moved as his head bent to kiss my breast and roll his tongue around and flick my nipple. My chest lifted toward him as he settled between me. I ran my finger over the head of him, as he groaned, then nipped at my breasts.

"Princess, careful. It's been a while, and I'm not gonna last long." His teeth grasped my nipple and the gasp that came from me as the pain flowed through me made him chuckle. His tongue swirled around, easing the pain away. He repeated the motion with the other breast as his hand slid between us, and his bare fingers circled my clit.

"Fuck." My head tipped back, feeling the first shred of an orgasm I've had in weeks. His fingers dipped lower, and I spread my legs further to allow easier access.

There was another hummed groan that reverberated in his chest when he felt just how wet I was. His eyes met mine, and he leaned down to kiss me as he slid two fingers into me. My hips rocked up involuntarily, and he spread his fingers into a V, then curled them repeatedly within me. When his thumb pressed against my clit, I tightened around those fingers as they pumped in and out of me.

"Atta girl." He kissed me again, and the sound of his voice in that moment rocketed me a little further. "Now give me one more, Princess."

"Are you serious right now?" I was panting, and when he kissed that spot on my shoulder, pressing against my clit, he said, "I do not get mine, until you've a few. Now I think you've only had two, so give me another one, Princess, then I'll fuck you over the edge."

It didn't take long, and I wasn't sure if it was just from the lack of sex lately, if it was Ian, or if it was just the ability to have the true skin to skin contact that set me quivering.

"That's my good girl." He kissed me, and as our tongues danced around each other. He tasted of honey and whiskey. He leaned back before reaching over and pulling a condom from the dresser and slipping it on.

Running his lips along mine softly, he slid against me, lining himself up to my entrance. I couldn't help but lift my hips. I wasn't waiting for him to tease me one damn moment longer. Ian groaned into me, and I couldn't help the smile that crossed my face.

"That wasn't fair, Princess."

"What's that?" I whispered against his lips. "You don't have to always be the one in charge."

He pushed the rest of the way into me, and my eyes rolled back into the back of my head at the feel of him filling me. His tongue ran up and down my neck as he set a steady pace, sending shivers across my skin. It was so different than from how it was with Jesse.

FUCK! Get him out of your head!

I opened my eyes, and Ian was staring at me. He gave me a quick peck on my nose and leaned to rest his forehead on mine. "Gods, you are stunning, my Princess Madilyn." It was a whispered prayer on his lips as he picked up speed, and when I felt him tightening within me, he reached down and pinched my clit, sending me over the edge once again. He pounded me through my orgasm, and then growled as he reached his release as well.

We were both sweaty, and he pressed his lips to mine as we laid there panting. Slowly, he retreated from me and said, "I'll be right back before there is a mess."

"Of course." I laid there, soaking in the feeling of being sated. I rolled over, and pulled the blankets up and when he returned, he had a pair of boxers on and sat down next to me, laying his hand on my back and rubbing it softly.

"Want some water or something to eat?"

I looked up at him and smiled. "Can we just lay here for a bit? Just hold me, and then when our alarms go off, we can get up and be responsible adults?"

"Anything you want, Princess." He kissed me again, and crawled over me and under the blankets, pulling me close.

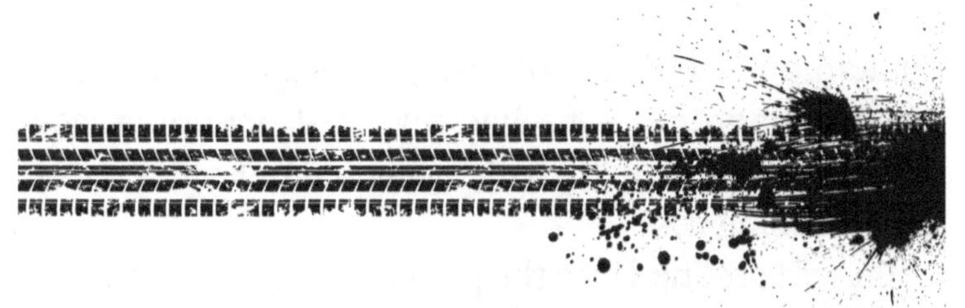

CHAPTER 37

JESSE

It had been three days since I had called Maddie. Three days since my world crashed down around me. After taking a day to just drink it all away, I dove headfirst into the Ashton Clarke assignment. That didn't stop me from drinking my weight the last couple of nights, and stumbling into my room to pass out cold on the too hard bed.

Sure, I had made some phone calls and called in some favors for people to keep an eye on her. Make sure she was taken care of. I extended out the contract for the grocery deliveries and set up payment for her rent through my app. If she was breaking it off with me, who knew what was happening. Flinch would find a way to take advantage of this, and I was going to make sure she could at least eat and have a roof of her own over her head.

Jonathon had finally gotten a hold of me this morning, and the ringtone alone had my head pounding, as if the amount of tequila I had consumed last night wasn't already doing it.

"Jesse." I groaned into the phone in answer. "Shit. I just talked to Maddie. How much have you had to drink? Just how hungover are you?"

"I'm fine. Just need to splash some water on my face—"

"And drink a faucet worth of water." There were a string of curses that flowed through the phone. "Damn it, Jesse. Sober up. This isn't like you."

"She left me, Jonathon."

"That's what she said. Something about you killing Sean? Did you really kill her brother?"

"It was an accident. Okay, so the death itself wasn't an accident. I was on an assignment. He fought me, and I took down the threat. I didn't fucking know it was Sean." My voice caught, and I swallowed the pain down.

"For fuck's sake, Jesse. If it weren't for bad luck, you'd have none at all." He sighed heavily on the phone.

Not wanting to talk about Maddie, and already too sober, I asked, "So is there a reason for calling that doesn't include talking about the woman who has shattered my heart?"

"I have been trying to call you for days. Though I guess now I know why you haven't been picking up. You are in Prince George, aye?"

"Aye." I sat up, realized I really was parched, and got up to get a glass of water.

"Talk to Chief Sesi. We talked to him and he said he could give you some info on where he thinks your Exorci is hiding out."

"Text me directions?"

"Yeah, no. He'll meet you at your hotel. Send me the info and he'll be there within a few hours." Jonathon waited before he spoke again. "Our sister clan is a bit hesitant of outsiders, and they certainly won't let an Exorci in."

"Noted. I'll shower and be waiting for a visitor. Yes, I'll get food and down some more water. You know I'll sober up within an hour, regardless of how much I drink. Though, I wouldn't mind a few more drinks."

"Jesse. Just remember, the bottom of every bottle looks the same. I know it's only been three days, but don't cope like this."

I let out a heavy sigh. "It hurts, Jonathon. Maddie is my forever and I'm not giving up on her. I'll find a way to make this right. I don't know what it is, but I gotta finish this assignment so I can get home and start."

"Okay. Finish up and fix it if you can. If not, you know you can hide out here for a bit."

"I know, thanks."

Chief Sesi was a short plump man who had two words, and only two words to give me. When he knocked on the door, all he said was, "You Jesse?"

"I am." He simply handed me a file, turned, and walked away.

I stared at the file in my hand for a long moment before shutting the door and taking a seat on the edge of the bed. When I opened it, there was a photo of Ashton Clarke getting out of a red Camaro in front of a very modern house and a note written on a sheet of paper.

EXORCI,

HE'S BEEN CREATING THE SAME PROBLEMS HE DID AT OUR SISTER CLAN'S TERRITORY. WE WOULD BE MUCH APPRECIATED IF YOU WOULD RELIEVE US OF THIS HARDSHIP.

DINNER IS USUALLY TAKEN AT THE ISLAND GARDEN, THEN HE GETS ICE CREAM AT THE LOTUS. HE RETURNS TO THE HOUSE IN THE PHOTO AFTER THE INDULGENCE.

THE ADDRESS IS ON THE NEXT SHEET.

MUCH APPRECIATION TO YOU AND THE AGENCY FOR YOUR SERVICES.

-CHIEF SESI-

Presumptuous much? Shit, it was like he just demanded that I to take care of his local problem. I mean, I was, but... damn.

I looked at the second sheet of paper, and it just had an address.

84568 RUSTAD ROAD

Bringing up the map app on my phone, I punched in the address. When I looked, it was only about a mile from here. Tonight. I'll sleep today, pack my shit, head up there tonight, take care of business, and be well on my way back to the states by the time they ever find his body.

Maddie. Get back home and try to fix things. Try to… before…

"I need a drink." The thought alone of that wolf moving in on her made my blood pressure rise. It wasn't that Maverick was a wolf, but that I knew he had it bad for Maddie. How could he not? She was beautiful, smart, sexy, and had enough sass to hold her own against anyone. I ran my hands through my hair and tipped my head back to the ceiling. "Fuck!"

I grabbed my phone, and as my fingers brought up her contact information, they froze. Instead, pulled up the information for Brandon and hit the call button.

"Hey, man."

"I'm losing my damn mind." I breathed.

I heard a door shut, and him sit down on what sounded like the squeakiest bed ever. "Why? What happened?"

"You know what happened."

"What do you need, Jesse? Want me to tail her when I get back? I'm planning on being back in town tomorrow mid-morning."

"Nah. I already got eyes on her. Not to stalk her, but just to make sure that if she ends up in too much trouble, that she's safe. I can't do shit though once she is in Ivy Grace. I know Flinch has her doing shit, not that I know what it is, but I can't stop it. Then there is the fact that I know the wolf is gonna step in."

"Ahhh. And *there* is the problem." Brandon's chuckle wasn't judgmental, but more in understanding. "You know that even if the wolf does, her heart will always be yours."

"That was before she knew I killed Sean. I think that broke what we have."

"Jesse. I'm going to be blunt here. Are you going to be okay if she ends up with the wolf?"

I clenched my fists and forced myself to take a deep breath. "I want her." I huffed out a hard breath. "Fuck that. I need her like the very air I breathe, Brandon. If I could change who I am, I would do it in a heartbeat to be with her, but I can't. I can't change that my very touch would kill her."

"But..." He let the word draw out and sit in the open silence.

"But if she can have someone to love and cherish her... and be able to properly give her the physical satisfaction she deserves..." my breath was shaky and I could feel my nails digging into my palms. "I love her with every cell in my body, but she deserves to have all that love and affection in the world. I always have to hold back. Always have to be overly aware of where every bit of exposed flesh is. Always have to make sure I keep that beautiful woman alive."

Brandon didn't say anything. He knew what I meant. He was borderline on the scale of being able to be with humans. So borderline, he didn't even chance it until he had his own set of special equipment made. He'd asked me who I used for my equipment after we had sat for hours and hours discussing how I was able to be with Maddie. It was exhausting, but it was worth every fucking minute.

"The fact you are willing to walk away to allow her to be happy... Jesse, there are not many people who love their partner so much that they would do that."

"I love her, Brandon." A piece of fuzz on the blanket next to my thigh caught my attention and I picked at it. "I need her happy. If that is with that piece of shit wolf, then as long as he keeps her happy and worships the ground she walks on... I won't kill him."

"Promise me, Jesse Westbrook. I don't want to have to get a file with your name on it. I'm not so sure I'd be able to go through that."

"I promise that as long as she is happy and healthy, that I won't kill him for keeping her that way, Brandon."

"Alright. Now get some sleep so you can come home."

"Thanks man." I rubbed my face and leaned back onto the bed. "I owe you."

"Nah. That's what friends are for. You'd be doing the same for me. Good night, Jesse."

"Night, Brandon."

With that, I flopped back on the bed and tried to sleep.

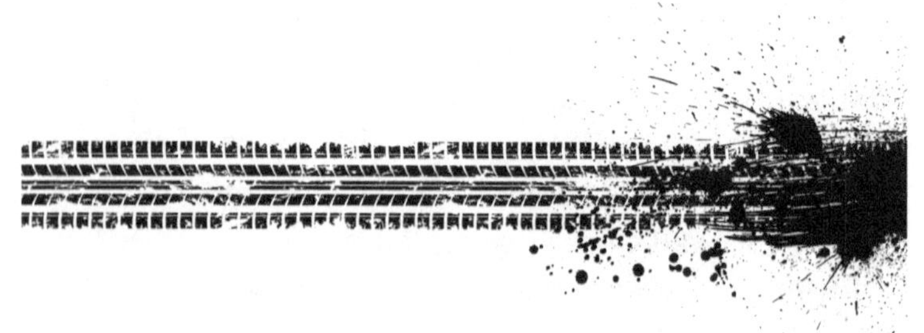

CHAPTER 38

JESSE

The house's porch was barely lit, and when I twisted the knob on the front door, it turned easily. Stupid fuck didn't even lock the damn door. There wasn't much light from the moon either, and so it allowed me to easily slip into a dark room that was lit with only the small beam of light from a hallway off to the right. As quietly as I could, I went to the hall and saw the door to the bathroom open and light spilling out. There was the faint sound of sloshing of water from the bath, and I shook my head.

I slipped off my gloves and stuffed them into my back pocket before heading to the bathroom, where I leaned against the doorjamb, arms crossed over my chest.

"Oh, they sent you. I knew someone was on my tail." He leaned back and took a swig of the fifth of Jack. "At least they sent the best."

Ashton Clarke looked comfy as hell in the bathtub. He laid there, head leaning back against the wall, arms and feet sticking out over the top opposite of him.

"I do appreciate you making this easy on me."

Rolling his head in my direction, he asked, "Can I finish my bath?"

I huffed a laugh and shook my head. "No. This is the perfect setup. You have to see that."

His eyes looked around the room and landed on the bottle of Jack. "It is. The whiskey will help kill me faster, too. I guess that's a good thing this is the second bottle" There was a deep sigh that had water sloshing as he moved a foot under the water and a knee popped up. Then he took another long drink before looking at me again. "What was the straw that broke the camel's back?"

"The file was pretty extensive, Clarke."

"A file? Shit. Didn't even go through the app, huh?" I shook my head. He gave me a smile, then his eyes trailed to the room behind me. "You should look at the black backpack next to the front door. Surprised you didn't trip over it coming in."

I raised an eyebrow. "You set up a bomb in case someone came out?"

"Gods, no. Like I said, I knew someone was coming for me. Kind of hoped it was you on my tail. I suspect it was the bears who told you where I was. Saw one of their scouts taking pictures the other day." I just shrugged non-committedly. "The backpack has some information that you might find interesting when trying to save your girl. Flinch isn't who you think he is. He isn't human, and we are both taking orders from someone much higher on the food chain."

"There isn't anyone higher than us except for the Minstrels and the Primes." I would be lying if he hadn't piqued my interest, but I also knew that we would keep the information to ourselves even to death.

"Read the file. You can get Flinch, but you won't be able to touch the one pulling our strings."

"Why are you even telling me this?"

He shrugged. "You'll kill me either way. I know I'm not in the best place amongst the gods. Might as well give you the information to start down the road to stopping him."

I felt my hand squeeze against my bicep and restrained myself as I said, "Who?"

His mouth opened, closed, and when he opened his mouth again, I saw the strain in his jaw before he sighed. "His power binds me even now, from speaking his name or even title."

I raised my eyebrows. "Title?" His whole body stiffened and I could see him fight against whatever command was in him to not respond.

"Just kill me, Jesse." His eyes were almost pleading.

"The black backpack next to the front door?"

He nodded. "Swordfish. You'll need it to get into the documents."

Without another word, I took the three steps to the bathtub, and as he looked up at me, his whole body relaxed as I pressed a single finger to his forehead. It took 45 seconds before he slumped under my touch, and his head slid under the water. No bubbles. No struggling. Just slid away.

I looked around the bathroom and, not seeing anything strange, I went back into the main room and found the backpack on a bench in the entry way.

After pulling the laptop out and entering the password he gave me, I clicked through a bunch of files before finding one labeled, '*Ivy Grace Parties*'.

I skimmed over the information in the file, and when I clicked on one labeled Party Favors, I froze.

"Oh, holy fuck." I stared at the screen until the computer's low battery warning popped up. Shaking my head, I looked at the clock and realized it was already pushing 11. I threw the computer back into the backpack and strode out of the room, not bothering to even close the door.

It was only three minutes before I had the pack strapped to my gear, and I was heading south, back to the States.

I sat there, leaning back in Carlos' chair two and a half days later. I had hardly stopped after reading those files. The two nights I had stopped to sleep, I had spent hours combing through the files on the laptop. The things that were in there were enough to have Flinch on a short list for extermination.

I had the laptop open and scrolling through the other documents as I waited for Carlos to make his way into his office. The monitors on the wall were a new addition since I was here, and I was able to track him as he made his way through the office, stopping by a few desks before reaching the door to his office.

"Nice of you to show up to your office, Minstrel." I drawled. My feet were still up on his desk as I leaned back with the laptop in my lap.

"First, what the fuck are you doing here? I just got word last night they found your assignment. Drowned in a bathtub. Nice touch, by the way." I shrugged before he put his bag down and crossed his arms. "Second, why the ever-living fuck are you sitting in *my* chair?"

"It's more comfortable than the guest chairs."

"Well, no shit. I'm sitting in it all day. If I wanted guests to sit there all day, I'd have more comfortable chairs." When he raised an eyebrow at me, and I returned the expression, Minstrel Carlos Medina rolled his eyes and said, "Get out of my chair, Westbrook."

With an overly dramatic sigh, I lowered my feet, but in the process, queued up the document on the laptop, leaving it on his desk for him to see when he sat down.

When I walked past him, he shook his head with a small smile. He was halfway to sitting in his chair before he froze, looked at me, and then back at the screen. "Are you sure about this?"

"It's not my laptop. It's Exorci Ashton Clarke's."

Carlos' eyes popped up to mine. "*That's* the file I delivered to your apartment?" I nodded as he studied me for a long moment. "Why didn't you report this to Primal Emma?"

Lifting a shoulder, I focused on the corner of his desk and tried to sort out a way to get Maddie out of Ivy Grace. Would she even be willing to go? How she found out about me wasn't even the problem. The problem between us was that I was the one who killed Sean. She was right. If Beth hadn't been at the funeral, she would probably still be alive. I was the sole reason the only people she had left in her life were dead. I couldn't even blame her for pushing me out of her life.

That didn't mean I was going to give up on her, though. What I had told Brandon was the truth. I would watch over her, make sure she was taken care of, and if she decided to be with...

I gulped, and it hurt to swallow. If she decided to be with Maverick, as long as he kept her happy and healthy, then I would keep my distance.

"Jesse." Carlos' voice brought me from my mental dive, and I looked over at him. "Why didn't you go to Primal Emma?"

"I reported the assignment complete, but when I saw this." Jerking my head toward the computer before continuing. "I had to come to you first. You and I have been working on the Flinch problem for a while."

His eyes crossed the screen over and over and he read through the information that I had already read four times.

"Maddie is stuck in there. I have scored all the documents in the *party file*, but haven't found a way to get her out of an Agency contract."

Carlos' face drained of color, and I took a deep breath. I knew exactly what section he had just gotten to. His eyes scanned further down the page as he sat down and rubbed his face. The lines in his face were getting deeper, and I worried how many more years he would be able to handle being a Minstrel. "Minstrel?"

"Flinch is a Phenric?"

"The ancestral documentation is there. What we need to know is how it got wiped from the system. He's obviously used those abilities to convince someone to do it, but they would have to be pretty high on the hierarchy to have permissions to do it, and the tech knowledge to do it."

"Wait. Stop." He leaned his head back on his chair, and the shift in weight had it squeaking slightly. "I need to think."

His index finger tapped against the leather clad arm, as he ran through scenario after scenario. After a few moments, he turned to his computer, and a few clicks and a couple seconds of drumming his fingers on the desk later, I heard Jade's voice come across the speakers.

"Carlos?"

"*Mija*, you got a moment?" He asked, as I heard Jade screaming at Kolton to just go outside. Kolton was shouting a colorful reply of his own, and my eyes widened when I thought I heard him utter a certain phrase. I could just barely see Jade on the monitor as she winced. Carlos' eyes narrowed before he asked, "What did he just say?"

A bright smile crossed her face. "Knew I shouldn't have answered until after he calmed down."

"Please tell me he said what I think he said."

"I'm pregnant. You are going to be a grandfather again." A joyous chuckle came from her as a full smile beamed across her face. "I just told Kolton. As you can tell, he's a tad bit excited."

Carlos got up and jumped for joy, and when he almost fell over his chair, I said, "Carlos, you gotta make it to the baby being born. Calm down, or at least be more careful."

"Jesse? What are you doing in Carlos' office? Last I heard, you were up north somewhere."

I stood and rounded the corner of the desk so I could see her. "First, congratulations Jade. I'm so incredibly happy for you."

An adorable blush crept across her face as Kolton bounced back into the room. He looked like a kid who was just told he could buy out the whole toy store. "Did you hear Jesse? I'M GOING TO BE A DAD!" He kissed Jade on the top of the head and then ran from the room.

"Good luck with Kolton and the babe, Jade. That's two kids there." I chuckled as she looked off in the direction Kolton ran off. There was nothing but love and adoration on her face. Kolton was still running around saying, '*I'm gonna be a dad! I'm gonna be a dad! James! I'm gonna be a dad!*'

"I'll manage. I babysat all you kids down there. Babysitting a whole slew of them up here, too. This one will just end up sassing me back, and I won't be able to put a dagger to its throat to teach it a valuable lesson that there is always someone higher on the ladder. No, this one, this one... oh, may the Gods help it." Then she turned to face the camera again, and narrowed her eyes before saying, "So, why is Carlos calling me out of the blue, and why are you sitting in his office? This can't be good."

I stepped back, and Carlos sat back down, reeling in his excitement. "Flinch." Jade's back got very straight, and she was instantly the Astral Primal Alpha sitting there. Carlos looked at me and I nodded. "Did you ever experience any headaches around him? Have the urge to do things you wouldn't normally do? Gaps in time?

Jade blinked, looked out toward the left, and then got up. I heard a door shut before she came back into view and sat down. "You think he's a Phrenic? I thought Flinch was classified as a human. In fact, I'm sure he is."

"We know he is classified in the Agency as a human." I said carefully as Carlos' lips pressed into a thin line.

"Jesse was on an assignment that has provided us some evidence of a family line that connects all the way back to the inception of the Agency."

Jade's face was a mask of professionalism that had been cultivated over many years. "This is solid evidence?"

"It is, but now that you are pregnant, I want you to stay as far from him and this situation as possible. Though you didn't answer my questions."

"It's been a long time since I was standing in the same room with Flinch. I don't remember, but is that because of time, or because he didn't want me to?" She shrugged like it was the most obvious answer in the world. It was when she put it like that. "What do you need me to do, Carlos?"

"Stay there where you are safe. I want you far away from him."

"Is that the Minstrel talking or the man who raised me?"

I laughed and got a glare from Carlos. Shrugging, I answered, "Both, but the sentiment is the same, Jade. Don't want to chance the babe."

"I am eight weeks! Don't you two start acting like I'm freaking made of glass. I'll get enough of that from my bonded. I'm a fucking Astral Primal Alpha, for fuck's sake. I can take care of myself. Plus, I have no doubt the fucking wolves with be overprotective shits... actually it explains why they have already started being overprotective shits. Probably already smell it on me."

"You are rambling, Jade." I rolled my eyes.

"Fuck you, Jesse."

"First, I would rather not piss off Kolton, and second, I don't think I want to kill you, at least not today."

"That would be preferred." Jade laughed. "Seriously though, I'll be okay. Unless he comes up to the Ranch or the compound, I should be alright." She turned to look at Carlos, and followed up, "I got Astrals and the pack to help. I'll let the pack council and Aaron know as well. I'll be pretty well covered, Carlos. *Te amo*."

"*Te amo, mija*."

Carlos turned back to the laptop, and his eyes narrowed. After about ten minutes, he said, "Why would a North American Exorci have multiple itineraries for flights to London?"

"You don't think the Fae Primal is involved, do you? He met with him in Oregon, and Clarke was going to London? That's close enough. It's only a few hours' drive up through the territory."

"I don't know. I'll scour through this and let you know what we find." He looked at me for a long moment, and I knew where the conversation was going. "I heard some things last night, Jesse."

"Yes, I've talked to Maddie, and she told me she found out about me killing Sean. Yes, Maddie said she couldn't be with me because I did. No, I'm not going to let it lie. I'm going to continue to take care of her. My motivation is still to keep her safe. She isn't safe in Ivy Grace."

"She has been staying with one of her co-workers."

"Maverick. I know who he is."

"I don't want to be the one to tell you, but you have to know." My stomach sank, and I knew what he was going to say. "They have been looking 'comfortable', Jesse."

"I can't say I'm surprised, but I'm still going to try to talk to her. I'm still going to make sure she has a roof over her head, and I'm still going to make sure she is taken care of. If he's wrapped up in Ivy Grace, he's probably under a contract too, and that means he is owned by Flinch. Not that I want anything to happen to him, if it causes Maddie pain, but..."

Carlos just looked at me and blinked. "You aren't angry."

"I'm pissed. I'm hurt. I'm fucking breaking. I have also fought through our entire relationship to understand why she would continue to risk her life with me. I've always known there could be a day that she would walk away, not wanting to take the risk anymore. I'd prepared for that. Then I killed Sean..." I ran my hand through my hair and rubbed my face, willing the knot of emotions at my throat to stay there, but it came out in my voice, anyway. "I've been waiting for the day she found out and walked away. If she is happier with that wolf, then I love her enough to let her be happy there."

Nodding, he turned back to the laptop. "I'll be in touch when I've looked through this. I'm assuming you've already made a copy."

"Of course." The corner of my mouth twitched up.

"Be careful, Jesse."

CHAPTER 39

JESSE

I was leaning against Maverick's truck, waiting outside Maddie's complex for him to come out. I saw Maverick kiss her through the window, which had me balling my fists and reminding myself that I did not want to make repairs to my bike. It had been a week. I had stayed away for a week, and I'd seen them together almost non-stop.

"I'd appreciate you relinquishing the tail, Exorci."

"That is for Maddie's protection, not yours, Maverick." I met his gaze and there was nothing but fury and rage on his face. I pushed off the hood and put my hands in my pockets. "Look, I'm not here to kill you, beat the snot out of you, or anything. I only want to talk."

Maverick came over and leaned against the hood, and asked, "What about? I'm not leaving her. I told her I would wait for you to fuck shit up, and I would be there. I'm here, and I have no intention of ever leaving her side."

There was a slight twist of the light in his eye, that something primal in him was saying that. "I love that woman with every ounce of my being, Maverick. I won't do anything to hurt her. That includes hurting you."

"Except for killing her brother."

I took a long, deep breath. "I swear, I don't know how many times I have to say it. I didn't know it was Sean until after I removed the ski mask and saw his face."

"The video—"

"The video from Flinch?" There was a quick nod from him, and I continued, "Where did it cut off?"

His head twisted to the side, in that way that dogs did when they were trying to figure things out. His voice was slow and hesitant as he said, "You were reaching for the ski mask, and took it off."

"So, it didn't show me freaking out over the fact I saw Maddie's face in male form laying there, knowing that I was the one who did it?"

"No, it didn't." His hands balled up into fists, released, and then balled up again before he slammed it down on the hood.

"Are you really surprised Flinch cut that part out? It doesn't matter. He was likely throwing you a bone, giving you the opportunity for something good and wonderful in your life." I looked up at the apartment, and I thought I saw her standing there watching us, but Maverick's eyes were fixed on her. I swung my head back around and she was gone.

"Here is the thing, Maverick. This is your chance. As long as you keep that woman happy and healthy, you won't have me as a friend, but I will be there to help with anything you need regarding Maddie. I will continue to provide for her."

"You really do love her?" I only gave a single nod of my head. "You love her enough to let her go and to be with me?"

"You apparently loved her enough to wait for me to be out of the picture. Figure turnabout is fair play."

Maverick's face was a little shocked, but held respect too. His eyes narrowed. "You are the one paying her rent and making sure that she has food."

"Flinch is going to take advantage of her. No matter what happens, I want to make sure she has a roof over her head and food on the table." I rubbed the back of my neck, and then looked back to the man I was allowing to have Maddie. "Just keep her happy, Ian. As long as she still looks at you the way she does, then my gloves stay on."

"I will never do anything to hurt her. If she wants to be with me, then you'll let us be?" His eyes did that animalistic thing again, just as I heard the apartment gate doors slam.

"Jesse Westbrook, you need to leave. Now." Maddie's voice was like a raging song to my ears, but I forced myself to keep Maverick's stare.

"If she were a wolf, you would mate her, wouldn't you?"

"In. A. Fucking. Heartbeat." He growled. Maddie reached us then and froze. "She is mine."

"What?" Maddie said, looking at Maverick.

"You haven't told her, have you?" His eyes narrowed. "I'm not here to start trouble. I merely wanted to talk. She would understand, though. Bacri are the same." My eyes looked down at my little bird, who was still looking at Maverick. "But you can't help who your heart and soul belong to. You just do what you can with the time you have with them."

Her face slowly turned to mine. "Jesse."

"Little Bird, just because you have pushed me out, doesn't mean I have stopped loving you with every ounce of my being. You've made it clear that I don't make you happy because of what I have done. If Maverick makes you happy, then I will step aside. All I want is my little bird happy. I was only here to let Maverick know that."

I pulled her against me, held her close for a moment, and kissed the top of her head. As I turned to walk off, I nodded to Maverick, who pulled her in close, protectively.

It was probably the hardest thing I've ever had to do. Walk away from Maddie, and allow her to be with Ian Cade Packard. Taking a deep breath, and holding back the tears that were clouding my vision, I put my helmet on, started the bike and roared out of there.

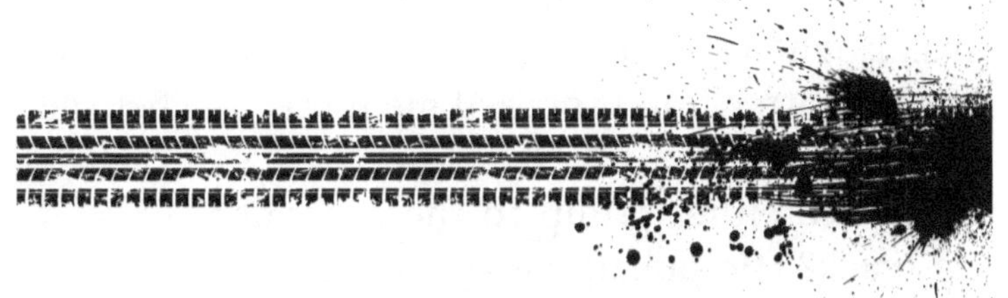

CHAPTER 40

MADDIE

"What did Jesse mean, I would understand?" Maverick was still staring off at where Jesse was peeling out of the parking lot. Even with my arm wrapped tightly around Maverick's waist, and him pulling me in close, there was a part of me that broke at Jesse's words. Did I still love Jesse? Yes, I did. Maverick knew that, too, but as I turned to look back up at him, I asked again, "What did Jesse mean, I would understand?"

"Sweets." His eyes flashed.

I reached up and put my hand on his cheek. He leaned into it before turning and kissing my palm. "Please."

"You were supposed to go back to sleep. Why did you come down here?"

"Don't you deflect, mister. Talk. Tell me what Jesse meant." When he narrowed his eyes at me, I huffed a small laugh. "Of course, Jesse knew I would ask, but it doesn't matter. You promised me no secrets between us, Ian."

"Can we either go up to the apartment or sit in the truck?" He pulled me against him and wrapped both arms around me. My arms tightened around him, and I nodded. "Upstairs." He kissed my forehead, then pressed his to mine for a long minute before taking a deep breath and leading me up.

His hand didn't leave mine, and when we got inside, my arm pulled tight as he planted his feet at the door. Turning, I looked at him, and he took a deep inhale of breath before sitting on the couch.

"Madilyn." I sat there waiting. "Jesse totally knew what he was doing, but it doesn't change the truth. As much as I hate to admit it, you should know."

"What did Jesse say?"

He stared at me long and hard, reached up and ran his thumb against my cheek before running it along my jaw and pulling away. "He asked if you were a wolf, if I would mate you."

I blinked. That was a serious declaration. Wolves only mated once. Once done, it wasn't undone. Bacri were lifetimers as well, so I knew the seriousness of that statement. Did I even want to know the answer to that?

"I told him I would in a fucking heartbeat."

I stared at him. "Wolves are like Bacri, though. You only mate with one of your own species. You physically cannot knot with someone who is not your mate."

"Madilyn, nothing in this world would make me happier than to be able to mate you. I would bite right here." He leaned forward and ran his tongue over my shoulder, and then clamped his teeth right on the tender part of flesh, capturing the muscle as well. I couldn't help the moan that emanated from me. I felt a small sharp prick, and he froze.

"What would happen if you did bite me in the midst of an orgasm and completed the mating... without it being a mating?"

"I don't know. I don't know anyone who has done it. I've heard stories where the non-wolf dies within twenty-four hours to a festering wound, but I've also heard that nothing happens to you, but I die. I won't take the chance with you, Sweets."

I couldn't help the chuckle that came from me. "Exchanged one danger for another."

One second, I was sitting there next to him, the next he had me straddled over his waist, running his hands along my hips, up under my shirt, and along the bare skin of my back. He knew what he was doing to me.

"No. I can and will fuck you raw. I can touch you. I..." He moved a hand around to the front of me. My hips instinctively moved and allowed him to run his hand through my middle and pinched my clit, causing a wave of heat to pulse through me. "I can bring those sounds from you with nothing between us. The only thing I have to be careful about is not to bite you. As long as I don't, there is no issue."

His fingers dove into me, and I tipped my head back, pressing my chest into his face, where he bit down on my nipple. When I moved off his lap, he growled as I stood, turned, bent over, and slowly slipped my shorts off. Maverick's hands were instantly on my ass, and there was a slap that went through the room, before then his face was pushing my legs apart. I caught myself on the coffee table, and when his tongue flicked my clit, I would have fallen if his arms didn't wrap around my thighs.

His tongue lapped and sucked at me, and I couldn't help my hips moving against his face. When he pulled back and kissed my ass on the right side, I stood up, pulling my t-shirt off as I did.

Maverick all but tore his jeans off, and when he sprung free, I fell to my knees before him. The look in his eyes was feral, and I knew I wouldn't be able to fully enjoy this, because he was an impatient bastard. Didn't mean I couldn't torture him for a hot minute.

Taking his balls into my mouth and humming, his cock twitched and his head flew back as his mouth opened in a silent howl. I repeated the motion, and his hands threaded through my hair, gripping tightly, which only caused another moan to come from me.

"Fuck, Sweets."

Slowly, I licked and ran my tongue along the bottom line of him, and just before I reached the head, I paused, looking up at him. Eyes were full of that animalistic feralness he was trying to keep at bay. The grip on my hair tightened as I wrapped my lips around the head of him. I sucked on only the tip of him before he growled and thrust himself down my throat. He sat there a moment, and I chuckled.

Impatient indeed.

We worked in tandem with me bobbing up and down and him thrusting himself down my throat. I had never known how much I loved sucking cock until Maverick. The pure power it gave me over him was something I relished.

I felt him tightening, and he pulled from me with a growl that I was sure had rattled the windows. Pulling me up, I licked the taste of him from around my lips as I straddled him.

I had barely lined him up with me before his hips rose, filling me in one stroke. My back bowed, and once again my nipple was in his mouth, tongue swirling, and sharp delicate pricks of pleasure on either side.

"Fuck." I rolled my hips against him. His lips pulled back, and when I looked down at him, he thrusted up into me again. Small beads of blood coated his canines, and I couldn't help but smirk.

Over and over again he pounded into me, and just when I was about to fall over the edge, he lifted me, and said, "Not yet, Sweets. Turn around and lean on the back of the couch." When I was in position, he pressed himself into me slowly. Painfully slow. Hips met my core, and he bent down, kissing his way up my spine.

"You going to cum for me, Sweets?"

I let a smirk cross my face as I looked over my shoulder. "If you do your damn job, and fuck me, right."

That wolf growl rolled through the room and I felt it in my chest, goosebumps peppering my skin. He pulled out and slammed back into me. I let a moaned scream go through the air as he pounded into me again and again.

Ian pulled me up against him, not relenting, and ran his tongue along my neck. His teeth clamped down on that spot on my shoulder, and I tipped my head to the side. There was a small prick of pain and I fell over the edge, groaning his name into the apartment. A few more strokes, and he followed me.

Sweaty and sated, we collapsed on the couch.

Just as we pulled up to Ivy Grace, I noticed someone standing next to the back door. Maverick opened the car door, took my hand, lacing our fingers together, kissed the back of my hand, and pulled me close to him.

I stopped short when I recognized who it was. One of the Bacri Primal's guards. His eyes met mine, shifted to their eagle form, and then he took three steps toward me. "Madilyn Taylor."

Dropping to one knee, with my hands stretched out to either side of me, I said, "Yes, Soldier."

"You may rise."

I swallowed, and Maverick gave me a concerned look as I saw Bell and Chip step out of the van and make their way to stand next to Maverick. I knew better than to say much of anything to the Prime's Soldier, but kept my head down.

"Madilyn Nikole Taylor. As you have spilled blood of innocents, by the laws of the Ashstrike Sanctorum," I heard Bell, Chip, and Maverick gasp beside me, but I refused to show any emotion. "and by the laws of the Bacri Council, your protections are hereby revoked."

"No. You can't do that. She was under orders on a contract bound by the Agency!" Bell shouted.

"There has to be a—"

"Stop." I said simply as I raised my head to meet the Bacri Primal's Soldier. "I understand and acknowledge the laws of Bacri and Ashstrike Sanctorum. I understand that the revocation is by my own actions. Considering the circumstances, I would do it again, and again, because if I did not..." I felt my anger rise, but saw respect shine in the Bacri soldier's eyes. "then my family would not be standing beside me in this moment. So, I accept the banishment."

I held my hand out, and he placed the paperwork in my hand. "I will always protect those I love."

The soldier nodded his head and said, "Good luck, Madilyn Taylor."

When he was out of sight, I turned to find Maverick just staring at me, fear, admiration, lust, and something else I couldn't place in his eyes. Bell and Chip, however, were rambling about different ways we might get my protections back.

"I love that you are willing to try to find the answers to me being under Agency law again. However, I would, and will probably do it again. If it is to protect you three, the only three in my life who matter, then yes, I will do it again. I told you all that night, when Maverick was laid out on that gurney, that I knew I was a dead woman. Now it's official. That is all that changed."

I forced myself to look at Bell until he nodded and did the same with Chip. "Good. Now that we have an understanding, I'm assuming it's a night on the town and I should change."

"It is, Sweets." Bell's voice was sad and sorrowful.

"Alright, give me ten minutes and I'll meet you back at the van."

"Madilyn..." Maverick's voice was thick, and it hurt a little to hear him say my name like that.

He reached for me, but I took a step back and didn't meet his eye. "Give me ten minutes, Maverick."

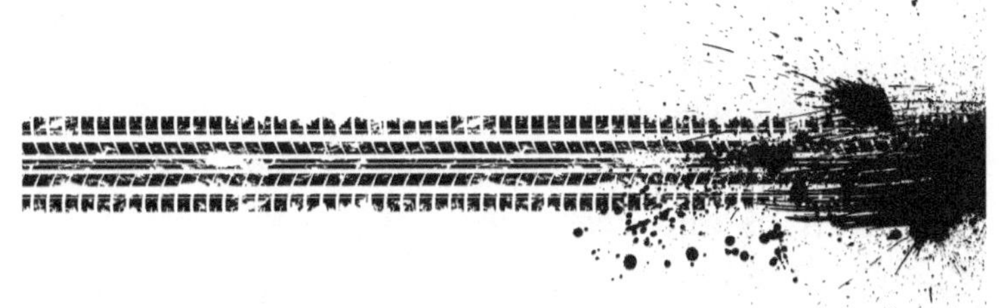

CHAPTER 41

JESSE

THREE MONTHS LATER

I pushed open the inner door to the strip club just off the 880. The Edging was known by the Agency for where a lot of species would come to watch humans and creatures alike do whatever they could for a few extra dollars. It wasn't that I had anything against the strippers; it was more the bouncers I had a problem with. They were usually arrogant assholes who thought just because they were the bouncer, they could push anyone around they wanted.

Tonight, though, I was looking for a Calassei, an air elemental, who was connected with Jaysen Flinch as well as known for killing humans at will. I stopped and scanned the room for her. Carlos and I had taken a deep dive into the laptop with all the information in there about Flinch and a mysterious *His Highness* or *Overseer*. It was always those two titles. Never a name or hint as to who he actually was.

The Calassei, Julietta Sanchez, had been murdering both humans and creatures in the name of Jaysen Flinch. Clarke had extensive lists of executions and job duties for a long list of creatures. We had been slowly making our way through them, but nothing was really all that helpful. I had looked for Maddie's name, even Maverick's, but couldn't find either of them mentioned in any of the documents, lists, or otherwise.

I found Ms. Sanchez sitting in a chair watching a tall bleach blonde hanging upside down on the pole, legs spread. After a few casual strides toward her, she never second guessed the person walking right next to her back. Her focus was so wholly on the bleach blonde that I almost laughed. If I hadn't wanted information, this would have been one of the easiest assignments I have ever done. Flipping the chair next to her around, I sat astride it, and leaned on the back. "Hi, Julietta."

"I don't know you." Her voice was wistful as she watched the woman move and dance along the pole. I watched the woman for a moment. She was pretty and graceful. Gods, the talent and flexibility of these women.

"You don't." I said carefully. "But I know you are not eyeing that woman because you enjoy the performance, or are imagining what she would look like with your head between her legs."

"I don't know what you are talking about. Of course, I'm imagining tasting her." I huffed a laugh as she actually licked her lips.

"So, this time you plan on enjoying her, before you prevent air from going into her lungs?" I said smoothly, watching as every muscle in her body froze. It took a good eight seconds before she took an inhale of breath, pulling it from around me, and then slowly looked toward me.

"Again, I don't know what you are talking about."

"Of course, you don't." I slowly removed my gloves, Juliette watching the movement, and ran my hand through my long brown hair. "You also don't remember killing about a hundred different people over the last two years, slowly suffocating them."

A small smile lifted the left corner of her lip, as she said, "When they deserve it, why not use what the Gods gave me?"

"Jaysen Flinch. What can you tell me about him?"

She tipped her head to the side and said, "You are Jesse Westbrook. Well, don't I feel special. The Agency sent their best."

"Jaysen Flinch." I hissed through my teeth.

"I know he has a special interest in someone very special to you." Why does everyone know about Maddie? "Well, she used to be. She's with a wolf now. Flinch loves tormenting those two. Heard he makes the wolf watch while she services him. You know she's doing jobs for him now, right?"

I knew Flinch had Maverick, Maddie, and two others out doing jobs almost daily, and I hated it. The problem was, I didn't know *what* they were doing. The last I heard, she was nothing more than a lookout, but who knew what happened in Ivy Grace. Exorcis couldn't get past the bouncers. I knew that because I had tried to get Julietta there just last week. The bouncers weren't the problem. It was more some serious wards had been placed on the building and Exorcis couldn't get past the threshold.

"Shall I just kill you now, or are you going to say what you really want to torment me with?"

"She's become a bit of a prized possession of Mr. Flinch. He *really* likes her." She leaned forward, and I felt the air around me thin. "Lets a few people enjoy her. I've seen her at work. She just takes it all. She's a bit of a screamer."

I willed myself to stay calm. She was trying to get me angry, and I took a slow, methodical, deep breath. My lungs were already burning, and I knew I had maybe sixty seconds before I would be visibly struggling.

"She's here, ya know. Maybe you should ask for Nikki." Then she smiled, tried to get up, but my hand snapped out and wrapped around her wrist. She instantly went limp, and one of the waitresses stopped and looked at me.

"Got up too fast after having a few too many drinks, I suppose." I smiled at her.

"I'll get Darren to help her. What's her name?"

"Julietta Sanchez. She's a friend of a friend."

I stood and headed toward the bathroom, when I saw a redheaded woman bent before an older greying man, shaking her tits at him. He slowly slid some bills into the bra strap, and ran a finger over the top of her right breast, then between them before I heard her purr, "Ask for Nikki."

As the woman stood, her eyes lifted and met mine. I slid my gloves back on just as one of the waitresses dressed in a sparkly bra and white shorts walked by with a tray.

She noticed me looking at her, and I asked, "Hey, can I get a private room with Nikki please??"

"She's one of the premiums, sir."

I reached into my jacket and handed her a few hundreds. "Not a problem."

I saw 'Nikki's' eyes tighten slightly, as the woman said, "Go down the hall to five. I'll tell her she has a private showing."

CHAPTER 42

JESSE

After pacing the room for a full five minutes, I had finally lowered my blood pressure from seeing her up there dancing for tips. It wasn't the dancing that was the problem. It was the way she allowed the *guests* to touch her. Regardless of what had happened between us. She was mine. She would always be mine. Finally, I leaned against the far wall, arms crossed over my chest, with my right ankle crossed over my left, and waited for 'Nikki' to walk in.

I only had to hold it together for another few minutes before the door opened and I took one last long deep breath in, before letting it out slowly through my nose. It took a lot of deep breaths and concentrating on not laying into her as soon as she walked through that door. She walked in, hands in her long dark purple sweater pockets, which covered her outfit, as she kicked the door shut with her barefoot before leaning back on it. We stood there just staring at each other for way too long before she finally sighed. "What do you want, Jesse?"

"You know what I want." The words were out of my mouth quicker and much too feral than I anticipated. Her eyes narrowed at me. "What are you doing here, little bird?"

"Jesse." She drew out my name as a warning, but when I just looked at her and waited for her answer. She pushed off the door, and took three steps toward me, finger outstretched. "I have bills to pay, Jesse. I don't work for the Agency and make enough to pay cash for a $25,000 motorcycle."

"If you need money, all you had to do is fucking ask. You know I'll help you out any way you need it. I told you that when we were still together. I will do anything I can to help you out. Just tell you how much you need?"

"Cuz I'm gonna ask *you* for money." She threw her hands up and turned around exacerbated and put her hands on her hips.

Pushing off the wall, I said, "Madilyn Nikole Taylor."

She whirled around toward me, and I had to stop short before her outstretched finger hit my nose.

"Don't you full name me, Jesse Westbrook. There is nothing wrong with stripping and dancing. It's really empowering, and believe it or not, freeing, actually."

"I don't care about the dancing. What I care about is how you allow your fucking *patrons* to touch what is mine." I took a step toward her, and she mirrored it backwards. I could feel myself growing hard for her. Gods, this woman was everything to me. Just the sight of her was enough to get me going. Then she matched my ferocity... and I was a dead man for her. But I had to stay on track.

"I don't need my ex-boyfriend to lecture me on how to live my fucking life."

"It isn't like I had a say in being your ex, Maddie. You are my forever."

There was a flicker of shock on her face, before she whispered, "Well, maybe you shouldn't have killed your forever's brother then, huh?"

It was a stab to the heart, and she knew it. Refusing to react, I took another step toward her, and again, she matched it backwards as I stared her down.

Step.

Step.

Gods, how I still craved this woman. Every ounce of me needed her. When she was against the wall, I took another half step toward her. She flattened herself against the wall, her chest taking quicker and deeper breaths, her breasts rubbing against my leather jacket.

Placing my hands on either side of her, I caged her in. I leaned close, and whispered, in that husky voice that I only used with her, "Dammit, Maddie. I didn't know it was Sean until it was too late. Didn't Maverick tell you that Flinch had cut the video short of me freaking out when I removed the ski mask and saw it was him? I would never hurt you, little bird."

"You still killed my brother, Jesse." Her voice shook, and when I glanced down to see her hands balled up into fists, I pulled back and stared her down.

Her heated eyes held mine for a moment, before her gaze settled on my lips, and she licked hers, biting her bottom lip. I let my gaze drop between us, and languidly come back up to settle on her lips.

I blinked quickly to clear my head, because damn if I wasn't close to losing every ounce of control. Slowly, I stepped back to the middle of the room. "What are you doing with Flinch?"

Again, she narrowed her eyes at me, and then finally let out a resigned heavy sigh, "Paying off Sean's debts. Even in death, I'm still paying for his stupidity. You know Sean signed a contract, and I was the collateral. The Token, but again, it is none of your concern, *Exorci*."

The door burst open at that point, and Maddie jumped. The bouncer who had taken my target off walked in and said, "Is there a problem, Nikki?"

"No."

"He didn't touch you, did he? If he did, I'll get Johnny on the line and have him arrested."

"No. He won't touch me." Her eyes hadn't left mine, but then slowly, as if she was pained to do so, she turned to the bouncer and said, "I have another set to do before I go home for the night. Excuse me."

The bouncer held open the door, and as I watched her leave, I took a deep breath, and just said, "You know how to reach me, Little Bird. If you need anything, don't hesitate to ask."

"Good bye, Jesse."

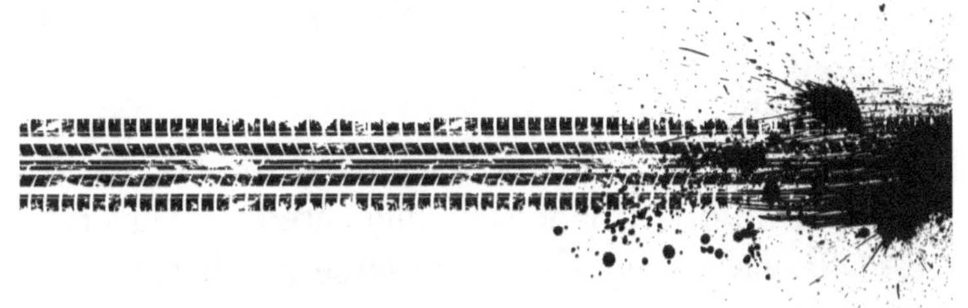

CHAPTER 43

MADDIE

"You don't have another set, Nikki. I thought you were done for the night." Darren whispered, but then he kicked his head to the side. "Unless you want one. I'm sure we can get you a pole."

"I just needed to get out of there."

He pulled me to a stop halfway down the hall, and I looked back to the door. "Seriously, if he's a problem, I'm sure we can help you out."

"He... We have a history. It's fine. He just wanted to talk." I took another settling breath and saw Jesse open the door. My heart hitched, and the sound of him calling me my pet name almost undid me.

Our eyes met before he nodded and I turned toward the dressing rooms, Darren quick on my heels. "Seriously, I'm okay, I said when I reached my chair. I just need a few minutes, then I'll page you for a walk out."

"Okay, Nikki."

I put my elbows on the bench table in front of me and put my head in my hands. I really cared for Maverick. He made me happy, but seeing Jesse was harder than it should have been. I'd been busy. Flinch was keeping me extra busy lately, and it helped to keep my mind off of not having Jesse in my life anymore, and Maverick... well he tried, but while I cared a lot for him, I was questioning if I was okay with him being the rebound, but tonight... tonight Jesse had my whole body revved and ready to go instantly. He'd always had that effect on me.

'*Little Bird.*' The words rang through my head again, and I squeezed my legs together. Whether he realized it, he had me on the edge with just those two words. Damn, when his gold eyes met mine, my whole body had flashed hot and cold, and hot again. It was everything I could do not to pull him to me, and beg him to make me scream like he had so many times.

Sex with Maverick was good. It was. I just didn't get that tingly rush of endorphins when I orgasmed. I didn't collapse from exhaustion after having sex with him. It was quick, rough, and usually what I needed at the moment, but it was nothing like it had been with Jesse.

Jesse and I were over.

I really needed to stop comparing them.

Maverick was what I needed right now.

I grabbed my phone and opened the text thread I had with Maverick. I smiled at the pictures we had sent back and forth to each other, most highly inappropriate for other person's eyes, while others were just moments from our everyday life.

Feel like being my chauffeur tonight or have you started already?

Just laying here thinking of your sexy ass

Well then come pick me up.

Maybe you can kiss it before we start tonight.

Anytime, Sweets. Love you. Be there in 10.

Putting my phone down, I took a deep breath. He had been telling me he loved me for a month now. He knew I couldn't say it back, and wouldn't unless I was completely sure. After my reaction at seeing Jesse tonight, I'm not sure I would ever be able to.

"AHHHH. I hate this!" I growled through my teeth.

Jackie, one of the other dancers here, put her hand on my shoulder, and asked, "What's wrong?"

"Ever think you are finally getting over someone, and then you see them, and realize that you haven't made a damn bit of progress?"

"Every time I see my ex. That man can get me going physically and emotionally quicker than anyone on this planet." She let out a heavy sigh. "I just can't deal with the drugs. That's a hard line for me."

I smiled at her. "I know that one all too well. My best friend was with my brother and broke up with him for the same reason. Hell, I hardly talked to Sean for a long time before he died. Then she died, and ... well, ever since my life has fallen down the toilet."

"Anything I can do to help?" Jackie was a 45-year-old mom of three who looked better on the pole than I did. She took care of all us girls, and there had been many a night when she took one of the girls home with her so they wouldn't have to go home to whatever hell they were living with.

"Not unless you have a travel machine, and even at that, I don't know if I would want the consequences of that." I smiled at her. Even if I had Sean and Beth back, it would mean, yes, I'd likely still be with Jessie, but I wouldn't have Maverick. He was there for me every second of the day if I needed him. Jesse hadn't been.

Jackie tipped her head back and laughed. "If I had a dollar for every time someone told me that, I'd have my own club with rooms on the second floor so that these troubled souls would always have a safe place to stay."

Both of our eyes moved to where Kaytlin's chair was. It sat empty again. She'd been missing for three days, and the police weren't doing anything. We had told them we thought her boyfriend was behind it, but nothing had been confirmed.

"Anyways, you sure there isn't anything I can do?"

"Thank you, but no. I just have to sort out my feelings, which are a crumbling, twisted mess." The lump in my throat made the words hard to get out.

She wrapped an arm around me, giving me a side hug, and I twisted into her, tears filling my eyes.

"Oh, honey." She pulled me in tight, and I just let it out. "It's alright."

When there was a knock on the door, Darren popped his head in. "Nikki, your ride is here."

Jackie answered for me, as another sob wracked through my body. "She will be out in a few minutes."

"It's not fair to Maverick, Jackie. Why does he still stay with me even when he knows I can't tell him that I love him back?"

"Because he loves you." She laid her cheek on the top of my head and squeezed. "It's okay, sweetheart. Let it out."

She held me while I cried for another ten minutes, before there was another knock on the door. Jackie separated from me, pointing me to the bathroom. "Go wash your face with some cold water."

Waiting until I was in the bathroom, she opened the door, where I heard Maverick's voice. "What's wrong? Why is she crying?" The worry in his voice undid me and fresh tears fell down my cheeks.

"She's fine. Just a rough night. Give her a minute?" Jackie told him.

I heard him stride over to the door and the wood groan as he leaned against it. "I know Jackie said you are okay, but you are crying and I need to hear from you that you are okay, Sweets."

A big snotty sniff wracked through me, and I muttered, "I'll be fine, Ian. Please, just give me a minute to pull myself back together, okay?"

Jackie's voice was next to the door. "How did you know she was crying? There is no way you could have heard her."

"Good hearing... plus, that sniff was way too wet not to be from tears."

I heard the pat on the shoulder she gave him and then him sit down next to the door. "I'll be here when you are ready, Madilyn."

Taking a shuddering, deep breath, I let it out slowly to keep myself together. I didn't deserve him. Either of them. I looked at the door though, and could almost see him sitting there, head against the door, forearms resting on his knees, and worry on his face. I smiled. That was what I needed. Someone who would not only love me fully and wholly but also be there when I was falling apart. They're here to pick up the pieces. I didn't have to do this alone.

I quickly cleaned up, scrubbing off all the make-up, and patting my eyes with a cold cloth to get some of the puffiness down. I ran my hand through my hair and threw it up in a ponytail. When I looked at myself in the mirror, I wasn't sure what I saw.

Thinner than I had been six months ago, there were heavy bags under my eyes. The grief alone would do it. Add in the near sleepless nights, and as Ian so often liked to remind me, my inability to take care of myself, and it was no wonder I looked like hell. I took a deep breath, closed my eyes, and let it out. "I'm opening the door, Ian."

By the time the door was open, he was standing and his arms were out to wrap me up. I let him, but swallowed down the tears that wanted to flow again. "You sure you are, okay?"

"Yeah. Like Jackie said, hard night."

I looked up at him, and his eyes were sad, "And I've already heard from Flinch. We are going back to the main campus."

Burrowing my head in his chest, I whispered, "Is he trying to get us killed?"

"I don't think he cares one way or another, but I will keep you safe. I'd never forgive myself if something happened to you." Kissing my nose, he smiled at me, and it was the breath of air I needed. "I got you, Sweets. I'll always have your back."

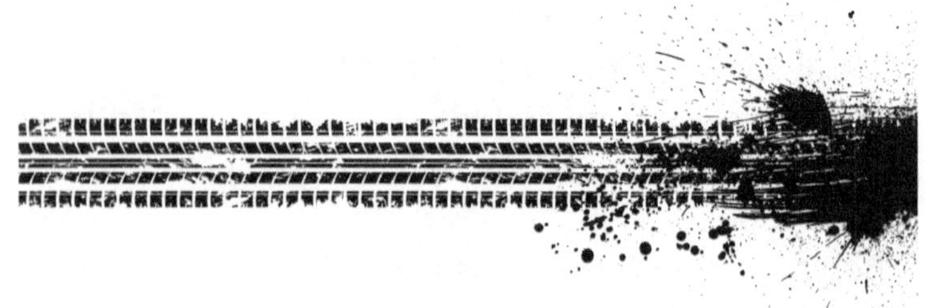

CHAPTER 44

MADDIE

Maverick had been overly protective of me since I saw Jesse at *The Edging*. I couldn't not tell him what had happened, even though I knew it would make him like this. It had been over a week, and it was driving me a little crazy, but I also knew it was in his wolf nature to be protective of his non-mate mate. That protectiveness was also why he wasn't letting me in the building tonight. I was going to be a lookout across the street like it had been at the beginning.

"No, Sweets. You aren't going anywhere near the building tonight." We were still packing up at Ivy Grace, and we'd been *discussing* the matter for almost ten minutes now.

"Maverick. We've done this a dozen times. I've even saved your hide on more than one—"

"No."

"Don't you go all wolf on me, mister." I raised a finger toward him, and even Bell and Chip looked at each other and took a step back.

He stared me down for a long moment, doing nothing but causing a pool of wetness between my legs. My hands were on my hips, and Maverick's eyes dropped to them when I cocked one out to the side before taking a long, deep breath. "Sweets, no matter how fucking amazing you look and smell, I am not budging on this. When we get there, you will be our eyes and ears."

His hands landed on my hips, and I let my hand slowly trail up his chest, palms flattening against his pecks, before reaching up and wrapping my arms around his shoulders. I raised an eyebrow at him, and he mirrored it.

"Yeah, we are going to pack up the van." When I gave Chip a questioning look, he smiled brightly. "Sweets, I can smell you, and I don't think Maverick is into allowing others seeing you get railed."

I tried to hide it, but heat flashed through me, and I saw the moment it filled Maverick's eyes, too. He pulled me closer, and I felt the hard on he was now sporting. The door behind us clicked, and he lifted me, thumbed my pants, and pulled them off in one fluid movement.

"We don't have much—" His lips were on mine, effectively cutting me off.

"I don't give a shit. If I have to smell your heat all damn night, I'm going to go insane." Maverick lifted me so my legs wrapped around his stomach, as he undid his belt and lowered his pants, enough for him to release his cock. Moments later, he was thrusting into me. Flipping us around so my back was to the wall, he pounded into me over and over.

"Fuck." I groaned out.

Maverick's lips trailed along my jaw as he continued his assault. When he ran his tongue along my neck, I felt myself tighten around him, and this time it was his turn to growl. "For all the Gods, Sweets."

He repeated the action, and when he clasped onto that spot at my neck, he sucked and ran his teeth over it hard. He was marking me, making me his, without the concerns of actually mating.

Kissing the spot quickly, his tongue ran up to my ear as he slowed and rolled his hips against my clit. "I promise to always be here for you, Madilyn. I love you, and I will always have your happiness and safety, my number one concern."

"Ian..." I moaned as he pushed me further and further to the edge.

"You are mine." He said, picking up speed and sucking that spot on my neck again. His teeth pricked the skin as I felt him release deep within me. The feel of his release and the pain at my shoulder were just that push that had me clamping down around him, screaming his name into the room.

Bell and Chip were quiet the entire way to the job site. Maverick, however, wouldn't stop eyeing and kissing that spot on my shoulder. The words he had said were ones you say to a mate, yet I wasn't his mate. He'd call me his non-mate mate a few times, but now he wasn't looking at me. I reached over and made him look at me.

"What is going through your head?"

He shook it, and when I forced his gaze still toward me, he finally said, "That was the closest I've gotten to losing control of my wolf side with you, Madilyn. I'm sorry."

"Why? I'll heal, and you did maintain control."

His control slipped for a flash, as a growled, "I don't want that spot to heal. I want it to stay there forever. Let the world know you are mine, and I am yours."

"I think everyone at Ivy Grace knows that." Chip chuckled.

"She screamed your name loud enough for everyone on the block to know that you two fucked each other's brains out, even without the supernatural hearing and smell."

"Fuck you, Bell." I laughed and threw a cup at him.

"Hell, if you need to go again. I mean..." He shrugged, and Maverick huffed a laugh, shaking his head.

Chip pulled into the little dark spot of the parking lot, and I felt an uneasy feeling go through me. I must have physically tensed because Maverick asked, "What's wrong?"

I looked around, studying the layout and where lines of sights were. "You're going into the Sun Electronics building?" There was a quick nod as I looked at the neighboring buildings. Maverick slid one of the earpieces into my ear and then into his own before I reached up, turned it on, snapped, he nodded, and I turned it off. "You want me on the Honeybar roof?"

"Yes. That will give you direct sight of the main road, and where we will be going in and out, but that doesn't tell me what is wrong?"

"Just a bad feeling, is all." I looked at all three of them. "Be safe in there, okay?"

"Always, Sweets." Chip smiled brightly.

"Your wish is our command." Bell said dramatically. Formal bow and all. There wasn't a force in this world that would have kept the eye roll from my face. I loved the boys, but damn if they weren't sassy as hell.

I climbed out of the van, Maverick right behind me. He pushed me against it, and kissed me until we were both gasping for breath. "See you in a few, Sweets."

I took off for the club's roof access, and when I was in position at the corner, I clicked the comm and said, "Eyes in the air."

My gaze trailed them, climbing the Sun Electronics' stone building and opening a door on the rooftop. I stared at that spot for a minute too long before I scanned the area.

An alarm down the street went off at the convenience store, and eight minutes later, three cops and two sheriffs rolled into the parking lot.

"Flashers down the street at the convenience store. Eta?" I asked, and it was Bell who answered, "I need a few more minutes. This isn't an easy pick."

Ignoring the gnawing feeling in me that something wasn't right, I focused on my one job. Watch for trouble. It was another thirteen minutes before I saw the boys slide out of the door and make their way down the side of the building. I stood, only to see a black SUV barrel through the alley and block us in. "We got company and are blocked."

"Madilyn." I turned to face a man dressed in solid black. I sidestepped so I would have both the man and my boys in sight.

"Who are you? What do you want?"

"It's time for you to learn some hard lessons." His head turned toward where the boys were.

"My life has been hard lessons since my brother was killed."

"This is a lesson not to get too close to others when you work for him." Then the man had me in a headlock, gun at my temple, forcing my gaze down to the fight that was occurring in the parking lot.

There were a hundred different ways to get out of that choke hold, but I couldn't move as I saw one man put a gun to Bell's head and as a shot rang out, Bell fell to the ground. My chest caved in as I watched the same happen to Chip.

"Ian…" I prayed, as I saw him freeze with a gun pointed at his face.

"*I'm assuming she can hear through the comm system?*" Maverick had blinked as he stared down the person standing before him. "*Answer me.*"

"*She can.*"

"*Good. Now. Only one of you will live through tonight. Tonight is a lesson in not getting too close to someone. You and your team were entirely too tight knit. Two of them are already dead.*"

I saw Maverick's head twitch toward where Bell and Chip lay in the parking lot. My gaze flicked to them quickly, and my stomach roiled.

"Let me go, Ian." I whispered, but there was a small shake of his head.

"*This will be your choice, Maverick. You or Sweets.*"

"Ian. Let me go. You have a family. Let me go."

His head turned toward me, a smile crossing his face, and then his words came through the earpiece as he bent down to kneel. "Easiest decision of my life. I love you, Madilyn Nikole Taylor. I will always be watching over you."

It was the last thing I heard before I saw the bullet exit the other side of his head and his body fall to the ground. Before I was able to scream, there was a needle in my neck as the last shreds of my heart crumbled to dust.

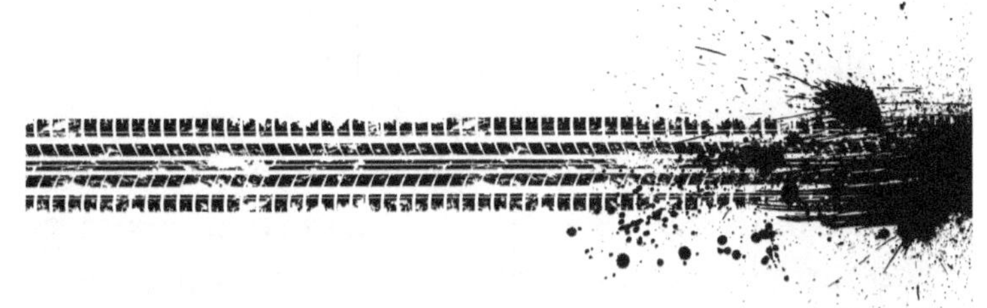

CHAPTER 45

JESSE

FOUR MONTHS LATER

"Carlos, I need a job."

"Jesse, you have done nothing but work for the last year. You need a break." His face was sad as he studied a file. Closing it, he huffed a puff of air and turned back toward me.

"I can't just sit in my condo."

"Well, you need a hobby, then." He looked at me and I had the distinct feeling he was trying to get a read on me as I paced the front of his office. "Take a vacation. Take that motorcycle of yours and go explore something beautiful. Go up the coast. Go down the coast. Go to the Sierras. Do something fun."

That was the problem. Nothing held my interest since Maddie was gone. I flopped into the chair in front of his desk and leaned my head back. "Nothing matters anymore. I need to keep my head busy. I'm going nuts since all our trails died out on Flinch."

He leaned back in his chair and there was an edge to his voice. "He's wrapped up with some of the lower demons, but I can't sort it out. I had some contacts try to tap his lines, his emails, and it's all high tech protected."

"The Fae? They are the only ones who have that kind of tech, right?"

"That's just it. Other than the meeting in Oregan, I can't connect Flinch to the Fae Primal. I've been looking." Carlos rubbed his face in frustration.

"So the Primal is nothing in this. Noted. What about proving the allegations of him being a Phrenic?"

"With the digging you've been doing the last few months, and what I've been doing? There is nothing. We don't have anyone alive who can testify for it."

He hesitated for a moment, but I raised my eyebrows at him to continue. "What have your eyes told you about Madilyn Taylor?"

I took a deep breath. "Not much since her team died. Mostly things that hurt on a personal level. Making me want to rip Flinch's dick off and feed it back to him until he chokes on it."

"He would have to live through the touch first."

"There are ways for me to do great damage to one's carcass before ending their life." I knew my eyes had become cold death, because Carlos' eyebrows went up to his hairline. "You know as well as I do, that he has himself warded. You and I also know that whoever it is protecting him is high on the food chain."

"And you couldn't get through them?"

"Ivy Grace has long been warded against Exorci. When I got back from Orange, I went straight there after hearing what Flinch was making her do. I tried, even though I knew I couldn't get in. I had to try again." His face crunched in confusion, and I pushed aside the sour feeling in my stomach. "He's been having her fuck his clients as part of her 'services' to pay off Sean's debt. She's basically an indentured prostitute, but at least the ones out on the street are physically getting paid for their work, in some aspects."

"They also at least have the illusion of a choice. Flinch is likely getting in her head and making her do it." He paled and shuddered. "I hate to think how she sleeps at night."

"Not well or much, from what I've been told. She wakes up with nightmares every forty-five minutes to an hour." I looked down at my phone. That information I had only gotten two days ago. "She won't take my calls, likely blocked my number. I tried to go see her this morning to see if she would let me help, and she didn't answer the intercom. I won't force my way in."

Carlos' eyes didn't leave mine as he took a deep breath to say something, but his phone rang. Reaching over, he picked it up, with a quipped, "Medina."

His face was a careful arrangement of neutrality. "Yes, Primal Rebekkah. ... No ma'am." His eyes flicked to his computer screen, and he said, "I really rather not. ... I realize that Primal, but I respectfully, and professionally, ask that you reconsider. There are other—"

He took another really long deep breath before saying, "Yes Primal." He closed his eyes as he hung up the phone, and when he reopened them, he was staring at the file on his desk.

"Please tell me that's a job." I muttered.

"It is, but I'm not giving it you, regardless of what the Primal ordered. I'll wait for Brandon, no... Nikolas to come back. I'm not giving it to you."

"Minstrel, I need the work. Just give me the fucking job."

Carlos looked at the phone, then back at the file. There was a fucking file on his desk. "I've already handled one file this year, and it gave us vital information that I'm sure the Agency will want to move on, if we can gain any more evidence. You know I can do this."

"Not this one." He whispered as Carlos picked up the folded pressboard and handed it to me. "Please don't kill me for showing you this."

"No promises." Because there were only a handful of people on this planet I would not exterminate.

"Primal Rebekkah has ordered the person in that file be exterminated for criminal acts against the Agency and the murder of innocents. Their Primal revoked

Agency protection months ago." His voice was brittle, short, and full of professionality that sat wrong.

I took the file from him, and when I opened it, saw the picture on the inside, my heart raced, and I felt my breaths coming short and fast. I threw it back on the table, and said, "Burn it... Burn that file. Make it disappear. It's a file, no record right. It's a fucking file. Burn. It."

"Exorci."

"Fuck you. I'm not killing the only person I have loved my entire life. I won't kill Madilyn Taylor. I will stop Brandon, Nickolas, or anyone else you send after her. She's off limits."

"I told you I wasn't giving you that file, but you pushed it." He said, and I stared at him. He wasn't wrong, and I felt my chest tighten and my vision blurred before I shook my head, clearing it.

Fuck, Maddie.

"It's been ordered by the Primals?" I whispered as I tried to hold any resemblance of myself together.

Carlos nodded. I stared at the folder. "Little Bird, what have you been doing?"

"You haven't come across her name in any of your search for answers on Jaysen Flinch?"

"No. Nothing. She's been avoiding my calls. There has been zero contact. Not so much as a text since she broke it off with me." I grabbed the file and looked at the photo. Her hair was shorter, and there were bags under her eyes.

"Drugs?" I whispered. Drugs I could get her off of, if I could get my hands on her. I could get her cleaned up.

"The one sample we got, which confirmed her involvement in that particular infraction, was negative. That was two months ago, so I don't know if she's started using since then or not. That picture is from two weeks ago." Carlos' voice had taken on the cold, distant tone it usually did when we discussed my targets.

Only, Maddie was not a target.

I flipped the page up and saw the long list of murders that they had laid at her feet. "Have these been confirmed as being committed by Maddie?"

I looked up at Carlos, who just nodded his head slowly. "She's arrogant. Leaves a calling card. An eagle on the back of a death tarot card."

I narrowed my eyes at him. There was so much to unpack in that. The first being, "Maddie doesn't believe in tarot, though. Never has." I blinked and looked at the photos in the file. When I looked at the pictures of the Death card, I shook my head. "They are from the same illustrated pack."

"Look at the eagle."

When I did, I blinked. They were all the same. Every single one was the same illustrated eagle in cream and black. It looked like a personal drawing. "She can't shift, though. She's non-shifting Bacri."

"Yet she uses the Bacri illustrated symbol."

"Why would she use an eagle, more importantly, one that was more of an unofficial Bacri symbol, if they pulled all protections?" I looked through each of the six iterations in the file, and noticed on the first two kills, there was a small scribble on the top left side, and my heart sank. She literally signed it 'MNT'.

"If you think the irony isn't lost that she is using the Exorci's symbol backed by the Bacri, think again." There were very few who knew that the Exorcis used this particular illustrated cream and black Death Tarot card as our dealings. "The only ones who would know—"

"Are the ones who know an Exorci intimately, or are in the high ranks of the Agency."

"Wait, the Bacri Primal pulled protections?" Carlos nodded. "That means she spilled blood." A nod again. "How?"

"She was on a job with her team. Killed fourteen that night. Single Shot each. Guess all that time you two spent at the range was worth it."

That had a flood of conflicting emotions go through me. Pride at how she neutralized her target with a single bullet, but then hurt that she was even in a position that had her taking fourteen lives. "Fourteen in a single night?"

"Primal Berk was impressed, but said he had no choice. He had already warned her that if she spilled innocent blood, that he would be forced to pull protections for her. He said, though, that when his soldier went to deliver the news, she took it with pride and grace. Said that she would do it again, if it would keep her family alive."

Her family. Meaning her team. I nodded. I understood that line of thought, because I would kill anyone who would try to hurt my little bird. Was trying to figure out a way to get close enough to Flinch to do just that for the hurt he has caused her.

"What if I get her out? If I can…" My voice cracked slightly, and my eyes flicked up to Minstrel Carlos.

"It's been ordered by the Primals. I can't authorize anything else."

"Fuck the Primals, Carlos. This is Maddie." I looked down at her picture, and it got a little fuzzy. "Little Bird."

He just stood there, letting me process. Letting me read over that list of Agency calling card deaths. I blinked when I saw a Thergui demon on the list I know. "Patrick Johnson?"

"He was deep undercover working with the Santa Cruz County Sheriff's department. They found him on East Cliff near the point. Throat slit and a dagger through the bottom of his jaw straight into his brain."

I lifted the sheet to look at the rest of the file and saw the photo of the dagger. The hilt had a small eagle on it. "Why is she using the Bacri symbols? She was last line. Didn't really give two shits about the Agency."

"The Bacri Primal revoked her protections. Maybe she was a little bitter about that. Maybe she's lashing out because she doesn't have anyone else to."

"I tried to fight the revocation, Jesse. Went to the Primes about it, but it didn't go. Said it was a Bacri problem. Wouldn't give me jurisdiction."

"If this is a Primal order, they might as well sign mine. If she dies, I'll pierce my own heart. I can't… kill her. You know this, Carlos."

"And I know you will kill anyone who tries." He leaned back in his chair, it squeaking under the movement. "I'm assuming you are going to become her shadow?"

I gave him a droll look. "Do I even have to confirm that?"

"Find a way to stop her, Jesse. For both your sakes. I'll only be able to push off the Primes for so long. While you are at it, see if you can get any more evidence of Flinch being a Phrenic. If we can prove it, and that he has hid or removed himself from the Agency's eyes, then that will seal his fate."

"Oh, his fate is sealed."

"I expected nothing less." A wide, satisfied grin spread on his face. "Good Luck, Jesse."

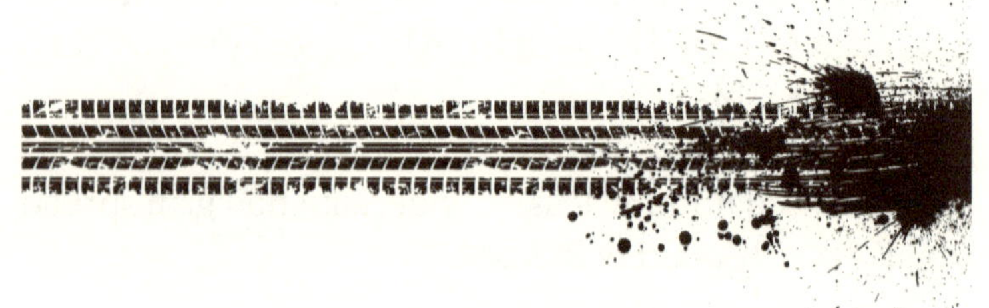

CHAPTER 46

MADDIE

For two weeks I've felt a shadow. Not my normal shadows who would come and go. I figured those were likely reporting to *him*.

No. This was a familiar shadow. That feeling would release when I got into Ivy Grace, but the moment I was outside the walls, I instantly felt it.

It didn't matter.

I was a wraith.

I was nothing.

I was death.

I was... nothing but a meat suit with dust inside.

It had been four and a half months since what was left of my heart blew away in the wind.

What was strange was that I had wanted *him* there. I wanted him to hold me as I cried for my other loved ones. Only, after waking up in a cold concrete room in the basement of Ivy Grace, I realized that if I was this ruined, I would do what I could to protect *him*.

Only once did I stop by his condo. I had refused to call *him*. I knew he would have answered. I had felt those shadows on me even then and reminded myself I needed to protect him. There was only one way to do that.

Keep him out of my life.

Keep him out of this mess Sean had dragged me into, even after his death.

Keep him safe.

If there was anything left in me, that was what I was going to do. I was going to keep him as far away as possible.

Only, that shadow... it felt like *him*.

I ripped open the black envelope, read the instructions, and strode out the door. No one made eye contact with me anymore. It wasn't like before, where everyone greeted me. No one wanted to talk to me. Ever. Shortly after that night, everything changed around here. Word had gotten out. Don't get attached to anyone, because they will die. Don't get attached to Sweets. Sweets let her whole team die so she could live. I was the plaguebringer to all.

I reached Flinch's office, and I felt that all too familiar pounding in my head. Opening the door, Flinch leaned against the front of his desk, feet kicked out, ankles crossed. There was a hitch of an eyebrow as his gaze traveled up and down my body again.

Two other men were sitting in the oversized chairs on either side of him, cocks in their hands, pleasuring themselves. All likely at Flinch's command. I reached behind me, making sure the door was shut. Just as I flipped the lock shut, those all too familiar claws entered my head, and I was forced to remove my clothing.

Once naked, I took the steps toward Flinch and saw the two knives on the table beside him. The pressure in my head increased, and I rolled my head slightly, but then the knives were in my hands.

'Twirl for me and slit their throats.'

My body moved, and as hot blood sprayed across us both, he muttered, "Atta girl."

I stood there, blood pouring down the front of the bodies in the chair, cocks still in their hands, staring at Flinch. He gave a simple nod of his head, and I dropped the knives and released him from his pants. The only thought I could think of was, at least *he* didn't have to see me like this.

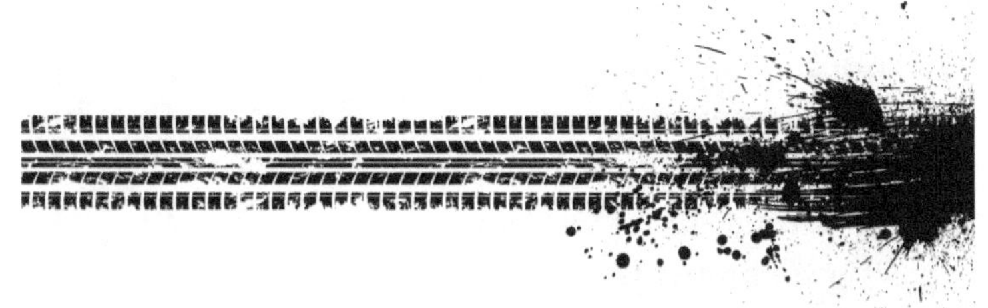

CHAPTER 47

JESSE

I had learned through my contacts that she wasn't working at the Edging anymore, and that after her team died, she didn't have the muster or pizzaz they required their dancers to have to be able to work the pole anymore.

I had been following her for weeks. There were times I was sure she knew it was me, but unless she was going to engage me, I wasn't going to disrupt her life. Well, if you could call this a life. She was spending eighteen hours a day at Ivy Grace.

It was as if Flinch knew I was following her, and had her working in the club only. She would leave Ivy Grace, only to go home, sleep on and off for a few hours, before getting up and heading back.

My little bird's building manager had come out and checked on what I was doing on the grounds one afternoon, but when I explained everything, he just nodded, and swore secrecy. The wad of cash I gave him helped in making sure he didn't talk. As we talked, he had mentioned that she knew someone was paying the rent, but he hadn't told her who.

Tonight, felt different. When she left the house, she was already dressed in head to toe black, and fuck if it didn't make my cock hard. Skin tight black jeans, black boots, and black long sleeve shirt. She looked in my direction for a hot second, but just shook her head and got in her car.

I pulled up to Ivy Grace five minutes behind her, and when I saw her leave thirty after that, I was thankful for Brandon allowing me to use his M5 while he was on assignment somewhere in Mexico. The bike wouldn't have been able to follow her inconspicuously, and this was more comfortable for sitting and watching a building for hours on end. Let's face it, the heated seats and heater alone helped.

Maddie bounced across the parking lot and got into the driver's seat of a small Civic hatchback with blacked-out windows. I bent over the seat as the headlights passed over the M5 on the way out of the parking lot and then started the car.

Wherever she was going, I knew it wouldn't be good. She hadn't left the damn club in weeks, and now she was randomly going out? I followed Maddie as she got on 280, then up 85 and into downtown Mountain View. She parked near an alley and was out of the car quicker than I could blink.

I parked around the corner and took off in the direction she had gone. When I got to the alley, there was a metal door just slightly open, where shouts filtered through.

Stepping through the passage, I felt death's presence and sighed as I found two men at my feet, throats cut. One was already dead, the other taking his last breath before death ushered him away.

"Flinch required the information a week ago." Little bird's voice carried down a long hall and I swallowed, trying to steal myself. If she did this, I would end it. I would end it for both of us. If I completed that execution order I'd been sitting on for weeks now, then I would take one of her daggers, and plunge it through my own heart.

"We don't have it. We need more time." One man begged. I toed up to the corner and what I saw almost brought me to my knees. My little bird was splattered in blood from the men who were behind me, and she had another on the ground with a knee to his dick and a knife to his throat.

"Flinch said he needed that info a week ago. Your time is up."

My heart broke. Nothing within me could reconcile the woman I had loved with what I saw before me.

This was Nikki, not my little bird. Nikki needed to be stopped. I stared at her for a long moment, as she continued to discuss things with the man at her mercy.

Stop her.

No. There had to be another way. I couldn't kill the only woman I have ever loved.

I didn't know when it happened, but my gloves were off, and my hand was reaching for her. "I'm sorry, Little Bird."

Only when my hand was inches from her, I froze. I didn't want to do this. I pulled my hand back half an inch when she turned and growled, "What did you just call me?"

"Little Bird, please stop this." I begged her. It was the least I could do. I would follow her into death. I couldn't do this anymore. This would be the death that would kill me.

"Jes—" She stopped and chuckled. "Of course they would send you. You *are* the Agency's best, after all. You've been following me for weeks, and now you step up?"

I couldn't move. I wanted to reach out and touch her, feel the soft caress of her under my skin, to hold her and truly kiss her as she slipped from this life. Then, I would plunge the dagger currently at the man's throat into my own heart.

"Just do it then. It's what you are good at, right? Destroying families. Killing those you *love*?"

"I didn't know it was Sean until he was gone, and I removed the ski mask." My voice was thick, and I knew that there were tears in my eyes as she studied me through the cold look in hers. "When I saw your name on the execution order, I refused."

"Yet, here you stand, reaching out to me. Without your gloves, Jesse." She smirked, and the next thing I knew, she had me against the wall, with a dagger to my throat. I leaned against the wall and stretched my neck out. "Do it. That way, I don't have to kill you. I love you, Maddie. I always have. Since you grabbed me by the jacket and demanded I meet you for lunch that night. I will always love you."

Something flickered behind those hazel eyes of hers, making them brighter than they had been. It was just a spark. A small shake of the head, and the dagger lowered a fraction of an inch, and her arms relaxed slightly. Pulling my arms up and disarming her, I held her by the shoulder against the wall, and the knife against her heart.

"Just do it Jesse." The defeated tone of her voice wrapped around my heart and squeezed. When my fingers twitched at her shoulder she said, "The best Exorci in the America's can't kill a simple broken girl?"

"Maddie... Little Bird."

"You have your orders. I have mine. He's always controlling me. I can't stop it. You can. You can stop *me*." She blinked again, and the muscles in her body relaxed slightly, her vision cleared, and her face took on more of the way I had remembered her.

I didn't even register that she had both hands around my wrist at her shoulder until she pulled my hand toward her face. I twisted my hand away from her skin, but she surprised me by quickly flattening her hand against mine and pressing it against her cheek.

Tears fell as I felt the smoothness of her skin for the first time. I ran my thumb along that apple cheekbone as I looked into her eyes. "I love you, Jesse."

"I love you, Little Bird."

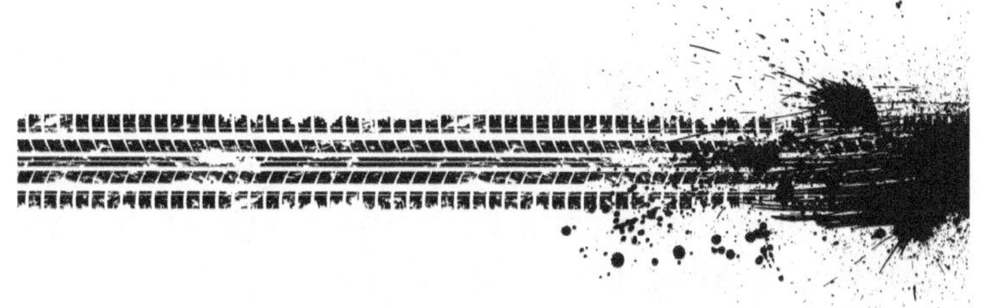

CHAPTER 48

MADDIE

His forehead came down to meet mine, and I kissed him quickly on the lips, knowing it would quicken my death, but needing the softness of his lips on mine, just this once. A real kiss from the man that would always carry my heart.

Everywhere our skin touched, mine tingled to life. The feel of his hand on my cheek was exquisite as I waited for the pain, for my breath to fade from my lungs, for death. Only, nothing came.

Confusion crossed his face. "Little Bird?"

"Why am I not dead yet?"

His eyes met mine, and I couldn't stop looking at him. My heart sang at his touch. His thumb continued to run along my cheekbone, and I reached out to kiss him again. A spark ignited between my legs, and I moaned into him.

Jesse grabbed both of my hands and pinned them above my head, and put a hand to my throat. He put just enough pressure to make me lengthen my neck and push my chest toward him. Gods, this man knew exactly what he was doing. How could this man, only this man, bring me to the brink of an orgasm so easily? It didn't make any sense.

"Why can I touch you?"

"I don't know."

"Why can I touch you, and you not die, Madilyn Taylor?" To anyone else, his voice would have been fueled by anger, but I heard it for what it was. A fire fueled lust that I knew had him hard as a rock.

My skin prickled where he touched me, but it made every nerve in my body hum and warm. If this was how I was going to die? Jesse touching me, and me feeling the most alive that I ever had, it was worth it.

He murmured against my lips and said, "I can touch you." He ran his thumb along the length of that vein in my neck, feeling my rapid heartbeat. He placed soft gentle kisses along my jaw and said, "I have never craved being able to touch someone more than I have with you. To know what it feels like to truly fuck you. Those mewling sounds you made before? I need to know what they sound like unhindered."

I melted to his touch. "So do it Jesse. If fucking you like we've both needed for so long is how I go, I will accept my fate."

A dry chuckle floated across my skin. "If you haven't died to my touch yet, Little Bird you aren't going to." He kissed my neck, "Now that I can do this..." He ran his tongue up the side of my neck, causing my entire body to both ignite and shiver within the same second. His hold on me was the only reason I didn't fall.

"Now that I have you, I'm never letting you go, Madilyn Taylor."

"I don't want you to."

"Ah, aren't you adorable?" He chuckled and smiled at me. It was the heat in his eyes, though, that had my nipples hard and my pussy pulsing in anticipation. "Thinking you have a choice in the matter."

His free hand ran down and cupped me, letting one finger press against that bundle of nerves. A light, needy moan escaped my lips as he said, "You are mine. No one else will ever touch you again. I let you go once, and it nearly killed me. I won't be able to again. Not that I can finally do this." His hand slid between my pants and my skin and dipped two fingers into me.

"And if they do?" The words came out breathless. I knew the answer, but I wanted to hear him say it. I could see the answer clearly in his eyes as he flicked my clit and had me moaning.

"My gloves come off, and my hands go around their throat." He pressed hard against that bundle of nerves and I rolled my hips against him, feeling my stomach tighten, my body now craving and screaming for that release.

My knees gave out beneath me and if it hadn't been for his leg between mine, and the grip he still had on my hands above my head, I would have fully collapsed on the floor.

There was a sound behind him, and Jesse just growled, "If you don't want to die, I would suggest you leave this room and forget what you have seen and heard."

His head turned to look over his shoulder, and I swear he made eye contact with the asshole as he nodded and ran from the room. When Jesse turned back to me, I moaned when his fingers truly moved against me.

My mind was fuzzy and clear all at the same time. I hadn't felt this way in Gods; it had been months and months. Moving against him, I groaned, "Fuck, Jesse."

CHAPTER 49

JESSE

The feel of her skin against mine was more exhilarating than I ever thought possible. "Cum for me, little bird. Scream my name." I commanded her and plunged my fingers deep within her. Her walls clamped down, and I fingered her through her orgasm.

"Jesse!" Maddie screamed, then she was panting, and leaning against me.

"That's my good girl." Her walls spasmed at my words and a crooked smile came upon my lips. I pulled my hand from her, and maintaining eye contact, licked my fingers clean.

Fuck, she tasted like heaven. Yeah, this woman was never leaving my side again. I had allowed her to be with Maverick so she could be touched and loved the way she needed. Now that I could give her that, there was not a force on this planet that would keep her from me.

I released her hands above her head, and they wrapped around my shoulders, as she leaned forward and rested her forehead against mine.

"Jesse, why can you touch me now?" Her voice was a whispered prayer, and she kissed my neck and moved up to my jaw. I turned to capture her lips, a hand cradling her cheek, kissing her softly. She set my entire body alight. Every connection of where our bodies met skin to skin felt like a song to my soul.

"I don't know, little bird." I pulled back and looked around the room. "We need to get out of here, though."

She nodded, and froze, blinked, and then asked, "Where do we go? I can't go back to Ivy Grace." Her eyes widened. "Flinch! He's a Phrenic. He needs stopped."

"I know. Minstrel Medina and I have been working on it for months to get proof and take him down. We haven't..." I looked around the brick room. "Not here. Come on."

I took her hand, threading her fingers through mine, and pulled her out, checking to make sure there wasn't anyone outside, and noted one lone camera sitting at the end of the alley. When we got to the car, I sent a text to Carlos and told him to wipe the camera footage. He confirmed and asked for a report in the morning.

Looking at Maddie sitting in the passenger seat, I ran through a million scenarios. "All identification of yours is at the club, right?"

"Yes. I never bring anything with me on a job... We never brought anything other than what we needed." The shadows that crossed her face had me reaching out and rubbing her cheek.

"You cared for him. It's okay. I don't hold that against you. He loved you, and he took care of you when I couldn't."

"It was Bell and Chip too. They were..." A tear fell down her cheek, and I reached over, kissing it away. I nodded. They were important. It was what had broken her completely and allowed Flinch to control her so easily. A broken mind was so much easier to manipulate.

"You aren't going home, little bird. When you don't show up back at the club and he realizes you didn't finish whatever it was that you were supposed to do in there, which we will discuss by the way,—"

"Jesse, you are rambling." Her smile was one that I had missed, but then she shook her head. "I can't believe I'm sitting in a car with you right now. I'm still so mad at you, but..." She looked at me and her mouth opened, closed, and I smiled at her.

"We have time to talk, Maddie." I pulled my phone out and texted Carlos again.

I'm taking a trip north with a passenger. Tell Exorci that I'll return his car eventually.

I'll advise destination to expect you at sunup.

"I can't take you back to my place for long. You need to shower and change, though. You'll be more comfortable."

"I'm fine."

"Maddie, we are going on a road trip. I'm not going to let you sit in those clothes for hours." I pushed the button to start the car, and pulled out onto the main road.

"I'm fine."

"If I hear you say that one more time, I'm going to get very pissed and you will find my temperament hasn't gotten any better over the last year."

She actually laughed at that. It was harsh, like she hadn't laughed in months, and she reached over to take my hand, squeezing it tight. "You think my temperament has gotten better? I've been under the control of a raping sadist almost since Sean died. I've been forced to do things I would never do under normal circumstances..." Her voice hitched, and the rage and fury on her face mixed with the tears that streamed down her face as I pulled onto 85 broke my heart.

"I'm going to kill him." Gripping the steering wheel so tight, I was surprised it didn't crack under the pressure.

"If you can get close enough without him taking control." She barked through her exasperation. "Jesse, he is strong. I tried to fight him. Really, I did. Then, after my boys died, it was just easier... I didn't care anymore."

I took a deep breath to calm myself down. My focus landed briefly on the tattoo on my hand Maddie was holding before popping back up to the road. I had gotten it a couple months ago because, while I couldn't be with Maddie, she was always going to be with me. "I wonder..." I muttered.

"What?"

I lifted my hand so she could see it through what little light came through the windshield.

"When did you get that? How? You can't..."

"There is an artist in the agency who is technically human, but not."

"An Immortal?"

"No. He's... different. He's under special protection with the Agency and has abilities that are unlike anyone else registered."

Her fingers traced the wings across my knuckles and down toward my wrists before freezing in the body of the eagle. She turned the cab light on, and I shook my head. My skin was a blaze of fire where she traced her name weaved into the feather design of the tattoo. It was a direct link to the blood flow to my cock, making me harden for her even more than I already was.

"Fuck. I can't wait to see this in proper light." She clicked off the light, leaned back, and turned her head toward me. "When?"

"Few months ago."

"Before or after they..."

"About a month before." I turned onto 280 heading toward my condo. I actually felt bad for Philip. It took him a few days to recover from inking me.

"I don't remember seeing it when you came to see me at The Edging."

"Well, we were otherwise occupied in not ripping each other to pieces at the time." I said with a chuckle and brought her hand up to my lips. I pressed a long kiss to the back of her hand and held it tight.

She just stared at me the rest of the way home, and when we got there, she got out of the car and looked up at the building. "I came here about a week after Maverick, Bell, and Chip died."

My head whipped around to her.

"I stood right there." She pointed next to the gate, took a deep breath, before continuing. "My fingers hovered over the keypad for a long time. I knew the code would work. I knew that you wouldn't have locked me out. This was a safe place for me to go, I knew that. Only I couldn't do it. I turned and walked away." She turned, and I wrapped my arm around her waist, pulling her toward the condo building. "I found out later you weren't home, anyway. Out on assignment."

When we stepped into the elevator, she turned into me, and wrapped her arms around me. It was habit to avoid the touch of her skin, but when she kissed my neck, I groaned. "I haven't changed it. That is your code. You will always have access to my place, little bird."

Nodding when the elevator stopped, I pulled her along the hall. She stopped short of the door, and when I looked back at her, she looked a little lost. My hand reached out toward her, and she paled. The blood splatters on her face were stark against her skin. "What is it, Maddie?"

"What is going to happen now?"

"That is a very loaded question, little bird. You should be a little more specific, but first, you are going to come inside, take a shower, get some clean clothes on, and then we are going on a road trip to keep you safe, while we figure out a lot of those answers."

"What is going to happen to you?" She slowly stepped into my apartment and didn't stop on the way to the shower. After turning the water on for her while she stripped herself of the blood covered clothes, she met my gaze. She was skinnier than she had been with me, but there was muscle definition, which helped. I knew she hadn't been eating right. My eyes and ears had told me that. "You were under orders from the Agency to kill me. What are they going to do to you for failing?"

Reaching over and running my thumb across her cheek. "Get in the shower."

"Yes, sir." Her voice was way too heated as she looked me up and down.

"Oh, Little Bird. Be careful with the way you say those words." She turned to step into the shower, but looked over her shoulder and, with a smirk, met my eyes. "Yes, sir."

I slapped her ass. The yip she gave and the look over her shoulder was enough that I had to bite my knuckles.

I leaned on the counter, watching her lean her head back into the water. Maddie was in my shower. I could touch her. There was no way that the amount of my toxin that had penetrated her skin shouldn't have killed her. Yet, there she was, now running a washcloth over her body... in my shower... after I had held her, kissed her, fingered her to release, and... fuck, I needed her.

"Jesse."

"Yeah? I'm still here."

She opened the shower door and peeked her head out. Those golden eyes lighting mischievously. "Why aren't you in the shower with me?"

I blinked and stripped. There was no way I wasn't taking that invitation.

CHAPTER 50

JESSE

I stepped into the water, and this time it was my turn to yip. "Good Gods, Madilyn. How hot do you need it?"

"Enough to melt the stress out of my shoulders." She pressed her chest against mine, and I sighed contently. "But this I think does more than that hot water could."

I wrapped my arms around her and rested my cheek on the top of her head. "Can I ask you something?" A contented hum came from her. "What does it feel like to you when our skin touches?"

"It tingles. Every fiber of me is acutely aware of where our skin connects." Her hand moved between us, and when she gripped my cock, I gasped at the feel of her hands on me. "I feel the silkiness of you against my palm." Her thumb rubbed across the head of me before her gaze met mine, and there was a bold fierceness in those eyes. "But there is a current that runs up my arm and hits in my nipples and clit."

She pumped the head of me a couple times before smiling and dropping to her knees. I moved the shower head, and leaned back as she wrapped those beautiful plump lips around me, and in a couple quick bobs of her head, swallowed me whole. Maddie's head moved in quick synced movements between sucking and swallowing, and I couldn't help but move my hips. This woman.

I felt my balls tighten, and I pulled back. My cock released with a pop and the moan from her almost had me releasing right there. I fought it with everything I had.

"I need to be buried deep in you when I cum, Little Bird." I kissed her, and when she opened for me, I felt the fire that was brewing between us. Lifting her against the wall, I lined myself up, and slowly lowered her onto me.

"Oh, fuck." I breathed when I pulled back. "Madilyn."

"Jesse." My eyes met hers, and they were full of a raging inferno, one that I had never seen in her before. My cocked twitched at the sound of my name on her lips, and I felt her walls tighten against me. "This. This is what I need."

Slowly, I pulled from her and pressed back into the only woman that would control every part of my being. "I will forever love you, Little Bird. My soul is yours. Always has been, always will be."

Her hips rolled against mine when I was deep within her, and she whimpered. The glazed look in her eyes was everything, as she muttered, "Mine. You are mine. I am yours."

I repeated the slow and steady retreat and refilling of her. She was my everything. I could never go back to what I was before. Not what *we* were before. This would be new. This would be... Fuck. Her eyes heated as I felt her stomach pull in, and her breathing increase.

"That's it, Maddie. Let go, my good girl."

"Jesse... I..." Her breathing quickened, and I felt her walls grip me tight. Slowly I retreated from her, and thrust hard into her and she whimpered, again, and again I repeated it, that tingling feeling at the base of my spine rising.

Then I was releasing with her as she gripped my cock and milked it for everything I had within me. The feeling of releasing into her was euphoric. Nothing but the two of us. Skin to skin. No equipment. No double checking where every inch of my body was. No worries. Just *her*.

"Good girl." I kissed her neck and up to her jaw as she panted against me.

She had finished getting cleaned up while I stepped out to make her something to eat and packed a few things. When she walked out of the bathroom wrapped in a towel, I couldn't help but stare at her. "It feels like I'm in a dream. You standing there, in my bedroom, wrapped in a towel."

The corner of her lip lifted, but she said, "Can I borrow some sweats?"

"I still have some of your clothes from when we were together before." Nodding my head to the corner of the bed where I laid out some of her clothes for her.

She took a few steps to the edge of the bed and fingered the undergarments, leggings and t-shirt sitting there. A small sniff and her head raised to look at me, tears slowly rolling down her cheeks. "You kept it?"

"Of course. I told you that this would always be a safe place for you, little bird." She nodded. "Why does that bother you?"

"I guess I just expected that when you let me be with Maver... with Ian, that you were fully walking away."

I grit my teeth, took a few deep breaths, and said, "I told you I would always take care of you. I did that as best I could even when we weren't together. He knew that as well. Thanked me for it even."

She blinked back a few tears, and I gave her a sad smile as I stepped up and wrapped an arm around her. "We have a lot to work through, little bird, but I'm not going anywhere." I kissed her temple and nodded to the plate of cheese and lunch meat on the dresser. "Eat while you get dressed. We need to get on the road before they sort out where you might have run off to."

CHAPTER 51

MADDIE

I woke up to the car slowing and light shining through some tall redwood trees. Jesse lowered the window and pushed a button on the keypad. A moment later, a woman with long brown hair and brown skin popped up on the screen.

"Come up to the office, Jesse."

He nodded and put the window up as the iron gate rolled back. Squeezing my hand, I couldn't help but smile as I looked at it. For over an hour, I had traced the tattoo when we got in the car. We had stopped in

Ukiah to get a few things for me, but otherwise, Jesse had driven non-stop to wherever we were. When we hit the redwoods, I had nodded off.

It couldn't have been more than a mile up the gated gravel road when I saw a newly constructed building with a very pregnant woman standing out front with her hands on her hips. A tall blond-haired man stood next to her, as well as an older black- and grey-haired woman. No sooner were we parked and Jesse was out of the car, was the older woman wrapping her arms around her. Jesse froze, but there was a smile on his face as I rounded the corner.

"Ms. Rose. Please. I don't want to kill you. Please give me a little warning."

"Jesse Westbrook, I will do what I wish, when I wish." The woman said, stepping back.

"I am just asking for some warning. Minstrel Carlos and this woman over here would likely kill me for killing you. Then Kolton would kill me for upsetting his pregnant bonded!"

"Damn straight. Ain't no one gonna hurt Ms. Rose on our watch!" He said, smiling brightly at Jesse.

Jesse's hand reached out toward me, and I took it, lacing my fingers through his. They all noted it, and while the pregnant woman and the male's eyes widened, it was the older woman, Ms. Rose, who smiled and said, "See, I told you, you wouldn't kill her."

Jesse rubbed his face and sighed. "You and your splitting of words."

"Jesse... how? How are you touching her and she's not be dead?" The pregnant woman asked.

"We don't know. By the way, Maddie, this is Mrs. Rose Porter. Everyone calls her Ms. Rose. Well, except for Jade."

My eyes bugged out of my head. Everyone knew who Rose Porter was. I stretched my hand out to shake hers, and said, "Nice to meet you, Ms. Rose."

"The one who is almost ready to pop with a little Astral of their own is the impeccable Astral Primal Alpha Jade Romero Webster. The overprotective human next to her is her bonded, Kolton Webster."

I shook both of their hands, but Astral Primal Alpha Jade said, "Please, just call me Jade. I keep begging Carlos to shorten the title, and when I married this one, I wanted to drop ninety percent of my name, but he refuses."

"Carlos? As in Minstrel Medina?" I looked at Jesse, who nodded.

"He is her cousin."

"That explains why you contacted him last night and why we are here." It was then I realized I didn't really know where *here* was. "Which is where exactly?"

Jade socked Jesse in the arm. "You brought your girl here and didn't even tell her where in the fuck she was going?"

He ran his hand through his hair and smirked at her. "Yeah, I guess I did. It was the only place I could think of that would get her away, and could protect her if they found out she was here."

Jade sighed and lifted a corner of her mouth before saying, "Well, let's go inside. I'll get that overprotective shit on video and we can talk about *why* you brought her here, and what exactly you expect us to do."

"Kolton, I'm sorry. I may have brought a shit show down on your home, but—" Jesse tried to say.

"Just as long as we can keep Jade out of the firing line, let's see what we can do to help." Kolton told him, putting a hand on his shoulder.

"I'm growing a little human. Not crippled. I can still whoop your ass, Mr. Webster."

"Oh, okay, Darlin'." Kolton muttered just loud enough for her to hear, and her cheeks flushed.

We headed inside, and when we sat down, Ms. Rose handed me a cup of tea. "You look exhausted. This will help."

Jade, Kolton and Jesse shook their heads and smiled. I met Jesse's gaze. "It's fine. It's like an energy drink on crack without the crack. You will crash, but hopefully by then we will have a game plan, and a comfortable bed for you to sleep in."

"I've already prepared one of the guest quarters for you. It's yours as long as you need." Ms. Rose said.

"Glad you made the drive safe, Jesse." Carlos' voice came through the speakers, and I leaned against Jesse's shoulder. He wrapped an arm around me and pulled me tight against him. "How are you doing, *mija*?"

Jade rolled her eyes. "I'm fine. This isn't about me today."

"What I can't check on you?"

"*Cabron*." She rolled her eyes again, in dramatic fashion and then looked at Jesse. "This is really Jesse's go."

When the camera turned toward him, it showed me leaning on my shoulder. "Exorci?"

"Don't Exorci me." He pulled me closer and Minstrel Medina's eyes widened. "I told you when you handed me that file, I wouldn't kill her."

Minstrel Medina's eyes blinked in shock and I knew he was focused on where Jesse's arm rested on my bare elbow and was running a thumb over it. I could also feel everyone's eyes on me, and then what he said clicked.

"A file. They sent you a file. Orders didn't come through the app?" My voice was low, but there was no doubt everyone in the room heard me.

"A file, Jesse Westbrook. You were given a file on the woman in your arms, and yet she is sitting in this office. You are able to touch her, and she doesn't die." Jade's face had gone pure Astral.

"I did. Astral or not, I hoped my friend would be able to help me, considering she has been under the control of a Phrenic since the time that Phrenic had called in a contract. A contract she had no say in, but her brother signed her over, anyway. A contract bound by Agency law, and no way out except for the issuing beings' death."

Jade studied Jesse closely, then looked at the monitor, where Carlos nodded. "Jesse is right. We have been able to confirm that Flinch is indeed a Phrenic. We have been working for months to find proof other than what was provided to Jesse in another assignment."

I blinked. "You need proof?"

"The problem is because he is apparently pretty powerful, that there are no testimonies available to give to the Primes to prove it."

"Not to mention that even if the Primes ordered his extermination, no Exorci can enter Ivy Grace, nor would they walk out of there either alive or be able to get to him. If he's as powerful as it would seem..." Jade's eyes went back to Jesse.

I laughed. "You cannot be serious right now. Of course he is. Have you ever been in his presence? Have you ever been forced to get on your knees and pleasure him, and whoever else is in the room, because he *wills* it?"

Jesse's hold on me tightened. I looked up at him and rested my hand on his cheek. "Later, we can discuss all that later."

He rested his forehead on mine, and whispered in a voice hard enough, I was sure it could have cut glass, "Why didn't you tell me?"

"Later, Jesse." Then I kissed him quickly before turning toward Astral Jade. Gods, I could kiss Jesse. "Astral, you have to understand what that is like. Half the time you walk out of that room, you're feeling the aftereffects, but not fully remembering what may or may not have happened."

"Madilyn." I turned toward Minstrel Medina and raised my eyebrows at him in question. "Would you be willing to report to the Primes on this? Here and now?"

I opened my mouth, but Jesse said, "Only if they rescind the extermination order and allow us to go away and lie low for a while."

He picked up his phone and after a couple of minutes of typing, he said, "Jade, adjust the camera so not everyone is showing. I want to keep this limited if possible. Just you and Jesse should be shown to the Primes. "*Comprende?*"

She nodded and adjusted it so only she was showing.

"Minstrel Carlos Medina. Do you have an update on the extermination of Madilyn Taylor?" The blonde said.

"I have a formal request from the Exorci who has been handling the matter." Minstrel Medina said.

Jesse's hand gripped my hip, and he kissed the top of my head before bending down and whispering in my ear. "I love you, Little Bird. I will not let anything happen to you. Regardless of what the Primes say today."

"I love you too, Jesse." I looked at him and his golden eyes swam with fear and determination. "But I've earned that extermination, regardless of the circumstances."

"Exorci Jesse Westbrook." A male voice said, and Jesse stood and went to sit next to Astral Jade. "Please report your findings."

"Primal Primes. As you know, the order is to a woman who I have a previous relationship with, and I refused the assignment."

"We are aware." The woman stated. "We are also aware you would kill anyone else who tried to complete the assignment."

"That is true. I stand by all of that. However, there is new evidence that has come to light, that I wish to share with you and I have some accompanying demands." I was in awe at how calm his voice sounded. His eyes flicked to mine, and then back to the screen.

"Madilyn Taylor has been under the influence of a Phrenic who has been able to hide himself from the Agency. We know he is being protected by someone high in the hierarchy of the Agency, however, we have as of yet, have been unable to determine who that person is."

"Who is this Phrenic?" The woman said.

"Jaysen Flinch." There was silence and the faint clicking of keys. "He will be shown in the Agency records as human. He runs a creature club called Ivy Grace in Santa Clara. Exorci Brandon and I were called to a meeting in Oregon to dispatch someone on behalf of the Fae Primal, and while there, he met with Jaysen Flinch. I do not know what the connection is. However, Brandon and I both felt the power rippling off of Flinch."

"Are you sure it wasn't just residue from the Fae Primal?"

"We are sure." Silence, then Jesse continued. "While handling a special assignment, I came into the possession of a laptop that showed ancestral lineage from Jaysen Flinch, one hundred percent pure, back to the creation of Ashstrike Sanctorum."

My eyes widened. Being so completely undiluted would explain why he was so powerful. Jesse's eyes met mine. He knew I had put it together, too.

"Minstrel Medina and I have been working on trying to gather enough evidence to bring this matter to you. The only evidence I can offer you is the evidence of someone who has been under that influence and will testify."

"Then bring this person forward." The male said.

Jesse let an evil smile cross his face. One I had only seen when he was on the verge of taking his gloves off. "Maddie?"

My heart was pounding, but Jade got up and let me have the seat next to Jesse. When I sat down, the faces of the three Primal Primes all met mine.

"Exorci Westbrook, you are under orders of the Ashstrike Sanctorum to exterminate the Bacri next to you. You have reviewed the file—" The male said, but a red-haired female raised her hand and said in a singsong voice that I hadn't heard yet, "I am Primal Rebekkah. Please explain why the Bacri lives?"

Jesse took a large deep breath and said, "I have been following her since I received the file."

Three and a half weeks. It had been him that had been following me. I knew it felt familiar. I reached over and put my hand on his leg and squeezed in assurance.

"During that time, she had been completely holed up in Ivy Grace except for a few hours of sleep, which she didn't get much of, by the way." His hand rested on mine under the table. "Last night was the first night she left. I followed her to Mountain View, where I walked in on her following her orders while under Phrenic Flinch's control."

I gripped him tight and tried to control my breathing. He had told me as we headed out of the city, but it still hurt to know he would have done all of it.

"When I saw what was happening, I reached out to do it, with the full intention of then ending my own life." He turned to face me, and the love in his eyes was all I would accept there. "She saw me. We had a bit of a scuffle, and when I touched her, she didn't die."

"What do you mean, she didn't die? No one survives your touch, Exorci Westbrook." The female that I had heard earlier said.

Jesse turned to the camera and said, "I touched her, and she didn't die."

The confusion on their faces was one that I cherished. So much so, I said, "You don't believe him?"

Their eyes narrowed and so I reached over, placed my hand on his cheek, making him face me. The mischief in his eyes was delightful, as he leaned down and kissed me with so much passion that it stole the breath from me. His essence was so deep within me I almost didn't care we had an audience, and pulled him closer. He met it, wrapping his hand around my throat and squeezing just that bit that had me moaning into him.

A chuckle from Kolton brought me back to my senses, and I was pulling back from Jesse, but not far. His hand was still there, and I kissed him quickly before turning back to the computer monitor. Jesse's forehead leaned on my temple, breathing ragged, as his hand still held my throat. "As you can see, his touch has no effect on me... well, in the way you want it to."

"She is the only one that I can touch and not kill. The fact she also holds my heart is a separate matter. I would like to know how she can, though. When..." He paused and looked at me, then back at the screen.

"When I fought Sean Taylor in the witch's cabin in Grand Junction... it took a minute for my touch to affect him."

I had noted that when I watched the video. Gods knew I had every detail of that video in my head. Maverick hated how often I had watched it. "It did."

"Excuse me, Ms. Taylor?" The male Primal said. I believed that was Primal Kobe, but wasn't sure.

"Jaysen Flinch gave me a thumb drive with a video of Sean killing a witch in Grand Junction, and the subsequent interaction with Sean and Jesse. I had paused the video numerous times, trying to sort out how Jesse's touch had taken so long to kill Sean. I had counted it a hundred times. It took twenty seconds of touch, and then almost a full minute for Sean to die."

I felt Jesse's eyes on me, but he said, "That sounds about right."

"The fact that Exorci Westbrook's touch does not kill you, Ms. Taylor, does not excuse your actions, which called for your extermination."

I took a deep breath, because they were right. "True. It was my hand that killed those people."

"Maddie..." Jesse said, but I cut him off with a hand to his cheek.

"Regardless of the fact that Flinch's effects were controlling me. Well, toward the end at least."

"Can you explain that, Ms. Taylor?"

I leaned against Jesse as he pressed a kiss to my temple and sat back, letting me do this.

"After Sean died, Flinch approached me and told me that I was under contract, and there was nothing

I could do about it under Agency Law. Eventually, I forwarded it to Primal Beck, who looked into it, and again, said it was ironclad, and gave me the warning that should I spill blood, that I would no longer have Agency protections. At the time, I had only served drinks, done some dancing, and was being a lookout for a team of shifters who were also under contract with Flinch.

"One night, they needed help inside, so I ran the mission with Maverick, Bell, and Chip. They had become my family, and I knew they would do anything to protect me, and I them. That was tested that night. We were caught, ambushed, whatever term you want to use, it's moot." I sat up straight in the chair and rested my elbows on the desk in front of me, staring straight at the camera. I wasn't going to sugarcoat this, and I had never apologized for protecting them, and I wasn't going to start now. "I killed fourteen that night. I'll never forget it. But I'd do it again to protect my boys. Maverick was severely hurt that night and he almost died. I knew I was a walking dead Bacri at that point. I knew my protections would be revoked, and I *still* would do it again."

I watched as they processed all of that, and when I had given them the time to, I said, "I was of my own mind until the day that we were ambushed again by Flinch's men and I was made to watch as they killed my boys. As Maverick, as Ian Packard, sacrificed his life for me." I will never forget the sound of Maverick's voice as he told me he loved me seconds before he died. "My life crumbled to dust at that point."

Jesse's hand covered mine, and I stopped. He, however, was looking sternly at the Primals. "She won't say more until you agree to rescind the execution order and allow us to hide away for a while. Regardless, Maddie and I are going into hiding for a long time after this. It would just be nice not to have to look over our shoulders waiting for the Agency to catch up with us."

"Exorci." The male admonished.

"No. You are not going to put her through the trauma of reliving all of that, without some reassurances of her safety and freedom." He growled.

"Jesse." I whispered. Jesse was growling at the Primal Primes.

"No, little bird. You've hinted at what you've had to go through, and this is the only thing we've got."

We had a bit of a stare off, before one of the Primes cleared their throat. We looked back at the screen and Primal Rebekkah said, "Consider the extermination order vacated, provided this leads to information to terminate the being known as Phrenic Jaysen Flinch. The ability to go into hiding afterwards is still up for negotiation."

Jesse relaxed next to me. He knew this was going to be the best offer we were going to get. I took his hand and threaded my fingers through his, gripping it tight. Kissing Jesse one more time for strength, I turned to the camera and told them what happened after Maverick, Bell, and Chip died.

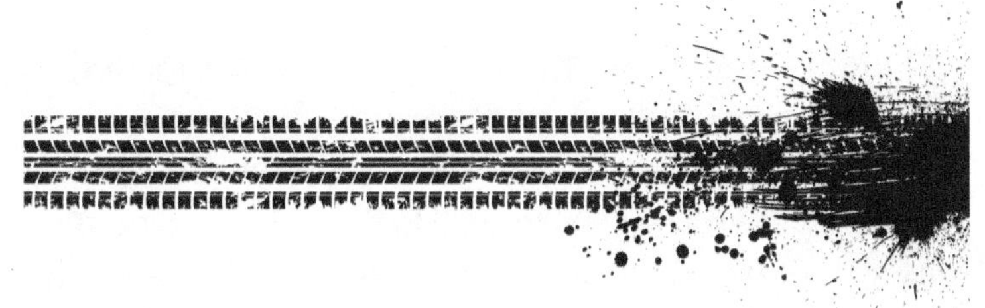

CHAPTER 52

JESSE

"After my boys were executed for loving and protecting me, I was held in a concrete room below Ivy Grace for a week. I tried to bash my head into the concrete as a way to end my grief, but they had a guard stationed with me preventing it."

I knew things had gotten bad, but I didn't think she had tried to end herself. I closed my eyes and tried to let some of the tension out of my body. I knew this story was going to get a whole lot worse, and I had to let her do this. It was the only way for us to move forward.

"I would occasionally get headaches and this clawing sensation in my head. I knew it was Flinch. He had used his abilities on me before. Only I didn't fight it anymore. There wasn't any use. So what if it killed me? I didn't have anything left in my life anyway, except for my love for Jesse."

Maddie's fingers tightened in mine, and I looked at her. They were sad, full of tears, and then she said, "It hurt to think of Jesse. He was just *him* in my head. I knew he was still out there. Still loving me. I had pushed him away after I found out that he was the one who killed Sean. Besides, when we were ambushed, the man who forced me to watch my boys die told me that this was the price of caring. Everyone we care about was used against us. It's the way of those in power. So yes, I realize you will use how Jesse and I feel about each other against us. I expect it, though I hope you are better than Flinch and don't."

I had to restrain myself from not smiling at her. She had laid the gauntlet down and called them out on their own strategies.

"When I was released from my cell, I received nightly black envelopes."

"Black envelopes?" Primal Rebekkah asked.

Maddie nodded. "It is how everyone who works at Ivy Grace receives their duties for the night. Usually mine said, '*Meet at the van*'. When the boys were still alive, there was the rare occasion it would tell me to report to Flinch's office."

Shadows passed across her face, and it was Primal Kobe who asked, "Tell us what usually occurred during those visits."

Her fingers tightened, and I could almost hear her heart beat faster. She was breathing quicker, and I readjusted our hands so that she was holding my hand in both of hers, as I wrapped an arm around the back of her.

I ran my fingers along her back trying to calm her down, and after a few minutes she said, "Before my boys died… it was usually specialized instructions, or to taunt me. On rare occasion, he would require me to service him orally." My hand stopped moving, and I felt every muscle in my body go taunt. "After… their deaths, I was required to service him almost nightly, him and any of his guests in any way they pleased. The ways were rough, violent, and no, I won't be itemizing out those details."

"You were raped, repeatedly." Primal Kobe's was gentle but firm.

"If you had been in that room, you would have thought I enjoyed every moment. That is what Flinch does. He gets into your head, and plays with your thoughts, emotions, and the chemicals in your body so that you are projecting all the enjoyment. Anyone who walked in would see me enjoying being used. My mind was broken. It was easy to use and manipulate.

"You don't understand what it is like to be sitting in the back of your brain. Seeing yourself enjoying what is being done to you. To see yourself moan and cry for it to be harder, or faster… To see yourself as someone you don't want to be." She took a deep breath and stood up straighter. "When I wasn't entertaining his guests, he had me working with trainers on how to kill in the easiest and most efficient way. He would have me practice on people I assumed displeased him in one way or another."

I saw her mind go through some of those instances, but she bit her bottom lip, before she continued. "Those are hazy memories. I remember them, but I can't pull one up and give you details. I'm sorry."

I looked up at my friends. Jade and Kolton's horrified reaction said it all. If the Primes didn't call for his death after this, I would literally die trying to end him myself.

"Last night, I received my black envelope and went to Flinch's office as usual. He opened my head like a nutcracker and told me what I needed to do, wiping all inhibition, all reservation, anything that would have any self-preservation in my life. Then Flinch sent me out to meet with Angelo DeCarlo, a Therugi Demon, to get some information on some tech being stolen from the Fae division in the Bay Area. I was supposed to retrieve a flash drive or other drive and give it to him. He gave me instructions to kill anyone I encountered until DeCarlo handed me the drive. If he gave me the information, then he was allowed to leave, and I was to take the drive back to him. If he didn't have it, I was to kill him. It was all programed into my head.

"Yet, when I saw Jesse, something clicked in the back of my mind. Seeing him. Feeling him next to me. Something pulled all that away long enough for me to beg Jesse to kill me. When his hand pressed against my face, I felt the control Flinch had put into my head slip and fade away. All there was, was Jesse.

"I didn't die. Jesse kept touching me, kissing me, and holding me like I mattered, like I wasn't something to be used and abused. That I was worth something, and all the commands that Flinch had put into my head vanished."

She stopped talking and stared at the monitor. I just looked at her. The things my little bird had to go through. She had forced my hand onto her cheek, willing to go. Knowing that if they sent me, there was no going back to anything normal again.

I swallowed the knot in my throat and tried to breathe through the rage and band that sat in my chest. Slowly, I turned my head to the screen and hissed, "I don't care if it's assigned or not. Flinch is a dead man. The question is now, how do we do it? How do I get close enough so that he can't prevent me from touching him?"

Primal Rebekkah didn't even hesitate in saying, "I agree. If he has the ability to manipulate your mind to the point that you don't even have to be in the same room with him, let alone the same building, to bend to his will..."

"That isn't something the Agency can permit." Primal Kobe said with a hint of fang showing through. "Primal Selene, how do you believe we should proceed?"

I blinked, and Maddie shifted slightly in her seat. I ran my hand down her back and rubbed my thumb back and forth.

"Primals." It was Ms. Rose who spoke, and there was just a split second of shock on their faces before Ms. Rose stood beside me.

"I'm going to assume that the Astral Primal Alpha Jade Romero Webster's bonded is there as well." Primal Kobe chuckled.

"He is, Primal." Ms. Rose laughed.

"Hello, Primal Primes." Kolton said just loud enough that they could hear him, but his hand circled around Jade's waist, and she leaned into him. There were four chuckles that came from those in attendance on the video call.

Primal Kobi allowed a fang to show, "Ms. Rose Porter, what idea did you have?"

"I have a certain specialist who is protected by the Agency who may give Jesse something to allow him in. I would have to discuss it with him, of course. The last time he worked on Jesse, it took him out for a few days."

Maddie rubbed along the tattoo on the back of my hand and I looked at her as she turned toward me. The small smile on her face was one of the most beautiful things I have ever seen.

The Primes looked at each other, and there was some clicking of keys and a menacing chuckle came from Primal Kobe before he said. "Seer Rose Porter, please speak to him and see if he will create what Exorci Jesse Westbrook needs to complete this task."

"One for Maddie as well." I said before they could close the video. "I won't leave her vulnerable again. Also, is it decreed she is to remain among the living and we are allowed to go into hiding for a while after this assignment is completed?"

"It is decreed that Madilyn Taylor shall live a long and happy life with Exorci Jesse Westbrook. It is also decreed that they are to go into hiding for the foreseeable future until such time that Minstrel Medina and Exorci Jesse Westbrook see fit. Henceforth, Minstrel Medina will oversee this assignment."

With that, the Primes signed off, and Carlos was left on the screen. "Well, that was interesting."

"Jesse..." I looked over at Jade, and the symbols on her arms glowed. "If I were not pregnant..."

"I know Jade. Don't worry, I will do everything I can to make him suffer."

"I want to help." I could see the rage in her eyes.

"Astral Jade—" Maddie started to say, but Jade cut her off, "Look, if you are going to be sticking around with this jackass, one that I love dearly, mind you, please drop the title. I'm so fucking sick of titles."

"Darlin'" Kolton raised an eyebrow at her. Jade stuck her tongue out at him and then turned back to Maddie.

"Seriously, please just call me Jade."

I huffed a laugh as Maddie nodded and said, "Jade, we appreciate it, but I think your bonded here would be a bit pissed if we put you in harm's way. I'm surprised he is tolerating us being here at all. Flinch's arms have a far reach, and high up the hierarchy of the Agency. Bringing you anymore into this isn't really up for negotiation."

"I know… If I weren't pregnant, though, I would be there. Please know that."

"I do, and appreciate it, but I think this will be something that Jesse and I *need* to do, if you know what I mean." She rubbed the tattoo again, and I felt that warmth go through me.

"Jesse, Maddie, go get some sleep. I'll talk to Philip and see what he can come up with and we can talk tonight."

"Tonight is Family Game night." Kolton said. "You two are welcome to join us."

"I appreciate it, Kolton, but I think it would do us good to sleep till morning. I'll need to make sure this one eats. She hasn't been great about her eating habits."

"I've been under some stress, Mr. Westbrook." Maddie rolled her eyes.

I turned toward her, shock and amusement on my face. "Mr. Westbrook?"

A flash of playful fear ran across those eyes of hers, and I said, "Watch it, Little Bird, or you may enjoy that punishment."

"First it was Jade and Kolton, now we have to watch you two?" Carlos scoffed. When I turned back toward him, he said, "Get some food and lots of rest. We will touch base tomorrow."

The video logged out, and Kolton started chuckling. I stood and was careful to navigate back into the open space of the room.

Ms. Rose went to her desk, retrieved a key, and handed it to me. "Up the stairs, door on the end. It's a studio. You guys can stay as long as you need."

"I'll bring you some chili and cornbread when we come back down for game night. It's cooking in the crock pot now, so you can stop with the 'We don't want to be a problem.' I've made enough to feed the ranch for a week. I'll bring some by around 6."

Nodding, I took Maddie's hand and headed up to the studio.

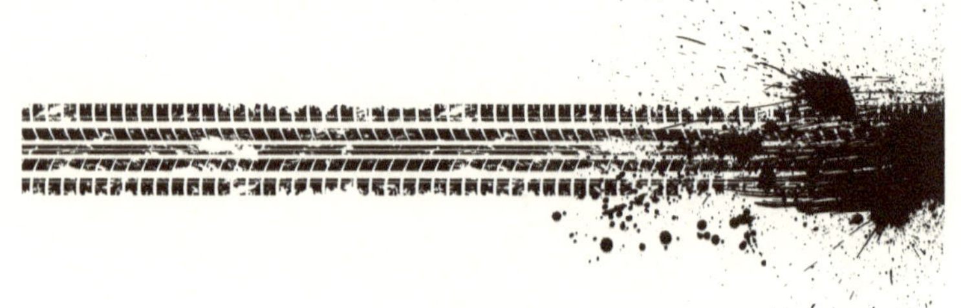

CHAPTER 53

MADDIE

We slept for hours, and waking up in Jesse's arms, naked, and not a stitch of clothing on between the two of us, was well, I couldn't think of a better way to wake in the morning... afternoon... whatever time it was. Hell, my whole sleep schedule was off.

I was starting to not notice the tingling sensation whenever he touched me, but as I laid there, listening to his gentle breathing, I remembered all the times he would kiss me and there would be that small tingling where he kissed me, or where he would be fingering me, and I would swear I felt his skin, and there was that tingling sensation. Shit, that first night we met, when his skin touched my forearm, and he panicked. There were signs to this.

"What are you thinking about so hard?" He murmured into my hair before kissing the back of my neck. He had spent the entire time sleeping with my hair over his face.

His hand moved and cradled one of my breasts, and when he pinched my nipple, I rolled over and glared at him. His hand shifted, moved up and down my spine, and I just smiled at him.

"I can't believe I can do this. I know I keep saying it, but... I can really touch you, Little Bird." His voice was full of so much amazement that it made my heart swell.

"It's sometimes the little things that we take for granted." I whispered.

"Did you—"

"Don't. I'm not going to talk about my time with Ian while we are laying in bed. I was happy with him, but... it wasn't you."

A smirk lifted the corner of his mouth. "Thought you said you weren't going to talk about him in bed with me?"

I pushed away from him and stood up off the bed, hands on my hips. "Fine, you wanna have this conversation, Jesse? Let's have it."

He looked me up and down, and when he looked at me with that heated gaze through his lashes, I almost felt my will crumble.

"You want to know about my time with Ian? Or do you want to fuck?"

His gaze fell to the floor, and I saw him seriously consider which way to go first. He slowly raised his gaze up the length of my body, and there was a ragged breath before he stood up off the bed. I reached out and took his hand. Leading him out around the small wall that separated the sleeping and living room, we went to sit on the couch. The studio was comfortably furnished, and when I sat on the tan cushions, I brought my knees up to my chest.

He sat and turned to face me. "Yes. I do want to know. Did he make you happy? Did he treat you well? Did he try to protect you from Flinch? Yes, I want to know all of those things."

"Why though? Does it even matter?" My voice was sad, even to my own ears.

"Because that was what I wanted for you. Because that was the one thing I asked him to do. To make sure you were happy and healthy."

"When my boys died..." I noted the confusion on his face. "Yes, they were my boys. I was only *with* Maverick... Ian, but Bell and Chip... they were just as important. It destroyed me. I realized just how much I loved them all afterwards. Ian, though, I cared for him a lot, but I wasn't in love with him. He loved me. Very much. I know that, but I couldn't give him my heart, because it was always yours. To answer your question though, yes, he kept me happy and healthy. Even tried forcing food down my throat once when I had almost passed out from a long shift and hadn't eaten the entire day. He was there for me when Flinch got in my head. He held me, protected me the only way he knew how."

Jesse sat there and waited. Didn't judge me for what I said. Just listened.

"The night Flinch pulled me into the office to tell me about Sean, he called for Maverick, too. I have these flashes of memory of Maverick turning to Flinch and screaming at him. Telling Flinch how he loves me, but didn't want me by default or because…"

"Because I killed Sean." His gaze dropped to the cushion between us.

I nodded. "Maverick and I talked about it. He had told me that he had a hard line. He cared for me a lot, but that he wasn't going to actively get between you and me. I think he knew…" I took a deep breath as the feeling settled within me. I looked up and said, "I think Maverick knew my heart and soul were yours. I think he knew he was a bandaid. That we would work to fix whatever was broken between us. He wouldn't let me go easily, but I think he knew."

"He wanted you as his mate."

"I know. We talked about that too. If I were a wolf… I'm not going to lie Jesse. Where I was emotionally, I might have let him."

Jesse smiled and reached over, taking a hand in mine. "I know. I broke your heart by killing Sean."

We sat there in silence for a long moment before he said, "I am sorry that I was the one who killed him, little bird. I owe you that apology. I also owe you an apology for not telling you the truth right away. I knew it would come out at some point, but I thought I could mend it. I didn't expect there to be a Maverick factor. Then there was, and I had to let you be happy... I made a whole series of bad decisions. I am sorry, Maddie."

"I know that now. I've done a lot of thinking in the last twenty-four hours. I believe you when you say you didn't know it was Sean behind the mask. Does it hurt any less that he died by your hand? No, but I think I accepted a long time ago that you didn't know until after he died. I think it was the night you found me at The Edging. That night was hard. It strained things with Maverick, because he could tell how much I still loved you. How much you still affected me." I looked up at him and his eyes were glazed over. "So, where does that leave *us*?"

His fingers squeezed mine. "Like I said, I don't think I can walk away from you again. I know I made love to you in the shower, that you said you were mine, but... Are you? Are you willing to have us start over? I know things will never be the way they were. I know that there is still a lot of hurt we have to work through and trust I need to gain back. I am willing to put in the effort, because you are my forever, Maddie. There will never be anyone else for me. I told you that back at the Edging. None of that has changed just because I can touch you. You have been since that first night at the bar. It just took me some time to realize it."

My heart squeezed, and my chest tightened as tears filled my eyes and started streaming down my face. I rolled up onto my knees and put his face in my hands. "You still want the broken bits of me?"

"Yes." There was zero hesitation in his voice.

My gaze bounced back and forth between his gold eyes. I looked for anything that would tell me he doubted that answer. I searched for any falsehood in his words.

"Your forever." I whispered.

Nodding, his voice shook, but there was determination in his eyes. "You are my forever, Madilyn Taylor. My Little Bird."

"Then yes. I am willing to make this work." Then I leaned down and kissed him softly, letting my lips linger. His lips wobbled slightly, and then there was a small hiccup that came from him. I opened my eyes, and tears were flowing down his cheeks. I kissed each cheek and rested my forehead on his.

"Can I just hold you?" His voice was trembling, and I smiled at the vulnerability of it.

Crawling up onto his lap, his arms wrapped around me, I rested my head on his shoulder. I smiled as the feeling of his skin touching mine rocketed through me. Every muscle in my body relax at it. It was then I realized that this was going to be a feeling that meant that I was home. I was safe.

CHAPTER 54

MADDIE

The next morning, Jesse got up and kissed me like he was trying to breathe life into me again before getting up, and heading to the shower. I stretched, feeling the stiffness in my muscles that I knew I needed to work out.

Stretches. That will help.

Position after position, I felt myself relax and loosen up. I stood, bent over, put my head between my knees, and pulled my head through, wrapping my arms around as well for leverage.

Breathing through it, I heard Jesse turn off the water and close the shower door. I reversed my position and bent backwards, placing my hands on the bed. I felt my back pop, and I let out a small moan. Standing, I worked my shoulders and looked around the small bedroom. The queen bed was right next to the door to the bathroom, but there was a little bit of wall space near the foot of the bed before the dresser.

I took a deep breath and flipped forward on my hands next to the wall into a handstand, letting my bare ass hit the wall. I walked my hands out a half step and bowed my back so that I was almost sitting on the wall. My back popped again, and I let out a contented sigh.

"You okay out there, Little Bird?"

Smiling and my voice a little breathy as I said, "Yup. Just stretching."

I saw him step out of the bathroom... take two steps and freeze. Toothbrush in his hand going limp, and his gaze trailing down the length of me, and when I kicked my feet out to stand, he blinked, and said, "Don't you think of moving."

"What?"

He took three long strides as he threw the toothbrush on the bed, pulled the towel from his hips, wiped his mouth, and had the towel on the bed with the toothbrush. Jesse pressed against me and I felt him hard against my stomach as he wrapped his arms around my thighs, pulling some of the weight from my arms, before kissing the inside of them.

"Fuck, Little Bird." A large open-mouthed kiss landed either side of the inside of my thighs, and I moaned. He took half a step back and spread my legs wide. "Do you have any idea how fucking delicious you look?"

I shifted my hands to keep from collapsing when he bent down and licked me from one end to the other. He chuckled against me, wrapping his arms firmly around my waist, taking all my weight and lifting me higher from the ground. When his tongue flicked against my clit, the combination of my skin's reaction to him, and him really tasting me, had me moaning and biting down on the inside of his thigh. He held me as his lips wrapped around my clit and sucked, moving me over to the bed.

After he dropped me on the bed and stepped back, I rolled onto my stomach to face him. My eyes froze on the hardness of him, just inches from my face. I licked my lips, but when I used my arms to pull myself forward, his finger landed under my chin, forcing me to look up.

"Now, now, Little Bird. You let me have a taste, and you want me to sit back and not have more?" He smirked and let out a little tisk. "Up and spread them."

I stood on my knees and crossed my arms under my boobs, intentionally making them stand up. His gaze heated and once again trailed up and down my body.

He took a step toward me and bent slightly to look me straight in the eye. "One way or another, little bird, I'm going to finish my breakfast. The question is, do you want to be the brat you are, or do you want to be my good girl, and lay on your back to allow me to finish..." His finger ran through the center of me, and my breath caught. "what I started?"

Every ounce of me was fighting the good girl in me, and so I didn't move, couldn't as Jesse's fingers flicked my clit, ran through the center of me again, and past my entrance to my ass. He circled it, and gently pushed.

My mouth fell open as heated pleasure burst through me. "There's my good girl."

His other arm wrapped around my legs and he swooped me back onto the bed. "Now, I'm going to say this once. Spread those beautiful legs for me."

I did, and he pulled me to the edge of the bed, kissing down the inside of my thighs. When his face was a mere inch from my core, I smirked, primed to be the brat I loved being, but his mouth latched onto my clit, and instead of the smart-ass words I had planned to say, a breathy, "Yes" came from me.

Jesse chuckled as his tongue snaked through me. Curling his tongue within me, he hit a spot that had me bowing my back off the bed in pleasure. His arms wrapped around me as his tongue fucked me, swirling it around and within every inch of my core. His fingers entered me, when he returned to my clit, and when they pressed on that spot within me, the orgasm hit me and the vibrations from his chuckle had me tightening around his fingers even more.

Jesse didn't hesitate and drank up every ounce of me. As I came down, his fingers continued to move in and around me as he lifted his head and met my gaze. His fingers moved lower and when he pressed two fingers into my ass, and pressed his thumb against my clit, working both in rhythm. "Give me another one, little bird."

I was already panting and grinding with him. When he lowered his head and flicked my clit with his tongue, I exploded. "Fuck!"

Jesse chuckled again and slowly removed his fingers from me, but before coming up, he kissed my clit, flicking it. Then slowly, so very, very slowly, he left a trail of open mouth kisses on my stomach, kissing each and every scar that had been placed on me in the months I had been away from him.

When his eyes met mine, there was heat, pain, and something else I couldn't place in that gaze. I reached down and ran my hands through his hair, cradling his head in my hands. I pulled him up, and when his lips met mine, I felt him sliding against me. My legs wrapped around him, and when our kiss broke, he said, "Damn, you taste like a fucking dream. Every inch of you is the sweetest treat I could ever have."

I smirked at him, and used the slight bit of leverage I had on him to roll him over, but Jesse was quick, and had me face down, my arms pulled back in his grasp. "Oh, my little bird, thought she was going to take over, huh?"

"Jesse." I breathed.

Rocking his hips so that his cock slid through me, I moaned. "Little Bird is getting demanding."

"Fuck..." I drawled as he positioned just the head of him at my entrance and fucked me with just the head of him.

He pulled on my arms and I lifted my shoulders, looking over behind me, and there was a smirk on my face as I started to say, "Jesse, just f—" He plunged into me and stilled.

He took a steading breath and looked at me as I bit my bottom lip. "Atta girl."

Using my arms as leverage, he drew out of me slowly and then slammed back in, over and over again. I felt another orgasm coming, but he froze, just when I was about to go over that edge. "I didn't tell you, you could cum yet, little bird."

Pulling out of me, he grabbed my hips and said, "Feet on the floor, elbows on the bed."

I did, and he ran a finger through me again. His cock rubbed a few times over my already sensitive clit, and he groaned as he bent down to kiss my shoulder. "Fuck."

He entered me slowly, but when he was fully seated in me, he wrapped his hand in my hair, and pulled my head back. "You've been so good."

I felt my stomach tighten at the words, and then he pinched my nipples as he pulled back and slammed into me. "But I think she wants to be truly rewarded."

"Yes, Jesse." I could only breathe the words as he slammed into me again and again. He hit that spot deep within me and it had my toes curling as he released my hair with a kiss on my shoulder.

A moment later, a smack rang through the room, quickly followed by my moan of pleasure. I felt myself tighten around him, as he repeated it over and over again, at each connection of us. I felt the heated sting on my ass.

His pace never stopped as his hand ran down my spine. There was another smack, and my legs quaked. "Please, Jesse. Please let me..."

Smack.

"That's my good girl. Cum for me."

Smack and then his hands were on my hips pounding into me. I was in a daze. I couldn't think past the blinding pleasure that coursing through me, and when my pussy clamped down on his cock, his roar of pleasure was everything that I held dear.

His hands still gripped my hips as we came down from our respective highs. My legs had completely given out, and as if I weighed nothing, Jesse picked me up and laid me on the bed.

"Don't move, my good, good little bird." He disappeared, and then I felt a warm washcloth between my legs and his hands lifted my legs. My thigh muscles quivered under his touch, and he just bent down and kissed the spot where the skin moved. A small, content smile on his lips.

Slowly, he lifted from me, giving me a quick kiss on the tip of my nose. "I love you, Maddie."

"Love you too, Jesse."

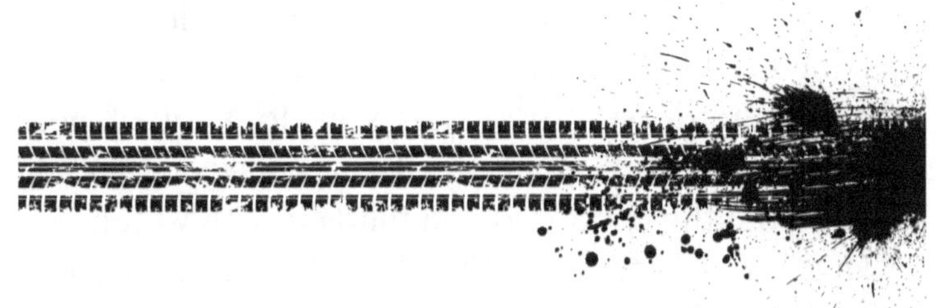

CHAPTER 55

JESSE

There was a knock on the door, and as Maddie finished getting dressed, I crossed the studio and opened it to find Ms. Rose standing in the doorway with Jade.

"Good morning." I looked between them.

Ms. Rose held up a bag and said, "Food for a couple of days."

"Oh, well, thank you. Come on in. I'll get it put away."

Maddie came out from behind the divider and I stopped. "Dammit, woman." She was in a pair of yoga pants and a crop top and one look at her, made me want to go back into that bedroom and cherish every inch of that body.

"I wish I could wear that again. Not too much longer, but I'll never look that good in it." Jade said and smiled.

"Umm, thank you, Jade." The blush on Maddie's cheeks was downright adorable.

"It's my understanding that you do a lot of pole dancing? Is that how you stay fit?" Jade asked, grabbing a glass from the cupboard and filling it with water.

"That and the training Flinch had me in so I could defend myself while doing things for him." Maddie shrugged it off, but when I looked back at Rose, her hair did that swirly thing.

"Ms. Rose, what are you seeing?" I asked as I stood in front of her, arms crossed.

She blinked and looked up at me, smiling. "I saw... you and Maddie standing in Flinch's office. That was it, though, just the surprised look on his face as you two walked through his doors."

"So that means Philip can do the tattoos? That they will work?" I asked, looking back to where Maddie and Jade were talking in the makeshift living room.

"That's what Jade and I came over to talk to you two about." She nodded toward where the two girls were at the couch. I raised my eyebrow at the position they were in. Their hands were on the back of the couch, and the balls of their feet pressed against the bottom of it as they pulled themselves back. I heard an audible pop, and Jade's whole face relaxed. "Oh, my god. That felt so good."

"You okay there, Jade? Need a minute?" I teased.

"Fuck off, Jesse. That pop just released a whole bunch of pressure down my hips and legs. You wait until Maddie is pregnant."

Maddie blushed, and I met her gaze. The thought of her carrying my child filled me with both fear and joy. Taking a deep breath to throw that thought away, I ran my hand through my hair. "Yeah, well, before we talk about anything too long term, there are some other matters we need to sort out. The first being how to rid the world of Jaysen Finch."

"That is something Philip can help you with. He is asking that you both be down in the game room mid-afternoon today, and he'll get you inked."

"I'm getting tattooed?" Maddie's questioning look was both adorable and amusing. "I mean, I'm not opposed to it. I've often thought about getting a couple of tattoos, but never really had the ability to move forward with it."

Her eyes landed on my hand and I smiled. "Depending on where it is, it won't hurt as much as they say it does."

"The vibration usually numbs it for me, but everyone is different." Jade interjected, and when she looked at my hand, she chuckled, "Though Jesse's hand is one of the more painful locations. I would suggest another location. I won't lie, though, he has to put a special kind of salt in the tattoo to keep the incantations he uses to make it work in the wound. That stings. Sometimes, like high heaven, so fair warning there."

"What have you thought of getting, Little Bird?"

She smiled brightly at me. "I want fine line leaf work that goes from my shoulder here." She pointed to just over her right breast, over her shoulder and behind her. "Around my back and up over my ribs, and over my heart."

I blinked at her, but her lip kicked up. "What else?"

There was a blush that rose into her cheeks before she lifted her shirt and pointed to the spot just above her heart below her breast. "A little bird, right over my heart."

Our eyes met, and there was determination, understanding, and a world of hurt laying there. That is when a thought went through my head. "They called you sweets, right?"

Her head rose and fell slowly, and Jade and Ms. Rose looked between us. "Add something to the leaf design for them. They should be honored for being there for you, when I betrayed you, and couldn't be there."

"What?"

"Put something within the leaves that honors them. Whether it be their names, or something else more artistically added. Do it." I ran my fingers along the line she was projecting, and bent down to kiss along her jaw, and whisper in her ear, "Just not anywhere near your heart. That belongs to me."

She chuckled and reached up to cradle my cheek. "You are sure about this?"

It sort of surprised me just how much I was okay with it. How much I wanted her to do it. "I am. Add something for Sean and Beth too."

She wrinkled her nose, shaking her head. "Not Sean. We wouldn't have to be doing any of this shit... I wouldn't have to be honoring Beth, Maverick, Bell, or

Chip if it were not for Sean. So no, he's not going anywhere on this body."

"See, I knew you would work out your shit, Jesse." I had almost forgotten that Jade and Ms. Rose were in the room, but my head swung to look at Ms. Rose.

I glared at her and shook my head. "What time does Philip want us down in the game room?"

"Mid-afternoon."

"Okay. We will be there about two–thirty." My fingers laced with Maddie's, and she squeezed them tight.

"Well, we will leave you be until then." Jade stretched some more, and turned back to Maddie. "Before you head back to the Bay Area, though, can you show me some of the stretches you do to get so limber, and show me some pole techniques?"

Maddie laughed and said, "I will give you personal lessons just to make Kolton beg on his knees."

"I'm usually the one on my knees, but... it would be fun to see him beg for once."

"In the meantime... enjoy the quiet. The guys are working up near the wildland, so it shouldn't be too loud downstairs. See you in a few hours." Rose said over her shoulder as she walked out.

I watched them stride out of the room and shook my head. When Maddie's arm circled my waist, and her hands ran up my back, I tipped my head back, reveling in the feel of her hands on my skin.

"How about we watch a movie for a bit?"

"Anything you want, little bird. Just don't stop touching me."

Maddie's leg was bouncing up and down when Philip walked in with his bag. "Hey, Jesse. Good to see you again, though I really wish it wasn't to ink protection runes on you."

He looked over at Maddie and stuck his hand out. "I'm sorry. I'm Philip. The one who has the pleasure of working on you."

"Nice to meet you, Philip." Her eyes narrowed as she asked, "How is it you can work on Jesse and not die?"

His lips twitched as he looked pointedly at where our hands were joined. "How is it you can touch Jesse and not die?"

"Well..." She looked at me and I shook my head.

"We don't know, Philip."

"How's your hand healing? Need a touch up while you are here?"

"Couple spots maybe." Shrugging, I pushed back my long sleeve t-shirt to my elbows on both arms, as Philip put his bag down, grabbed a pair of disposable gloves, and slipped them on. I looked at Maddie, who was looking at me with heated eyes, and bit her lip.

"Little bird?" I said it as a warning and a question, but she crossed her legs and shook her head. "What is it?"

"Do you have any idea how fucking sexy it is for you to just roll your sleeves up to your elbows? It doesn't matter who does it. Man, woman, or they-be, someone rolls up their sleeves to their elbows..." She let out a long breath through o'd lips. "Fuck, it's sexy as hell."

Philip took my hand and looked at it. "Just a couple spots." He looked at both of us before taking a deep breath. "So here is the thing with this rune. For it to work, I have to put it between your breast bones, and at the base of your skull. It's the only way to have protection against the physical aspects and the brain."

Maddie looked down and asked, "Can you do some other artistic work while you are at this? I know it's going to take hours, but..."

"Maddie, I've already been given authorization to give whatever pieces you want or need." Maddie relaxed. "So what do you want done?"

Maddie explained the piece, including telling him where she wanted a small blacked out wolf, bell, and computer chip on the vines on her back, opposite her heart. They were close to her heart, but in her past. She wanted the bird over her heart in front of her, looking to her future. When she was done, Philip had his chin between his fingers looking over the area. "That works. The protection rune goes here, so it will tie in the rest."

"What does the rune look like?"

"Points in four directions with smaller ones between. There is a small dot in the center, but the points don't have to be one specific style, so it should be able to make it cohesive. It does have to match on the base of the skull though." Maddie nodded. After Philip drew it up, Maddie made a few small modifications, including adding some decorative dots to tie the leaves together and a thin red droplet from the bottom of the rune.

"Anything for you Jesse? Other than Phrenic protections?"

"The male version of whatever little bird she picks for over her heart, over mine." He nodded, but I said, "What about the rune to get me into Ivy Grace? I need one that will allow me where Exorci are prevented."

He took a really deep breath and let it out slowly through his nose. He reached over and took my arm and waved his hand over it. A swirly mess of various skin-colored tattoos glowed across them.

"Shit, Jesse. I didn't realize you had that many. I'd seen some, but thought most of them were just scars." Maddie's voice was a mix of awe and worry.

"I'm fine. Comes with the job description."

"Not the point, Jesse." I reached over and kissed her on the cheek, and she leaned into me.

"Kiss ass."

"I'll do more than kiss that ass of yours." A mischievous smile crossed her face as Philip chuckled.

"Who's going first?"

"Do Maddie first. That way, you are fresh. She is having a lot more work done, and mine don't have to be pretty. They just have to work."

"Have you eaten?" Philip asked, turning to Maddie and offering her a re-encouraging smile. Her leg was still bouncing. Not as much, but I knew it was nerves. She'd been so strong for so long. Been through so much, and a tattoo was what she was being nervous about. I couldn't help but smile at her.

Maddie nodded and said, "Jesse made me eat and drink a lot of water before we came down."

"Well, let's get started then."

Five hours later, I couldn't have been prouder of Maddie. It was her first tattoo, and she didn't get a small one. Not to mention the salt that Philip had to put into it for the incantations to work. She just laid there and met my gaze, wincing occasionally, but never once asked him to stop. Even as he went over her rib cage, adding in the bird.

The faces she made while he did the one on the back of her neck were completely hilarious. She kept reaching up to wiggle and rub her ears when Philip would move. When I teased her about it, she just said, "It tickles, okay?"

Philip ate a quick sandwich that Ms. Rose brought in, and then he touched up my hand and inked on the three runes I needed. The access one was just a lightning bolt with a curly top, and my Phrenic protections were more solid bold geometric shapes, compared to the more delicate design he did on Maddie. The bird was small, mostly completely blacked out, but it matched hers, and that was all that mattered.

When he finished up, Philip went over the aftercare procedures for Maddie. He looked at me and, with a meaning that I knew Maddie wouldn't understand, suggested, "Wait at least a week before heading back for that real life experience. When you cross the threshold, Jesse, expect some tingling on the entrance rune. The Phrenic one... well I don't know if it is the same for everyone, but mine burned like a hot match getting too close to the skin, but if what Carlos says is true..." He ran his hand across his face, and tapped his cheek for a moment. "Mine was strong, but I don't know... I mean, it sounds like Flinch is just as..."

"Can I ask how you ended yours?"

Philip's eyes turned dark. "Dagger through the throat and a rock to the head... repetitively."

I smiled at Maddie, but I couldn't help but read the expression on her face. "You are wondering what Flinch is doing."

"I've been gone over twenty-four hours and haven't reported back at all." I took her hand. "He has to realize I'm not dead. He would have sent scouts to the meet point. Would have seen who I'd dispatched, and the one I hadn't. Would know that my body isn't there."

"He's searching, I'm sure."

I stared at her, not knowing really what to say. Philip's voice was soothing as he tried to reassure her. "The Ranch has special wards. He won't be able to find you here."

"Don't leave the ranch. Got it." She let out a large huff. "Just another cage."

"I promise, little bird—"

"No. Stop. It's... look. I get it. Hopefully, a short-lived cage." Looking up at me, her eyes held understanding, but they were tired as well.

I knew the exhaustion wasn't just physical. The emotional bullshit this woman has been through in the last year alone was not something I would wish on anyone. Well, except for Flinch. He wouldn't live another month if I had my way.

"Come on. Let's get you back upstairs. You need to rest."

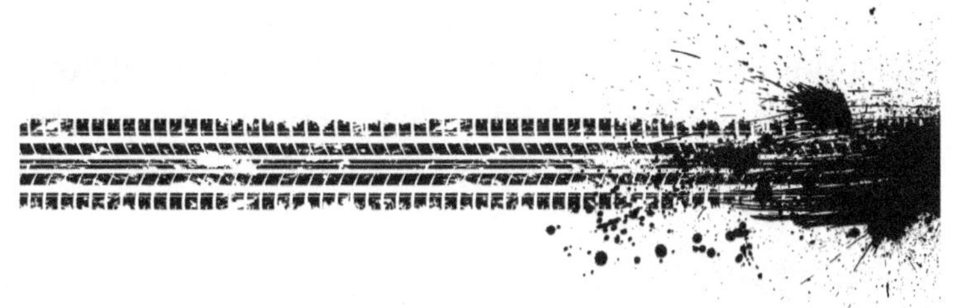

CHAPTER 56

MADDIE

We spent a week and a half at the ranch. Philip wanted to make sure that there weren't any parts of the runes peeling anymore, and before we left, he asked that we come back in a couple months so that I could have anything touched up that needed it. The hardest thing was not to scratch it.

Jesse applied the antibiotic moisturizer that Ms. Rose gave us often, and it helped, but at night I would wake up scratching myself, and Jesse would grab my wrists to stop me. That usually ended in us having raging, rough, amazing sex.

I took a deep breath to shove that out of my mind.

"We can wait for another night." Jesse said, reaching over and playing with the fingers on my hand.

"No. We need to get this done and over with." I looked up at the entrance to Ivy Grace, and fear and anxiety rushed through me, but when Jesse squeezed my hand, a calm sense of determination settled within me.

Jesse.

I had Jesse.

"I'll go, and do it myself if you don't want to go in there."

"No. I need to do this for not only myself, but for us and the boys. For everyone who is in there. There are good people in that building, Jesse." He gave me a small smile as pride filled his eyes. "I need to watch the light leave his eyes."

"What are the chances he knows we are sitting out here?" His head turned toward the front doors.

"I don't know. I would say fifty–fifty. Depends on whether he thinks I'm dead or not. I wouldn't think he'd believe I'm sitting with you right now, let alone walking in, hand-in-hand tonight with you." Jesse huffed a laugh. "Okay, possibly sitting in the car with you, but no way he would imagine us walking in together."

"Well then, Little Bird," He leaned over and pulled my chin around and said, "No matter what happens, remember, I love you. You are my forever. Just remember that. If none of these runes work, remember, you are mine. You are my forever."

"Forever." I whispered against his lips. "I love you too, Jesse."

His kiss was soft and lingered in the sweetest way. I felt every ounce of his love in that kiss. When he pulled back and rested his forehead on mine, his hand gripped the back of my neck tight.

"Gods, I love you, Little Bird."

I kissed him quick and turned to get out of the car. "I know. Now let's do this so you can take me home and show me just how much you do."

I was at the driver's side corner of the hood when I froze and looked at him. Jesse had left his jacket and gloves in the car, and my eyes trailed down the length of his body. I bit my lip, enjoying the view. He was just in a pair of dark blue jeans and a black t-shirt that pulled across the muscles on his chest. Honestly, I'm not sure how I had kept my hands off him as much as I had. Not only was he the sexiest man I had laid eyes on, I *could* touch him. He took his hand in mine and threaded his bare fingers through.

We strode past the long line, hearing the grumbled complaints of those thinking we were jumping the line. I just smirked and kept my head high. When we got to the bouncer, he blinked and startled, jumping up from his stool. "Sweets. We thought..." Then his eyes met Jesse's.

Fear filled them as he noted we were holding hands. "Nathan, I would appreciate it if you just let us walk through and not alert *him* to us arriving."

"Sweets, the Exorci will not be able to pass through the wards. You know that." He looked at Jesse, who had plastered a bored look on his face.

I shrugged and moved to go past him, but his hand rested on my shoulder. I looked down at it, then up at him. "Flinch will kill you, Sweets. You walk in here, and Flinch is going to take you over. He was livid when…"

"I know." I turned and smiled up at Jesse, who smiled down at me with a knowing look. I reached up on my toes, kissed him quickly, and turned back to Nathan. "He can try."

I pulled Jesse along and left a very stunned Nathan gawking behind me. I felt the tingling at my neck and between my breasts as soon as I turned down the hall toward Flinch's office. "He knows we are here."

"Are you really surprised?"

We reached the doors, and two of his usual guards were standing there. The blonde's eyes widened slightly before he said, "Nikki. Nice to see you are alive."

"Only because you enjoyed my pussy so much." I felt Jesse stiffen beside me. When I reached for the door, his hand stretched out to stop me, but stopped short when he heard Jesse's baritone voice come through low and dark.

"Are you sure you want to do that? See, it seems I left my gloves in the car. Wouldn't it be a shame if I stopped you and accidentally put my hands around your neck?"

"Flinch has protections against that." The brown-haired guard said, his voice almost hopeful.

"Like there are protections from Exorci entering Ivy Grace?" Jesse's face was pure droll boredom, and I had to suppress the smile from reaching my face.

I turned to the blond whose name I couldn't remember. In fact, I couldn't remember either of their names. I remembered the lust in their eyes as they took me repeatedly, but not their names. I looked between them. "Why can't I remember your names?"

"Because we never give them to our whores." The blond spat with distaste.

All I heard was a heavy sigh before Jesse grabbed him by the balls and punched him across the jaw. The blonde was dead before he hit the floor. "Guess your protections don't work."

Jesse turned toward the brown-haired guard and raised an eyebrow. The guard opened the door with a hint of a smile, and I strode in, with Jesse's hand on the small of my back. When Flinch's head raised, there was a flash of surprise, before he tried to cover it up with a slow evil smile across his face.

CHAPTER 57

JESSE

The dark-haired guard quickly figured out I wasn't going to be playing around and opened the door. Seeing Maddie's shoulders twitch and then out of the corner of my eye, I placed my hand on the small of her back in reassurance as we walked into Flinch's office. The muscles in her back tightened under my hand, and I ran my thumb back and forth, trying to calm her. The tingling at my skull and chest grew stronger, and Maddie's head tipped back just an inch as she suppressed the feeling.

Flinch's eyes narrowed slightly, before saying, "I'm glad to see my investment hasn't been a total loss. Though I am surprised to see you standing with the man who killed your brother."

"Flinch." I gritted through my teeth.

"He did kill him, just as you showed me on the video. What you *didn't* show me was how he realized who he killed afterwards." Maddie shrugged, crossed her arms, pushing her breasts up, and I had to push the thoughts out of my mind. This was not the time or place. "Jesse and I have an understanding."

Flinch's eyes flashed, and Maddie stiffened under my touch. A ripple went down her spine, and I couldn't help the swell of pride that I felt for her. She was fighting every instinct in her to turn and run. There was a small light out of the corner of my eye and as I watched it from my peripheral vision, I could see the tattoo at the base of her neck start to glow.

The protection was working, and yet Maddie hardly showed any indication of it. Flinch's eyes narrowed on me and I felt those runes burn like an eraser had been taken to my skin. I took a slow breath to steady myself, and I knew he was trying the same with Maddie. He stood, walking around the glass-topped desk I wanted to smash his face against, before leaning on the front of it, crossing his arms and ankles, and smirking at me.

"Let's have a little fun, shall we, Nikki? On your knees." His tone was pure command, and Maddie rolled her neck and smiled at him.

"No."

"I said, on your knees, whore."

Sighing, I took a step forward. "I'm getting really tired of you and your staff calling her a whore."

"That's what she is. She is mine to do with what I please. I *own* her."

"No one owns a woman. Women are not meant to be owned. They are to be cherished and worshiped for the amazing creatures they are. You wouldn't know that, though. You just jump into someone's head and force them to *pleasure you.* You probably don't have the first clue how to make a woman writhe under you in pure pleasure. To take pleasure *in* that pleasure."

"Why would I need to when Nikki is bound to me by Agency Law, and I can do whatever I please with her? I'm not sure how much she told you, *Exorci,* but Sean Taylor owes me a substantial amount of money. Under the contract he executed, that debt passes through to one Madilyn Nikole Taylor. She becomes my property until such time the debt is paid off. She is mine. I own her. She is my property, my *whore,* to do with what I wish."

I pulled my arm back to punch him, but blinding pain burst through my groin. I bent over and saw Flinch lower his foot to the floor. Somewhere through the pain and ache that was spreading through my core, Maddie was cussing Flinch out and there was some satisfaction in that.

"As I said, I own her. Now, *whore.* On your knees before me."

Her muscles shook, and I saw her hands bawl up into fists as I groaned through the ache. Her legs quivered in restraint, and I realized she was fighting the commands, even as the runes burned bright. Fuck, Flinch was a strong mother fucker.

"No." Her voice was strong and fierce. One I had only heard her use when she was completely and utterly livid with me.

I took a deep breath through the pain and forced myself to look up. I blinked, and Flinch lunged for her. It was instinct to reach out, but I only caught his pant leg. He fell forward, and Maddie moved, lodging a knife into his shoulder.

He gripped it and looked between us. "How?"

"We made some friends." Maddie cut through her shirt and bra, showing her the rune between her breasts. His eyes focused on it, and I swear I saw her flinch as it started to glow slightly.

"You... You really are a powerful Phrenic, aren't you, Flinch?" Maddie's voice shook only for a second before it found its resolve.

His eyes glared at me, but then he lunged again for Maddie, who met him with that blade. He froze just before it lodged in his throat. Damn, my little bird was a deadly one.

She looked at me quickly, and back to Flinch before saying, "Do you want to do the honors? Or shall I?"

"Little Bird, you are a right, deadly creature. I'll make it quick. The question is, do you want it quick or do you want it painful?"

She tipped her head to the side, her hand twitched, nicking his throat, a small well of blood rising to the skin. Her other hand moved to her boot, where she pulled another blade. This one was serrated, and when she smirked, I saw an evil determination cross her face. It was one I had seen in so many others.

"Hold him." I stood, breathing through the ache in my balls, and kicked him in the jaw. He fell back on his ass where I used my legs to trap his arms under me and then held his shoulders down.

"Hurts, don't it?" I chuckled as Maddie's determined eyes met mine.

She stood, knives in both hands, "This is for every time you raped me." Her arm sliced through the air, and cut his left ankle.

"For every time you forced me to endure your clients." Her arm moved again, and that serrated blade went through his right ankle, and I saw bone.

Flinch screamed, but I felt the runes heat in a quick blast that sent ripples through the room. Maddie's lip curled, and she laughed. I had never heard such an evil sound come from her that even my heart raced as I whispered, "Little bird?"

Her gaze met mine, and something cleared in her golden eyes that shifted to love. Flinch groaned under me, and her focus flicked back to him, some of that hatred and pain coming back to the surface. A vindictive tilt to her lips practically sent a shiver down my back and she continued.

"For every time you forced anyone to do anything they didn't want to do." A slice to his knees in quick succession. Bone and tendon showed through the slice and spray of blood.

"For every one..." She cut his pants open, and my eyes widened.

"For killing my boys." Then she plunged the serrated blade into his dick.

There was a blood-curdling scream that filled the room, as Maddie's eyes met mine. The gold in them seemed to swirl with deadly resolve.

The doors to his office shuttered against the force someone was putting against it. I huffed a laugh, noting the pieces of lock that sprayed into the room. When someone kicked it in, about twenty different creatures came through. I let my senses fill the room, and while death hung heavy in the air, I realized it was only centered on the piece of shit under me. My eyes locked on a raven-haired woman with large brown eyes, who smiled at Maddie. "Hi, Sweets."

My gaze met Maddie's again, and she just said, "Hi Raven."

"If anyone thinks of taking one step closer to us, just know I will stop you." I warned.

"Stop you?" Scoffed, a burly man with bright blue eyes. "He called us to him, but that released as we heard a scream ring out. Now that we see what is going on. Please continue. We would like the show."

Flinch's screams broke through the room again and cracked as Maddie twisted the knife at the man's words. She frowned at me, and I tipped my head at her with a shrug.

"Ah, his vocal cords went out. I wanted to hear him scream like we had in our heads. That was going to be part of the fun." Maddie stood, leaving the knife embedded in his dick attaching it to the floor. If he so much as moved, he would filet it.

I stood, holding Flinch down with a booted foot to the shoulder. I looked at him with the most malicious smile I could bring forth, and said, "This doesn't end until my little bird says it is over."

Maddie stood there looking at me, before glancing back at the creatures that crowded the doorway and said, "He will never suffer enough for the people he has taken from us. He will never suffer enough for what he took from us. He will never suffer enough for what he has done to us. He needs to rot in hell."

There were agreeable mummers from the throng of creatures, but my gaze hadn't moved from the piece of shit under my boot. Maddie reached up and cradled my cheek, making me look at her as she took my hand, lacing our fingers together. "I was lucky that you loved me so much that you didn't give up on me."

"I am lucky you were able to forgive me." I whispered against her lips as she stood on her toes and kissed me carefully. The movement to meet her put more weight on Flinch and he moaned.

I felt that tingling sensation again at my chest and neck. Maddie did too, and she threw another knife down where it landed with a thud in his throat. I knew she had brought several knives, but the accuracy and skill she wielded them shocked me. Just how much training had she been doing under Flinch?

A collective release of breath came from the creatures behind us, as Flinch's wet gasps of breath came from our feet. My gaze crossed the crowd, and all of their shoulders seemed to relax, and there were a few holding each other up.

Maddie looked down at Flinch. "I want you to suffer. I want you to know in these last seconds of life before death claims you, hopefully taking you to the deepest depths of the Underworld, that what you did was cruel and vicious. You deserve to be torn into the smallest pieces and fed to the pit demons who eat souls like yours." She looked down at our joined hands and let out a content sigh. "But there has been enough violence."

Bending down, pulling me with her, she took our joined hand and splayed them over the top of his head. There was a gurgling intake of breath as he pointed to his computer and pointed to his heart.

I watched as my hand touched his skin. It was just as it had been with Sean. A simple brush of my fingers did not take him. He just kept pointing between his chest and computer, as my hand sat there for almost a full twenty-five seconds before the last wet breath silenced.

CHAPTER 58

JESSE

When we stood, I wrapped Maddie into my arms, and felt her hands fist my shirt at my shoulder blades as she held me.

"It's over. He can't hurt you or anyone else again." I whispered against her hair and kissed the top of her head. There were a few shuddering breaths from her, and I could feel the tears seeping through my t-shirt.

"Sweets?" A woman with almost really short white blond hair and bright red lipstick asked carefully. I lifted my head to look at her, and she met my eye. She opened her mouth, closed it, then her head tilted to the side. "You are the Exorci Jesse Westbrook."

I nodded once, and there was a flash of fear that went through the crowd. In the same instant, two large men, probably bouncers, stepped forward, but they stopped halfway to me, as they saw how I was holding her.

"She can touch me." I breathed, and Maddie looked up at me, her face streamed with tears and smiled.

"I can, Brent. It's fine." To prove it, her hands wrapped around my neck, and her fingers dove into my hair as she pulled me to her to kiss her. It was strong, fierce, and full of purpose.

When she pulled back, I smiled against her lips. "I think they get the point."

Those gold eyes of hers filled with heat and of all the love she had for me as a smirk crossed her lips, and she said, "Do they, though?"

"Later, little bird. Later."

The most adorable little pout crossed her face, and my eyes flicked to where Flinch laid at our feet. She let out a big sign and nodded.

Turning to face everyone, she smiled. "As you can see from the interaction with Flinch and just now, I am perfectly safe with Jesse."

A strawberry blonde with a big messy bun on the top of her head, and black thick-framed glasses looked to a dirty blond with piercing blue eyes and said, "Well, at least we don't have to worry about our contracts anymore."

A woman with hair every color of the rainbow turned to face me. "What happens with the club, Exorci?"

I blinked. I needed to call Carlos. He could answer that. He could figure out what was next.

"I was not in as deep as everyone else here," she said, interrupting my thoughts. "I was getting a cut of my earnings. How am I going to pay the bills?"

"I've got an eight-year-old at home." Another woman next to her with bright purple hair said. "This is my only income. Small as it is, if I don't have it..." She swallowed as another blonde with ruby red lips and milky white skin came and stood over Flinch.

"He gave us just enough. We couldn't get financial assistance from the County or State." The blond standing next to Flinch said before looking up at me. She kicked him with the toe of her shoe. "Knew that if we made just too much, that we wouldn't qualify, but wouldn't be able to make ends meet in the Bay Area either."

"Cherry—" the woman held a hand up, stopping Maddie.

"Don't think that there is a single one of us here that are sorry this piece of shit is dead. We are just now wondering, in the midst of processing all of this," her hand waved over the body at our feet. "How we are now going to pay our bills?"

I nodded. "Let me make some calls. Keep the club going tonight. Let me see what I can do."

Nathan, the bouncer from the front door, stepped forward. "We basically locked the main room with a handful of bouncers in it. Made an announcement that there was a disturbance outside, and for everyone's safety, that they were to stay in there. We kept the music up so they could still enjoy themselves, and opened the bar."

The strawberry blonde with the messy bun said, "But all of us dancers came up here."

"You mean he made us come up here?" The long dirty blonde-haired woman next to her said.

There were blinks and a few nods. Maddie huffed a laugh though and said, "Of course he would. He thought to use you guys against us."

"I... regained control when you put that knife through his dick." The pixie cut blond said.

I kissed Maddie on the top of the head. "Go. I'll call Carlos and work this out."

She nodded and slowly the people she had become closest with over the last year filtered out. Pulling my phone out, I called Carlos.

"It is almost midnight, Jesse. What is it now?" Carlos' sleep-addled voice came through the line.

I chuckled and said, "You have one less Phrenic to deal with in the world. "

"It worked?" His voice was instantly clear and attentive. I heard him get out of bed and a door close behind him. "The runes worked? You got in and he didn't take control?"

"He tried." I chuckled. "I took care of him."

"Why don't I believe you single-handedly relieved the world of him?"

"It was my touch that killed him." I looked at Flinch, and then remembered what he was doing when he took those final breaths.

"That is all I'm getting until I get there, isn't it?"

"As I said, it was my touch that made his heart stop beating. Eta?"

Reaching down, I pulled open his shirt and had to peel it back. Blood soaked the shirt from the neck wound, the wet sound of the blood starting to dry against his skin. When I pulled it away, there were black lines through the layer of blood shining through. "What the fuck?"

"What are you talking about?"

"You are going to have to see this yourself. Again, what is your eta?"

"Fifteen." I heard a door shut, and keys jingle in the background.

"See you then." I stared at the tattoo of... my eyes widened as my mind flicked through any other possibilities, but only came to one conclusion. The outer edges looked almost like a fae ear. I stared at it, and blinked when I made out a single word, interlaced in the decorative swirl of lines.

Standing, I went to the computer and brought up the password prompt. Looking at Flinch, his chest, and then back at the computer, I slowly typed in s-u-l-e. Noting the small camera sitting in the corner of the monitor, I tore a piece of fabric off my t-shirt and covered it, before pressing enter. As the monitor came on, there was a faint light that came through the fabric, and his home screen came up.

I spent the next few minutes glancing through the financials and through some of the other folders. I found one labeled, 'Ivy Grace Parties'. It couldn't be a coincidence that both of them would have the folders named the same.

My shoulders tightened as I saw folder after folder of video and photos of Flinch's "special parties" with the workers here at Ivy Grace. Many of them I recognized from the group that came in. Some I did not. I purposely did not click on the file for Maddie. I didn't know if I could bring myself to not beg the gods to bring him back just so I could repeat what she did.

Forcing myself to get out of that particular folder, I went back to the folder with all the financials in it. My gaze snagged on a folder named 'Destinations', which opened to another file 'Special Projects'. I blinked when I opened it and saw a list of files, each named with the separate creature Primals. Hovering over the file, I noted it was a ftf file. "You've got to be shitting me."

Carlos walked in at that point, Maddie on his heels. His eyes trailed across the floor to where Flinch still laid, but when he looked at me, he said, "Do I even want to know what you found on his computer?"

I instantly started going through the desk drawers, looking for a backup drive. Not finding one, I looked at Maddie. "In my bag, back seat." I tossed her the keys. "There is an external drive. Grab it for me please, little bird."

Her eyes narrowed, looked at the computer, face draining of color. Nodding, she ran out of the room. I had no doubt that she knew exactly what I found.

"Carlos, I'm not sure if there are still cameras or audio being record right now, but these are *fae tech fundamental* files." I whispered so lightly that I hoped that if there was audio, it wouldn't be picked up.

I moved aside, pointing to miscellaneous files that I had seen and needed him to look at before Maddie came back. He cycled through them quickly, noting key points. I could feel the rage and anger that rose the more he looked. When Maddie came back, she handed over the drive, and I copied everything over. It took a few minutes, but when it was done, I took the drive and stuck it in my pocket.

Carlos stood up and looked between Maddie and I. "You two need to disappear. Tonight. Do whatever you did in Mexico all those years ago, Jesse."

I watched as Maddie came next to me, wrapped an arm around my waist, as I pulled her close. "What did you find on his computer?"

"Nothing I want you to see, little bird." I kissed her temple, and she leaned into me, nodding and letting it go for now.

"I'll get a copy of the files to you and contact you through burners. We will be ghosts by morning." I looked at him for a long minute before asking, "Is there a way that the club can keep running? Get some legit crew in there to run it? A lot of these guys, it's their only income. They need every dime."

Carlos nodded and pulled his phone out as he looked at me and then Maddie. "Consider it done. Now you two get the fuck out of here. Good luck."

Then I was dragging Maddie out of the room.

When we got to the end of the hall, she pulled short and asked, "Can I go to the backroom to say goodbye?

See if my wallet at least is still in there? I mean, I assume he took it, looking for clues where I could go, but..."

Smiling at her and giving her a quick jerk of my head for her to go, she disappeared down the hall. While I waited, Nathan rounded the corner, looked at me for a half second, and when I lifted an eyebrow at him in question, he said, "I didn't realize you were the Jesse that she and Maverick fought over. I see it, though. She never looked at him the way she looks at you."

I couldn't help the small smile that fell on my lips, but said, "She loved him. Bell and Chip, too." Nathan looked shocked by my expression. "They were there for her, when I wasn't. I can't blame her for how she fixed what I broke. The fact she *can* look at me like that, after everything... I am genuinely the luckiest man alive."

Nathan's eyes darkened for a moment before he looked at me and said, "Nikki... Sweets is special to all of us." Then he let out a long breath. "I'm assuming you two will be disappearing for a while."

I nodded. "Minstrel Carlos is upstairs working on keeping the club open so you can still pay your bills."

"Thank you for that, Exorci."

"Please call me Jesse."

Maddie bounced around the corner and held up her wallet. "Pinkie had grabbed it and stowed it away the night I didn't come back."

I put my hand out, and she gave it to me without question. I ran my fingers along the seams, along the edge of the fabric, and removed each of the cards.

"What are you looking—"

My fingers stopped as I cocked an eyebrow at her. I reached over and pulled the last remaining knife from her belt, and tore into it. Fishing out the little wire. The little red light blinked, and as I took the knife to the end of it, it stopped glowing. "Pull what you want out of the wallet, and put it in the trash. I found one, but that doesn't mean there aren't more."

Nathan's eyes widened. "I'll have everyone on staff do the same."

"Thank you, Nathan." Maddie said, pulling him into a hug, and then said, "Tell the crew I'll see them soon."

"Be safe."

We walked out of Ivy Grace and didn't look back.

CHAPTER 59

MADDIE

I sipped on my cup of coffee as I stood out on the white washed deck over the ocean. For three days we took flight after flight, bouncing around the Pacific before we landed here in the Maldives. Getting Jesse on a plane was a feat in itself. He was so wholly against it, for fear someone would accidentally touch him. We bought out the row of seats with us, and I always sat on the outside to help mitigate the problem.

While we were sitting in the airport in the Philippines waiting on our flight to Qatar, he was super twitchy, but when I asked, "Why don't we just stay here? We've gone far enough. We can hide among the throng of people."

"You deserve to be on a beach somewhere. Trust me, where we are going, you are going to love it. A few days of discomfort are worth it. I have to keep you safe."

"We should have just taken straight flights instead of zigzagging around the Pacific. You are having to spend more time out in public than either of us are comfortable with, and you on a plane isn't the least stressful thing I've been doing for a day and a half."

"The people who would be hunting us down for Flinch's death... they are going to look for us to take the easy route. Even the little more complicated route. We've also changed our passport nation. It will be harder to track, not impossible, though. Not to mention that it isn't likely they will be looking for plane tickets with my name. It's pretty well known that I don't fly." His knee had bounced as he looked around the airport non-stop.

I hated to see him like that, but I had to admit, waking up this morning to nothing but turquoise blue waters, fresh air, and Jesse's arm firmly around my waist... I couldn't wish for anything more.

I stood there sipping my coffee, breathing easy, cool breaths for a long time, occasionally playing with the ring on my left hand. I smiled as I remembered we had been walking through the airport in Doha, Qatar, and he stopped dead in front of the shop. He didn't say anything, just pulled me in there, had them pull three out from the counter, and when he found one that he liked on my hand, he paid for it, and we walked out.

Standing in one of the waiting areas overlooking the ocean, Jesse lifted the hand to his lips and whispered, "Forever."

I looked at my hand, and knew what he was asking, without asking. Looking up at him, I teased him for it. "No grand gesture of asking me to marry you, telling me how I am your everything?"

The corner of his lip had curled up, and he said, "Why do I need to, when I've already told you all that, and you just said it?"

Laughing, I reached up on my toes and whispered against his lips, "Forever."

Then Jesse was kissing me, making the world fade away to nothing.

I sighed as I took another sip and felt Jesse behind me just before one of his hands landed on my hips. I kept looking out over the ocean and smiling. Jesse moved my hair off my shoulder and bent down to kiss the base of my neck, before running his lips up the length of it and kissing just below my ear. My toes curled along the edge of the deck as his arms curled around my waist, pulling me back against him.

I hummed as I leaned back. His lips kissing my temple as he held me close. There was a content sigh that came from him, and I smiled.

"I could get used to this." He whispered.

"Which part?"

"This." He squeezed me. "Waking up next to you. Smelling the ocean in the air. I can see how someone could get lost in this life."

The Agency would never let him be. Sure, we have ducked out of the world for a bit, but I knew Jesse would be pulled back into it soon. Too soon.

"Whatever it was that went through your head, you can let it go. I realize you have lived in a fight-or-flight response for months, and so it's going to be hard." He whispered it against my shoulder, and I took a deep breath and tried to let some of it go. "We will be here for a few months at least. So, try to relax. We can get whatever it is you want delivered here. We just have to be careful."

"Have you talked to Minstrel Carlos about Ivy Grace?"

He nodded, and let his lips graze across my jaw as he said, "He has them all set up. Says when we return, you can return to working there... running the place. With Nathan and Pinkie."

I had to smile. "Please tell me they finally told everyone they were a thing. Seeing them try to hide it was painful."

He nodded, and nipped my earlobe quickly before saying, "According to Carlos, the club was very excited to hear they would run it with you. They have agreed to hold it together until you got back. We've also secured some video chats so that you guys can talk in a few weeks. We need to stay silent until then." His lips lingered on the spot that Maverick used to mark me at, and he kissed it before pulling away and making me turn to face him. "That's where he would mark you, right?"

I nodded, but kept his gaze. I wasn't ashamed of it, and he didn't seem to be angry either, but still tried to say, "I'm sorry—"

I held up my hand to him, twirling the ring around. "You've said that, and I've forgiven you. Never apologize for that time again. Just like I won't apologize for that time either. This here?" I moved the ring again. "This means that I am yours, and you are mine. What is in the past is the past, Jesse. I love you, and you love me. That is all that matters anymore."

"Forever." He whispers.

"Forever, Jesse Westbrook."

THE END

Song Inspirations

Must've Never Met You – Luke Combs

Too Far Gone (feat. Svrcina) – Hidden Citizens

THE ASHSTRIKE SANCTORUM

THE ASHSTRIKE SANCTORUM
CREATION STORY

www.kimberlymringer.com

It was supposed to be a simple assignment. Astral Jade Romero was supposed to fix the werewolf problem at the Porter Ranch.

Only there was a problem, she hadn't prepared herself for, the human foreman Kolton Webster. He occupied all her thoughts and sucked her in like she never had been before.

When the wolves attack and Jade is injured will it be Kolton or the wolves that destroy her?

Exorci Jesse Westbrook can't touch anyone with his bare skin. If he does, they die. Such is the curse of an Exorci, the executioners for the Ashstrike Sanctorum.

His job is as simple and complicated as that. Receive the name and location of the person, and with a simple touch, the extermination is complete.

Jesse's life isn't all death and destruction. He has Maddie Taylor. The woman is his forever, but he's never dared to truly touch her. When her brother dies, her life spirals out of control, to the point she pushes Jesse from her life. Now... Now she's his next assignment.

Books Also By Kimberly M. Ringer

The Ashstrike Sanctorum Series

The Astral's Bonded

The Exorci's Touch

The Five Angels Trilogy
The Five Angels
The Ash'bani

The Helena Crystal

A Five Angels Novel

Duchess' Crown
Duchess' Throne

Other Books

Ashes and Flame

Weekend with Rylie

Kimberly M. Ringer lives in Santa Cruz, California with her husband, little human, and two furballs, Wall-E (a Jack Russell mix) and Pippin (a Pomeranian Terrier mix). When she isn't writing, she is reading, playing with the dogs, playing video games or down at the beach. She's a bit geeky and nerdy, so sci-fi references and other things going on in the science world will often end up in her stories.

Contact Kimberly M. Ringer:
www.kimberlymringer.com
Instagram: @kimberlymringer
Facebook:
https://www.facebook.com/kimberlymringer

Sign up for my newsletter and receive freebies, coupon codes, and stay up to date on all things Kimberly M.

Ringer and K.M. Ringer
Newsletter Signup

www.ingramcontent.com/pod-product-compliance
Lightning Source LLC
Chambersburg PA
CBHW060942190726
48286CB00005B/1385